Somewhere in Time- trilogy part 2

SOMEWHERE IN TIME

BY RICHARD TERRAIN

Somewhere in Time- trilogy part 2

Somewhere in Time- trilogy part 2

Chapter 1:

Esselle laughs. Then again Esselle always laughs when she's with Mardrin. She grabs her purse back and he takes her hand. The cold had never bothered Esselle. But she was glad the winter months were over. May 1, 2017 was Esselle's favorite day. Her anniversary with the love of her life Mardrin. Sure, everyone says they're in love. But it had always been different with them. They were meant for each other. never fought, never raised their voices past the subtle whisper of the wind. Only eve screamed when they laughed too hard. Esselle looked up and saw Mardrin's golden blonde hair shine around his head like a halo in the sunlight. His yellow-green eyes twinkled when he smiled at her. She loved it when he smiled at her. Esselle had been quite different from Mardrin physically. But she guessed that's why everyone thought they looked nicer together. Mardrin was all sunlight and golden colors. Mardrin was tall, which didn't work for Esselle who was only around 5 foot 4, with the body of a jock. She hated sports. But he did and she didn't mind. But she definitely teased him about it. On the other hand Esselle was Latina. Although the complexion of her skin made you think other wise. She was light skinned. But she was curvaceous. Not too much but just right. She had long. long thick brown curls that turned red in the light and golden brown in the moonlight and hazel almost honey colored eyes that changed with the light. Sometimes they were brown others they were a forest green other times hazel other times a mix of all those colors. Mardrin found it odd. But loved her for it anyone.
You see Esselle and Mardrin weren't your typical high school sweethearts. They were going to get married one day it was a

Somewhere in Time- trilogy part 2

definite. Everyone knew it. They had their entire life planned out. They were going to graduate high school. Start college and get an apartment together. Then when they graduated college they'd get engaged start their career and a year late get married. Everyone knew. They all joked about it. But they knew it was serious anyway. Even their parents knew and encouraged it. Mardrin and Esselle had known each other their entire lives. Their parents were both world renowned scientists studying the art of preserving the body and one day bringing people back.

Esselle and Mardrin didn't care however. They just wanted to be together. All day everyday. Forever and always.

They were very mature for 17. Then again as mature as 17 year olds can get. Point was they were matured and knew what they were going to do with their lives. After they got married 3 years later after traveling they'd settle down and have a family with four kids. A girl first her name was to be Elaina and she would have eyes like Mardrin's and hair like Esselle's. the next would be a boy. He was to be named John with an attitude like his mother's and passion like his father's. The next would be twins. A boy and a girl. Their names would be Alexander and Veronica and they'd be a random mix of Esselle and Mardrin. Yes that was them alright always planning ahead. Always knew what they were to do with their lives. Always.

But Esselle was young and in love and had based her future on perfection because that was what her present was. Perfection. She had money, love, a great family, she lived in a beautiful mansion in Manhattan. One of the very few. Esselle had it all. But now she was just enjoying it with the man she loved more then anything in the world.

Somewhere in Time- trilogy part 2

"Ok" Mardrin said putting the blanket under their favorite tree in Central Park. He had a quizzical look on his face and firmly placed his hands on his hips. "I'm not good with blankets" he said and Esselle laughs. No he wasn't very good at all she thought and fixed the wrinkled edges.

"There" she says "All better"

She sat under the tree and pulled her apple out from her picnic basket. "You know next time I'm picking the apples" she says and he sits behind her "I love you my dear but your apple picking is quite awful" she says examining the apple and Mardrin laughs.

"Fine then, you're awfully picky" he says and pulls out his grapes. Her jaw drops. The little snipe bought grapes and didn't tell me! she thought.

"You're not going to share?" she shrieks and he laughs shaking his head.

"You insulted my apple picking skill" he says and she tosses her apple.

"That's because you have no apple picking skill!" she ranted. he laughed and shrugged his shoulders then took more grapes.

"Don't criticize me next time" he says and she places her hands on her hips. He is just trying to be difficult.

"Mardrin give me some!" she says and reaches over the blanket. He pulls back.

"Nope!" he says and smirks.

"Mardrin!" she says and climbs over the blanket reaching for them. He brings his arm in the air and shakes his head.

"Nope" he says. She climbs unto his lap and reaches. he brings arms behind him and she reaches.

"Mardrin!" she says but can't help but giggle despite being

annoyed. "Give me some!" she says and he shakes his head again. He puts his hand on the back of her neck and pulls her down to kiss her. She wraps her arms around him and he does the same. With his fingertips he grazes the bottom of her back making circles the way he always did when he kissed her. it was comforting.
Esselle yanked away from his warmth. "Ha!" she said grabbing the grapes.
"Real slick" he says and his face glows in the sunlight. She gets up making a run for it down the hill and shrieks.
"Hey give me my grapes!" he calls after her and soon he's running too. She laughs when he grabs her and they roll unto the flower. They fall to the ground Esselle still holding the grapes and laugh. She looks to the sky and watches the clouds move as the sunsets.
"Do you think there is really anything up there?" she asks and they look at each other.
"What do you mean?" he asks and she pops a grape into her mouth. he grabs his grapes back makes a face and she giggles. She turns over and places her elbow on the ground and the side of her face in the palm of her hand.
"You know. Like God heaven and all those angels and stuff. Like how they talk about in school" she says. She and Mardrin attended Private school all their lives. They always had religious education.
He shrugs "there must be" he says and her eyebrows press together. He smiles a corny smile "Because you have the face of an angel" he says and taps her nose.
"Wow how charming" she says rolling her eyes. Esselle had been

pretty at certain angels and awful at others. Over all she always thought she was normal. A sweet kind of pretty.

"Well of course there is Elle" he says. Elle was what everyone called Esselle. Elle.

"There has to be. There is so many things the world can't explain that the belief in a God could. Like," he says and looks at her

"How much a person could be in love with another"

She smiles "That has nothing to do with it you dope" she says but feel flattered anyway.

"Oh I know. It was just that time of day I had to confess my undying love for you Esselle. We have to stay on schedule" he says and smiles. She rolls over and laughs to the sky. Perhaps there is a God or maybe there isn't. She didn't know. But Mardrin was always so logical and if he believed it had to be true. So therefore she would believe.

She turns her face and his an inch from hers.

"I love you, you know that?" he asks as if he really meant it.

"Who doesn't love me?" she says and he softly laughs. After a moment of silence he shakes his head and takes her face in his hand.

"No I mean it" he says and her face falls serious.

"One day I promise you Esselle, I'll spend the rest of my life with you. You can count on it" he says and she smiles.

"Well now that we've established that there is a God instead of getting married in a court we can get married in one of this big churches. And you can see me in a white dress" she says and he laughs.

"Yes, I've always wanted to see you in one of those" he says and rubs his thumb over he cheekbone.

7

Somewhere in Time- trilogy part 2

"You know just going back to the whole love thing" she says and his eyes meet hers.
"I know you do" she says and he lets out a deep breath "And I love you too. Just thought you should know"
He opens his mouth to speak but no words escape. Instead he shuts his eyes and kisses her and the world seems to not exist anymore and its just Esselle and Mardrin. Mardrin and Esselle. The way it will always be. Forever and Always. All day everyday. Perfection.

sselle with a glowing smile sits on the stool next to the kitchen counter and stretches. Her eyes were half shut from slumber and she was floating on a cloud. It was Saturday. Of course she was floating on a cloud. Her mother made a funny smile and put her breakfast down in front of her.

"What are you so happy about?" she asks and Esselle sighs.

"Oh just another day of life!" she says. She throws her arms in the air and spins. The light shone through the large windows like gold and everything had the movie in imax glow to it. Esselle loved mornings like those.

"You're going to work today mom?" she asks. her mother had her white lab coat on. The one that hugged her curves. Her short brown and bangs were combed into her usual bob and her green eyes twinkled.

"Yes, I am. You're father and I are on a break through with some new aging formula using a rare melon" she says and washes the dishes. I nod. Always working.

I tap m skin "Maybe you can make me look young!" Esselle says. Her mother smiles and picks her daughters chin up. She always did that when there was something on her mind. Esselle opened her eyes. She's hoped everything was alright. Speaking of alright her father came in. His golden blonde hair was everywhere. His brown eyes had bags under them and he seemed frantic. His tan skin glowed and he had his lab coat on as well.

"Hey dad" I say. He looks around and absent mindlessly kisses my forehead.

sselle with a glowing smile sits on the stool next to the kitchen counter and stretches. Her eyes were half shut from slumber and she was floating on a cloud. It was Saturday. Of course she was floating on a cloud. Her mother made a funny smile and put her breakfast down in front of her.

"What are you so happy about?" she asks and Esselle sighs.

Somewhere in Time - trilogy part 2

"Oh just another day of life!" she says. She throws her arms in the air and spins. The light shone through the large windows like gold and everything had the movie in imax glow to it. Esselle loved mornings like those.

"You're going to work today mom?" she asks. her mother had her white lab coat on. The one that hugged her curves. Her short brown and bangs were combed into her usual bob and her green eyes twinkled.

"Yes, I am. You're father and I are on a break through with some new aging formula using a rare melon" she says and washes the dishes. I nod. Always working.

I tap m skin "Maybe you can make me look young!" Esselle says. Her mother smiles and picks her daughters chin up. She always did that when there was something on her mind. Esselle opened her eyes. She's hoped everything was alright. Speaking of alright her father came in. His golden blonde hair was everywhere. His brown eyes had bags under them and he seemed frantic. His tan skin glowed and he had his lab coat on as well.

"Hey dad" I say. He looks around and absent mindlessly kisses my forehead.

"Hi mami" he says. "Um, have you seen my-?" he says ready to break a sweat and mom pulls something out.

"Your phone?" she asks and he lets out a deep breath of relief.

"That's why I married you" he says taking it and kissing her cheek.

"Mhm" she says with a raised eyebrow.

"I'll see you in the office!" he calls and runs out the door. When it slams shut her mom rolls her eyes.

"Your father woke up late" she says "Again"

Somewhere in Time- trilogy part 2

Esselle laughs "Have you seen my-?" she says and her father comes running through the door again.
"Vitamins?" her Mom says and hands me a bottle.
"I forgot my suitcase" her father says and stops in front of them on his way out.
"Um Vivienne those-" he says and Vivienne shoots him a look.
"These aren't my vitamins" Esselle says and she looks at her mother awaiting an answer.
"Your father and I made these in the lab. We like them better" she says and raises an eyebrow at her husband. He nods and breathes in.
"I'll see you at work sweetie" he says and walks out. Esselle shrugs and pops her vitamins down her throat.
She looks at her phone and practically chokes.
"Elle!" her mother says.
"I have to meet Selena in 20 minutes!" Esselle says with a mouth full of food and runs to her bedroom. Esselle couldn't help but wonder how odd her new vitamins were.
"Hi mami" he says."Um, have you seen my-?" he says ready to break a sweat and mom pulls something out.
"Your phone?" she asks and he lets out a deep breath of relief.
"That's why I married you" he says taking it and kissing her cheek.
"Mhm" she says with a raised eyebrow.
"I'll see you in the office!" he calls and runs out the door. When it slams shut her mom rolls her eyes.
"Your father woke up late" she says "Again"
Esselle laughs "Have you seen my-?" she says and her father comes running through the door again.

Somewhere in Time- trilogy part 2

"Vitamins?" her Mom says and hands me a bottle.

"I forgot my suitcase" her father says and stops in front of them on his way out.

"Um Vivienne those-" he says and Vivienne shoots him a look.

"These aren't my vitamins" Esselle says and she looks at her mother awaiting an answer.

"Your father and I made these in the lab. We like them better" she says and raises an eyebrow at her husband. He nods and breathes in.

"I'll see you at work sweetie" he says and walks out. Esselle shrugs and pops her vitamins down her throat.

She looks at her phone and practically chokes.

"Elle!" her mother says.

"I have to meet Selena in 20 minutes!" Esselle says with a mouth full of food and runs to her bedroom. Esselle couldn't help but wonder how odd her new vitamins were.

Somewhere in Time- trilogy part 2

Somewhere in Time- trilogy part 2

Selena!" Esselle said barging through the doors of the Macy's on 34th street with open arms and a Spanish accent.
"Esselle!" Selena said imitating her and they laughed. Selena was Esselle's best friend for as long as she could remember. Esselle's family and Selena's had their mansions in Puerto Rico next to each other. Ever since they'd been inseparable.
"My darling Elle" Selena says. They walked through Macy's arm in arm and looked around like they owned the place. Which in all reality they did. Everyone knew and loved them and vice versa.
"How are you?" she asks and Elle imitates her British accent. Esselle had secretly wanted to be British. Always.
"Just dashing and you?" Esselle asked. Selena stopped reached over to straighten a perfume and kept walking.
"Just smashing" she said.
****
******
"You know," Esselle said looking up from her Elle magazine. Selena looked up from her Vogue one. "I want you to be the maid of honor at me wedding in 5 years"
Selena snorts "Honey I was going to do that whether you liked it or not" she says going back to her magazine and biting into a Twizzlers. Selena was very blunt. She was all hotness all attitude all sarcasm and all of the things that made her Esselle's fabulous best friend.
Esselle rolled her eyes. "Hey Elle?" Selena said.

"Mhm" Esselle responded flipping through the pages of her magazine. Turns out The ripped up jeans look is out of style. I never like it anyway. What is in though is stitch lines style. Where the stitches are all around the jeans carving the desired shape to the woman's body. Hmmm Esselle thought they could be useful.

"What kind of wedding ring do you want?" Selena asked. She shrugged. How was she supposed to know? She doesn't plan *Everything* out. But she could see why they thought so. She had her heart set on David Tutera planning her wedding. Which he totally will.

"Whatever he gets me I'll be happy with" is what she said and flipped more pages.

Selena smirks "Ya well I'll be damned if its anything less than ten carats"

Their eyes meet. For a moment there's silence and they burst into hysteria.

"I pity the man who marries you Selena. He'll definitely have his worked cut out for him. You're a challenger" Esselle says and Selena bows her head.

"You're damn straight" she says kicking back in her chair and flinging her legs over her bosses desk.

"Hey where's Eve??" she says. Eve was Selena's boss. She let Esselle and Selena hang out in her office all the time but she was nowhere in sight.

"Probably starring at the marketing guy Tim in the Tommy Hilfiger section" Esselle says and flips a page.

Selena laughs "You're such a bitch!" she says and Esselle laughs with her.

"Its true. She's probably getting all googly eyed near the perfume and sprayed herself in the eye!" Esselle says running out of air from laughter along with Selena. The door opens and they quickly hide their faces and sit back.

"Oh hey guys!" Eve says and walks towards the window yanking the curtains open "What are you laughing at?"she says passing by them

"Nothing" they say like mischievous little children and laugh behind their magazines.

You know one day I'll be on top of the world" Esselle says and stares at the sky "I'm going to be the first female president of the

Somewhere in Time- trilogy part 2

United States and I'm going to have my beautiful family and I'm going to make a difference in the world"
Selena laughs "Of course you are babe!" she says and goes back to he makeup.
Esselle had been sitting at the table in the yard of her school wit her elbows on the back and staring at the sky.
"Don't tease me" she said looking back at he friend. Selena had he cute preppy uniform on with the grey shirt white button down tie and red blazer. She had her feet across the bench and was working on her make up. I"m serious" Esselle said and turned back to the sky. Esselle and Selena were waiting for the guys to come pick them up and Esselle took the time to relax. The day was that of her favorite kind. Beautiful, bright blue sky, pretty white clouds, and a huge shining sun. The days had grown longer and she was absorbing it all in.
"Of course I know that! Sweetie, I know you better than you know yourself" Selena says.
Esselle turns in her seat to face her. "Do you think Mardrin knows me that well?" she asks in pure curiosity. Esselle had never doubted their love or anything the other one said. She never had too. She never doubted the faith within each other. But it had never stopped ehr from wondering.. She knew enough about the man she loved to write a biography on him. could he say the same for her?
Selena sighs and brings her feet to the ground with a thump.
"Elle, you hit the jackpot with that one. He couldn't live without you. He just lives through you. I'm telling you. Elle doesn't see it but Selena does. Sometimes I just wonder if God forbid anything happened to you" she says and her tone becomes softer "what on

Somewhere in Time- trilogy part 2

Earth he'd do without you. Sometimes I think he just might kill himself" she says and her eyes are distant. Esselle takes her hands and chuckles.
"selena why are you talking like that. Nothings going to happen to me I'm fine!" she says. Selena swallows hard and meets Elle's eyes dropping her distant look. She nods.
"Ya you're right" she says with a hint of uncertainty. Esselle opens her mouth to speak but there's a shout.
"Hey gorgeous you come here offten?"
Esselle looks behind her and she breaks out into a wild smile. Mardrin smiles back at her. Selena rolls her eyes.
"Oh God!" she moans and grabs her bag.
Mardrin stood at the gate with his partner and crime Stephen by his side. Stephen was somewhat like Mardrin body wise. But Stephen had chocolately brown hair and grey eyes compared to Maardrin's yellow-green eyes and golden blonde hair.
Esselle yanked her bag right of the bench and darted down towards the gate.
"Elle you know I don't do running!" Selena called from behind her.
"At least she runs to great her boyfriend!" Stephen calls up and Selena makes a face.
Esselle falls into Mardrin's arms and she's lifted from the groudn when he kisses her. Selena laughs in the background. It had been Esselle's favorite part of day seeing mardrin after school. School was always such a drag it was nice to see his face at the end of the day. It was the one part of day she had anticipated everyday since junior high. She had never loved anyone else. And never loved anyone more. the feeling for him was mutual. His fingers grazed

the bottom of her back the way the always did and Selena finally caught up and kissed Stephen's cheek.

"There" she says and Esselle's feet touch the ground when Mardrin releases her.

"So how was school?" he asked and Esselle snorts.

"I'm with you. So I'm better now" she says and slips her hand into his.

"In other words it was awful" Selena said and Stephen wrapped his arm around her.

Mardrin nodded "Ahh I see!" he says.

"How was your day at school" Esselle asked truly curious. He kissed her again.

"Oh Elle, I'm with you now so I'm fine. Let's just say I'm glad its over" he says and tugs at her hand.

"Come on. Its Friday." he smiles "Let's go have fun"

sselle slept in her bed and drepmt of sweet kisses, love, and lovely lullabys. Esselle had gone on a double date the other night with Selena and Stephen and it was She and Mardrin. It ended the same way it always did. Selena and Stephen 'somehow'

Somewhere in Time- trilogy part 2

'mysteriously' got seperated and the innocent Esselle and Mardrin were left alone. Which was ok Esselle thought it just made it easier to kiss without judgement.

But now esselle had been burried deep under her silk chiffon cushions and thick blanket in her glamrous bedroom. She had been tossing and turning all night and finally fell asleep. She was talking to Mardrin all night on the phone. Which ruined her sleep schedule. But she didn't care. She just loved hearing him speak and the sound of his voice was soothing. Sometimes she'd sit up in her bed all night and wonder how she could have been lucky to be so happy?

There was a shearing pain in Esselle's side and she sharply took in air. Her sleepy eyes began to peel open when she began feeling masueated. There was now a searing pusling pain in her head. her skin began to crawl and she felt the urge too...

She rolled over in her bed and she banged into the night stand. her Tiffany Lamp fell to the ground and shattered. She clutched her stomach and vomitted. She was so dizzy and light headed and tired she leaned back against her bed. Her insides felt as if someone took there hand shoved it through her grabbed everything then squeezed and twisted.

"Mom!" she called "Dad!" But her voice was drowned out by her insides being pucked out from her mouth.

She rolled over because the pain was too much. she began coughing up blood when ehr bedroom door was flown open.

"Elle!" her mother gasped and fell to her daughters side on her knees. Esselle tried to speaking but her mind was spinning. She felt like there was and odd spark pinching her body in various places like electricity. Then the blood came from her mouth again and her eyes shut tight. She couldn't bear the pain she thought it was too awful.

"Vivenne" she heard her father say but everything was foggy "What have we done?" he asked and it was almost a whisper. Esselle's eyes burst into tears but not because she wanted them too. they just did. She looked at her parents and their faces were unreadble. half shock mortification the half curiosity and horro.

"What's wrong with me" Esselle moaned and her father stroked her hair.

"We have to get her to the lab" he said and Vivenne didn't protest.

"Now" was what her mother had said. And then Esselle blanked.

Somewhere in Time- trilogy part 2

sselle had felt as if she'd been dreaming. Where ever she was she felt as if everything around her had been spinning. She'd hear voices once in a while. She didn't know who though. They were just voices. Some sounded faint some were louder than others some stronger than others but what had heard over and over again is "What have we done?" And that was all Esselle had thought about for a while. Really, what had they done?
Esselle began to slowly grow concious. Her eyes slowly peeled open and it pained her to do so. When she got a speck of light into her eyes she squinted then forced them open again. The colors of whatever was around her just swirled like it did in the movies she liked to watch. The govenrment movies where the good guy gets drugged and they couldn't see straight. That's how it was like for Esselle. It especially hurt Esselle when she fully opened her eyes. She moaned and took in a deep breath. it had taken a while for Esselle to notice and grasp the fact that

Somewhere in Time- trilogy part 2

someone was holding her hand and tight. As if in anticipation. the anticipation of awakening from whatever daze she had fallen under. Her vision finally was no longer fuzzy and she could for the most part see clearly. At first she thought she was in a strange place until everythign started taking its place. She was in her parents lab. In the medical room there. She recognized the feeling of the bedsheets where she slept because when she was younger and went to work with her parents she had slept in the medical room. She liked naps very much so.

Esselle turned her head only to be rewarded by a sharp pain running down her spine.

"Hey Elle" someone had said. Her vision began to focus and she could see a golden halo around someone's head.

"Mardrin" she moaned. he had looked...different to Esselle. He looked as if he hadn't slept for days. His eeys were yellow-green and red. His perfectly groomed hair was losse in locks pushed to the side. His face seemed to be drained of color in the light. Besides herself Esselle laughed. "You look like a mess. But since you're so hot I'll you a hot mess" she says and he laughs. Esselle knew he knew that a hot mess was worse then just a mess. They have joked about such things before.

"Look who's talking. You look awful" he says and the smile on her face is weak with sickness.

"Is it alright if I..." Esselle began. But Mardrin was already nodding. He took her shoulders and helped her sit up.

"So" esselle groans. Mardrin laughs and pushes the hair from her face. "How long was Sleeping Beauty out?" she asks. He let's out a deep breath.

"A few days. Although I have to talk to you about something very

Somewhere in Time- trilogy part 2

serious" he says and her blood runs cold.

"What is it?" she asks.

"I think I'm going to have to beat some guy up" he begins and Esselle's mind drowns in confusion "I tried kissing sleeping beauty and she didn't awaken from ehr slumber. I wanna know who this guy is and where he is so I can kick his ass" he says and Esselle bursts into hysteria. Her head begins to thump and she stops laughing with a sob.

The room falls silent for a moment and then their eyes meet.

"What happened? To me, I mean. Why am I here?" she asked and glanced around. They were the only two in the room and she hadn't heard anyone outside.

He took her hand in both of his and placed his mouth an chin on them. Then he looked up at her.

"What do you remember?' he asked. Her head was beginning to pound and she was annoyed with the pain constantly coming up. She shook her head "No, almost nothing at all" she said. Esselle had never seen Mardrin look so broken and lost before. But even hurt he still looked beautiful. Like something heaven sent. She remembered when they were younger and would attend parties with their parents. They were always the only children their age. Every other child had either been in diapers or old enough to participate in the adult conversations. They would sit in a corner. It hadn't been what usual children would do. They never believe in cuddies but they were very formal and cordial with each other. Until they had gotten older and talked more. And then one day during the spring May 1st to be exact they had realized they had fallen in love with each other. And it was history ever since.

He let's out a deep breath "Elle, your sick" he says as if there's a

Somewhere in Time- trilogy part 2

knife in his throat. Esselle's heart stopped.

"What do you mean?" she asked. When he looked at her his eyes daid it all. He knew something she didn't. And he wasn't about to tell her.

"They don't know with what or how. They've seen such a thing before that's inside of you this sickness they say is or maybe uncurable. They just know there's somethign wrong. You passed out your parents said that night in your bedroom and you hadn't opened your eyes since. Its been days. This is your first time waking up" he says and Esselle could hear his voice deep scratchy and almost choking.

"Oh Mardrin" she croaked nad laid her hand on his face. Was this true? it hadn't felt true. Esselle was shocked but for some reason he had seemed more distaught then she. He turned his face deeper into her hand and left it there.

"Mardrin I-" she said and stopped. She had no idea how to comfort him. He was suppoesed to be comforting her! Not the other way around. She had been the one that just discovered she was sick not him. But it was natural she guessed for her to think of him before herself. She always had.

He turned his face in her hand and kissed her palm.

"I'll be alright" she whispered even though she wasn't sure.

"No!" he said and took both her hands. "You don't understand you don't know what has been done"

Esselle laughed a bit "What are you talking about? Millions of people get sick every day Mardrin and they work through it. Whatever it is our parents will find out and I'll be all better" she said.

He shook hsi head again "No, you don't understand this, this, is uncurable you can die" he says and the tears burn in the back of Esselle's eyes. "Oh Elle I can't loose you. I can't!" he said oh so softly but with so much emotion it broke her heart. She swallowed hard. Was this true? Was the time left in her life just ticking away and sliping through her fingertips. This sickness he was talking about would it really end her life? Would it cut the time she had with the man she loved her friends her family short? Would she ever get to live her life? Will she even make it through high school all the thoughts surfacing her mind.

She reached over despite the pain pulsing through her viens and hugged him and he wrapped his hands around her. She let herself cry in his arms and she didn't move.

"I don't want to die" she said and she felt him nod. "I don't...I don't want to leave you here! Without me!" she said. She had been crying so much she had been gasping for air and short of breath. He stroked her hair which just made her cry more. One day probably soon she wouldn't be able to feel that again. She wouldn't be able to hear him laugh or hold his hand or love him or kiss him or be near him. She wouldn't be able to look into her mother's eyes when she smiled and hugged her father when he was filled with an overwhelming joy.

"Elle," he said and began to tear away. Esselle sniffled and clung harder "Esselle" he said and tilted her head back.

"What am I supposed to do?" she asked.

He took in a deep breath and didn't stop looking at her "I love you Esselle I want you knwo that. No matter what I love you and I will always love you. I don't care I'll be with you until the end. I won't leave your side you hear me? I want it to clearly reach your eyes and stick in your mind. Elle," he says and takes her hands

Somewhere in Time- trilogy part 2

again "I'll find a way" he says.

Esselle nodded. He tilted his head. "Alright?" he asked. She nodded again and he wipped the tears from her face. He brought his hand to the back of her neck and kissed her forehead. She looked down at her hands in his one hand and swallowed hard.

"I love you too" she said and looked at him. He nodded.

"Oh I know" he said. Despite the arrogance in his tone Esselle smiled. He knew she hated his sarcasm but tolerated it anyway because she loved him.

"You'll be alright" Mardrin said reassuring her. She nodded

"Ok?" he said and kissed her. For a moment Esselle felt better and the worls melted away. She felt at peace. He pulled away and pressed his forehead to hers.

"You'll be alright" he said and Esselle couldn't help but catch the doubt and uncertainty in his voice. It made her stomach turn.

Somewhere in Time- trilogy part 2

sselle had placed herself in seclusion. She didn't let any in her room. She had locked all the doors in her part of the house. She locked the doors to her private living room, study, library, and lounge. Esselle kept all the windows shut depriving herself of warm spring air and breezes. She kept all the beatiful french doors to the balconies shut leaving the latch locked. Her mother Vivenne had banged the door until it practically came down. But it hadn't. Words were just echoing through Esselle's mind. "rare form of cancer" "Only one of its kind" "Uncurable" "Not responding to treatments" "Just try and go about your life like normal" "There is no definite amount of time you have left" "Death?" "Soon" All the words had made Esselle sick to her stomach.

Selena had came a few days ago. Maybe 2 or 3. She pounded on the door and cursed Esselle until her hands grew dumb and she broke into sobs and she was unable to open the door. Esselle had heard her slide against her bedroom door bang her head against it and cry. Eventually the pain had been too much for Esselle to bear and she pushed the sliding doors and went into her study. Her father had came by earlier that day. Esselle didn't want to think about it but his tone of voice just broke her heart and stood there in the back of her mind. He had begged and pleaded for hsi daughter to come out. But she still wouldn't. Esselle didn't think she'd ever come out.

Somewhere in Time- trilogy part 2

How could they all just say that to her? Say that life would go on? Say she'd be fine and she just needed to live her life? Of course life would go on. For them. For them it always would. They weren't the ones with their lives ticking away. They weren't the ones that the next time they'd see sky might be the last or the next breath they took would be their end or the next sunrise or sunset they saw would be the only one left in their lives. How was she to go on living that way? It had seemed so impossible for her. She did not want to be swarmed by people and sympathy. If she were going to die one day soon at least she'd die in peace. But against her will she still managed to take those awful vitamins everyday. They were slipped under her door every morning at 8 o clock on the dot.
Never failed.
But now Esselle needed to do something because she was ready to die of bordeom. So she sat at her piano and played Fur Elise. Esselle had always done very well with playing piano. It had been her skill. Her fingers poudnign on the black and white cures out of pure anger letting the anguish escape her viens. She was angry. She was mad she was hurt she was burning with emotion on the inside. She had banged in they keys so hard the ground below her vibrated and the piano made a hard loud noise that vibrated in her ears. She sighed when the song came to an end. She flipped through her music sheets and pulled out something with a softer higher sweeter tone.
Her fingers were so fast when they glidded across the keys it looked as if they were flying or just weren't even touching they keys. This is what she had done when she was angry. When she was furious.

Somewhere in Time- trilogy part 2

So with with Esselle always having been so happy her playing this way was not often.

Esselle hadn't noticed at first but she heard a clicking noise and eerr sound and then another click. She took in a deep breath. She already knew who it was. Mayjor jerk face must have picked the lock. He always did that. God now she'd have to talk to him. She loved him but her just didn't understand what she was going through. Or maybe she had not given him the chance to do so. Either way some company right now she wouldn't mind its just that she couldn't help but feel her stomach turn.

She didn't know just his presence was alone was comforting yet sickening.

His arms wrapped around her and she smiled continuing to play. He placed his chin on her shoulder and she let out a depe breath. She hadn't talked to anyone in days and she didn't know what to do or what to say or what he'd say. She didn't want to talk about what was wrong with her and that she was potentially dying. It was just awful.

"Hey Elle" he said and kissed her cheek. She sighed and continued to play.

"Hi Mardrin' she says and he slides into the seat next to her.

"You know I'm awful at playing piano" he says and she laughs a little "So I can't play alonjg with you"

Esselle shook her head "No, its alright" she says.

"Elle" he said and she ignored him. If it weren't for the fact that she hated crying mostly never did the tears would come pouring out right about now. "Esselle" he said and she continued to ignore him.

"Esselle!" he said and took her hands. She looked up at him. It was the most heartrending look in the world. her eyes glossy with tears her jaw clenched tight and her breathing speading up hiding the sobs. He sighed.

"Oh Elle please don't cry" he says. She presses her lips together and the tears streak her face. "Esselle please" he said and took her into his arms.

She knotted her fists in his shirt and cried into his shoulder without restraint letting the sobs and whimpers and pain surface. She didn't care she could be herself in front of him. It didn't matter not to her not to him. That's why she loved him.

"What am I going to do?" she sobbed so hard she had to catch her breath. He stroked her hair and swallowed hard.

"I don't know Esselle" he says.

"How can they just say that to me?" she whimpered "Say that I'm fine and that to just go on with my life?"

"Esselle..." he said

"I can't Mardrin I just can't! I don't want to die! I want to stay and be here with you! I don't want to leave!" she cried and he held her tighter.

"What am I supposed to do now?" she asked and pulled away to look at him. He opened his mouth to speak but then shut it again. She sat up straight and looked down at the piano keys. Soon the tears began coming again. They were so consistent and warm that it felt as if Esselle had her face under a warm shower. Mardrin wrapped an arm around her shoulder and pulled her close while she laid her head on his. She had begun to cry so much there was a shortness of breath and she couldn't cry anymore because she was struggling to breath. She cowered up and rolled into a ball putting her feet up.

"I can't believe this is happening to me. I'm going to die" she said so low it was a whisper.

"Oh Esselle. Stop. Please don't talk like that. I can't loose you I won't" he said.

"Well I don't know why everyone's making such a big deal out of it anyway! Telling me to go on ahead and just live my life! With whatever is left of it anyway! I'm just as good ten feet in the ground!" she snapped to no one in particular. At that moment Mardrin snapped. He hated all this talk of death of loosing the only person he had ever loved more than anything in the world. Yet Esselle knew that and she said it anyway. All this anger and animasity was bottling up inside her for so long she was ready to burst under the pressure. But she didn't care she let it out anyway and she was glad that she did.

Mardrin grabbed her shoulders "Stop That" he said.

"Stop that right now. Stop talkign like that. Nothing is going to happen to you. There's is nothing bad or wrong. I'm here. I won't let anythign happen to you you hear me Esselle? nothing. I don't care sickness, to hell with it. I'm not loosing you. You'll be alright I know you will" eh said with the only softness she had ever heard but still hard and stern it made her shiver. his eyes softened "You just have to be strong" was what he said to her. She looked away again at the piano and felt her eyes burning like a thousand suns.

"It's all over for me Mardrin" she said and looked him. She covered her mouth when the powerful whimpers came and the tears once again. This time it was so much she had a hand over her stomach and almost fell forward crying and gasping for air practically shrieking with pain. He pulled her back into his arms and she cried there. She could feel his heart rate slowing and him swallowing hard.

"I'm never going to get married! I'm never going to have children!" she cried.

"Of course you are" he said and looked at her. Esselle had always wanted to be a mother to four children. Mardrin wanted two so they compromised on three.

"I'm going to tell you exactly what's going to happen to you Elle" he said and turned her to face him.

"You are going to grow up and graduate high school. Top of your class. Then you'll go to college to be a writer then graduate and start your career. You'll get engaged and then married. TO me. Just like we've always wanted. Nothing is ever going to change that. And then sometime after that you'll be a mother and we'll raise our children the best we can. Elle, everythign will be fine and the same. I won't let anything change that" he said and she swallowed hard.

"You can even have that fabulous car you wanted" he teased and she laughed. WHen she did she realized she hadn't laughed in a while.

"Mardrin" she said fidling with fabric of his shirt.

"Hm" he said.

"Do you really think I'll have that fabulous car?" she asked and he laughed. His laughter lit up the room like a hundred stars. Just like it always did.

He kissed her "Of course you are!" he said like he hadn't been more sure of anythign else in the world.

He leaned down and whispered into her "You'll even get the diamond ring you've always wanted" he teased. She smiled.

sselle had always loved the way the trees swayed in the wind. She loved the peace and joy that had gone along with it. It was a beautiful but warm day the day she had decided she wanted to be a writer. She was around 13 years old. She had many jobs before that she wanted to be. For a while she tried so hard to be a singer. But she realized she should just sing at the church masses her Catholic school sent her to and that was it. She had wanted to be an actress. Now that she was good at. She always got the lead in the school play. It took a lot to get herself out of that mind frame but the thought was always there. And then teacher was on her list for a while because she had two teachers in junior high that changed her life. She truly did love those wonderful teachers and had always said one day when she hit it big as a writer they'd be there at her book signings. And by her side on the red carpet. Because lets face it she was determined to one day be an Oscar winner as a free time. Esselle had always been a writer. Since she was an infant all her parents did was read to her. When she was three she wrote on the walls and said it was a story about a flower. It wasn't until she was 8 in the second book when she realized she was good at writing. She had used up all the paper in the class room for her story. Then as the years had gone by and Esselle looked back in her memory she just found more and more evidence of ehr being an execellent writer. That was her true talent. And she was always determined to stick with it. Then when she was in fifth grade she wrote the very first story she ever cared about and it was writing ever since until she turned 12 and got published in poetry books a few times and won contests for her writing. And then she was 13 and she had set her midn to it. Typing away for long hours in front of a computer screen. That was Esselle. The beauty of today had just reminded Esselle of the day she decided to be a writer. It was night time she was sitting on the stoop of her cousins house in Ridgewood, Queens and she was watching the trees sway. It gave her inspiration. But she couldn't say the same. Now, she was lying on the grass in central park with Selena watching the trees sway and there was no inspiration. nothing that gave her the spark to go on. just plain old simple. Nothing.

The sky was the bluest it had ever been and the clouds were so white they hurt your eyes. Selena lie there by her side with her hands behind her head. And she lie there with her hands folded over her stomach. Finally Esselle turned over to face her.

"Sel," she said picking a blade of grass.

"Hm, her friend replied and looked at her.

Esselle took in a deep breath. It had been a week since Mardrin dragged her out of her bedroom. Now she was just living everyday like it were her last. Literally.

"Do you think," she began and felt her stomach turn. She cleared her throat "Do you think I'll make it?" she asked and Selena fully turned to face her. "Be honest" she said as she already saw the look in her friend's eyes.

"I don't usually think about it. I just try being there for you" she said and every word seemed like it killed her. over and over again.

"Its going to happen eventually" Esselle said blandly. Why was everyone not facing the truth already? She was. Selena shook her head.

"No, Elle, You just don't understand the thought of loosing you...' she said and stopped searching for words "The thought of you not being here-" she said and Esselle took her hand.

"Selena you know its going to happen" she said.

"No!" Selena snapped and sprang up. "I don't want it to happen!" she said and sounded like a mounring child nagging.

"I don't want to loose my best friend Elle! You've been here through everything! I want you to stay here and be here through everything! I want you to be by myside when my future fiance gets down on one knee, I want you to be my maid of honor, I want you holding my hand in the delivery room when I'm about to give birth to my first child, and I want you at the baby shower for my next!" she said.

"I want you to be the God mother of my children! I want to be there for you too! I want to be there when Mardrin gets down on one knee! I want to be your maid of honor! I want to squeeze your hand tight when you're popping out your kid and I want to be there at the baby shower for the next! I want you to be my kids God Parents" she said and sat back on her elbows while the tears rushed down her face.

She bit her lip and her eyes scoured the grass. "You have no idea how much this is hurting me Elle" she said and Esselle just

Somewhere in Time- trilogy part 2

looked at her trying to figure out what to say.

"I don't want you to die. I want you to be right here by myside. Who's, who's gonna be there to stick up for me for my stupid ass mistakes" she said starting to cry and Esselle slowly sat up. "Who is going to be there those late nights on the phone when my heart is broken or the early mornings when I have so much gossip i'm going to burst. Who's going to be there to borrow lip gloss from or paint my nails with or buy clothes or for God's sake fix my bra when I need them to because the damn strap keeps sliping!" she said flinging her hands in the air. Esselle just laughed.

"Who's going to be there for me?" Selena whispered.

Esselle took her hands. "Selena I'll always be there for you. Always watching over you when that time has came" she said softly.

"No!" Selena snapped and took her hands back "I don't want that" she said through gritted teeth and crying eyes "I want you right here by myside where I can feel you and touch you and punch your shoulder when you get out of hand" she says and Esselle laughs.

Finally the reality had caught up to Esselle. She swallowed hard. Sometimes it was hard for her too to try and be realistic. But sometimes you just can't.

"You didn't deserve this Elle" Selena said ferociously wiping her tears "You really didn't" she said and her hands pounded hard on the grass.

Esselle sighed and looked to the sky "Selena" she said and her friend looked at her.

"What?" Selena asked.

"I'm glad that before I die' she says and meets her eye "At least I got to be friends with you"
Selena looked at her "me too" she croaked.
Esselle laid down on the grass once more. "I wonder when I'll die" she said.
"Stop saying that" her friend pleaded. Esselle laughed a little. She extended her arm showing her friend the inside. Her forearm was pale very pale and the viens were so visible it was like looking at a big ink smudge on a white wedding gown.
"I'm getting wekaer, no use in hiding it" she said and took her arm back and turned to the sky once more.
Selena grabbed her purse and pulled out her makeup bag.
"You're fine" she sniffled. She took out bronzer and foundation and covered Esselle's arm in it.
"There" she said and gave her a sorrow ful smile. "You're fine"
Esselle shook her head. She grabbed a napkin and wiped it right off.
'No!' selena shrieked and grabbed her arms tears pouring out of her eyes.
"No stop it! You're fine! You're Esselle you're my best friend and you're not dying you're fine!" she said and broke out into a whimper. so much so her body looked as if it were vibrating.
Esselle gently took her arm back. "Just accept it. You'll make it harder on yourself" esselle said. Suddenly she felt like a ghost.

Somewhere in Time- trilogy part 2

Somewhere in Time- trilogy part 2

"Mardrin" Esselle said. Mardrin continued to do what he was doing, chew on his pen and read from his text book, and responded by saying "Hmm?"
"Do you think there really is a God?" she had asked him and at that he looked up. Demeanor unchanging but his eyes locked on hers he said "Of course there is. Its all I believe in" he said and she remaind silent "Don't you?" he asked.
Esselle continued to rock in the hammock on the terrace in his penthouse and looked out over the city. Esselle was never raised to believe in a God. Her parents were but they said they wanted her to decide. Now she was dying and it was time to decide. Is there or is there not?
Mardrin sighed and slammed his textbook shut. Finals were this week and he always studied. And hard. But he didn't mind doing it with her. The setting sun was adding layers to his hair and face. His face was all angles and shapr structure. Nothing fine and smooth about it. His hair was a golden halo around his head when the sun glistened upon him and his hair had some kind of sparkle or glow. His yellow-green eyes in the sun resembled that of a cat. Beautiful.
"Esselle," he said and she cut him off.
"Mardrin don't patronize me. I may have gone to private school but I wasn't raised that way. I wasn't raised to believe. You were." she said. Of course Esselle always felt like there was some kind of higher power up there watching over them. Her granparents were by the book catholics and everyone else in her family were dedicated religious freaks. It was in her blood. But with lack of support from her scientist parents...well...things like that get hard.

"I believe it with all of my heart, mind, body, and soul" he said rising from his chair. She smiled.
"Well aren't you a little goody two shoes" she said and he stood over her. He shrugged.
'More or less" he said and stole a kiss.
"So," she said and he looked at her. 'Do you have all of your, what's those called sacramentals?" she asked. he laughed shutting his eyes. he had his fists in the hammock at her sides and then he looked at her.
"Sweetheart, you mean sacraments" he says.
"Well whatever! sacraments! don't tease me about it!' she said and he laughed. She slouched with a wry smile.
"You know I'm getting a little sick and tired of you picking on me with all of that sarcasm' she says.
He made a face and nodded growing closer "Ya alright mhm" he said and she made a funny face two bringing her arms around her neck.
"Uhu!" she said with a laugh. They both smiled in the warm sunlight. It was times like these Esselle would miss when she was gone. but she quickly pushed the thought aside in her head. She was not going to let such a morbid thought ruin her moment with Mardrin. it could ruin any other moment but not when he was about to kiss her. Those times are sacred.
Their lips touched and Esselle felt tingly everywhere. She wanted to laugh. She thought about what would happen if his parents came in right at that moment. Esselle would laugh then be mad for interrupting the moment then laugh all over again.
He enveloped her in his arms and she rose from the hammock with her fingers getting locked with his golden hair.

Somewhere in Time- trilogy part 2

Finally the air and space between them was gone when he hugged her and kissed her at the sametime. Esselle didn't want to die. She had decided she was going to fight to live. Just so that moments like these there could be more of. She ready to pull away but then she went sick with dizziness and happiness and didn't bother. His fingers grazed the bottom of her back tracing the circles the he always did. Always did. And always will. Because at that very moment Esselle had decided she was to live and she wasn't going to die. She would survive for him. She would survive for Selena. She would survive for her parents. Most importantly she was going to live for herself. Because she wanted to see it happen. She picked her feet up from the ground and he held her not stopping their kiss. that was it. One more thing and Esselle was sure to budge she was sure to laugh. He hated holding her in the air. mardrin thought it was such a cliche movie thing. but Esselle didn't mind. In fact she loved it more than anything. So the very few moments Mardrin held her in the air she cheerished them. But then they were over and she was urging for more. she tugged on his hair and smiled against his mouth. he hated that too. he did the same and finally she broke away to laugh. Her feet touched the ground and she was standing on her own completely again.

"I hate it when you do that" he said with a chuckle. Esselle on the verge of hysteria nodded.

"Oh I know" she said and kissed him "That's why I did it" she said and kissed him again.

"Please don't do it anymore!" he said and kissed her. This time longer. It was mid May that of Esselle's favorite when the weather is the most beautiful. Well, her second favorite.

She pulled away and kept her eyes shut.
"I want to ask you something" she said.
"Anything" was his reply. She opened her eyes and smiled.
"Oh no, I take that back. I know that look" he said and her smile just grew wider.
"Well you have your sacramental thingys" she said and he rolled his eyes "Well I want them too" she said and he smiled.
"I think its a great idea"
****
****

Esselle had gotten what she always forgot were sacraments and not sacramentals quickly because Mardrin knew a guy. The thought made her roll her eyes. He always knew a guy. It had been in a beautiful church with pretty everything. From that moment on he rtaught her what he knew in his faith and Esselle learned that religion contained healing powers but only if you attended a mass. Whatever that was. So she did. Every sunday from that moment on. It never failed.

Somewhere in Time- trilogy part 2

Mardrin you don't like it?" Esselle asked and Selena's face fell. Mardrin shook his head "Esselle why did you dye your hair it lookws awful" he said.

Esselle stomped hard on the ground "It does not! And its a simple blonde highlight!" she faught back.

Mardrin shook his head and took one of her curls.

"How could you do this to your beautiful hair Esselle? Not only did you dye it you cut it to practically nothing!" he said. Esselle jerked away from him.

"It hits my shoulders! I didn't want it below my butt anymore!" she snapped and Stephens lips flattened to a flat line when he pressed them together. Selena, Stephen, Mardin and Esselle were on Mardrin's Terrace in the setting golden sunlight. Esselle had been exicted to show Mardrin her new hair but he seemed so annoyed but what she had done. It was her head what the hell?!

"Esselle I want you ti dye it back" he said and sat in one of the pretty metal chairs.

Her jaw dropped "Dye it back? But I like it" she said and he shrugged.

"Elle I really hate the way it looks. You ruined your hair" he said. She rolled her eyes.

"Sorry dad!" she said.

"I will break up with you Elle don't test my patience" he said and looked over the city.

She snorted "Right, because you'll break up with me" she said and he smirked.

"Why you scared?" he asked.

She shot him a glare.

"I think it looks fine! It looks awesome with her new dress" Selena said coming to her defense.

"That's another thing that dress looks like she should have someone's phone number written across her leg. I don't mind but I don't want any other girl looking at her" he teased. Esselle looked down at her fitted summer dress. She had thought it was fine.

"You know you're being a real asshole today" Esselle said crossing her arms.

Mardrin laughed "I loved you but I'm sorry it looks awful. And please stop crossing your arms. I hate it when you do that" he said and Stephen made an unpleasant noised. Esselle looked over. he was trying not to laugh.

Mardrin laughed and soon Selena broke into a smirk.

"What yhe hell is this pick on Elle day?" Esselle snapped.

Mardrin laughed. He reached over grabbing her wrist and pulling her over to sit on his lap. She did so but kept a face to show her annoyance.

Somewhere in Time- trilogy part 2

"You look as mad as the time I told you I hated those stupid books you were reading" he teased. She smacked her hands on her thigh and looked back at him.
"I love literature! How do you not?' she said and he shrugged.
"I love sports how do you not?' he said and she rolled her eyes.
"You also love that Molart guy" he says and everyone laughs.
"His name is Mozart!" she ranted. She hated when he did that. Teased her because their likes and interests were so different. It annoyed her to the point she'd want to wrip his head off.
"Or how about all those old movies she loves watching" Selena teased. Mardrin with wide eyess nodded.
"God, what was that dear awful like 5 hour movie she wanted me to sit down and watch with her? Gone with what?" he asked.
"Gone with the Wind" Esselle corrected.
'ya that! I wanted top shoot myself" he said.
"You know that's not fair Mardrin! good boyfriends do stuff like that wuth their girlfriends! I sit and watch your games becaus I know it makes you happy and thats what girlfriends do. Would it be a little too much to ask you do the same" she said.
His eyes widened sardonically "Yes!" he said "Elle not five hours! And watch movie after movie with you! They are not even in color half the time!"
She ignored his stupid remark and began twisting her ring on her finger. Mardrin's hand covered ehrs.
"Stop that its annoying" he said and went on and conversated with Stephen.
"You know I was thinking I might want to go into fashion one day" Esselle said. The terrance was silent for a moment. Mardrin was the first to laugh a little dismissing her comment.

Somewhere in Time- trilogy part 2

"Esselle you in fashion?" he said and looked at her "With that outfit" he teased and her heart sank. Gees, a little support would be nice.

"You're going to be a writer and a house wife Esselle. Fashion isn't for you. You don't have what it takes to make it. You'd never be able to do it"

"You never know" she protested and he rolled his eyes,

"Right, because Esselle can make it in the fashion industry" he said. She sighed and looked around. She began to fiddle with her hair. Mardrin took her wrist gently and placed her hand on her lap.

"I hate it when you do that" he whispered and continued to talk to Stephen. All she wanted was a little bit of attention. Sometimes that was rather hard woth Mardrin. In fact a hundred percent difficult.

"Come on" Esselle said rising from her seat on his lap. She took his hand.

"Let's go inside and freeze some popcicles or something" she said.

"Like five year olds?" he said and Selena got up from her chair and took Esselle's arm.

"I'll go with you" she said and her friend smiled at her. They walked inside together.

"Judging by how he's acting" Selena said grabbing juice from the fridge "He's in one of those moods"

"Yes, and now Esselle is the punching bag" she said rolling her eyes. She grabbed the cartain of grape juice and gently poured it into some popcicle trays.

"I really love your hair Elle" Selena said. Esselle looked up and

Somewhere in Time- trilogy part 2

smiled.

"Thanks" she said.

****

Night had fallen and everyone was inside with the a.c on watching the Bugs Bunny cartoons on rerun.

"I hate these" Esselle muttered. Mardrin had his arm around her on the black couch. His entire penthouse was beautiful with high ceilings and the walls were made of glass so you could see outside. There was a big stone fire place and the mantle was intricate.

Mardrin looked at her "I love these" he said.

"I'd rather watch Tom and Jerry on rerun" she said and he made a sound.

"I hated that show when I was a kid!" he said and she laughed a bit.

Being with Mardrin not only was out of love but secretly because of how easy and convinent it was. The parents knew each other they knew each other. It seemed easy enough. When Esselle found she liked him she didn't even bother with anyone else. She had decided it was him. Period Amen.

"Ice cream and milk!" Selena said and put the tray on the table.

"Mm chocolate ice cream" Esselle said and took a bowl.

Mardrin made a face then smiled. 'Vanilla is better" he said and smiled at her.

"Strawberry milk" he said and grabbed a cup. They liked mixing odd things for snacks. Esselle shook her head.

"Strawberry is awful. Chocolate milk is better" she said and took a cup.

Somewhere in Time- trilogy part 2

"We can totally warm this milk up and give ourselves stomach aches." Stephen said and everyone laughed.
"I can put marshmellows in mine" Esselle said and Selena tossed a bag to her.
"Got that covered" Selena said.
"Eww! Marshmellows!" Mardrin teased.
"You're just odd. Saying you don't like marshmellows is like saying you hate joy and smores" she said.
"Its because I do hate smores" he said and Stephen laughed.
"You guys make such an odd yet cute couple" he said and Esselle made a scrunched up smile.
"Thanks doll" she said.
"Hey, I'm the boyfriend here" Mardrin said. She sat back and rolled her eyes.
"Whatever" she muttered. Mardrin smoothed his hand over her hair. She looked at me.
"I still can't believe you cut it all off" he said.
"Would you get over it already!" she said.
He shook his head with heavy eyes. You're curls look sad" he said and she laughed. Not as sad as she had been right then and there. There was a knock on the door.
"I'll go get it" Mardrin said standing from his spot on the couch. Esselle grew annoyed. She had been warm and snuggled up by his side and when he stood up she felt cold.
"Don't be long" she teased as he stood over her.
He bent down "I'll take forever now" he said and her jaw dropped. He took her face in his hand and kissed her with warm lips that tasted sweet like vanilla. Esselle kissed him back. He straightened up and walked out.

Somewhere in Time- trilogy part 2

Esselle heard him walk out of the living room down the long hallway and the door creaking open. She heard whispers and murmurs. She frowned and scanned their friends faces.
"Martha" she heard Mardrin say. Her friends faces gave it all away. They held a secret aching to be kept inside. They were hiding something and knew somethign was going on. yet they said nothing to her. She gently put her bowl down.
"Who's that?" she asked them. They shrugged and quickly looked away. She eased out of her seat and Selena looked sick to her stomach.
"Elle its not what you think" she said right away standing. Esselle frowned and geared toward the hallway.
"Elle please don't" Stephen said but it was too late. She was already out of the living room and aiming for the front door.
'Mardrin-" she said softly peaking past the corner but she stopped dead in her tracks.
She had never seen him do that with anyone before. With that much passion and love and fire it was beautiful. But deadly. Esselle felt the life slowly leave her body. She chocked slowly where she stood. She didn't know what to do or what to say. There in the door way a beautiful woman one of the most beautiful she had ever seen. She was around their age. She had beautiful blonde short thick straight hair. She had her arms wrapped around his neck and his arms were around her waist and they were kissing. It looked like something magical like that of soemthign taken out of a movie. Beautiful so beautiful. She was ready to kill him.
He gently pushed the girl away. "Martha" he said and she looked at her. Esselle had never seen Mardrin look at another woman

like that. Ever. Not even her.

'Mardrin who's that?" she asked and looked at him.

Mardrin looked over and he instantly realesed her and geared toward Esselle.

"Elle" he said when he reached for her. She yanked her arm back.

"Who is that?" Esselle demanded. Martha slowly came behind him.

"Who's she?" Martha asked.

"Martha stop it!" he snapped. "Elle its not what it looks like"

Esselle could feel her cheeks burnign with rage and her eyes itching with tears. She was not going to cry in front of him or anyone. They didn't deserve her tears. She smacked him. She smacked him so hard and fast it might have hurt her more than him. Then she darted for the living room grabbing her bag.

"Esselle you saw" Selena said slowly and painfully approaching her with the most sorrowful look on herface. Esselle's eyes burned through her when she gave her the look of death.

"Elle," Stephen began as if seeing the look on her face but she cut him off.

'You knew?" she asked.

"Elle" Selena reached for her but she brushed her off. It disgusted her being anywhere near any of the,. Esselle couldn't even think straight. Had she seen what she had just seen? Her stomach was turning and she had to leave. She had to get her mind straight. Wherever her mind was. She was everywhere. She thought she might besick and vomit all over the floor. She aimed for the door.

"Esselle!" Mardrin ran out after her. Esselle stepped into the elevator. Before it shut in front of him she shook her head unable

Somewhere in Time- trilogy part 2

to do anything else and managed to get something out.
"How could you?" she asked
"Dear God its not what you think!" he said. She pressed harder on the elevator button to shut the doors. She clenched her jaw tight. "I hate you" she spat.
"Elle" he said stopping in front of the elevator doors but they had already shut.
****
****

Esselle yanked the door to her Mercedes opened and just flew down the streets on New York City. She didn't know where she was going she just knew she had to get away. How could he do that to her?" she thought. It was a gorgeous warm night with beautiful stars and a full moon. The tears began to streak her face and she swallowed hard. How could he just betray her like that? She fiercly sratched the tears right off her face. She gripped the steering wheel so tight her knuckles went white. The window next to her was open and the wind was rushing through the car making her feel as if she were flying. She was so hurt and betrayed. It felt as if someone had taken either part of her heart and was slowly tearing it apart so that she may feel every separate tear.
She had given him everything all she had. He was the only love she had ever known. She gave him her heart and world and more. yet he stabbed her in the back. Martha was beautiful. Far prettier than Esselle he knew that. It was as if he got someone like her just to spite and tease esselle on purpose but why? What had she ever done to him? all she did was love him.
She looked at her rearveiw mirror. She had been driving at 90

mph. She couldn't stop. She was on a highway going God knows where. She could see the city and the water in the distance. New York was beautiful at night. There was a car growing far to Close to Esselle. She tried to speed up and hit 105 mph. Speeding and zig zagging around cars. She was going too fast. She tried easing down. She panicked. Something was wrong. The car was just going faster. She screamed. The car behind her hit her bumper fast and hard. The cars speed went to 125 mph. She couldnm't stop. She slammed her foot on the brake. Nothing happened. She just kept goign. Esselle's hands scoured the controls on the car. She tried yanking her door open and jumping out but nothing happened. Soon enough the car behind her hit her hard in the back again and she shrieked. She reached for her hadn and lost grip of the steering wheel. The black car rammed her right side. She dropped her phone.
"Damn it!" she shouted and grabbed the steering wheel again. The wind from the open car window was blowing her now short curls everywhere. There were headlights in front of her. She screamed her for her life. The black car rammed into her. The car was at 200 mph. The steering wheel was turning uncontrollably and there was a huge truck driving straight into her. She jerked her arms and screamed. She saw lights. Big bright white lights and she felt as if she were flying. Flying right off the high way. There was only the sound of shattering glass and her heartrending scream.

Somewhere in Time- trilogy part 2

Somewhere in Time- trilogy part 2

t was cold. Wherever it was that Esselle was at. Her breathing was slow and normal but somehow she felt warm clam and tingly everywhere. For a while ever moment in Esselle's life had been going on. Over and over again on reply. From her very first memory to her last. Her first memory she can recall is being two years old in the park with her mother and father. They were smiling and laughing in the sunlight. She remembered being happy. Her last memory was noise, screams, and shattering glass. That had been it. She remembered no more no less. Suddenly her heart was breathing. she felt warmth pulse through her veins. Her fist knotted in what felt like bedsheets. She lie still on what felt like a bed. Her eyes were shut but she was very slowly and calmly breathing. Her grip on the bedsheet loosened. Then her eyes flew open.

Somewhere in Time- trilogy part 2

sselle could see lights over her head. She looked from side to side. The room she was in was all white with bright lights. She slowly sat up and she some how felt an odd hollow inside like she was out of place. She had a white tank top on and white stretch pants that stopped at her knee. Esselle looked around once more. there was a door and that was it. No windows or anything. Across from her was a cabinet made with a metallic kind of glass where she could semi see its contents. Where was she? It had been a stranged place to awaken. Esselle's head began to hurt a bit and her hand touched her head. Esselle's eyebrows furrowed. Her hair. She ran her fingers through her hair until it came all the way down to the tips. Her hair it was so odd. It was no longer blonde. All of her huge beautiful blonde highlights were gone. Her hair was its natural color. And her hair was no longer short. Its was long very long so long the way she had it before it was cut. Esselle felt off. Like when you took too long of nap and now when you wake up you regret sleeping soo long. She looked at her hands for a moment. Her nails were long and well groomed. Her hands felt soft and delicate. Esselle pulled the blanket off and slidded off the side of the bed. Her feet didn't reach the floor the bed was so high. Her toes, oddly, were painted red. She swung her feet back and forth the way they did when she was on the swing and her toes just barely grazed the floor. Her palms her pressed against the bed on either side of her with her shoulders hunched over. she tilted her head. Her favorite color was purple not red.

"She's awake!" esselle heard someone shout. She looked over and saw a man, who was probably middle eastern with no hair and a lab coat, frantic looking in front of the door she saw through the glass.

She frowned. She looked at her arms and very thin clear things were attatched to her skin. When she pulled them off they almost resembled wires. The odd looking machines on either side of her stopped doing whatever she was doing and she turned to look at the door again.

Everyone frantic some running around some craming around the door. She couldn't see much through the long narrow glass window on the door but she could see enough to know that something was going on.

"Get the docotrs!" she heard someone shout. She slid off the bed and walked over to the door slowly. She tilted her head and her eyebrows pressed together. As she walked closer to the door the faces through the glass turned with mixed expressions of awe and horror.

She stopped for a moment in front of the door and looked at them. Where on Earth was she?

She reached for the door knob.

"Elle?" she heard from behind her. She turned her head with a snap. All the way in the back of the room. Stood a figue in front of a door she had not noticed before she knew that figure and there was another one by the figures side. Her mother and father.

"Mom! dad!" She said with relief. Blinded by joy she ran into her arms. She hadn't noticed before but her mother's breath and

Somewhere in Time- trilogy part 2

heart beat against her chest was steady yet leaping. She could feel her breathing hard and her father's grip on her was tight.
She looked up ready to say something but her eyes widened.
"Mom, Dad" she said. Her mother was smiling with the teariest eyes she'd ever seen smiling and her father with deep sincere eyes fiilled with tears and a parted mouth.
"YOu look so old!" she said and her mother laughed. Her parents still looked young but old. Her mother's skin had aged at least ten of maybe even fifteen years as did her father's. His hair was turning salt and pepper. Their eyes were droppier with fine lines and her mother's hair color was dulling.
"You look exactly the same" her mother said.
"Well duh!" Esselle said. Her father smiled a bit. He stroked her hair.
"I knew we'd be able to do it one day" he said.
"What are you talking about?" she asked.
"Sweetheart, its been... a while" she said.
"Since what? I fled Mardrin's house?" She said all too sarcasticaslly. Mardrin. Her heart ached and raced at the same time. How was he not there? Where was he? Oh no maybe he was here and she wasn't awake yet. She had to find him for two reasons. One, she just had to she was in love with this man and she just woke up, and two he owed her an explination.
"Mardrin!" Esselle said and broke from her parents embrace. Her mother swallowed hard gaining her composure and her father stiffened.
'Where is he that wonderful loving two timing evil little maggit! I have to talk to him!" she said and darted towards her bed. Surely there were shoes she could slip on somewhere.

Somewhere in Time- trilogy part 2

"Elle sweetie" her mother said softly and slowly approaching her. "Dear God I must have been out for days!" she said. She looked over and saw a mirror. She flew over and checked her reflection. She was fixing her curls when she stopped. A few days. The last thing she had remembered was a car accident. She had not one bruise or scratch or anything on her body indicating that. Her hands carressed her skin and her eyebrows pressed together. Her face was full and glowing. Her body looked healthy and she looked healthy. No sign of being sick. Something was wrong. Her mother and father slowly stood behind her.

"Why aren't I-?' she said and her mother spoke.

"elle there was an accident" She said.

"Well I know that but..." Esselle said and began touching her skin again.

"What?" she whispered to herself.

"It was on the highway" he said.

"Ya, I was going home a few days ago. Where are we the lab? I've never seen this part" she said and her father looked at her.

"You were driving home and you were going too fast you drove right off the highway" he said.

"I know-!" Esselle began but her father cut her off.

"28 years ago" he said. Esselle froze. What had he just said to her?"Excuse me?" she said.

Her mother swallowed hard.

"Esselle 28 years ago you got into a car accident" she looked at her mother in a twisted horror "And died"

Esselle slowly stepped back "You're crazy I don't believe you. Where's my phone?" she said.

"Esselle that was 28 years ago no one uses iPhones. The company closed ten years ago" he said. She looked at them funny.

"What year is it?" she asked.

"Elle honey-" her mother said gearing toward her but Esselle spoke louder stopping her.

"I said what year is it?" she asked more forcefully.

Her mother stopped and held her hands together.

"2045" Vivenne said. Esselle's mind went blank again.

Somewhere in Time- trilogy part 2

2045" Esselle whispered "2045" she repeated. Before she knew it she was gripping hard on the bed to keep from loosing her balance. She was breathing hard and deeply. She looked at her parents.
"How the hell is it the year 2045?" she said. Esselle was ready to snap and loose her sanity. How do you just tell a 17 year old kid that they were asleep for 28 years?
Vivenne swallowed hard. "Esselle-" she said. Her husband looked at her and spoke instead.
"After your car accident you died. We couldn't loose you" he said. Esselle's eyebrow softly raised. "We had been working on an experiment here in the lab" he said.

Somewhere in Time- trilogy part 2

"We thought it was a long shot but we just had to. We had to try and save you. You were our only daughter left" his wife continued. Esselle put a hand up.

"Let's not" she said. Her mother looked down for a moment. She nodded.

"Anyway we froze you. Until we could bring you back one day" she said.

Her husband took her hand. "And it worked. Last week we removed you from your chamber. You were showing signs of predefrosting in the cold. You were awakening. Your heart had started up again on a normal pace all on its own. Luckily we froze you before you technically died died. Your heart almost stopped before we froze you" he said.

"Almost" his wife said. They smiled at each other then faced their daughter.

"But now you're here" Vivenne's tone was light and her face was beaming eyes still watery on the verge of tears "You're alive and still with us we thought we'd lost you" she said.

Esselle crossed her arms and looked around. How could this be? Esselle didn't know what to think. Where would she even begin?

"What is this place?" she finally asked. Her father had his arm around her mothers waist and her hand was on his chest like a pose for a pretty picture.

Her mother looked around with a frown.

"Um, around what was it Henry 7 years ago we made an extention on the lab" Vivenne said.

"Yes, almost eight now in what January?" Henry replied and his wife nodded in agreement.

"What's today's date?" Esselle asked and eased on to the bed. She

Somewhere in Time- trilogy part 2

was sure to faint. She was already light headed. At least she'd fall into pillows and not tiles this way.

"June 1, 2045" Vivenne smiled "You're favorite month" she said. Esselle swallowed hard. June was her favorite month for reasons she hadn't the desire to think about. HEr eyes met her parents. Esselle felt out of place like she didn't belong. Her heart was aching and breaking and she could just feel home sick.

"I want to go hom. I want my room and my house," she said "I want it all back"

Vivenne smiled "I was hoping you'd say that"

Somewhere in Time- trilogy part 2

So what happened?" Esselle asked walking up the steps of her townhouse in Manhattan. On the way driving home she breathed in the beautiful city air. The city's buildings were so different but so the same. The people dressed a bit differently. It was like walking into a whole new world Esselle. She was dressed in her favorite blue jeans and her yellow ruffle shirt and beige flats. Looking around the wardrobe to her was quite odd. People had looked at her a bit funny. Was her hair alright?
Her father slipped some kind of card into a slot. Esselle frowned. "Another future thing I don't know about" she said. Her father looked as if he wanted to say something then Henry looked almost uncomfortable and just pushed the door open.
The lights when on inside and Esselle stepped inside. The cool air hit her like a breaze and home still smelled like home. Even 28 years later. Esselle felt so odd saying it. 28 years later. It felt so unreal. Well for god sakes even the cars were so different! When the lights came on Esselle expected to see beige colored walls and a beautiful persian rug with a mohagany table near the door. Her heart sank. Everything was glowing. Sparkling

Somewhere in Time- trilogy part 2

dazzling. The style was so off. The staircase even seemed different. It turned with a beautiful iron banister thats design reminded her that of the curly intricate lines on lace.

She sighed. This was going to take a lot of time to get used to. She just might break before it happens.

****

Her mother pushes her bedroom doors open. The room smells the way it did last time she remembered.

"We haven't changed a thing" her mother said and smiled. Esselle smiled softly to herself. she walked over running her fingers along the lacy dresses in her closet. She looked over to her book case. All of her favorite books lined up the way she left them.

She sat on her bed and the feeling was the same. Plush and fluffy. Her beautiful mirror was the same but the reflection had changed a bit. Her pretty perfume bottles were nicely arranged and her room smelled like roses. She loved roses. She walked over to her night stand and smiled.

She took the picture frame in her hands. It had been taken on her 14 birthday. Selena by her side. They had boas on and cute little party hats. They were making the duck face. That must be so out of style now.

She put it down. Next to it was a beautiful pearly colored picture frame. HEr heart raced and she took it in her hands. It was her most favorite picture in the whole world. Mardrin was kissing her cheek and she was laughing. You could see her 17 birthday party in the background. It must have been the last picture they had taken together. Her heart sank. She wanted them right in front of her more than anything in the world. She wanted to wrap her arms around them. Hug them and kiss them and never let them go. She put the picture down.

"Where is she?" Esselle asked. Her mother shook her head.

"Esselle I don't think-" but her daughter cut her off.

"Mom she's my best friend! I have to see her talk to her" esselle said.

"You don't understand Esselle it would be like seeing a ghost for them" Vivenne said.

Esselle gave her mother an accusing look. 'What do you mean?" she asked.

"I mean everyone thought you died 28 years ago. We didn't tell anyone we froze you. It would just be worse. Do you really want to cause that heart ache" she asked. It was too much for Esselle to absorb. She didn't care.

She shook her head "No, where is she. I want to see her now" she said.

"Esselle the streets of new York aren't the same anymore. You are a stranger in this place" he mother said.

"Just tell me where she is!" esselle snapped.

"You won't be happy with what you find" she said hard and stern. Esselle planted her foot in the ground

"Oh well" she said. Her mother took a deep breath. Then after silence Esselle ran out the door. She was going to find Selena.

Somewhere in Time- trilogy part 2

sselle's New York had changed. Very much so. It was like she was some alien in a whole new world. It was like a whole new place she never knew. But yet she somehow found her way. The Empire State building was the same. The beautiful old buildings she used to marvel at were still there but that was only in a certain area. She could see the Empire state building in the distance. That's how she knew it was still there. Then again she was in dowtown. She didn't know what Midton and Uptown would look like 28 years later. Esselle climbed up the stairs to what her mother told her was Selena's town house. It was beautiful small and humble. In the distance Esselle could see the skyscrappers that seemed almost to be glowing. She squinted but in the sunlight it hurt her eyes and she stopped. The buildings were made of dark glass. She was the freedom tower far off. She swallowed hard and rang the doorbell. At least that stayed the same. Hopefully opening the door was too. She had counted about a handful of times while she was walking to Selena's house when people rang bells they opened on their own. Esselle shivered. It was kind of creepy.
"Hello?" Someone said and opened the door. Esselle's heart stopped. Then when she saw the head peeking out from behind the door her face broke out into a smile.
"Selena" she said.
Her friend looked so much older. But she didn't look 45. No not

Somewhere in Time- trilogy part 2

at all. In fact she looked exactly the same. Super strangely exactly the same. Except her long wavy dark hair was shirt and hit her shoulders. She had reading glasses and her wardrobe was far too mature to look like any Selena outfit Esselle had seen before.
Then again that was years ago. Esselle felt light headed when she thought about it. years ago.
The door opened wider and her friends eyes were escaping their sockets.
She looked her up and down and the whole moment felt like a dramatic revelation.
"Esselle!" she exclaimed with eyebrows pressed together and her jaw dropped. 'Oh my God you're alive!" she said and looked too shocked to be anything else.
"You, you look..." Selena said. Esselle opened up her arms and smiled.
"The same way you did 30 years ago' she said.
Esselle laughed "Selena you haven't changed a bit you know"
The moment must have caught up to Selena becuase all though her eyes were wide with shock with confusion and fear they began tearing up. Her hand covered her mouth.
"It can't be" she said.
"Sel its me?" she said and Selena shook her head in disbelief.
Esselle let out a deep exaspperrated sigh clearly annoyed. "Its me. When we were 13 years old we snuck a bottle of Vodka from your dads liquor cabinet and finished the whole thing. Next thing we knew we were walking down fifth avenue shouting out in song S-----E-----X-------Y------G------I------R------L-----S Laughing in hysteria" she said blandly. "and we never did it again"
"Oh my God it is you!" Selena exclaimed. She yanked Esselle into

Somewhere in Time- trilogy part 2

her arms and hugged her. Esselle smiled. Selena smelled and felt the same. She smelled like sweet candy and her hair was very short but soft and her hugs were just as warm. This Selena may have been a grown woman but she was still her best friend.
"Esselle its you, its really you" she whimpered into Esselle's cotten white cardigan. She laughed "You're outfit is soooo 30 years ago" she said and Esselle laughed in her arms. They pulled away,
'Ya just 17 year old me back from the dead" Esselle said. Selena's black sharp eyebrow arched when she raised it and looked around with a hard superior look.
"Calm inside. It isn't safe to talk out here" she said. She took Esselle's wrist and pulled her inside.
****

****

Esselle sat at Selena's kitchen table with a mug in her hand. Selena walking over took a sip of her coffee and sat down in the bronze metal chair across from Esselle. She placed her cup down. "How did this happen?" Selena asked.
"They froze me" Esselle said far too nonchalant. Her friend's eyes widened. Esselle sighed and began to explain. Everything. What happened the day of her car accident. What her parents told her about dying. The way they froze her. How everyone thought she was dead. She just poured her heart out to Selena and it felt good. She felt like they were 17 again in Eve's office gossiping and talking the day away, When Esselle was done Selena looked at her empty coffee mug.
"I think after what you just told me I need something stronger than coffee" she said and turned in her seat.

Somewhere in Time- trilogy part 2

"I need a drink" she said.

"You think you need a drink?" Esselle asked and Selena met her eye.

"I just woke up from being what do you even call it frozen half dead half alive for 28 years!?" Esselle said. Selena began shaking her head. She turned in her chair again and took Esselle's hands in hers. She was looking down with shut eyes.

"Elle, you have no idea" she said.

"What?" she insisted.

'What you put us through that day you ran off. The only heartbreak everyone went through. It was like everyone was a meaningless zombie without you just mopping around. You know what Mardrin did after you left?" she asked and looked at her. Esselle shook her head.

"He ran out after you. He drove in his car for hours trying to find you, didn't come home until mid night. It took around an hour after that when we got the call. Can you imagine what is was like for him for me? Even Stephen was distraught. Can you imagine hearing *"I'm sorry but she's gone. There was nothing we could do for her. She was going way too fast lost control and flew right off the free way. The car exploded and she burned to death. It was unfortunately that of a long and painful death. There was nothing we could do for her. She was already gone. We found her body a few feet away from the vehicel she flew right through the windshield. When the car exploded the fire spread and burned her along with the rest of the trees the fire took. It was awful. A huge devestation"'* Selena said.

Esselle felt sick to her stomach.

"I remember that day as if it were yesterday. I rememebr that

phone call word for word" she said and Esselle looked away.
"I'm sorry" Esselle finally said "I didn't mean to I was just mad and hurt and angry I didn't...." she said and trailed off.
'I saw Mardrin" Esselle began. Selena brought her hands down on the table with a smack and rolled her eyes.
"Dear God that?" she said.
"But I saw him-" Esselle began but she cut her off.
"Elle do you remember when you had just turned 16 and your parents moved to England for a feww months?" she asked.
Esselle nodded. Research purposes.
"Well you and Mardrin had broken up. That's when he dated Martha. It was nothing huge. She was French like him. Then she moved back to France and wasn't coming back. It was undefinite. Thenn you came back and you got back together. Then before your accident she came back to the states permenately. She didn't knwo about you. She came to see Mardrin that's why she kissed him I mean hello to her they were once together" she said. Esselle shut her eyes. Mardrin's voice rang in the back of her mind. She could have imagined what it was like for him. The last thing he wanted to do for her was explain. The last thing she had said to him was that she hated him. HOw could she have been such a fool and just run out liek that? Not even give him a chance?
Esselle looked away. "Elle that man died the day you did." she said and Esselle met her eye forcing herself to. She felt shameful and her punishment she decided for herself was to sit and listen. "He locked himself in his room and wouldn't come out. He was on suicide watch for a year!" Selena said. Esselle practically fell out of he rseat.

Somewhere in Time- trilogy part 2

"A year?" she asked and selena nodded with wide eyes and attitude. She was so a spanish girl. Not even age could take that away from her.

"He didn't care after you died. Almost got killed in a car accident three times. Finally I got him on his ass and he finished high school and college. But Elle he was nothing without you everyone knew. You knew how long it took for him to even think about dating again when I shoved it down his throat?" Selan asked. Esselle thought. 3 years?

"10 years Elle 10" she said and Esselle lost it.

"But why!" she shouted.

"Because of you Elle! Because he loved you!" Selena yelled back. The room fell silent for a moment. Selena looked away and licked her lips.

"I'm sorry I didn't mean to yell at you" Selena said.

"Where is he?" Esselle. Selena gave her the only look like she had lost her mind.

"What?" she asked.

"Where is he? I have to find him!" Esselle said rising from her chair.

"Elle what are you crazy? You'll put him through hell if you do that!" Selena snapped.

"And what let him go on thinking I'm dead when I'm alive!" Esselle snapped back faster. Selena's face fell.

"Either you tell me where he is or I'll find him on my own either way I will Esselle said. There was a moment of silence. Selena sighed defeated.

"Its the anniversary of your death" she said and looked at her.

"For an entire month usually two weeks before and two weeks

after your death everyday around this time he goes to your tree in central park and he sits under it. He has been doing it every year for the past 30 years Elle. Sometimes he'll walk down the hill by the fountain. But he's there he's always there. You'll find him" she said.
Esselle touched her friends arm. "Thank you Sel" she said and aimed for the door.
"And one more thing!" Selena called after. Esselle turned around to face her.
"You might not be happy with what you find" she said. Esselle laughed. It didn't faze her anymore.
"I've been hearing that alot" she said. Selena didn't smile.
"Just know he loved you. And a lot. Be gentle with him. He hurts worse this time of year" she said. Esselle froze feeling her heart yearn for him. Her eyes were to the floor then met Selena's. She nodded and bolted out the door. Mardrin was what she thought over and over again. Mardrin.

Somewhere in Time- trilogy part 2

Somewhere in Time- trilogy part 2

he day had become partly cloudy. I hoped on to the nearest train and rode until I reached Central Park. Odd enough the subways were spotless. Everything even the trains were now glossy and sleek. It was odd the way the new new train system worked. Esselle got lost several times. She hated it. But loved it odd enough at the same exact time. When Esselle stopped in front of the entrance to Central Park she smiled and took in a deep breath. Finally she felt home. Finally she found one place she could call home that hadn't changed one bit at all. The trees were a vibrant green and the paths were cobble stone. People zoomed by her riding odd looking bikes. Even the bikes looked so different. It didn't matter point was they were riding them. Mother's held their babies in their arms with their husbands smiling at them. Esselle felt a pinch at her heart. That could have been her. Esselle took in a deep breath and went on her way walking down the path. The trees above her arched into a

Somewhere in Time- trilogy part 2

beautiful arc over her head. The willows in the distance witht heir hanging swaying branches draped over the water and little skimmed the surface. She looked off to her side and noticed the sun was half set in the sky and the light was so golden everything looked goldish yellow and a bit green in the light. Kind of the way it did in movies. When it has that glossed touched up look to it. Like in the Transformers. She loved that movie. Then again if she stopped anyone and asked them about it they'd look at her as if she had ten heads. Esselle took a very brief walking through the park she had once known even as a child she grew up here. Esselle climbed to the top of the hill where her tree was. From the top of the hill you could see the beautiful bridge where Stuart Little was filmed. She had loved reruns of that movie as a child. The water glistened in the light and Esselle smiled. THere used to be a stand over by the water where you rented a boat and you could row around in the water. Next to it was this stunning resturant. The resturant was still there but the bost rentals were gone replaced by what looked like an outdoor eating area with beautiful iron tables and chairs. There was a wall wiht pretty vines and flowers.

The light from the sun bounced off the dark green leaves in the tree and hit random places. Esselle leaned against her tree and let the warmth of the sun overwhelm her. She sighed. She felt at home. Finally at peace. The thought of her being gone for such a long time made her sick to her stomach again and she quickly shook the though from her head.

Essselle saw a couple walking by the water hand in hand. The girl was on the smaller slimmer side with a head of dark hair and light eyes. The man by her side was tall and well built blonde with light eyes. This made her stomach turn. They had reminded her so much of how she was like. She looked away in shame. What had she done? Not only did she screw up her life by being an idiot she ruined everyone else's. To hell with ruining her own life who cares btu she was to blame for everyone else's heart ache. How could she? And Mardrin. She wanted to find him. And hold him and love him and kiss him to her heart's content and never let him go. Ever not ever again she didn't care.

Esselle's eyes scoured her tree and she smiled. It looked the same and smelled of bark and late spring. She found a carving in the tree and broke out in a wide smile. She ran her fingers over the carving and felt every curve and dent in it. Her and Mardrin's names together with forever. It had been a comedic joke at frst because Mardrin thought it was such a tacky cliche movie thing. But Esselle loved it and thought it was sweet so he left it there anyway.

Mardrin hadn't been by the tree and it made her heart sink. She let out a deep breath. It had been a long shot anyway. Esselle turned to catch a vew of the bridge. Then a face caught her eye. A face she knew like the back of her hand. All triangular angels and hair like a golden halo. Esselle knew those yellow-green eyes and jock like build. Esselle knew that face and those lips the way she knew herself. It was Mardrin. Against her will she smiled. She smiled like she'd never smile again. Then her feet gave out below her. She was running, falling, flying down the hill it didn't matter. She was growing closwer to Mardrin with every step. Esselle ran so fast she almost bumped into people she didn't care. In fact she even laughed. Anyone else would have thought she was insane. But Esselle guessed that was what she loved

Somewhere in Time- trilogy part 2

about her home. It and the people would never change. They were all new Yorkers so it was all good. Esselle's heart was practically escaping her chest reaching for him.

"Mardrin" she whispered to herself as she ran closer. He was leaning over the edge with his hands folded. Oh how he looked the same. Exactly the same odd enough like he had been frozen along with her. Except he had a button down long sleeve shirt with the sleeves pulled up to his elbows. He wore dark long black pants and work shoes. His hair was long and slicked back. Long so that it curled in short locks in the back of his neck. His face was much more matured and masculine. His skin looked golden in the light and his hair lit up. He had, Esselle wanted to laugh, almost like a 5 o'clock shadow.

"Mardrin" she said again to herself. She couldn't say it enough. She ran faster so fast she might have flown.

"Mardrin!" she said louder but he didn't hear.

'Mardrin!" she shouted. She had forgotten how deaf he was. But she loved him anyway. He looked up with an arched eyebrow. He was so handsome looking at him sometimes Esselle felt like she were falling in love all over again. She smiled.

"Mardrin!" she shouted. The look on his face was unreadble. He stood up straight. She just laughed. She couldn't help it. She ran into his arms and almost knocked him over. he wrapped his arms around her waist tightly and she was feet off the ground. Without hesitation Esselle took his face in her hands and kissed him. For Esselle the world just blew up into fireworks and the light from the sun wamred her skin. The light wind whisped through her hair and she smiled against his mouth and kissed him again. It had been so long. She could only imagine what he was thinking.

Somewhere in Time- trilogy part 2

She ran her fingers though her hair something she hadn't done in such a long time. Her fingers twisted around his locks at the bottom. His mouth against hers was warm and familliar and a sound emerged from deep in his throat. She smiled against his mouth again and kissed him harder. She wanted to speak but didn't want to take her mouth off of his. Then she noticed something had been wrong. The tips of his fingers tips weren't tracing circles on the bttom of the back. he always did that. There wasn't a kiss that he didn't. Not ever had it happened before. She frowned. She put her hand at the side of his face and the other at the back of his neck and brought him closer. She felt his hands slowly and hesitantly move. She softly nodded and pressed her mouth harder to his so much it hurt. She ran her hands through his hair again. Her feet were still above the ground. She slowly touched the ground. His hands were now slowly tracing circles and then it became consistent. This was him. Then he hugged her while he did it. Tight as if he didn't want to let her go. She did the same and he kissed her back. Finally, Esselle thought, it only took long enough. She took his face her hands and his skin was still rugged the way it always was. He pressed her body closer to his and Esselle felt the only giddiness.
"hey!" someone called. Esselle ignored. She was having a very intimate reunion here could people kindly shut up and not ruin the romantic moment?
"Mardrin!" she heard again. This time it was a female's voice. Esselle didn't fool away. She felt Mardrin slowly doing so. Like he didn't want to but had too.
"That's my husband!" she said again and at that she oulled away. She looked at Mardrin.

Somewhere in Time- trilogy part 2

"Husband?" she said. His eyes were wide with shock confusion and somethign else she knew. It was always there when they kissed but she never got around to figuring out what it was. "Esselle" he said looking her up and down still holding her in his arms. She looked over.

There stood a woman giving them a funny look. Her hair was blonde she had pink lips big brown-blue eyes light skin and a pretty figure. She looked more mature but Esselle couldn't help bet recognize her beauty. It was Martha. Her hands slowly slid down Mardrins face and chest ashe pulled away. She looked at him accusingly. Ok, no Esselle couldn't help but think this but she couldn't help but love the heart broken look on Martha's face. Esselle called it a deja vu/ karma coming back 28 years later to bite her in the ass. She didn't like it now did she?

"You're married?" Esselle asked in a whispered disbelief. She was slowly backing away but stopped. She had not seen Mardrin and despite the circumstances she didn't want to be too far from him.

"Elle" he said and reached for her. She slightly pulled back. Enough for his face to have pain written all over it. He put his hand down "You're...alive" he said.

Martha walked over and locked her arm with his.

"Why you look, you look-" Martha said.

Esselle finished her thought off "Yes I know" she snapped. She looked at Mardrin "17" she said.

"but how?" Mardrin asked.

Esselle slowly backed away. She felt so exposed and violated. she swallowed hard.

"i-" Esselle said and looked at both of them. She pressed her lips together. She looked down off to the side and fought back a single tear. "um, I have to go" she said.

"Elle wait!" Mardrin called after her. But esselle turned and ran. She ran for the exit but took a wrong turn. Damn it. She found her self under a private bridge that looked deserted. she leaned against the stone wall. She placed her hand over her mouth and her back arched over. Her eyes squeezed shut tight and she sobbed. It felt like an awful pain in her gut. Like she couldn't do all she could do was scream from the pain. The awful heart wrenching pain.

"Elle!" Someone said forcefully. They grabbed her arm and turned aroind.

"No!" she groaned and tried to wiggle her arm out. "Leave me alone!" she said.

"No" Mardirn said. He took both of her arms in his hands tightly. He strained her out and turned her to face him completely. His eyes were wide and strong when he spoke "I let you get away from me once 28 years ago. I lost you. I'm not letting it happen again" he said.

"You're married" Esselle nagged trying to wiggle free.

He slightly shook his head "Oh Elle. God knows I've never truly loved anyone but you" he said.

Esselle squeezed her jaw shut tight and pressed her lips to a fine line. She probably looked like a bratty child. But who cared it was Mardrin.

"How could this be" he said.

"I'll tell you" she said "My parents stook me in a freezer for 30 years then took me out and defrosted me" she said sarcastically. His eyes widened. She forgot how gullible he was.

"Oh God Mardrin!" she said and threw her arms down hard. He

Somewhere in Time- trilogy part 2

still held her tight. Finally she was breathing hard. She was angry and hurt and everything at one time. But he was just looking at her with eyes of awe desire and love. Like he was just taking her all in.

"What are you looking at?" she blurted out. He smiled softly and took a lock of hair in his fingers.

"I never thought i'd see you again. I'm enjoying her view" he said. her heart soared. She wanted kiss him again and hard and this time not be interrupted.

"ya well" she said. That look in his eyes. She was slowly loosing her will power and slowly loosing her anger. "I don't think your wife would approve"

He laughed "Ya," he said and stopped smiling. He let her go "I don't think she would" he said. She got a glimpse of his wedding band. Another woman put it there., She should have been the to do so. It really should have been her.

'Of all people Mardrin you seriously chose to marry her" she said because it was all she managed to say. He shrugged.

"I had to try didn't I?" he said. Esselle tried to decipher what it meant. All she knew was that her heart started breaking and she was ready to cry.

He took her face in his hands "Don't cry Elle, don't" he said.

"Mardrin" she said and melted into his arms hugging him. She cried but softly.

"Elle I am so sorry, you have no idea" he said and she looked at him.

"Oh I know you are" she said and he laughed.

"You must know" he said. Esselle couldn't help it. She kissed him. She just had to. He kissed her back without hesititation and

Somewhere in Time- trilogy part 2

he traced circles on her back. She held him tight like if she didn't he'd turn for dust. Then it became too much for Esselle. She kissed him one last time and pulled away. She ran off as fast as she could into the subway and home. Home to where she could die in peace. This time permenately. Hopefully.

Somewhere in Time- trilogy part 2

he day had become partly cloudy. I hoped on to the nearest train and rode until I reached Central Park. Odd enough the subways were spotless. Everything even the trains were now glossy and sleek. It was odd the way the new new train system worked. Esselle got lost several times. She hated it. But loved it odd enough at the same exact time. When Esselle stopped in front of the entrance to Central Park she smiled and took in a deep breath. Finally she felt home. Finally she found one place she could call home that hadn't changed one bit at all. The trees were a vibrant green and the paths were cobble stone. People zoomed by her riding odd looking bikes. Even the bikes looked so different. It didn't matter point was they were riding them. Mother's held their babies in their arms with their husbands smiling at them. Esselle felt a pinch at her heart. That could have been her. Esselle took in a deep breath and went on her way walking down the path. The trees above her arched into a beautiful arc over her head. The willows in the distance witht heir hanging swaying branches draped over the water and little skimmed the surface. She looked off to her side and noticed the sun was half set in the sky and the light was so golden everything looked goldish yellow and a bit green in the light. Kind of the way it did in movies. When it has that glossed touched up look to it. Like in the Transformers. She loved that movie. Then again if she stopped anyone and asked them about it they'd look at her as if she had ten heads. Esselle took a very brief walking through the park she had once known even as a child she grew up here. Esselle climbed to the top of the hill where her tree was. From the top of the hill you could see the beautiful bridge where Stuart Little was filmed. She had loved reruns of that movie as a child. The water glistened in the light and Esselle smiled. THere used to be a stand over by the water where you rented a boat and you could row around in the water. Next to it was this stunning resturant. The resturant was still there but the bost rentals were gone replaced by what looked like an outdoor eating area with beautiful iron tables and chairs. There was a wall wiht pretty vines and flowers.

The light from the sun bounced off the dark green leaves in the tree and hit random places. Esselle leaned against her tree and let the warmth of the sun overwhelm her. She sighed. She felt at home. Finally at peace. The thought of her being gone for such a long time made her sick to her stomach again and she quickly shook the though from her head.

Essselle saw a couple walking by the water hand in hand. The girl was on the smaller slimmer side with a head of dark hair and light eyes. The man by her side was tall and well built blonde with light eyes. This made her stomach turn. They had reminded her so much of how she was like. She looked away in shame. What had she done? Not only did she screw up her life by being an idiot she ruined everyone else's. To hell with ruining her own life who cares btu she was to blame for everyone else's heart ache. How could she? And Mardrin. She wanted to find him. And hold him and love him and kiss him to her heart's content and never let him go. Ever not ever again she didn't care.

Esselle's eyes scoured her tree and she smiled. It looked the same and smelled of bark and late spring. She found a carving in the tree and broke out in a wide smile. She ran her fingers over the carving and felt every curve and dent in it. Her and Mardrin's names together with forever. It had been a comedic joke at frst because Mardrin thought it was such a tacky cliche movie thing. But Esselle loved it and thought it was sweet so he left it there anyway.

Mardrin hadn't been by the tree and it made her heart sink. She let out a deep breath. It had been a long shot anyway. Esselle turned to catch a vew of the bridge. Then a face caught her eye. A face she knew like the back of her hand. All triangular angels and hair like a golden halo. Esselle knew those yellow-green eyes and jock like build. Esselle knew that face and those lips the way she knew herself. It was Mardrin. Against her will she smiled. She smiled like she'd never smile again. Then her feet gave out below her. She was running, falling, flying down the hill it didn't matter. She was growing closwer to Mardrin with every step. Esselle ran so fast she almost bumped into people she didn't care. In fact she even laughed. Anyone else would have thought she was insane. But Esselle guessed that was what she loved about her home. It and the people would never change. They

Somewhere in Time- trilogy part 2

were all new Yorkers so it was all good. Esselle's heart was practically escaping her chest reaching for him.

"Mardrin" she whispered to herself as she ran closer. He was leaning over the edge with his hands folded. Oh how he looked the same. Exactly the same odd enough like he had been frozen along with her. Except he had a button down long sleeve shirt with the sleeves pulled up to his elbows. He wore dark long black pants and work shoes. His hair was long and slicked back. Long so that it curled in short locks in the back of his neck. His face was much more matured and masculine. His skin looked golden in the light and his hair lit up. He had, Esselle wanted to laugh, almost like a 5 o'clock shadow.

"Mardrin" she said again to herself. She couldn't say it enough. She ran faster so fast she might have flown.

"Mardrin!" she said louder but he didn't hear.

'Mardrin!" she shouted. She had forgotten how deaf he was. But she loved him anyway. He looked up with an arched eyebrow. He was so handsome looking at him sometimes Esselle felt like she were falling in love all over again. She smiled.

"Mardrin!" she shouted. The look on his face was unreadble. He stood up straight. She just laughed. She couldn't help it. She ran into his arms and almost knocked him over. he wrapped his arms around her waist tightly and she was feet off the ground. Without hesitation Esselle took his face in her hands and kissed him. For Esselle the world just blew up into fireworks and the light from the sun wamred her skin. The light wind whisped through her hair and she smiled against his mouth and kissed him again. It had been so long. She could only imagine what he was thinking. She ran her fingers though her hair something she hadn't done in

Somewhere in Time- trilogy part 2

such a long time. Her fingers twisted around his locks at the bottom. His mouth against hers was warm and familliar and a sound emerged from deep in his throat. She smiled against his mouth again and kissed him harder. She wanted to speak but didn't want to take her mouth off of his. Then she noticed something had been wrong. The tips of his fingers tips weren't tracing circles on the bttom of the back. he always did that. There wasn't a kiss that he didn't. Not ever had it happened before. She frowned. She put her hand at the side of his face and the other at the back of his neck and brought him closer. She felt his hands slowly and hesitantly move. She softly nodded and pressed her mouth harder to his so much it hurt. She ran her hands through his hair again. Her feet were still above the ground. She slowly touched the ground. His hands were now slowly tracing circles and then it became consistent. This was him. Then he hugged her while he did it. Tight as if he didn't want to let her go. She did the same and he kissed her back. Finally, Esselle thought, it only took long enough. She took his face her hands and his skin was still rugged the way it always was. He pressed her body closer to his and Esselle felt the only giddiness.
"hey!" someone called. Esselle ignored. She was having a very intimate reunion here could people kindly shut up and not ruin the romantic moment?
"Mardrin!" she heard again. This time it was a female's voice. Esselle didn't fool away. She felt Mardrin slowly doing so. Like he didn't want to but had too.
"That's my husband!" she said again and at that she oulled away. She looked at Mardrin.
"Husband?" she said. His eyes were wide with shock confusion

Somewhere in Time- trilogy part 2

and somethign else she knew. It was always there when they kissed but she never got around to figuring out what it was. "Esselle" he said looking her up and down still holding her in his arms. She looked over.

There stood a woman giving them a funny look. Her hair was blonde she had pink lips big brown-blue eyes light skin and a pretty figure. She looked more mature but Esselle couldn't help bet recognize her beauty. It was Martha. Her hands slowly slid down Mardrins face and chest ashe pulled away. She looked at him accusingly. Ok, no Esselle couldn't help but think this but she couldn't help but love the heart broken look on Martha's face. Esselle called it a deja vu/ karma coming back 28 years later to bite her in the ass. She didn't like it now did she?

"You're married?" Esselle asked in a whispered disbelief. She was slowly backing away but stopped. She had not seen Mardrin and despite the circumstances she didn't want to be too far from him.

"Elle" he said and reached for her. She slightly pulled back. Enough for his face to have pain written all over it. He put his hand down "You're...alive" he said.

Martha walked over and locked her arm with his.

"Why you look, you look-" Martha said.

Esselle finished her thought off "Yes I know" she snapped. She looked at Mardrin "17" she said.

"but how?" Mardrin asked.

Esselle slowly backed away. She felt so exposed and violated. she swallowed hard.

"i-" Esselle said and looked at both of them. She pressed her lips together. She looked down off to the side and fought back a single tear. "um, I have to go" she said.

Somewhere in Time- trilogy part 2

"Elle wait!" Mardrin called after her. But esselle turned and ran. She ran for the exit but took a wrong turn. Damn it. She found her self under a private bridge that looked deserted. she leaned against the stone wall. She placed her hand over her mouth and her back arched over. Her eyes squeezed shut tight and she sobbed. It felt like an awful pain in her gut. Like she couldn't do all she could do was scream from the pain. The awful heart wrenching pain.

"Elle!" Someone said forcefully. They grabbed her arm and turned aroind.

"No!" she groaned and tried to wiggle her arm out. "Leave me alone!" she said.

"No" Mardirn said. He took both of her arms in his hands tightly. He strained her out and turned her to face him completely. His eyes were wide and strong when he spoke "I let you get away from me once 28 years ago. I lost you. I'm not letting it happen again" he said.

"You're married" Esselle nagged trying to wiggle free.

He slightly shook his head "Oh Elle. God knows I've never truly loved anyone but you" he said.

Esselle squeezed her jaw shut tight and pressed her lips to a fine line. She probably looked like a bratty child. But who cared it was Mardrin.

"How could this be" he said.

"I'll tell you" she said "My parents stook me in a freezer for 30 years then took me out and defrosted me" she said sarcastically. His eyes widened. She forgot how gullible he was.

"Oh God Mardrin!" she said and threw her arms down hard. He still held her tight. Finally she was breathing hard. She was angry and hurt and everything at one time. But he was just looking at her with eyes of awe desire and love. Like he was just taking her all in.

"What are you looking at?" she blurted out. He smiled softly and took a lock of hair in his fingers.

"I never thought i'd see you again. I'm enjoying her view" he said. her heart soared. She wanted kiss him again and hard and this time not be interrupted.

"ya well" she said. That look in his eyes. She was slowly loosing her will power and slowly loosing her anger. "I don't think your wife would approve"

He laughed "Ya," he said and stopped smiling. He let her go "I don't think she would" he said. She got a glimpse of his wedding band. Another woman put it there., She should have been the to do so. It really should have been her.

'Of all people Mardrin you seriously chose to marry her" she said because it was all she managed to say. He shrugged.

"I had to try didn't I?" he said. Esselle tried to decipher what it meant. All she knew was that her heart started breaking and she was ready to cry.

He took her face in his hands "Don't cry Elle, don't" he said.

"Mardrin" she said and melted into his arms hugging him. She cried but softly.

"Elle I am so sorry, you have no idea" he said and she looked at him.

"Oh I know you are" she said and he laughed.

"You must know" he said. Esselle couldn't help it. She kissed him. She just had to. He kissed her back without hesititation and he traced circles on her back. She held him tight like if she didn't he'd turn for dust. Then it became too much for Esselle. She kissed him one last time and pulled away. She ran off as fast as she could into the subway and home. Home to where she could die in peace. This time permenately. Hopefully.

soon as Esselle got home it was already dark out. She had gotten lost on the stupid train again. When she stepped through the door and shut it behind her her mother stopped in front of her. She raised an eyebrow.

"I told you, you weren't going to like what you found" she had said. Esselle had ran past Vivenne and slammed the door shut to her bedroom locking it. Esselle hadn't cried. not at all. She just lied there on her bed staring at the cieling. Occasionally rolling over. She had no idea what to do with her life. Where to go what do. She was lost. She was confused. She was heart. It was going to take Esselle a while to fully absorb and grasp the fact that she was frozen. She had waken up 28 years later in a world she no longer knows. All night Esselle repeated that to herself getting herself used to it. Everyone I loved once before have moved on without me Esselle thought And now I have to find a way to go on with my life. Esselle sighed. She was dying inside and this getting used to it. Was going to take a while

Somewhere in Time- trilogy part 2

****
****

Esselle lazily moved her eggs around on her plate. Gees even the plates were different 28 years later. Dear God was nothing the same anymore?

Vivenne smiled somberly at her daughter "I missed making breakfast for you" she said. Esselle smiled back.

"Me too" she said. Technically she didn't. She hadn't remembered anything.

"What do you want to do today sweetheart?" she asked. Henry came in and Esselle turned to face her father.

"Hey dad" she said. Her father smiled. He walked over to kiss he forehead.

"Hey mami" he said. "I missed kissing you ing the morning" she smiled. She kept forgetting they were deprived of their only daughter for almost 30 years.

"Your father and I have to work today but for dinner when we get home. Where do you want to go? You know LaBelle's is still open. They are celebrating their 30 year in buisness" she said softly. Esselle looked at her mother.

"I know how much you liked to go there when you were younger" she said.

Esselle swallowed and looked at her parents.

"So how old am I?'she asked. The cup in her father's hand fell to the flower making a shattering noise.

"What?" he asked.

"Technically i'm still only 17 and technically i'm like old. What is it 45?" she said and Vivenne turned a sea green.

Esselle broke into a smirk "Does this mean I can have a drink if I

Somewhere in Time- trilogy part 2

want too?' she asked.

"No!" her parents both said. She slouched in her chair.

"You know technically I have been legal for 24 years" she said.

"No!" her parents said and again and she smiled a little. Now that she missed. Her mother ran her fingers through her hair.

"I think I might visit Selena again today" Esselle said. She waited vervously for their reply.

"You know, catch up" she said.

Her mother smiled taking her hand "I think its a great idea"

****
****

Selena took a scrap book and handed it to Esselle with a smile.

"Its me wedding album" she said and chocked a little. "You're in there. There was a picture of you there the whole time. And I made copies of pictures we had already take and cut them to fit into the wedding pictures I already had."

Esselle smiled as a sign of comfort to her friend. She opened the book and immediately broke out into a smile. She turned the page and laughed.

"I see you had david Tutera plan your wedding did you?" Esselle asked. Selena laughed teary eyed. She pressed her smile to a fine line and nodded.

Esselle noticed that Selena's dress was that of what they always talked about. Fitted at the top and flared out below the waste in ruffled layers that resembled waves. Esselle smiled. Her reception had been that of a beautiful one too. All red and white just like Selena wanted it. It hadn't shocked Esselle very much that Stephen was the one she had married. They were just bound to end up together. Esselle flipped some more pages and saw

Somewhere in Time- trilogy part 2

what Selena meant. A picture of Esselle had been cut out and taped to another. IT looked like she was at the wedding.

"How creative are you" Esselle said. Her friend nodded.

"He, uh, proposed at Rockefeller the moment the tree lit up for the first time" she said. Esselle softly smiled.

"That's sweet" she said. Selena nodded. She looked tired. Worn out even.

"How old were you?" Esselle asked. Selena's eyebrows furrowed in deep thought.

"22?" she said. Esselle nodded and flipped through the pages again.

"Then a year later my son David was born" Selena laughed a bit. "We got lucky he was born right after our wedding anniversary" she said.

"I'm not surprised. You always did want to get everything done young" Esselle said and they both laughed.

"Then 5 years later I had my daughter" Selena said and Esselle met her eye.

"Marie Esselle" she said.

Besides herself she smiled "You named her," Esselle begun in disbelief "After me?"

Selena nodded. "Elle you were never forgotten. We always thought of you always. There wasn't a day that went by that someone didn't mention you and smile or something happened that didn't remind us of you" she said and took her hand. "We never forgot about you"

Selena took in a deep breath. "Ten years ago though I had my twins. My last kids!" she said and Esselle laughed "Diana and John" she said.

Somewhere in Time- trilogy part 2

Esselle swallowed hard. "It's just hard seeing all of this. All it does is make me wonder. What if. It makes me think I should have been there. I was deprived of so much. I hurt you all because...I don't even know why. I feel like its so unfair! Everything was taken away from me! How am I supposed to even live after this? I can't even go to school. It just wouldn't even work. I could be my classmates mother! And I couldn't get a job. Not into todays world with what happened to me. And that's another thing everything is so different! I keep getting lost. Sel, I used to know this city like the back of my mind" Esselle confessed "I feel like an outsider now"

Selena nodded. "I understand. Elle, I know you're hurting a bit inside-" Selena said but she cut her off.

"No Sel I'm practically dying inside! You know what I saw yesterday?" Esselle asked. She could feel her cheeks burning red with anger her eyes stinging green with envy and her blood boil. Selena shook her head. "Mardrin" Esselle said "And his wife. Martha"

Selena rolled her eyes a bit "Elle, what'd you expect to see? He had to go on with his life" Selena said with an obvious tone.

"He was supposed to be with me Selena! That's the point not her! Dear God he couldn't have picked anyone but her?" Esselle said frustrated. She fell back hard into her chair and slouched.

"It was easy for him to be with her" Selena said. Esselle raised an eyebrow.

"He was already in love with her. I'm sorry Elle but its true he was. Not as much as he loved you but he definitely cared for her. And she felt the same. she never left his side. She was caring, good hearted, kind sweet. She was there for him when he needed

Somewhere in Time- trilogy part 2

a shoulder to lean on. Even after he made it clear they'd never be together she didn't care. She still kept up with him. Brought him whatever he needed. Elle, if anyone was going to end up with Mardrin besides you it deserved to be her. She's a wonderful person. Take it from me who really just couldn't stand her for a while!" Selena said. She met Esselle's eye and her face softened. "They loved each other Elle. That's what counts" she said.

Esselle ran her fingers through her hair. "Ya well I still don't like her" she said.

Selena sighed "It took ten years Elle for him to get over you. And that's because I forced it upon him. Plus he was just miserable I wanted to see him happy Elle. I suggested he get with her. Elle can you just imagine she stood by his side for ten years. It didn't take long at all. They didn't even date they just got engaged" Selena said.

Esselle rolled her eyes "How romantic" she said.

Selena made a face. "What!?" Esselle said.

Selena rolled her narrow eyes dismissing her. "Anyways Esselle he missed you but he found a way to cope with it all and be happy. Not long after that they had their son. Augustine. Then I think two years after they had their daughter Jacqueline. He was for the most part happy Elle. Shouldn't his happiness count for anything? Even if it wasn't with you?" Selena asked.

Her mouth formed a thin line and she said "It would. But do you blame me for thinking about how that should have been me?" Selena sighed. She sat back and after a moment she shook her head. 'No, I guess not"

"Alright then" Esselle said and shut the wedding album with a snap.

Somewhere in Time- trilogy part 2

'Guess who's here!" Someone called and Esselle could hear the front door shut. Selena gasped. Her face instantly lit up and she broke out into a huge smile and she turned in her seat to face behind her.

A man came through the door way. He had skin on the tanner side like Stephan did but he had his mother's strong eyes and features. He walked like his father and his built was the same. Selena clasped her hands together. "Oh! My son!" she said. He had what looked like a very odd carrier with a pick blanket peeking out.

Selena darted out of her seat. The man smiled at her.

"Hey mom" he said and kissed her cheek. How odd it was. Her best friend. The all hotness all attitude all fierceness and fire Selena all the things that made her, her best friend was being called mom. By someone older looking than her!

Selena turned and smiled at Esselle. "Elle" she said and Esselle slowly rose from her seat. "This is my son. David." she said. David smiled at her. "So this is the famous Titi Elle" he said en extended his hand. "Its nice to finally meet you" he said.

Esselle smiled and shook his head. "Its so nice to meet you" she said and looked at him with adoring eyes. "You look just like your father when he was younger" Esselle said. David laughed. 'But you have your mother's smile. From when she was younger" Esselle said. She looked at Selena. She was smiling with eyes glossy with tears.

Selena shook herself out of her daze. "Oh um" she said and clasped her hands together. She took the carrier from David and he smiled. "There's someone I want you to meet" she said. She gently put the carrier on the table and pulled back the silky pink

Somewhere in Time- trilogy part 2

blanket.

"This is my granddaughter. Isabella" she said. Esselle felt her heart warm. She was beautiful. She hard dark hair like Selena. She had a button nose light skin and rosy cheeks. She slept like an angel. She was a beautiful baby. Esselle covered her mouth with her hands as Selena gently took the sleeping baby out. Her throat was becoming scratchy and begun to burn along with her eyes.

"Oh Sel," she said. Selena smiled. Esselle looked up at David and his mother. "Oh could I hold her?" she asked.

"Of course!" David said softly.

Selena smiled and gently gave her to Esselle. The baby was warm and heavy in her arms. She smelled sweet that of lavender and baby powder.

Esselle laughed a little as the tears came down. She rocked her back and forth.

"Hi" she said. Esselle felt an overwhelming joy soft and sweet come over her. "I'm your Titi Elle" she whispered. Esselle swallowed hard. She let the tears go freely.

"You're so beautiful" she said and gently touched the baby's hair. She looked up at Selena and they both let out a laugh. Selena placed a shaking hand over her mouth and her eyes were so watery you couldn't see their color through her tears.

Esselle looked at the baby in her arms. "I promise you little one. I'll be here and I'm not going to be leaving your side. Ever. Consider yourself the thing that's gonna turn me around." she said and stroked her hair "I'll always protect you. I promise I won't let anything happen to you" she whispered and that the baby slowly opened her big blue-grey eyes. Esselle smiled and let the tear trickle down her face. What a beautiful blissful moment.

Somewhere in Time- trilogy part 2

soon as Esselle got home it was already dark out. She had gotten lost on the stupid train again. When she stepped through the door and shut it behind her her mother stopped in front of her. She raised an eyebrow.

"I told you, you weren't going to like what you found" she had said. Esselle had ran past Vivenne and slammed the door shut to her bedroom locking it. Esselle hadn't cried. not at all. She just lied there on her bed staring at the cieling. Occasionally rolling over. She had no idea what to do with her life. Where to go what do. She was lost. She was confused. She was heart. It was going to take Esselle a while to fully absorb and grasp the fact that she was frozen. She had waken up 28 years later in a world she no longer knows. All night Esselle repeated that to herself getting herself used to it. Everyone I loved once before have moved on without me Esselle thought And now I have to find a way to go on with my life. Esselle sighed. She was dying inside and this getting used to it. Was going to take a while

****
****

Esselle lazily moved her eggs around on her plate. Gees even the plates were different 28 years later. Dear God was nothing the same anymore?

Vivenne smiled somberly at her daughter "I missed making breakfast for you" she said. Esselle smiled back.

"Me too" she said. Technically she didn't. She hadn't remembered anything.

"What do you want to do today sweetheart?" she asked. Henry

Somewhere in Time- trilogy part 2

came in and Esselle turned to face her father.
"Hey dad" she said. Her father smiled. He walked over to kiss he forehead.
"Hey mami" he said. "I missed kissing you ing the morning" she smiled. She kept forgetting they were deprived of their only daughter for almost 30 years.
"Your father and I have to work today but for dinner when we get home. Where do you want to go? You know LaBelle's is still open. They are celebrating their 30 year in buisness" she said softly. Esselle looked at her mother.
"I know how much you liked to go there when you were younger" she said.
Esselle swallowed and looked at her parents.
"So how old am I?'she asked. The cup in her father's hand fell to the flower making a shattering noise.
"What?" he asked.
"Technically i'm still only 17 and technically i'm like old. What is it 45?" she said and Vivenne turned a sea green.
Esselle broke into a smirk "Does this mean I can have a drink if I want too?' she asked.
"No!" her parents both said. She slouched in her chair.
"You know technically I have been legal for 24 years" she said.
"No!" her parents said and again and she smiled a little. Now that she missed. Her mother ran her fingers through her hair.
"I think I might visit Selena again today" Esselle said. She waited vervously for their reply.
"You know, catch up" she said.
Her mother smiled taking her hand "I think its a great idea"
****

Somewhere in Time- trilogy part 2

****

Selena took a scrap book and handed it to Esselle with a smile. "Its me wedding album" she said and chocked a little. "You're in there. There was a picture of you there the whole time. And I made copies of pictures we had already take and cut them to fit into the wedding pictures I already had."

Esselle smiled as a sign of comfort to her friend. She opened the book and immediately broke out into a smile. She turned the page and laughed.

"I see you had david Tutera plan your wedding did you?" Esselle asked. Selena laughed teary eyed. She pressed her smile to a fine line and nodded.

Esselle noticed that Selena's dress was that of what they always talked about. Fitted at the top and flared out below the waste in ruffled layers that resembled waves. Esselle smiled. Her reception had been that of a beautiful one too. All red and white just like Selena wanted it. It hadn't shocked Esselle very much that Stephen was the one she had married. They were just bound to end up together. Esselle flipped some more pages and saw what Selena meant. A picture of Esselle had been cut out and taped to another. IT looked like she was at the wedding.

"How creative are you" Esselle said. Her friend nodded.

"He, uh, proposed at Rockefeller the moment the tree lit up for the first time" she said. Esselle softly smiled.

"That's sweet" she said. Selena nodded. She looked tired. Worn out even.

"How old were you?" Esselle asked. Selena's eyebrows furrowed in deep thought.

"22?" she said. Esselle nodded and flipped through the pages

Somewhere in Time- trilogy part 2

again.

"Then a year later my son David was born" Selena laughed a bit. "We got lucky he was born right after our wedding anniversary" she said.

"I'm not surprised. You always did want to get everything done young" Esselle said and they both laughed.

"Then 5 years later I had my daughter" Selena said and Esselle met her eye.

"Marie Esselle" she said.

Besides herself she smiled "You named her," Esselle begun in disbelief "After me?"

Selena nodded. "Elle you were never forgotten. We always thought of you always. There wasn't a day that went by that someone didn't mention you and smile or something happened that didn't remind us of you" she said and took her hand. "We never forgot about you"

Selena took in a deep breath. "Ten years ago though I had my twins. My last kids!" she said and Esselle laughed "Diana and John" she said.

Esselle swallowed hard. "It's just hard seeing all of this. All it does is make me wonder. What if. It makes me think I should have been there. I was deprived of so much. I hurt you all because...I don't even know why. I feel like its so unfair! Everything was taken away from me! How am I supposed to even live after this? I can't even go to school. It just wouldn't even work. I could be my classmates mother! And I couldn't get a job. Not into todays world with what happened to me. And that's another thing everything is so different! I keep getting lost. Sel, I used to know this city like the back of my mind" Esselle

confessed "I feel like an outsider now"
Selena nodded. "I understand. Elle, I know you're hurting a bit inside-" Selena said but she cut her off.
"No Sel I'm practically dying inside! You know what I saw yesterday?" Esselle asked. She could feel her cheeks burning red with anger her eyes stinging green with envy and her blood boil. Selena shook her head. "Mardrin" Esselle said "And his wife. Martha"
Selena rolled her eyes a bit "Elle, what'd you expect to see? He had to go on with his life" Selena said with an obvious tone.
"He was supposed to be with me Selena! That's the point not her! Dear God he couldn't have picked anyone but her?" Esselle said frustrated. She fell back hard into her chair and slouched.
"It was easy for him to be with her" Selena said. Esselle raised an eyebrow.
"He was already in love with her. I'm sorry Elle but its true he was. Not as much as he loved you but he definitely cared for her. And she felt the same. she never left his side. She was caring, good hearted, kind sweet. She was there for him when he needed a shoulder to lean on. Even after he made it clear they'd never be together she didn't care. She still kept up with him. Brought him whatever he needed. Elle, if anyone was going to end up with Mardrin besides you it deserved to be her. She's a wonderful person. Take it from me who really just couldn't stand her for a while!" Selena said. She met Esselle's eye and her face softened. "They loved each other Elle. That's what counts" she said.
Esselle ran her fingers through her hair. "Ya well I still don't like her" she said.
Selena sighed "It took ten years Elle for him to get over you. And

that's because I forced it upon him. Plus he was just miserable I wanted to see him happy Elle. I suggested he get with her. Elle can you just imagine she stood by his side for ten years. It didn't take long at all. They didn't even date they just got engaged" Selena said.

Esselle rolled her eyes "How romantic" she said.

Selena made a face. "What!?" Esselle said.

Selena rolled her narrow eyes dismissing her. "Anyways Esselle he missed you but he found a way to cope with it all and be happy. Not long after that they had their son. Augustine. Then I think two years after they had their daughter Jacqueline. He was for the most part happy Elle. Shouldn't his happiness count for anything? Even if it wasn't with you?" Selena asked.

Her mouth formed a thin line and she said "It would. But do you blame me for thinking about how that should have been me?" Selena sighed. She sat back and after a moment she shook her head. 'No, I guess not"

"Alright then" Esselle said and shut the wedding album with a snap.

'Guess who's here!" Someone called and Esselle could hear the front door shut. Selena gasped. Her face instantly lit up and she broke out into a huge smile and she turned in her seat to face behind her.

A man came through the door way. He had skin on the tanner side like Stephan did but he had his mother's strong eyes and features. He walked like his father and his built was the same. Selena clasped her hands together. "Oh! My son!" she said. He had what looked like a very odd carrier with a pick blanket peeking out.

Somewhere in Time- trilogy part 2

Selena darted out of her seat. The man smiled at her.
"Hey mom" he said and kissed her cheek. How odd it was. Her best friend. The all hotness all attitude all fierceness and fire Selena all the things that made her, her best friend was being called mom. By someone older looking than her!
Selena turned and smiled at Esselle. "Elle" she said and Esselle slowly rose from her seat. "This is my son. David." she said. David smiled at her. "So this is the famous Titi Elle" he said en extended his hand. "Its nice to finally meet you" he said.
Esselle smiled and shook his head. "Its so nice to meet you" she said and looked at him with adoring eyes. "You look just like your father when he was younger" Esselle said. David laughed. 'But you have your mother's smile. From when she was younger" Esselle said. She looked at Selena. She was smiling with eyes glossy with tears.
Selena shook herself out of her daze. "Oh um" she said and clasped her hands together. She took the carrier from David and he smiled. "There's someone I want you to meet" she said. She gently put the carrier on the table and pulled back the silky pink blanket.
"This is my granddaughter. Isabella" she said. Esselle felt her heart warm. She was beautiful. She hard dark hair like Selena. She had a button nose light skin and rosy cheeks. She slept like an angel. She was a beautiful baby. Esselle covered her mouth with her hands as Selena gently took the sleeping baby out. Her throat was becoming scratchy and begun to burn along with her eyes.
"Oh Sel," she said. Selena smiled. Esselle looked up at David and his mother. "Oh could I hold her?" she asked.

"Of course!" David said softly.

Selena smiled and gently gave her to Esselle. The baby was warm and heavy in her arms. She smelled sweet that of lavender and baby powder.

Esselle laughed a little as the tears came down. She rocked her back and forth.

"Hi" she said. Esselle felt an overwhelming joy soft and sweet come over her. "I'm your Titi Elle" she whispered. Esselle swallowed hard. She let the tears go freely.

"You're so beautiful" she said and gently touched the baby's hair. She looked up at Selena and they both let out a laugh. Selena placed a shaking hand over her mouth and her eyes were so watery you couldn't see their color through her tears.

Esselle looked at the baby in her arms. "I promise you little one. I'll be here and I'm not going to be leaving your side. Ever. Consider yourself the thing that's gonna turn me around." she said and stroked her hair "I'll always protect you. I promise I won't let anything happen to you" she whispered and that the baby slowly opened her big blue-grey eyes. Esselle smiled and let the tear trickle down her face. What a beautiful blissful moment.

Somewhere in Time- trilogy part 2

soon as Esselle got home it was already dark out. She had gotten lost on the stupid train again. When she stepped through the door and shut it behind her her mother stopped in front of her. She raised an eyebrow.
"I told you, you weren't going to like what you found" she had said. Esselle had ran past Vivenne and slammed the door shut to her bedroom locking it. Esselle hadn't cried. not at all. She just

lied there on her bed staring at the cieling. Occasionally rolling over. She had no idea what to do with her life. Where to go what do. She was lost. She was confused. She was heart. It was going to take Esselle a while to fully absorb and grasp the fact that she was frozen. She had waken up 28 years later in a world she no longer knows. All night Esselle repeated that to herself getting herself used to it. Everyone I loved once before have moved on without me Esselle thought And now I have to find a way to go on with my life. Esselle sighed. She was dying inside and this getting used to it. Was going to take a while

****
****

Esselle lazily moved her eggs around on her plate. Gees even the plates were different 28 years later. Dear God was nothing the same anymore?

Vivenne smiled somberly at her daughter "I missed making breakfast for you" she said. Esselle smiled back.

"Me too" she said. Technically she didn't. She hadn't remembered anything.

"What do you want to do today sweetheart?" she asked. Henry came in and Esselle turned to face her father.

"Hey dad" she said. Her father smiled. He walked over to kiss he forehead.

"Hey mami" he said. "I missed kissing you ing the morning" she smiled. She kept forgetting they were deprived of their only daughter for almost 30 years.

"Your father and I have to work today but for dinner when we get home. Where do you want to go? You know LaBelle's is still open. They are celebrating their 30 year in buisness" she said softly.

Esselle looked at her mother.

"I know how much you liked to go there when you were younger" she said.

Esselle swallowed and looked at her parents.

"So how old am I?' she asked. The cup in her father's hand fell to the flower making a shattering noise.

"What?" he asked.

"Technically i'm still only 17 and technically i'm like old. What is it 45?" she said and Vivenne turned a sea green.

Esselle broke into a smirk "Does this mean I can have a drink if I want too?' she asked.

"No!" her parents both said. She slouched in her chair.

"You know technically I have been legal for 24 years" she said.

"No!" her parents said and again and she smiled a little. Now that she missed. Her mother ran her fingers through her hair.

"I think I might visit Selena again today" Esselle said. She waited vervously for their reply.

"You know, catch up" she said.

Her mother smiled taking her hand "I think its a great idea"

****
****

Selena took a scrap book and handed it to Esselle with a smile. "Its me wedding album" she said and chocked a little. "You're in there. There was a picture of you there the whole time. And I made copies of pictures we had already take and cut them to fit into the wedding pictures I already had."

Esselle smiled as a sign of comfort to her friend. She opened the book and immediately broke out into a smile. She turned the page and laughed.

Somewhere in Time- trilogy part 2

"I see you had david Tutera plan your wedding did you?" Esselle asked. Selena laughed teary eyed. She pressed her smile to a fine line and nodded.

Esselle noticed that Selena's dress was that of what they always talked about. Fitted at the top and flared out below the waste in ruffled layers that resembled waves. Esselle smiled. Her reception had been that of a beautiful one too. All red and white just like Selena wanted it. It hadn't shocked Esselle very much that Stephen was the one she had married. They were just bound to end up together. Esselle flipped some more pages and saw what Selena meant. A picture of Esselle had been cut out and taped to another. IT looked like she was at the wedding.

"How creative are you" Esselle said. Her friend nodded.

"He, uh, proposed at Rockefeller the moment the tree lit up for the first time" she said. Esselle softly smiled.

"That's sweet" she said. Selena nodded. She looked tired. Worn out even.

"How old were you?" Esselle asked. Selena's eyebrows furrowed in deep thought.

"22?" she said. Esselle nodded and flipped through the pages again.

"Then a year later my son David was born" Selena laughed a bit. "We got lucky he was born right after our wedding anniversary" she said.

"I'm not surprised. You always did want to get everything done young" Esselle said and they both laughed.

"Then 5 years later I had my daughter" Selena said and Esselle met her eye.

"Marie Esselle" she said.

Besides herself she smiled "You named her," Esselle begun in disbelief "After me?"

Selena nodded. "Elle you were never forgotten. We always thought of you always. There wasn't a day that went by that someone didn't mention you and smile or something happened that didn't remind us of you" she said and took her hand. "We never forgot about you"

Selena took in a deep breath. "Ten years ago though I had my twins. My last kids!" she said and Esselle laughed "Diana and John" she said.

Esselle swallowed hard. "It's just hard seeing all of this. All it does is make me wonder. What if. It makes me think I should have been there. I was deprived of so much. I hurt you all because...I don't even know why. I feel like its so unfair! Everything was taken away from me! How am I supposed to even live after this? I can't even go to school. It just wouldn't even work. I could be my classmates mother! And I couldn't get a job. Not into todays world with what happened to me. And that's another thing everything is so different! I keep getting lost. Sel, I used to know this city like the back of my mind" Esselle confessed "I feel like an outsider now"

Selena nodded. "I understand. Elle, I know you're hurting a bit inside-" Selena said but she cut her off.

"No Sel I'm practically dying inside! You know what I saw yesterday?" Esselle asked. She could feel her cheeks burning red with anger her eyes stinging green with envy and her blood boil. Selena shook her head. "Mardrin" Esselle said "And his wife. Martha"

Selena rolled her eyes a bit "Elle, what'd you expect to see? He had to go on with his life" Selena said with an obvious tone.

"He was supposed to be with me Selena! That's the point not her! Dear God he couldn't have picked anyone but her?" Esselle said frustrated. She fell back hard into her chair and slouched.

"It was easy for him to be with her" Selena said. Esselle raised an eyebrow.

"He was already in love with her. I'm sorry Elle but its true he was. Not as much as he loved you but he definitely cared for her. And she felt the same. she never left his side. She was caring, good hearted, kind sweet. She was there for him when he needed a shoulder to lean on. Even after he made it clear they'd never be together she didn't care. She still kept up with him. Brought him whatever he needed. Elle, if anyone was going to end up with Mardrin besides you it deserved to be her. She's a wonderful person. Take it from me who really just couldn't stand her for a while!" Selena said. She met Esselle's eye and her face softened. "They loved each other Elle. That's what counts" she said.

Esselle ran her fingers through her hair. "Ya well I still don't like her" she said.

Selena sighed "It took ten years Elle for him to get over you. And that's because I forced it upon him. Plus he was just miserable I wanted to see him happy Elle. I suggested he get with her. Elle can you just imagine she stood by his side for ten years. It didn't take long at all. They didn't even date they just got engaged" Selena said.

Esselle rolled her eyes "How romantic" she said.

Selena made a face. "What!?" Esselle said.

Selena rolled her narrow eyes dismissing her. "Anyways Esselle he missed you but he found a way to cope with it all and be happy. Not long after that they had their son. Augustine. Then I think two years after they had their daughter Jacqueline. He was for the most part happy Elle. Shouldn't his happiness count for anything? Even if it wasn't with you?" Selena asked.

Her mouth formed a thin line and she said "It would. But do you blame me for thinking about how that should have been me?" Selena sighed. She sat back and after a moment she shook her head. 'No, I guess not"

"Alright then" Esselle said and shut the wedding album with a snap.

'Guess who's here!" Someone called and Esselle could hear the front door shut. Selena gasped. Her face instantly lit up and she broke out into a huge smile and she turned in her seat to face behind her.

A man came through the door way. He had skin on the tanner side like Stephan did but he had his mother's strong eyes and features. He walked like his father and his built was the same. Selena clasped her hands together. "Oh! My son!" she said. He had what looked like a very odd carrier with a pick blanket peeking out.

Selena darted out of her seat. The man smiled at her.

"Hey mom" he said and kissed her cheek. How odd it was. Her best friend. The all hotness all attitude all fierceness and fire Selena all the things that made her, her best friend was being called mom. By someone older looking than her!

Selena turned and smiled at Esselle. "Elle" she said and Esselle slowly rose from her seat. "This is my son. David." she said. David smiled at her. "So this is the famous Titi Elle" he said en extended his hand. "Its nice to finally meet you" he said.

Esselle smiled and shook his head. "Its so nice to meet you" she said and looked at him with adoring eyes. "You look just like your father when he was younger" Esselle said. David laughed. 'But you have your mother's smile. From when she was younger" Esselle said. She looked at Selena. She was smiling with eyes glossy with tears.

Selena shook herself out of her daze. "Oh um" she said and clasped her hands together. She took the carrier from David and he smiled. "There's someone I want you to meet" she said. She gently put the carrier on the table and pulled back the silky pink blanket.

"This is my granddaughter. Isabella" she said. Esselle felt her heart warm. She was beautiful. She hard dark hair like Selena. She had a button nose light skin and rosy cheeks. She slept like an angel. She was a beautiful baby. Esselle covered her mouth with her hands as Selena gently took the sleeping baby out. Her throat was becoming scratchy and begun to burn along with her eyes.

"Oh Sel," she said. Selena smiled. Esselle looked up at David and his mother. "Oh could I hold her?" she asked.

"Of course!" David said softly.

Selena smiled and gently gave her to Esselle. The baby was warm and heavy in her arms. She smelled sweet that of lavender and baby powder.

Esselle laughed a little as the tears came down. She rocked her back and forth.

"Hi" she said. Esselle felt an overwhelming joy soft and sweet come over her. "I'm your Titi Elle" she whispered. Esselle swallowed hard. She let the tears go freely.

"You're so beautiful" she said and gently touched the baby's hair. She looked up at Selena and they both let out a laugh. Selena placed a shaking hand over her mouth and her eyes were so watery you couldn't see their color through her tears.
Esselle looked at the baby in her arms. "I promise you little one. I'll be here and I'm not going to be leaving your side. Ever. Consider yourself the thing that's gonna turn me around." she said and stroked her hair "I'll always protect you. I promise I won't let anything happen to you" she whispered and that the baby slowly opened her big blue-grey eyes. Esselle smiled and let the tear trickle down her face. What a beautiful blissful moment.

Somewhere in Time- trilogy part 2

soon as Esselle got home it was already dark out. She had gotten lost on the stupid train again. When she stepped through the door and shut it behind her her mother stopped in front of her. She raised an eyebrow.
"I told you, you weren't going to like what you found" she had said. Esselle had ran past Vivenne and slammed the door shut to her bedroom locking it. Esselle hadn't cried. not at all. She just lied there on her bed staring at the cieling. Occasionally rolling over. She had no idea what to do with her life. Where to go what do. She was lost. She was confused. She was heart. It was going to take Esselle a while to fully absorb and grasp the fact that she was frozen. She had waken up 28 years later in a world she no longer knows. All night Esselle repeated that to herself getting herself used to it. Everyone I loved once before have moved on without me Esselle thought And now I have to find a way to go on with my life. Esselle sighed. She was dying inside and this getting used to it. Was going to take a while

Somewhere in Time- trilogy part 2

****

Esselle lazily moved her eggs around on her plate. Gees even the plates were different 28 years later. Dear God was nothing the same anymore?

Vivenne smiled somberly at her daughter "I missed making breakfast for you" she said. Esselle smiled back.

"Me too" she said. Technically she didn't. She hadn't remembered anything.

"What do you want to do today sweetheart?" she asked. Henry came in and Esselle turned to face her father.

"Hey dad" she said. Her father smiled. He walked over to kiss he forehead.

"Hey mami" he said. "I missed kissing you ing the morning" she smiled. She kept forgetting they were deprived of their only daughter for almost 30 years.

"Your father and I have to work today but for dinner when we get home. Where do you want to go? You know LaBelle's is still open. They are celebrating their 30 year in buisness" she said softly. Esselle looked at her mother.

"I know how much you liked to go there when you were younger" she said.

Esselle swallowed and looked at her parents.

"So how old am I?'she asked. The cup in her father's hand fell to the flower making a shattering noise.

"What?" he asked.

"Technically i'm still only 17 and technically i'm like old. What is it 45?" she said and Vivenne turned a sea green.

Esselle broke into a smirk "Does this mean I can have a drink if I

Somewhere in Time- trilogy part 2

want too?' she asked.

"No!" her parents both said. She slouched in her chair.

"You know technically I have been legal for 24 years" she said.

"No!" her parents said and again and she smiled a little. Now that she missed. Her mother ran her fingers through her hair.

"I think I might visit Selena again today" Esselle said. She waited vervously for their reply.

"You know, catch up" she said.

Her mother smiled taking her hand "I think its a great idea"

****

Selena took a scrap book and handed it to Esselle with a smile. "Its me wedding album" she said and chocked a little. "You're in there. There was a picture of you there the whole time. And I made copies of pictures we had already take and cut them to fit into the wedding pictures I already had."

Esselle smiled as a sign of comfort to her friend. She opened the book and immediately broke out into a smile. She turned the page and laughed.

"I see you had david Tutera plan your wedding did you?" Esselle asked. Selena laughed teary eyed. She pressed her smile to a fine line and nodded.

Esselle noticed that Selena's dress was that of what they always talked about. Fitted at the top and flared out below the waste in ruffled layers that resembled waves. Esselle smiled. Her reception had been that of a beautiful one too. All red and white just like Selena wanted it. It hadn't shocked Esselle very much that Stephen was the one she had married. They were just bound to end up together. Esselle flipped some more pages and saw what Selena meant. A picture of Esselle had been cut out and taped to another. IT looked like she was at the wedding.

"How creative are you" Esselle said. Her friend nodded.

"He, uh, proposed at Rockefeller the moment the tree lit up for the first time" she said. Esselle softly smiled.

"That's sweet" she said. Selena nodded. She looked tired. Worn out even.

"How old were you?" Esselle asked. Selena's eyebrows furrowed in deep thought.

"22?" she said. Esselle nodded and flipped through the pages again.

"Then a year later my son David was born" Selena laughed a bit. "We got lucky he was born right after our wedding anniversary" she said.

"I'm not surprised. You always did want to get everything done young" Esselle said and they both laughed.

"Then 5 years later I had my daughter" Selena said and Esselle met her eye.

"Marie Esselle" she said.

Besides herself she smiled "You named her," Esselle begun in disbelief "After me?"

Selena nodded. "Elle you were never forgotten. We always thought of you always. There wasn't a day that went by that someone didn't mention you and smile or something happened that didn't remind us of you" she said and took her hand. "We never forgot about you"

Selena took in a deep breath. "Ten years ago though I had my twins. My last kids!" she said and Esselle laughed "Diana and John" she said.

Esselle swallowed hard. "It's just hard seeing all of this. All it does is make me wonder. What if. It makes me think I should have been there. I was deprived of so much. I hurt you all because...I don't even know why. I feel like its so unfair! Everything was taken away from me! How am I supposed to even live after this? I can't even go to school. It just wouldn't even work. I could be my classmates mother! And I couldn't get a job. Not into todays world with what happened to me. And that's another thing everything is so different! I keep getting lost. Sel, I used to know this city like the back of my mind" Esselle confessed "I feel like an outsider now"

Selena nodded. "I understand. Elle, I know you're hurting a bit inside-" Selena said but she cut her off.

"No Sel I'm practically dying inside! You know what I saw yesterday?" Esselle asked. She could feel her cheeks burning red with anger her eyes stinging green with envy and her blood boil. Selena shook her head. "Mardrin" Esselle said "And his wife. Martha"

Selena rolled her eyes a bit "Elle, what'd you expect to see? He had to go on with his life" Selena said with an obvious tone.

"He was supposed to be with me Selena! That's the point not her! Dear God he couldn't have picked anyone but her?" Esselle said frustrated. She fell back hard into her chair and slouched.

"It was easy for him to be with her" Selena said. Esselle raised an eyebrow.

"He was already in love with her. I'm sorry Elle but its true he was. Not as much as he loved you but he definitely cared for her. And she felt the same. she never left his side. She was caring, good hearted, kind sweet. She was there for him when he needed a shoulder to lean on. Even after he made it clear they'd never be together she didn't care. She still kept up with him. Brought him whatever he needed. Elle, if anyone was going to end up with Mardrin besides you it deserved to be her. She's a wonderful person. Take it from me who really just couldn't stand her for a while!" Selena said. She met Esselle's eye and her face softened. "They loved each other Elle. That's what counts" she said.

Esselle ran her fingers through her hair. "Ya well I still don't like her" she said.

Selena sighed "It took ten years Elle for him to get over you. And that's because I forced it upon him. Plus he was just miserable I wanted to see him happy Elle. I suggested he get with her. Elle can you just imagine she stood by his side for ten years. It didn't take long at all. They didn't even date they just got engaged" Selena said.

Esselle rolled her eyes "How romantic" she said.

Selena made a face. "What!?" Esselle said.

Selena rolled her narrow eyes dismissing her. "Anyways Esselle he missed you but he found a way to cope with it all and be happy. Not long after that they had their son. Augustine. Then I think two years after they had their daughter Jacqueline. He was for the most part happy Elle. Shouldn't his happiness count for anything? Even if it wasn't with you?" Selena asked.

Her mouth formed a thin line and she said "It would. But do you blame me for thinking about how that should have been me?" Selena sighed. She sat back and after a moment she shook her head. 'No, I guess not"

"Alright then" Esselle said and shut the wedding album with a snap.

'Guess who's here!" Someone called and Esselle could hear the front door shut. Selena gasped. Her face instantly lit up and she broke out into a huge smile and she turned in her seat to face behind her.

A man came through the door way. He had skin on the tanner side like Stephan did but he had his mother's strong eyes and features. He walked like his father and his built was the same. Selena clasped her hands together. "Oh! My son!" she said. He had what looked like a very odd carrier with a pick blanket peeking out.

Selena darted out of her seat. The man smiled at her.

"Hey mom" he said and kissed her cheek. How odd it was. Her best friend. The all hotness all attitude all fierceness and fire Selena all the things that made her, her best friend was being called mom. By someone older looking than her!

Selena turned and smiled at Esselle. "Elle" she said and Esselle slowly rose from her seat. "This is my son. David." she said. David smiled at her. "So this is the famous Titi Elle" he said en extended his hand. "Its nice to finally meet you" he said.

Esselle smiled and shook his head. "Its so nice to meet you" she said and looked at him with adoring eyes. "You look just like your father when he was younger" Esselle said. David laughed. 'But you have your mother's smile. From when she was younger" Esselle said. She looked at Selena. She was smiling with eyes glossy with tears.

Selena shook herself out of her daze. "Oh um" she said and clasped her hands together. She took the carrier from David and he smiled. "There's someone I want you to meet" she said. She gently put the carrier on the table and pulled back the silky pink

Somewhere in Time- trilogy part 2

blanket.

"This is my granddaughter. Isabella" she said. Esselle felt her heart warm. She was beautiful. She hard dark hair like Selena. She had a button nose light skin and rosy cheeks. She slept like an angel. She was a beautiful baby. Esselle covered her mouth with her hands as Selena gently took the sleeping baby out. Her throat was becoming scratchy and begun to burn along with her eyes.

"Oh Sel," she said. Selena smiled. Esselle looked up at David and his mother. "Oh could I hold her?" she asked.

"Of course!" David said softly.

Selena smiled and gently gave her to Esselle. The baby was warm and heavy in her arms. She smelled sweet that of lavender and baby powder.

Esselle laughed a little as the tears came down. She rocked her back and forth.

"Hi" she said. Esselle felt an overwhelming joy soft and sweet come over her. "I'm your Titi Elle" she whispered. Esselle swallowed hard. She let the tears go freely.

"You're so beautiful" she said and gently touched the baby's hair. She looked up at Selena and they both let out a laugh. Selena placed a shaking hand over her mouth and her eyes were so watery you couldn't see their color through her tears.

Esselle looked at the baby in her arms. "I promise you little one. I'll be here and I'm not going to be leaving your side. Ever. Consider yourself the thing that's gonna turn me around." she said and stroked her hair "I'll always protect you. I promise I won't let anything happen to you" she whispered and that the

Somewhere in Time- trilogy part 2

baby slowly opened her big blue-grey eyes. Esselle smiled and let the tear trickle down her face. What a beautiful blissful moment.

Somewhere in Time- trilogy part 2

sselle looked through her albums. She smiled. Taylor Swift, Lady Gaga, Miley Cyrus, Eminem, Will.I.Am, Black Eyed Peas, Brittney Spears, Justin Bieber, Rihanna, Avril Lavine, Maroon 5, Arianna Grande, Kesha, Pitbull, Jennifer Lopez, Demi Lovato, Jonas Brothers, R5, Jason Derulo, Jordin Sparks, Katy Perry, Lana Del Rey, One Republic, Imagine Dragons, Avici, Swedish House Mafia, Selena Gomez, Paramore, Beyonce, Kanye West, Jay Z, Justin Timberlake, Timbaland, Keri Wilson, One Direction, Christina Aguilera, Kelly Clarkson, Christina Perri, and all of her other favorite artists. Esselle bet a good portion of them must be all wrinkly by now. Esselle had such a fun good childhood. Who would have known her life would take a turn for the worst not so long after. Esselle's best moments were when she was thirteen. That's when she had the most fun. When Esselle left Selena's home last week she had had a lighter heart. Selena had been slowly piece by piece updating Esselle on what has happened. Esselle missed her graduation and prom but heard it was ok. It was odd enough but Esselle wanted to know all the gossip from high school she missed. She couldn't help it. Selena laughed but filled her in anyway on everyone's lives. Esselle had seen Stephen again. He looked older more mature but the same. She had met Selena's other children and the twins. Esselle spent a lot of time home though. She was under a seclusion. She didn't want to leave her bedroom. She left once a day from her house to see Selena for an hour. That was it. Selena asked her if she wanted to watch the twins the next day. As a way to bound with them. Esselle immediately excepted. Things seemed like they were falling carefully into place again. Anything that was ever hers that she called mine she had lost. Now she had found it again. Now she just needed to find a way to live. A way to live with herself the way she was. Different.

Somewhere in Time- trilogy part 2

sselle looked through her albums. She smiled. Taylor Swift, Lady Gaga, Miley Cyrus, Eminem, Will.I.Am, Black Eyed Peas, Brittney Spears, Justin Bieber, Rihanna, Avril Lavine, Maroon 5, Arianna Grande, Kesha, Pitbull, Jennifer Lopez, Demi Lovato, Jonas Brothers, R5, Jason Derulo, Jordin Sparks, Katy Perry, Lana Del Rey, One Republic, Imagine Dragons, Avici, Swedish House Mafia, Selena Gomez, Paramore, Beyonce, Kanye West, Jay Z, Justin Timberlake, Timbaland, Keri Wilson, One Direction, Christina Aguilera, Kelly Clarkson, Christina Perri, and all of her other favorite artists. Esselle bet a good portion of them must be all wrinkly by now. Esselle had such a fun good childhood. Who would have known her life would take a turn for the worst not so long after. Esselle's best moments were when

she was thirteen. That's when she had the most fun. When
Esselle left Selena's home last week she had had a lighter heart.
Selena had been slowly piece by piece updating Esselle on what
has happened. Esselle missed her graduation and prom but
heard it was ok. It was odd enough but Esselle wanted to know
all the gossip from high school she missed. She couldn't help it.
Selena laughed but filled her in anyway on everyone's lives.
Esselle had seen Stephen again. He looked older more mature
but the same. She had met Selena's other children and the twins.
Esselle spent a lot of time home though. She was under a
seclusion. She didn't want to leave her bedroom. She left once a
day from her house to see Selena for an hour. That was it. Selena
asked her if she wanted to watch the twins the next day. As a way
to bound with them. Esselle immediately excepted. Things
seemed like they were falling carefully into place again. Anything
that was ever hers that she called mine she had lost. Now she had
found it again. Now she just needed to find a way to live. A way
to live with herself the way she was. Different.

Somewhere in Time- trilogy part 2

sselle slipped on her favorite red, yellow, purple, and blue spring dress. It hit right of above her knees and was very flowy. She tied her curls up in a pretty ribbon and stepped back. Her outfit was that of her favorite. But odd enough when she walked the streets of New York she stuck out like a sore thumb. She wasn't crazy about the rather odd attire of everyone else. If she wanted to be stuck in 2017 then she was entitled to damn it. She stepped out of her bedroom grabbing her shoulder bag and shut the door behind her.

****

"Here sweetie" Vivienne said and handed her daughter vitamins. Esselle frowned.

"Are these the same ones I used to take?" she asked.

Henry nodded "Yes, just have those they are fine" he said. Esselle was skeptical at first but took them anyway. She swallowed hard and a sordid taste stood in her mouth. Her face scrunched up.

"So what are you guys doing today?" she asked. As soon as her father put the orange juice on the table Esselle lit up. She frantically reached over and grabbed the orange juice chugging it down her throat. With a sigh she gently placed the empty cup down while her mother put a plate of pancakes in front of her. At least the breakfast remained the same.

"Well we are working in the lab today and won't be back until tomorrow" Vivienne said and handed Henry coffee and held a cup in her hand for herself. Henry picked up an odd looking newspaper. Esselle's eyebrows pressed together and she tilted

Somewhere in Time- trilogy part 2

her head to look at it. It read:

Breaking news: Government Secrets Revealed!

Her father quickly shut the paper and Esselle lost sight of it. Her father sighed "Yes, um if you'd like sweetheart you can just stay home. We know how much there is to get used to and well with you having a whole day alone it'll give you time to cope" her father said. Esselle nodded.

"That would be nice" Esselle said. Her mother walked over with a sweet smile. She touched her daughter's head.

'Don't worry Elle" she said "You'll get used to it"

****
****

Esselle was not going to get used to it. She turned on what looked like a television. She sat on the couch and started fiddling with a remote. She was sure it was a remote. At least she thought it was a remote. There was a huge rectangular screen so flat it was a sheet of glass. She crossed her legs under her and tried turning it on.

"Damn it" she said and started pounding the remote on her hand. She started shaking it and beating at all the buttons.

"Oh my god!" she said and frustration. She threw it hard on the floor and there was a flash then voices. She screamed and fell back over the back of the sofa. She crawled and leaned against the sofa that was now lying on its back. She carefully craned her head back. She heard speaking. She slowly placed her hands on the edge of the lopsided couch and looked over. She saw moving images on the screen. She popped her head back down. Wait a minute she thought. She raised and eyebrow and looked over again. The tv was on and some corny show was playing. Honestly the outfits nowadays were awful. That blue blaze did not go with her red shirt. It didn't match. She looked over the couch and saw the remote. Turns out it didn't look like a remote anymore. It looked like a mini tablet. So the big button in the middle wasn't the on button she thought. She carefully reached over to grab it. It felt heavy in her hands. Hmm, it could really knock someone out. It had little images and words on touch buttons on it. She gently touched something. There was a spark.

"EEEKKK!" She shrieked and tossed it on the sideways couch cushion. There was silence. Her eyes looked back and forth. She looked over the couch again. The TV was off. The remote was back in the shape she had seen it previously. This was going to take a while she thought and some practice getting used too.

****
****

Esselle had hopped unto the subway. She was determined to know her away around her New York like the back of her hand again if it killed her...again. She thought. When she came up out the subway she was overwhelmed. She turned with her head to the sky and smiled. Everything was the same but it was like a breath of fresh air. She could see the tips and halves of new looking buildings behind the ones in front of her. The Empire State Building was up the block. She semi-skipped semi-walked and semi-ran down the block to the corner. The build boards around her were colorful and lit up. She saw new white buses driving by and the double decker tourists buses. She looked at them and smiled and laughed at the same time. She opened up her arms and took in the sunlight. The early days of June were that of her very favorite. Her most favorite. She let the warmth of

Somewhere in Time- trilogy part 2

the sun overwhelm her in such a beautiful way. Oh she missed days like these. Wonderful beautiful ones.
she crossed the street and in the middle was a huge square with tables and chairs. people sat and talked. It was like a whole new world. Esselle just marched down the streets and took in all the new and old sights alike.
"Pretty flower for a pretty lady!" someone called.
Esselle looked over and smiled. An older man had a red rose extended to her.
"Oh thank you" she said and took it. He had very dark skin big eyes white hair and a warm smile. He nodded and continued with his business. Esselle continued walking down the streets with a big smile. She looked around. She just couldn't get enough. Enough would never come to her because she just wanted more and more.
****
****

Esselle had hopped unto a bus. She jumped right off and ended up on Wall Street. She laughed. She had always told Selena she'd run wall street one day. When she saw Selena's face on a build board she shook her head with a smirk. She knew it. Selena became a big business woman. She was glad her life ended up working out well for her. She skipped down the street past buildings. She smelled her rose again. It smelled sweet.
Esselle twirled once and giggled when her dress turned with her. Esselle loved the sound her beautiful red heels made when they clicked against the cement sidewalk.
"Elle!" she heard someone say. She frowned. Who could that have possibly been. She felt a hand lay on top of her shoulder and

Somewhere in Time- trilogy part 2

she turned around. Her eyes widened.

'Mardrin! What are you doing here?" she asked. He made a face.

"Esselle I work here" he said and pointed to the building next her "In that building" he said.

Esselle stepped back and his hand fell from her shoulder.

"Well I don't want to speak to you" she said and turned around.

"Elle!" he said clearly annoyed. He stopped in front of her.

"Come on talk to me" he said

"I'm sorry but aren't you supposed to be at work?" she said.

"I look out of my office window and see a girl with thick curly hair and an outfit from 2017 no one would be caught dead in and you think I'm not coming out?" he asked.

Esselle's jaw dropped "You used to love this dress!" she said defensively.

He gently took her face by her chin "I still do" he said "But let's be honest no one else from today's youth would"

She felt like she were on a cloud. She wanted to smile at him. She was about to. But wait a minute wasn't she mad at him for something?

She smiled at him and he smiled back.

Oh darn she had forgotten.

He grazed her cheek bone with his thumb.

Oh yes that was it! she was mad at him for no apparent reason. It was probably because he married Martha. Yes, that was it.

"If anyone saw us they might think this was odd" he said.

Esselle frowned "Why?" she asked.

He laughed a little "Because you look like you could be my daughter" he said.

Her jaw dropped to the ground 'Hey! I'm four months older than

Somewhere in Time- trilogy part 2

you!" she said and stomped hard on the ground.

He laughed "Esselle that doesn't count. We were born in separate years. If anything I'm four months older than you" he said.

She rolled her eyes "Whatever!" she said.

It had grown silent. He was just smiling at her in the yellow sunlight. She looked at him.

'Why do you keep looking at me like that?" she asked.

He shrugged "Because now I can" he said.

She shook her head. As much as she didn't want to she took his hand in hers and brought it back down to his side. She took his left hand and flashed his ring.

"No you can't" she said. He flexed his hand and looked at his hand as if remembering again.

"Oh right" he said bringing his hand closer. He mad an annoyed sarcastic face "Forgot about that" he said.

she walked past him and he took her hand.

"Elle wait" he said.

"Mardrin what do you want?" she asked.

His eyes widened "God Elle you just came back 28 years later from the dead what do you expect? I missed you I just want to talk to you" he said.

"No you don't you just want to kiss me" she blurted out. Instantly her cheeks became red with embarrassment.

He stopped up straight closer and smiled.

"Ok is there anything wrong with that?" he said "Not like you aren't thinking the same thing" he added. Damn the man he knew her too well.

"I'm not married!" she said and he laughed.

"Yes that's true. But I am a faithful husband Elle. Just because I want to kiss you doesn't mean I am. I care for my wife Elle" he said.

She came a bit closer without noticing.

"But If you keep looking like that you're eventually going to wear out my will power" he said. She wanted to smile so bad it hurt. The corner of her mouth rose for a second then softened out. Then the thought came back to her. he was married. And the worst part of it all was that it wasn't to her.

"Mardrin I have to go" she said and wiggled her hand free.

"But why Elle? Why can't you just talk to me?" he pushed.

She looked up at him. "Because I can't" she whispered "It just hurts too much" she said.

He looked at her with eyes so soft they looked vulnerable. HE sighed and tilted his head.

"Elle" he said. She looked away.

"Just let me go Mardrin its no use" she said.

He swallowed hard and against his will he nodded. "You know where to find me" he said and pointed the building. "17 floor, just ask for me" he said. She wouldn't look at him. Finally he couldn't help it.

He turned her head and kissed her cheek. Esselle shut her eyes and fought back her tears. He stood there for a while warm against her cheek. She gently turned her face and there nose gently touched and their lips grazed each other. Esselle caught her breath. But Mardrin didn't move just froze. Esselle turn and ran.

Somewhere in Time- trilogy part 2

Somewhere in Time- trilogy part 2

It had rained that day in the later after noon after Esselle had seen Mardrin. The night sky was dark and blue filled with clouds that were clearing out and stars peeking through. Esselle had spent the rest of the day with Selena and her family. She met the rest of her children and watched the twins until Selena got back. Esselle had met the ten year old twins and instantly fell in love with them. The entire time they called her Titi Elle and it had been beautiful. Now Esselle had taken another wrong turn and she was probably in the lower east side. The buildings were made of brick. Everything was wet muggy and sticky. Fog and steam were coming out of pipes sticking out from walls and there were very few street lights on. It looked like a narrow abandoned alley way. The street was deserted. Esselle had changed her outfit. She got milk all over her dress. When she did they all laughed. She wore a pair of Selena's dark blue sweetheart jeans vintage shirt made of sheer fabric with pretty poufy sleeves and a hanging bow. After the rain it had become a bit cold and so she wore a jet black leather jacket. All of it from her box in the attic of clothes from when she was 17. Esselle refused to wear modern day clothing. She liked her look.

Esselle had been fiddling with her nails when she heard something. She looked behind her. The top of a metal garbage

Somewhere in Time- trilogy part 2

had fallen to the floor. She rolled her eyes. Probably a stupid raccoon. She turned around and kept walking. She heard another noise. Like an ear wrenching noise. Like a sword across to a wire. Her heart stopped and her stomach turned. Her head snapped around and she stopped. There was nothing there. She swallowed hard turned on her heels and started walking again. There was a bang like a hammer to a metal bar. She gasped for air and stopped dead in her tracks. She turned around and her veins were pulsing.

"Hello?" Esselle. See now Esselle knew this was a stupid thing to do. She should be running for the hills. Esselle used to make fun of all the white girls in movies that did stupid stuff. Her and Selena used to always say how a Spanish girl would never do that. Now Esselle was struck with an utter fear. She didn't know what to do.

Esselle turned around and started walking quickly. As fast as she could. She looked behind her and she saw dark lurking figures. She turned around. It could just be other people. They could just be walking the same way. She turned her head to the side and saw from the corner of her eye they were coming closer. She ran. She heard them run behind her. She felt a hand grab her arm and she screamed. She screamed for her life. IT was two of them. All in black. They grabbed her and tugged at her. They yanked at her and she screamed. They covered her mouth and she felt punches and cuts. She saw the flickering of a knife silver in the street light.

"Another one down" she heard someone mumble.

She felt her bones cracking. She scratched and kicked and di everything they could.

Somewhere in Time- trilogy part 2

She saw one of them take out a contraption with a glowing liquid inside. Esselle felt so weak and in pain she couldn't do anything. "Ok lets take this one out" someone said. Esselle tried doing everything she could there was nothing. Until she heard a grunt. Out of nowhere they let go of her. She heard punches and kicks being flown. She fell to the ground with a thump on her knees. She fell to the floor coughing her guts out. She yanked the rope they had strapped around her throat off and rolled over. Someone, a man, she felt took her in her arms. He turned her over and she could see the stars. she felt herself bleeding and everything hurt. Then as if by angel she felt as if she had seen an angel of God. But it wasn't he was just a man a regular man. He had saved her.

His eyes were huge so huge and he had long full thick jet black curved eyelashes. His hair had been thick and straight and jet black. His eyes were blue, so blue. Not just blue. Like tanzanite blue. Not even they were like Elizabeth Taylor blue. Like The Hope Diamond blue. Just gorgeous and they sparkled like diamonds. He had big full beautiful lips and his skin was just glowing. It was that the same complexion of Esselle's. Light but had color. He had beautiful cheek bones. High and everything about his face was smooth and carved. He had a square jaw line everything down to his eyebrows and nose was beautiful.

"are you alright?" he asked. Even his voice, deep and strong sounded that of heavenly and hero like to a dying Esselle. Almost as if naturally Esselle brought her weak hand to the side of his face.

"Who are you?" was she managed to croak. She saw him smile. What a beautiful smile it was that he had.

She saw him slip something out of his pocket. She was slowly slipping away. She felt a burn on her skin.

"Daniel" he had said to her "Daniel carter" Esselle shut her eyes.

sselle had slowly been growing conscious. Very, very, very slowly been growing conscious. Esselle had a searing pain in her hand. Her eyes peeled open and she looked at the inside of her arm. It had been bandaged up. She looked to her right and so a black night stand. The bed she was lying in was grey. Everything she had seen had been modern. Everything was oh so modern. The room was painted a dark grey-blue and the walls were flat and sleek with no pictures. Esselle tried sitting up but pain traveled through her veins making them pulse.

"I wouldn't do that if I were you" someone had said. Esselle looked to her left. It was then man she had seen before save her. He was standing near a wall that seemed to be made of all glass one huge window. He was dressed all in black just like his hair. he had a belt around his waist with what seemed like little pockets zippers and weapons shoved into them. He was what a 14 year old boy crazy her and Selena would call a sick body. Esselle blinked the thought out of her head. But she couldn't help it. His t-shirt was black just like his hair and tight so that you could see every carve and mold of his body. 6 pack. dear God Esselle must have been on drugs she couldn't keep her mind straight. He had the broadest shoulders she had ever seen. And his arms were just fit muscles. He looked so strong he could probably crush a skull between his fingertips. So strong you could see his veins. Esselle always found that attractive.

"Wh-What?" she stammered. She had been slipping on black leather gloves without the fingers. Like the texting gloves she had when she was 15.

He walked over to her and sat in the chair at her bed side. He flexed his hand. 'I thought I should stay until you woke up. Figured you'd be less cranky if you had something nice to look at" he said.

Esselle couldn't help it. He came pouring out of her. "Well aren't you arrogant" she said. She was Spanish. These kind of things just came to her. He just laughed. Laughed like he was genuinely entertained. He had a nice laugh.

"well aren't you a bit snippy towards the open that saved your life" he said. Esselle slouched a bit. He had saved her life didn't he? yet he was a complete stranger. Esselle looked in front of her. There was a TV and a table under it a black one just square with sharp edges.

"Where am I?" she asked.

"Ehhhh" he said with a face "Call it my temporary apartment" he said.

"Temporary?" she repeated. He nodded.

He stood from his chair and reached over Esselle. She caught he breath. He was very close to her. They had only just met. But it didn't stop her heart from skipping a beat. he reached for something. A tube. He sat back down. He pulled his chair in closer and took the cap off.

'Give me your arm" he said and his voice was deep but soft. Like melting chocolate.

Somewhere in Time- trilogy part 2

Esselle cowered away a bit. HE met her eye. Finally after a moment he rolled his eyes.

"Listen Kid I'm not going to hurt you" he said.

"How should I know that? Why should I trust you?" Esselle said sliding off the side of the bed.

"I did just save your life" he said. Esselle approached the window and rubbed her elbow. Soon he was behind her. She could see his glowing reflection in the glass.

Esselle grew confused. She was looking out over the city but something had seemed odd wrong. Almost as if there was something there flashing before her eyes hut she couldn't quite grasp the image long enough.

"You can see it. Can't you?" he said.

"See what?" Esselle asked. It had been raining outside lightly. The sky was a very dark blue with the occasional lighting.

"The city. You can see it. I can tell by the way your eyes sparkle" he said.

"You think my eyes sparkle?" she asked. He nodded.

"When the city is seen for the first time we always have our eyes sparkle. Its how its known we first have the Gift. Its the first sign. We all have it. Unless you have to be trained for it. That takes a while" he said.

Esselle was drowning in confusion. "What Gift? What We?" she said.

His eyes fell for a moment then looked at her. He placed his hands on her shoulders and turned her to face the window.

"Concentrate kid. Try hard. You can do it. I know you can" he said.

Esselle couldn't help but think about how warm his hands were

on her shoulders and the little shocks of electricity it sent through her veins. She didn't even know his name yet she felt like she knew him. Or did he tell her his name? And she had probably just forgotten? But then Esselle was doing what he hald told her. She concentrated on the city. She saw the image before her flicker. Then before her eyes she gasped. She was no longer looking at New York anymore. She was looking at a city filled with buildings of all different heights. The city's buildings were black with glowing lights running down the, and slanted tops. She gasped. His grip on her shoulders tightened and her hands covered her mouth. She looked back at him and he was smiling.
"You're a special one aren't you? I knew you were from the moment I scanned arm" he said.
"What are you talking about?" she said. He took her arm. The white gauze wrapped around it was turning red. He sighed.
"They cut you pretty bad and you're bleeding again. Come on. Let me go fix it" he said. She shook her arm free.
"I don't even know your name" she said. he smiled and extended his hand.
"Daniel Carter" he said. He had a twisted little grin on his face. Esselle sucked hard on her teeth. He raised his eyebrows.
"What the little princess is above shaking the hands of commoners?" he said.
"Uck!" Esselle said and walked over sitting on the edge of the bed. He just laughed.
"You know I think I'm going to like you" he said. "we're definitely going to get along" he said and sat at the chair by the bed.
"Aren't you a confident one so sure right away that I'd like you" she said. HE just laughed a bit shaking his head

Somewhere in Time- trilogy part 2

"Oh ya" he said and took the tube in hand again. "I'm definitely going to like You" he squeezed something out of the tube. It was gel like and a translucent color.

"May I have your arm now kid?" he asked. She gave him her arm.

"I have a name you know" she said.

He smiled and took the gauze off her arm. "Well It would be my honor if you decided to actually tell me" he said.

she kept her eyes on her arm. "Esselle," she said and he looked at her "My name is Esselle Elunas" she said.

He nodded "I don't like it" he said.

"What?" she asked in disbelief.

"Your name. Esselle. It doesn't suit you" he said.

"You don't even know me" she said.

He shrugged "You can just tell by looking at a person. I'm not calling you that" he said. She rolled her eyes.

"Oh great" she said.

"I'll call you Essie" he said and she laughed.

"Essie?" she asked and he nodded. He was cleaning up her arm.

"Sometimes Ess for short but mainly Essie" he said.

'And what makes you think we'll be the best of friends after this" she said.

Daniel let out a deep breath and sat back nonchalantly in his chair.

"Well for one no one can stay away from me for very long after seeing me the first time" he said. She let out a deep breath.

"Second after seeing what you just saw did you honestly think you were going to get away that easily?" he asked. Esselle looked at him. He was right.

"There goes your reason" he said "In fact I believe there were two" he said and got up. WIth her eyes she followed him as he walked over to the window again.

"You were hurt pretty badly. You should be ready, if you choose to leave in the morning." he smiled "Not like you will" he said.

"Why is that?" she asked truly curious.

"Because" he said and pulled on his glove. "You aren't going to be able to stay away from this hunk of gorgeous very long after this" he said.

"Oh God!" Esselle said rolling her eyes. The door opened. A very peppy girl came in. She had ink black long straight hair and brown eyes. She was slender and of average height. She was pretty and youthful and vibrant. She was dressed all in black. She smiled "Oh yay she is awake!" she said.

"Jasmine you'll blind her with your rays of sunshine tone it down" he said walking across the room. Jasmine narrowed her eyes at him.

"Right Daniel let me just tone down your hotness" she said. She put air quotes around the word hotness. HE smirked walking next to her.

"That's impossible. Telling me not to be is stunning is like telling the world not to rotate. Impossible" he said and opened a door in the very small hallway. HE disappeared behind it.

Jasmine rolled her eyes. She looked at Esselle and smiled.

"I'm so glad your finally awake. You took quite the hit" she said walking over to the TV.

"Oh ya Um," she said and looked to where Daniel disappeared. "Is he always that arrogant?" she asked.

Jasmine shrugged and turned the TV on. "Sure he is. I ignore it though. Besides his arrogance is one of the things that make him

Somewhere in Time- trilogy part 2

so damn sexy" she said and sat in a love seat in the corner of the room. Esselle's eyes widened.

"Oh" she said and Jasmine looked at her. Jasmine had been very, very beautiful. The kind of beautiful Esselle always wished to be. "I didn't know you to were um.. so uh I mean... you're...?" but Esselle couldn't quite get the words out. Thank God Jasmine did. "Oh God no that's disgusting we're not dating!" she said and Daniel came back in clueless to the conversation at hand. "He's my brother" she said.

"Oh come on sis like if you didn't have the chance to totally call dibs on this hunk of hotness you wouldn't jump on it" he said and fell into the bed beside Esselle. She gave him a look. He had a rubber band in his hands and he shrugged. Had he no idea how awkward it was. Jasmine rolled her eyes "Ignore him" she said.

"You know I'm surprised that cut knocked you out so easily" he said.

Esselle looked at him "I'm human not titanium. They were ready to stick some weird contraption in my skin!" she said. Daniel's eyes became alert. HE looked at his sister and she looked at him the same way.

"We have to take her sooner than I thought" he said and flew out of the bed. Jasmine did the same and grabbed a belt from on top of one of the tables and wrapped it around her waist.

"You're right" she said.

"Wait a minute where?" Esselle said standing up. Daniel took her arm and drew her close like nothing. Esselle caught her breath again. His hands grazed her waist causing goose bumps to surface and for her to shiver when he wrapped a belt around her waist and snapped the buckle.

Somewhere in Time- trilogy part 2

"On a trip, oh! By the way Jasmine this is Essie, Essie this is Jasmine. But Jasmine You're not allowed to call her Essie only I am." he said.

"Please don't call me that" Esselle said softly.

"Jasmine you have to call her by her awful real name" he said.

"Hey!" Esselle said. He smiled and tightened the belt around her.

"Her name's Esselle" he said. She guessed it was the way he was it that made the corners of her mouth twitch.

Jasmine pushed Daniel to the side and shook Esselle's hand.

"Jasmine Carter. Nice to meet you" she said.

"Alright lets go" Daniel said by the door "Time to get Essie to headquarters"

Try to keep up kid" Daniel said from ahead. Esselle limped close behind.

"You try keeping up with a twisted ankle. Who are you? Speedy Gonzalez!?" she said. He looked back and laughed then kept walking.

"You know you whine a lot" he said. Jasmine hit his arm.

"Shut it! Can you be anymore rude?" she asked.

"No" Esselle muttered.

Daniel burst into laughter and Esselle felt her cheeks burn red with embarrassment. She had not meant for that to come out the way it did.

"Go ahead and open the door" he said to Jasmine. She nodded and darted down the dark narrow alley way in which they were walking and disappeared into the dark beyond the fog.

He stopped and Esselle stopped next to him.

"Where did she go?" she asked.

"Ahead, so I can stay behind with you" he said.

"Stay behind with me?" she said.

He nodded "Ya, you're limping and pretty bad. I don't want you walking to quickly" he said.

Esselle swallowed hard. "Oh thanks" she said.

"So," he said and they started walking slowly so that Esselle could keep up "Essie" he said and Esselle looked at him.

"Please don't call me that" she said. He smiled.

"Sorry Ess, you're screwed. Once I give a nickname it sticks" he said and looked at her.

"If anyone will call be a nickname that nickname is Elle. Short for Esselle" she said.

His face scrunched up and he shook his head "No, I like Essie" he said.

Esselle rolled her eyes and gave up. "So Daniel," she said and he looked at her.

"How did you find me?" she asked. He looked away.

"So you're one of those" he said.

"One of what?" she asked.

"The 'Million and one questions' type" he said.

Her mouth opened and her eyes widened "Its a good question!" she said and he shrugged.

"What should it matter?" he asked.

Esselle sighed "I just wanted to know. In all fairness you're a complete stranger to me and you're dragging me to some unknown place and I'm kind of against my better judgment letting you. So maybe if asking you a question would help me trust you a little more than I'd like an answer" Esselle said.

Daniel took in a deep breath and looked at her. "Here" he said

when Esselle winced. She had added too much pressure to her ankle. HE took her arm and wrapped it around his shoulders. "Anymore pressure to that ankle you'll break it" he said.
Esselle looked at him and pressed her lips together. "Thank you" she said. He nodded and it remained silent.
"I heard you screaming" he said.
Esselle looked at him. In the night the light from the moon reflected off his face and she could see his beautiful profile.
"You what?" she asked.
"I want you to trust me so I'm answering your question. I heard you screaming so anyone's extinct is to go see where all the commotion is at. So I saw those people and you so I knocked them out. You were hurt pretty badly so..." he said and trailed off.
"Thank you" Esselle said and he laughed a little.
"Essie I believe you said that already" he said.
'No, I mean it. I would like to thank you" she said and his eyes met hers . "For saving my life"
They ended up out in the open they had been walking so much they didn't notice. They were on a main avenue with cars, despite it being so late, were flying by.
"Had you not shown up when you did I would have been bleeding out in an alley right about now" she said. She saw him swallow hard.
"Ya well, I guess you can call me a Good Samaritan" he said. Besides herself Esselle smiled a bit.
"I guess you are" she said.
Jasmine showed up. "Um, I forgot my keys" she said. She had a cherubic look to her at that moment like an innocent little child

Somewhere in Time- trilogy part 2

that had done something wrong and was now saying something. Daniel rolled his eyes. "Dear Lord Jas!" he said. Jasmine shrugged. "Listen my job is to stand around looking pretty Danny Dan. Not to have the keys. That's your job you work here" she said.

Esselle looked up. She was standing in front of the Freedom Tower.

She frowned "What at we doing at the Freedom Tower?" she asked. It was lit up Red, White, and Blue. Esselle remember when it was first being built.

Daniel smiled and slipped a card into its slot. The door opened. "This is the home of The Invisibles" he said.

Somewhere in Time- trilogy part 2

Somewhere in Time- trilogy part 2

hen the doors of the elevator opened to the top floor of the Freedom Tower and she was overwhelmed with awe.
"Wow" she said. Jasmine smiled and took arm and gently led her out of the elevator.
"This is Head Quarters" she said.
Esselle was overwhelmed with the beautiful sight. Everything had been glowing white, silver, and an icy blue. People walking around in uniforms. The oddest machines and screens Esselle had ever screen covered the walls. In the center was a huge circle with a short white metal gate surrounding half of it. It looked like a semi circle shape on both sides and they were glowing graphed screens.
A woman looked over and smiled. She had blonde hair pulled up and brown eyes. She had a warm smile and was dressed in black.
"Well, I see you've managed to find an ice child" she said. She had an accent to her. A beautiful one too. It reminded of her of a

Somewhere in Time- trilogy part 2

European accent. Swedish maybe.

She walked down the stairs exiting from the circle her tall black boots clicking. She had to be probably in her early 40's. She was a very wholesome beautiful with a square face and bold eyelashes.

"Um, child of what?" Esselle asked. She laughed.

"I can also see you haven't informed her of anything" she said and extended her hand.

"This is Essie Char, but you're not allowed to call her that only I am" Daniel said.

"Please don't call me that" she said.

He ignored her "You have to use her awful real name Esselle" he said. Esselle took the woman's hand. She had a funny smile on her face and gave Daniel a look.

"I see you have already made a claim on this one" she said.

Daniel nodded. "Duh" he said.

The woman looked at Esselle and smiled "Its a pleasure to meet you sweetie" she said.

Esselle smiled softly. "Nice to meet you ma'am" she said. The woman laughed.

'Sweetheart ma'am is my mother. Call me Charlotte everyone does" she said.

Esselle nodded. "Charlotte" she repeated.

'Unless you're me and call her Char. Only I am allowed to call her Char though" Daniel said.

Charlotte rolled her eyes "Yes Daniel. Only you're allowed to call me Char" he smiled satisfied.

"Well sweetheart you must be lost completely" she said.

Esselle nodded and Jasmine laughed.

"You're sure about that" she said and yanked her gloves off.
"Is she-?" Charlotte began. Daniel nodded cutting her off.
"First thing I noticed about her. She has the Gift Char" he said. Her eyes widened.
"I see" Charlotte said.
"I think she's the one we've been waiting for. The one that set the chain reaction almost 30 years ago" Jasmine said.
"Jas, she's not that old" Daniel said.
Esselle's mind was spinning she could not quite grasp anything.
"Ok slow down!" Esselle said. "First off" she said taking a step.
"Ah!" she winced. Daniel took a quick step and grabbed her arm.
'What's wrong with her?" Charlotte asked coming to Esselle's aid.
"Her ankle. She was hurt" Jasmine said.
"Daniel take her to the medical room. Jasmine come with me. I guess we'll have to find doctor Matlock now" Charlotte said.
Jasmine nodded and they went on their way.

****

Esselle couldn't help but think about how cool the medical room looked. It was just glowing like neon lights. Everything about it so futuristic and unique and unknown to Esselle. It reminded her of how she saw the city for the first time change before her eyes and how it looked like a city pulled out of Tron Legacy. She sat swinging her legs feet above the ground as Daniel went through the cabinets.

"What are you doing?" she asked and tilted her head.
"Looking for the-" he said and pulled something out with a smile
"Ha, got you" he said and walked over to Esselle.
"What's that?" she asked.

"It's a scanner." he said and reached over. He shut the lights. Esselle quickly reached out and grabbed his arm. He chuckled. "Calm down, I need the lights off for this" he said. Suddenly a light came on and she saw Daniel in the dark. His eyes were sparkling. Esselle looked down. It was what looked like a long thing about the length of a ruler and thick with one dark line running across it. It gave off light.

"This is electural light. It helps us to see your mark. It captures the electrolytes in your skin wherever it maybe and captures its shape using the light to form it" he said.

Esselle frowned "You are speaking gibberish to me" she said. He laughed a bit.

"I know I'm sorry. You're probably completely lost" he said.

She nodded "I have no idea what you are talking about" she said. He nodded while taking the gauze off of her arm. "You will soon enough" he said.

Esselle's eyes widened. Her arm had been healed and clear of blood.

"But wasn't I-?" she asked and Daniel smiled.

"You haven't been awake for very long have you?" he asked.

Esselle felt her stomach turn. Awake? What did he mean? Did he know Esselle was frozen? But no how could he?

He ran the scanner down her arm. Slowly of course. She felt the tingling burning sensation where he held her arm. Esselle began to feel light headed. When he had her arm in his hand she could just feel his strength traveling from his touch to her skin.

"There" he said. He had stopped over the middle of the inside of her arm. Esselle's eyes widened. There in front of her was a beautiful glowing intricate curvy curly mark on the inside of her arm. It had to be around 4 inches big and beautiful. She looked at Daniel.

"What the hell is that on my arm?" she asked.

"You have the mark" he said.

Essie you're special. This mark you have no idea. I don't think you fully comprehend what you're now apart of" Daniel said. Esselle looked at him and he just looked at her. And it stood like that for a while and Esselle felt the oddest pull towards him almost an attraction. She had never felt that way before.
'Would you care to tell me what I've gotten myself into?" she asked after a while. He sighed.
"Something a nice girl like you I wish didn't have to go through"

he said. What was that supposed to mean. Esselle opened her mouth to speak but the lights went on. Daniel quickly pulled away shutting the scanner off. She had noticed how close they were until just then.

Charlotte, Jasmine, and a man with silver hair and light skin with grey eyes came in.

"So, where is she?" he asked and Daniel pointed to me. he leaned against the cabinets and began picking at his fingers.

The man smiled "You must be the new girl everyone is ranting about" he said.

"Matlock that's Essie." Daniel said.

"Please stop calling me that" she begged.

Daniel ignoring her said "But that's my nickname and you know the rules. You have to use her awful real name Esselle" he said and went back to her fingers.

"Ahhh Daniel" Matlock said and turned to face Esselle. "I'll never get used to your ahhh what's the word? Charisma?" he said.

Daniel thought "I think its dashing good looks and charm" he said and went back to his fingers. Jasmine made a face.

"I'm Doctor Matlock" he said and extended his hand to Esselle.

"Esselle" she said and smiled. He clasped his hands together.

"So your ankle is it?' he said and bent down to examine Esselle's foot. He whistled.

"You hurt it pretty bad. But nothing a healer can't cure" he said.

'Hey how is the Paula Richardson case going?" Daniel asked out of nowhere.

"Who?" Esselle asked.

He gave her a face "The sweetie the adults are talking. Just concentrate on your little booboo" he said. Esselle felt her skin sizzle.

'I'm not 5" SHE SNAPPED.

"No but with a few ribbons and pig tails with that squeaky voice no one would ever know" he said.

"It turns out she was not brought back. She lived once that was it she wasn't one of us" Charlotte said.

Daniel sighed. 'I guess it's true what they say. POLO. Paul Only Lived Once" he said.

Finally Esselle snapped "That's YOLO you jackass! You Only Live Once!" she said.

He rolled his eyes "Same thing!" he said.

Esselle exasperated rolled her eyes.

"Alright I think Esselle has had enough of this annoying silence" Jasmine said and approached her. "I think its time we explain everything to you" she said. Esselle sighed with relief.

"Yes please!" she said.

"We are The Invisibles" Jasmine said and smiled "We are an under cover society of genetically altered human warriors created by the United States Government" she said and her eyes were shining like neon lights.

"Excuse me?" Esselle said.

"Let me explain," Charlotte began "For the past 50 years the United States was been experimenting with humans. They have been trying to design, using microscopic electrical wires and electrolytes, to create the ideal human fighters. But, to the governments dismay it always causes disease in the people they are experimenting in. They become sick before they are able to show off their new abilities" she said.

"Ok slow down Char the girls mind is spinning" Daniel said

looking up from his hands. He looked at Esselle.

"It always ends up working but people become sick before the government can experiment on them. Test them if it makes more sense to see if the work they did on their body was efficient and successful" he said.

"What the government was doing was slowly turning the flesh of humans into cybor-gens. Computerized genetics that send sparks of electricity through the host's body when the changes have fully taken place. These cybor-gens work in your muscles and your instincts everywhere in your body even your brain to control your body. It helps with your reflexes your sense and strength" Jasmine said.

"Why did people start dying?" Esselle asked.

"Because these cybor-gens needed a lot of time to settle in the host's body. But they were so strong they eventually ended up killing them. So that's when the government and their elite inside scientists started with a new for of cybro-gens that had the same effect but instead of killing them to the point of no return it would stop the bodies processes but preserve it" Daniel said.

Esselle shook her head "I don't understand" she said.

"What the government did was freeze the people they were testing. To whatever extent they needed to be frozen. They froze the people before they died. Then the human body would regenerate and awaken on its own time when the cybro-gens had fully settled and the host was rejuvenated and ready to perform the duties the cybro-gens were programed to carry out." said Matlock.

Esselle nodded pretending she understood.

"But something went horribly wrong as they continued with he project. The hosts were just becoming uncontrollable. The government saw them as posing a threat and stopped freezing bodies around ten years ago. For the past ten years they had been killing off these people whenever they found them because as the government puts it they 'Pose a threat to the very form of the U.S and how it functions and therefore must be terminated'" Daniel said putting air quotes in.

'What does all of this have to do with me?" Esselle asked.

Jasmine spoke next "These people genetically altered-" she said and Daniel cut her off.

"We are not genetically altered! Are genes and DNA are fine. We have just had things added to our bodies therefore changing the ways in which it functions and works." Daniel looked at Esselle "Basically we are half computer" he said and Esselle shivered.

"Anyway!" Jasmine said shooting him a glare. "These people have gone in hiding. Even before they were being hunted down that was only recent. These people knew the government would find them and continue work on them. And then the society of The Invisibles was born. We are The Invisibles because we are unseen in the public eye and are in hiding. The world isn't as anyone thought. We have abilities no one else poses" Jasmine said.

"Has she seen the city yet" Charlotte asked.

Daniel nodded "Didn't even need help" he said and she smiled as if impressed.

"Most people have to be trained vigorously to have the Gift" she said.

"I'm still confused. Why did I see the city the way I did?" she asked.

"Because that is the way it all truly looks. It is hidden the reality of the U.S by the government. That's another reason they wanted to kill us off. We saw what they didn't want us to see thanks to their mistake." she said.

"There" Matlock said. "Wiggle your foot" he told Esselle and she did so. It didn't hurt. She had not even noticed he was doing anything to her.

"Excellent" he said.

"So what does this have to do with me?" Esselle asked.

Jasmine sighed "You're one of us Esselle. You have the mark. We all have it somewhere on our hands. Mine is on my back Charlotte has hers on her ankle. Its where the electrolytes collect and form a special pattern. The government programed it that way so that if they needed to tell us apart from others they could do it easily" she said.

"You were frozen weren't you? I can tell that outfit" Daniel said and made a face.

Esselle ignored the comment and just nodded.

"2017" she said. Daniel whistled.

"Damn" he said and Jasmine laughed.

"Hey you were frozen-" she began and he waved at her.

"Ehhh sh! child" he said and she giggled. When had Daniel been frozen.

"So now I'm pretty sure your mind is spinning" Charlotte said.

"Ha!" Esselle said and ran her fingers through her hair "Spinning isn't the word.

Charlotte nodded. "Daniel take her home" she said and met Esselle's eyes.

"I'm going to give you a choice. You know what you are now. You need training. What happened to you in the alley will happen again. But its up to. You can either go home and we'll never bother you again or Daniel can bring you back tomorrow night and we'll do more explaining. Go home clear out your mind. Think of what you want to ask and if you choose come back" she said and flicked her head at Daniel

He sighed. "Come on Essie child" he said taking her hand so she could hop off. Esselle looked at Daniel. 'What do you think?" she asked.

"About what?" he asked.

"Whether I should come back or not" she asked and he smiled.

"Oh you'll come back" he said.

Esselle raised an eyebrow "What makes you so sure?" she asked.

"Because you'll definitely want to see me again" he said. Esselle's cheeks burned. Was it wrong that she did? "Don't be embarrassed about it though most girls do besides. I'd like to see you back again too" he said.

Daniel d brought Esselle home that night. And after that she had slept. For the first time ever despite how tired she was she kept waking up. Her dreams were once filled with sweetness. Now they weren't even dreams just nightmares. She dreamed of being trapped in a small space. Several times she woke up to scream for her life. Then she had remembered her parents would not be home until morning. She lay in bed while the blue essence of twilight filled her room. Finally her eyes fell shut and she dreamed again. She dreamed of night black hair and tanzanite for eyes. The most beautiful thing in the world she had seen. A shiver went through her body when their hand rested on her shoulder. Esselle's eyes flew open. The sun had fully risen and it was 8:30 in the morning. Should could hear rush our in the city from inside her bedroom and she sat up in her bed. Her fingertips gently grazed her shoulder where she felt the burn of someone else's skin brush hers. She suppressed any feelings she feared coming on about the man that saved her life and pushed back all of her thoughts. She needed to decided what to do. Be with them or choose to no. Either way her life would never be the same. So Esselle dragged her self out of bed. She stopped in front of the long vintage mirror in her bedroom. She looked like a curvy, curly bed headed, hazel eyed mess. She went into her dressing room and flicked the lights on. Now the only problem was she had no idea what to wear.

****

Esselle held her bag in front of her. She had her pretty heels on the ones with the ribbon and were peek toed. She had a pretty early summer sweater with long sleeves wrapped around her neck hanging off her shoulders. She had on a pink and white polka dot dress with spaghetti straps and an a neck line. She took two pieces of her hair and pinned it back. The sun had been beaming down on Esselle. It was early morning in the city and it was always that way. Esselle against her better judgment let her heart lead her to where it had wanted to go. At first she went to the Freedom Tower. Then she snapped herself out of it. She had not been planning to go the Freedom tower in the first place she just somehow got stuck their. By accident. She had hopped back unto the train and went to where she wanted to go originally. She

stopped and looked up at the building where Mardrin worked. She sighed. She knew she could talk to him. He had always been one she could talk too. With the sound of her heartbeat and clicking heels she pushed the door to his building open.
****
****

Mardrin Vauge- Managing Partner/CEO
Esselle rolled her eyes. She knew it. Mardrin had always wanted to run his own company. Now he was. The plaque on the door outside his office shown in the sunlight coming in from the other side of the office. She pressed her lips together and slowly knocked.
"Come in" she heard him say. She took in a deep breath. Just the sound of his voice it felt like a rush of relief. She pushed open the door gently and shut it behind her.
"Judith if its about those reports I told you Carla has them" he said. He had his reading glasses on which made him look a lot older. Actually his age. He was working fiercely through some papers. The entire wall behind him was a huge glass window. It had the most priceless view of New York. It made her catch her breath.
"Actually Judith is a bit busy at the moment" she said. With a snap of his head he looked up.
Esselle smiled a bit. "Its just me. Sorry to disappoint" she said. He stood from his chair. Esselle took a step forward and shook her head.
'No, its fine sit please" she said. he made a face and walked out behind his desk and stopped in front of her.
"Esselle" he said. She looked up at him and the light hit him just

perfectly to make Esselle think he was just heavenly. He hesitantly brought his hands up. Finally without hesitation he placed them on her shoulders. He bent over and kissed her cheek. Esselle sighed. This was all it would be from now on. Then again until Esselle lost it. She shut her eyes and then all too soon he pulled away.

"I'm glad you came" he said. It all sounded far too formal to Esselle so she didn't like it. She shoved the lump in her throat down and nodded.

"So am I" she said.

'Come" he said and sat her down in the seat across from her. 'So," he said. He had taken a picture frame and put it into his desk. Esselle hadn't caught a glimpse of what it was. He reached for another one but Esselle smirked and took it before he did.

"You don't have to hide your family from me" she said. He made a distressed face and Esselle looked down at the photograph. At first she had thought he was putting away pictures of his family not to offend her but her heart stopped.

It was of them just smiling at each other. She had loved this picture. It used to hang in her locker. She looked at him.

"Where did you find this?" she asked. he sat back in his chair.

"When you...well...you know Selena and I cleaned out your locker. I took the pictures and Selena took the rest" he said. Esselle felt her heart ache. 'And you kept it this whole time and on your desk at that....why?" she asked.

He sighed "Esselle what do you think?" he asked. Esselle didn't want to answer the question although she knew the answer. She knew she'd just cry. She didn't want to cry not at all.

"Mardrin you make it so hard you know that?" She asked.

He raised an eyebrow "Make what hard?" he asked.

Esselle shut her eyes. "Trying not to love you anymore" she said and looked up at him.

"Because you're charm is so easy to fight" was his remark and he picked up some papers and had the tip of his pen like a true business man in his mouth just as he always did.

Esselle stood up and walked to the window where she stood.

'What was it like?" she asked. Mardrin turned in his chair. In one swift move he stood up and was at her side.

"What was what like?" he asked.

She looked at him "Being without me" she said.

His eye lids fell when he looked down at her. "Esselle burning to death would have been better" he said.

Esselle swallowed hard. "How about as the years went by?" she asked.

He gently took her face by her chin. He gently shook his head. "Stood the same. It just got easier to forget the reason why I was hurting. Then there were days I'd wake up and couldn't wait to see you and I'd forget I'd have to go to a cemetery to do so. There were days I would forget you were gone and I was just dying to tell you something. I used to think just wait till Elle hears and then I'd remember you couldn't. It was like that for years Elle years. I just never got used to being without you. I'm going to tell you a little secret. While I was writing my wedding vows I accidently put 'My dear love Esselle' instead of Martha. I felt so awful I burned the paper to ash" he said.

Esselle's eye lids fell "I'm sorry I ran off that day" she said.

He pressed his lips together. "It was my fault" he said. She shook her head a bit.

"No, it wasn't. All you wanted to do was explain and the last thing out of my mouth was that I hated you when in reality I loved you I still do. I love you" she said. Then in that instant her chest went tight. She didn't know if whether or not that had been the wise thing to say but then something in his face made her think it might have been the right thing to say.

"Oh Elle" he said and used his other hand to brush her cheek "I loved. I still do. Esselle I love you and I don't care if I get sent to hell for it I love you and I'll say it again just so you hear me clearly. I love you" he said.

Then it all happened slowly after that. Esselle slowly raised her hands and his body shifted. Then he had wrapped his arms around her in a huge embrace. Then he kissed her. She pulled his shirt bringing him closer and his hands rubbed her back before began tracing circles. She ran her fingers through his super fine soft thin hair and his lips were pressed hard against hers. If it were the year 2017 it wouldn't have been that forbidden but it wasn't 2017. They were just pressed hard together their lips and the pressure of teeth against teeth was so hard it hurt but they didn't care. At least she didn't.

Slowly as if painfully Mardrin detached his mouth from hers. "Elle I can't. I can't do this to my wife not her. She doesn't deserve this" he said. Esselle swallowed hard and nodded. They looked away from each other and pulled away. the warmth from Esselle's body left. Mardrin as if a life loss nothing sat at his desk again.

Angry, hurt, and confused Esselle looked out the window again. Her eyes widened. his hair was just shining in the sunlight black as ever. He was leaning against a car he looked so stunning as he pulled on his black leather gloves. He turned and Esselle could see his stunning profile. looking at him every time just put Esselle in a trans. How much so did Esselle just want to try and run her hands over that beautiful glowing skin to feel every curve and mold of his body against hers and just run her fingers through that black hair of his. She blinked pushing those thoughts far in back of her mind. His eyes blue as they were twinkled. Daniel was standing outside.

"Mardrin I have to go' she said aiming for the door. 'I'll talk you later" she said and ran out the door grabbing her bag.

****
****

He smiled at her. A big beautiful wide smile with perfect white teeth and blue eyes that twinkled.

"Hey Essie" Daniel said.

"What the hell are you doing here?" Esselle said in an urgent whisper approaching him

He shrugged "Just came to check up on you. Besides I totally called dibs on training you" he said and turned to face the car. She walked over to stand next to him.

"So you show up at my boy friend's office?" she said.

He turned to look at her. Something in his eyes screamed sadness and sympathy. Like, almost unreadable.

"He's not your boyfriend anymore" he said.

Esselle gasped for air to speak but stopped. She hadn't noticed she said that and he was right. He was another woman's husband.

"I mean ya my guy friend" she said.

He turned and looked at her.

"Its fine I get it. Don't correct yourself. It'll take a while trust me" he said.

"But..." Esselle said and trailed off when he opened the car door.

"So, have you made your decision yet?" he asked. Esselle looked around. Had she?

"I don't know" she said.

He sighed :Its him isn't it? You're afraid how it might affect him? Well you know what they say" he said. He slipped on his belt the one with all the compartments. "Under love's heavy burden do I sink" he said and slipped on the other glove.

Esselle's eyes widened "You can quote Shakespeare?" she asked baffled.

He nodded making an obvious face "You can't?" he said.

'Well its just I...I was always only the one to love literature" she said.

"I guess you've met your match then" he said and smiled "So you coming or what?" he asked. there was something about Daniel she found herself drawn to. Either way she liked it.

So she smiled and said "yes"

Somewhere in Time- trilogy part 2

Somewhere in Time- trilogy part 2

Although it was only the early days of June that of Esselle's favorite when she stood under the sunlight she could feel her clothes clinging to her body. Esselle had the car window pulled down. She stuck her hand out and the wind wisped through her fingertips as she made waves. While Daniel drove he glanced at her a few times usually with a funny face. Like a twisted smile. Esselle looked back a few times to gave the same twisted soft smile and she went back to making waves in the wind.

"The early days of June are my favorite" Daniel said and Esselle turned to look at him.

She smiled "Mine too" she said.

"When I was younger my mother to take a huge blanket and lay it out on the grass outside in our backyard. She would cross her legs like a pretzel and watch jasmine and I play in the backyard. she always had her sketchpad with her. She'd draw us. Our smiles, our faces, our hands, the way our hair would move in the wind when we ran" he said. he glanced at her with big eyes then looked back to the road "She used to do that. A lot" he said. Esselle smiled a bit "Does she still draw?" she asked. Daniel she had noticed took in a deep breath with an expression unchanging. She had begun to wonder if she said something wrong. They came at a red light and he tilted his head to look at her.

"No, she died a few years ago" he said.

Esselle in a quick moment brought her hand back inside the car and folded them gently on her lap.

"Daniel I am so sorry" she said.

He shrugged and grabbed hold of the steering wheel "I wasn't there when it happened so it hurts a lot less. At least I don't have that lingering memory to dwell on" he says.

Esselle swallowed hard and nodded. She knew what it was like. To mourn the death of someone. But for Esselle it had been her fault and she was there. And the person she loved the person she should have protected in the world she was the reason of her death. And she'd never forgive herself.

For Esselle she had been five and she could still smell the chlorine of the backyard pool. The sounds of scream still fresh in her mind and the softness of her wet hair still clinging to her lifeless body. The warmth dissolving from her body right there in Esselle's arms. She was only five.

She quickly suppressed the memory and looked at Daniel again.

"Loosing someone is just awful. A horrible wound comes about after that" she said.

"Time does heal all wounds" Daniel said and his blue eyes met hers. She had hoped he didn't notice her melt a bit. But she just nodded once.

"yes, I guess so" she said.

Somewhere in Time- trilogy part 2

Daniel effortlessly pushed through titanium doors and kept it walking.
"Whoa hot shot let's not push the doors to hard opened" Esselle says. He smiles a little.
"Ya well you have to with these damn doors they're a pain in the ass" he says.

Esselle made a face "Like you're not!" she said and he laughed. Finally he shrugged "So what?" he said "I'm selfish, impatient and a little insecure. I make mistakes, I am out of control and at times hard to handle. But if you can't handle me at my worst, then you sure as hell don't deserve me at my best."

Esselle smiled "That was one of my favorite quotes from Marilyn Monroe. Although I highly about you're insecure" she said.

He looked at her "Oh no absolutely not. Everything about that quote prevails true for me except that" he says and slides what look like huge metal doors to the side. He walks a few steps into what looks like a room. There are silver gates running down over a white wall. Daniel presses buttons on a control pad and the wall splits open revealing another hallway.

"There are a lot of doors here" Esselle says. The hallways were narrow and white just pure white.

Daniel looked at her "Safety is important" he said and made a right.

"At least I know its safe to read a book here" Esselle teased. All the security was insane to her. Because people are really going to guess the Freedom Tower of all places to look? Esselle was still very much in the dark with so many questions but she guessed she'd just have to take it day by day.

"You sure do read a lot don't you?" Daniel asks.

Esselle looks at him. "What's that supposed to mean?" she asked.

He shrugged "You are just about the only person I have met ever that can actually pick up on what I am saying and understand what it is I mean. You also know just about every quote in the book. Don't get me wrong I like that it's impressive. But you seem like one of those that never lives and just reads those stupid

Somewhere in Time- trilogy part 2

long ass books all day with the fancy words and drawing pictures in your head because there are no pictures on the page and you're screwed" he said and turned a corner.

Esselle stopped in her tracks "Excuse me" she said. He stopped where he was. Esselle frowned crossed her arms and kept walking. Sometimes he can just be so-

"Hey Ess it wasn't supposed to be an insult" he said.

Esselle stopped dead in her tracks to look him in the eye. "Its not a matter of reading a book, completely and totally submerging yourself in it. Feeling it, being it, and with every word fully design a scene and plot in your head because there are no pictures scribbled on a stupid book page. Its a matter of reading and looking at the words and even without understanding them or picturing them or imagining them finding them completely and utterly mesmerizing and beautiful and finding yourself lost in the words themselves hanging on every last syllable. It isn't just reading. So yes it is an insult." she said. He stood silent and eyes seemed a far deeper blue. All of a sudden the annoyance and anger Esselle had felt slowly melted away until it was a aspeck of nothing while she was looking at him. And then it disappeared all together and her face was finally said.

"Beautifully said Essie" he said. Esselle hadn't noticed there was a door behind her. Still looking at her Daniel reached behind her, his hand brushing her shoulder, and pushed passed another door.

"You sometimes its just fun to annoy you and you get mad" he says

"Oh really? Why is that?" she asks.

"Because" he says "You say the most beautiful things when you

Somewhere in Time- trilogy part 2

do so"

Esselle took in a deep breath. She just looked at Daniel and he looked at her. Like time had frozen. She could feel the heat and radiance of his body hitting hers because he was so close. And it hadn't been in the least bit odd or uncomfortable. In fact odd enough Esselle found herself wanting more. Even after he stood next to her and they continued walking down the narrow bright white hallways.

Daniel stood in front of a huge steel door that looked like nothing in the world could penetrate it.

"Finally!" he said exasperated. He walked over and grabbed the large handle and pulled back.

"This my dear Essie is the training facility" he said pulling it back. It made a rough noise and Esselle's jaw dropped in awe.

The bright light from inside the training facility had blinded her. Daniel took her elbow and guided her inside sliding the door shut behind him.

The room was just glowing with power. She saw people shooting bullets through mannequins. In the far right she saw two large polls with a string attached that people walked across to keep their balance. There were people flinging knives fighting dummies even each other. There obstacle courses and odd machines Esselle couldn't identify.

"That's where we get our marks" Daniel said close to her ear point to the far left corner. There was a black glossy door. "Come on let's go find Dawn." he said. Daniel put his hand on the small of her back and guided her to the front of the room. Esselle felt her heart race and pound so much it hurt. It felt warm where his skin touched hers and everything was tingly. Like a spark. She ignored it and tried to concentrate on the ferocious fighters she saw. Many of the woman wore what looked like those sports bras/shirts with short nylon capris. They were all dressed in black with ponytails. Most of them men wore lose black shirts with no sleeves and the trimming was a steel color.

"Hey Dee!" Daniel called. He was approaching a girl with booty shorts and a tight tank top. Odd enough she had been wearing a pink tank with black shorts. She had a platinum blonde pixie hair cut with her roots dark. She was beating at a punching bag. She had a heart shaped face with almond eyes a watery green color, light skin and long lips. She looked totally punk girly and hot. Complete badass.

She wiped her forehead which was beaded with sweat and smiled.

"Looky here. Mr. Carter I see you have found a friend" she said and yanked off her gloves.

"Dee, this is Essie" he said "Essie this is Dawn. You know the rules you can't use my nickname" he said.

Esselle rolled her eyes and smiled at Dawn. Dawn smiled back.

"She's a pretty one Mr. Carter" she said and extended her hand to Esselle. Daniel rolled his eyes.

"Don't call me that" he said.

Dawn shook Esselle's hand and laugh "Why? That's your nick name" she said teasingly.

Esselle's eyes widened and she looked at Daniel "So you do have a nick name!" she said

Dawn laughed "YOu haven't been here long at all have you?" Dawn asked grabbing a towel and a water bottle. Esselle shook her head.

"I don't suppose you have a nick name" she said.

Esselle sighed "yes, my name is Esselle but I'm working on trying to get him to not call me Essie or Ess" she said.

Dawn let out a long deep chuckle "Oh sorry babe you got a nick name from him now you're screwed! Its a nick name and its gonna stick!" she said.

Esselle grunted "Great!" she said and looked at Daniel.

He shrugged and ran his fingers through his hair. "Its true" he said.

Dawn sat on a bench and drank from her water bottle "So," she said coming up for air before taking another sip "Whatsup" she said.

"I'm just showing Esselle around. Dawn is one of our very few warriors in the New York office" he said.

Esselle frowned. "Warriors?" she said and Dawn smirked. Esselle meant to say New York Office but that meant more explaining as if her mind hadn't already been spinning.

"Remember what I told you about our body settling to the changes the government did?" he asked. Esselle nodded. She remembered that much.

"Well, Dawn is one of the very few that has been fully settled and fully trained. She is a full blown Tron" he said.

'Tron?" Esselle said. It sounded like a movie character.

Daniel nodded "Tron is short for Tronomatic Computerized Host Body. Tron is just for short. It means what the government did successfully worked on dawn and she is a full blown government weapon. Armed and dangerous" Daniel said.

"And sexy!" Dawn added "not to mention a total bad ass warrior" she said with a smirk of pride.

"She has all of her marks" Daniel said.

"You mean there are more marks?" Esselle asked.

Daniel nodded "The government is smart. In order for them to know who was who in their little experiment they programmed the lets just say virus to know when the host body had fully gone through all of its changes and was now half computer. Their flesh literally replaced by electricity. What happens is the mark morphs into something more electronic looking rather than intricate and beautiful. It also changes color. But that is very rare. only in extremely skilled Trons do the marks change from blue to green. That means that they are much more powerful than any other tron" Daniel said. Esselle supposed it kind of made sense. "There's also a special mark we give ourselves as a sign of accomplishment" he added.

Dawn jumped up from her seat. "Come on I'll show you" she said and waltzed over to the room with he black door. She pulled it open and Daniel and Esselle followed.

The room had been completely black. The kind of room that only neon colors would show. Like when Esselle was younger and went to go play laser tag. Like that.

"Here hold this" she said and handed Esselle her towel. Dawn walked over to the control pad on the wall and pressed a few buttons. She stood and without shame took her shirt off. She turned around to toss it behind her then she unhooked her bra. Esselle's widened.

"I don't think-" she began and Dawn snapped back around covering her breasts "oh hush" Dawn said. She reached over and pressed another button on the control pad. Then a sound like when lights in an old building go on making a zzz noise.

Suddenly Esselle could see them. Green marks. The room although still black lit up in an odd way and color. Dawn smiled. Her marks where green on her arms and chest tracing to her back.

"Wow" Esselle said.

"Pretty cool isn't it?" she asked.

"They're beautiful" Esselle said.

Dawn smiled. She turned around and in a snap was already dressed again. She turned the lights on and suddenly Esselle had to squint.

"I want those" Esselle said in a whisper of amazement. Daniel laughed.

"Sorry kid you'll have to wait a while" he said.

Esselle made a face "Why do you keep calling me kid? I'm probably older than you" she said and he opened the door. Something about his face made Esselle soften. He looked almost sad to speak and she felt her heart go out to him.

"Trust me kid I'm far older than you" he said and walked out.

Somewhere in Time- trilogy part 2

Somewhere in Time- trilogy part 2

The next day Esselle had spent watching Selena's twins. And it had been a good day. Then every night for a week Esselle had snuck away in the middle of the night. Daniel waited every day by her window until she came off and she escaped into the night. The Freedom Tower she learned was originally built but as an inside job. It was always going to be the home of The Invisibles. Making it look like something in honor of the Twin Towers made total sense and was a great cover up. At least that was what she was told. You see every night for the past week Esselle had been learning. Things seemed to make better sense. Dawn and Jasmine would spent hours on end teaching her the story of The Invisibles. It had all started in 1995. The U.S was in danger of terrorist threats and it was unknown to the citizens but rumors of war between several nations were rising. The U.S was in a rut. They didn't have the weapons or technology or enough soldiers for the kind of battle coming up. And with all of that days modern technology it was easy to wipe out an entire army. That's when the project came about. They wanted to create human warriors that were better skilled and harder to kill. They needed to replace their flesh making them part robot but maintaining their human qualities. It had explained what they said about starting the work on people. But what Esselle didn't understand through their countless hours of explaining was how it had happened to Esselle. They virus is distributed in two ways: by needle and by consumption. Esselle had done neither of the two so how she had obtained such a virus was beyond her. No one knew. But it turned out that Esselle was different from the rest of them. Her mark was different from the rest of theirs. They said around the time Esselle was frozen one person started a chain reaction. They were experimented on and that was how the government figured out a new way to alter the host body without killing them. But this caused another problem. The host body then became too hard to kill. And therefore started the new form of the virus which lead to ten years ago. When they decided the hosts were beyond repair and needed to start killing them off. But the one special person around 30 years ago. There is a code inside of them within their mind. The code that is key to riding all of the host bodies of the virus. Jasmine said she was unsure and they needed to do a lot more research after that. That was all they gave Esselle. Now she had been in a rut with no way out. The only time she truly felt better was when she was with Daniel. Despite his arrogance and annoying tendencies he was like a breath of fresh air. Something different for Esselle. She liked it. He made her calm he made her smile he made her laugh. He made her feel like everything going on around her wasn't so bad. There was a lot, a lot Esselle hadn't understood. But she just had to slow down and absorb everything slowly as possible. Esselle's brain hurt all the time. It was all far too confusing. Sometimes Esselle would climb to the roof and look at the stars to clear her mind. Besides who cared if anyone saw Esselle on the roof of a skyscraper. It was New York City people have seen far weirder and far crazier.

But now Esselle just wanted her mind to clear up. She had so many questions. So many it drove her mad but she just pulled down the car window and made waves while Daniel zoomed down the highway in the middle of the night.

"And when its coming closer to the end hit rewind all night long baby slow down the so-o-ong oh oh" Esselle hummed She had made Daniel put on all of her old favorite songs. And that had been one of them. The night sky was a dark blue and every star had a beautiful twinkle. Like a freshly polished flawless diamond. The arm early summer breeze filled the car and made Esselle feel at peace. The first time in a long time. her family didn't know no one did. And they weren't going to.

Daniel smiled "I can't believe I let you make me put this music on" he said.

Esselle looked over and smiled "That's because I'm awesome and you can't resist my charm" she said.

He laughed and looked at her "You're right I can't" he said and went back to the road. Esselle felt herself smile and quickly look away. She continued to carve waves into the wind.

"Daniel" she said.

"Yup Ess" he said. Esselle had finally given up on making him call her Esselle. It had been pointless.

"When were you frozen?" she asked. They were easing off the

highway in front of a red light and Daniel stomped hard on the breaks.

"What?" he asked.

She shrugged "Well you know when I was frozen. When were you? jasmine said she was frozen too a long time ago-" she said but Daniel cut in.

"Y well Jas says a lot of things" he said. The light turned green and Daniel stepped on the gas again.

"Why won't you tell me?' she asked.

"Because I don't think it matters" he says.

Esselle rolls her eyes and her hands slam against her thighs. "You know you're just being difficult" she said.

"Listen sweetheart when I feel good and ready maybe I'll consider telling you some things about that part of my life. Ask me anything else I'm an open book really just anything but that" he said and glanced at her.

She let out a deep breath and her lips vibrated making that deflated balloon noise. They drove up to her town house and Esselle made sure all of the lights were off and they were.

"Alright thanks, just pull up where you usually do" she said.

Daniel nodded and prepared to make a U-turn. Esselle looked in the mirror on the outside of the car and her eyebrows pressed together. A flash went off in the back of her mind. As if a memory she had forgotten. It was of a jet black Audi. The crazy thing was, was that this was a 2017 model. This car has been out of style for 28 years. That car she had seen before but where? There was another flash in the back of her mind. It was night time. She knew that car she saw it she saw it...her heart began to race. The night she died. Her hand went flying across the car and she got hold of Daniel's hand.

"Daniel" she said unable to say anything else. She had tensed up in her seat and her stomach was turning. The car was growing closer.

'Ess I'm pulling an illegal U-turn for you so please don't distract me" he said.

"Daniel!" she said trembling with fear. Her head began to hurt. She saw the flashes of light and it was as if she were brought back 28 years ago when she had flown off the road.

"Ess what is it?" he said. He pulled over at the corner down the block from her house and she grabbed hold of her shirt.

"Daniel look its them its them!" she cried "They came back for me Daniel look!" she said.

His eyes became blue wide awake and alert. He took Esselle's hands in his and he looked out her window.

"Essie where? Show me" he said. Esselle sat back in her chair and with her eyes trailed the path to where the black car had pulled over.

"Ess, that car is almost 30 years old" he said.

Esselle squeezed her eyes shut. The images began to appear her bleeding and the sound of car horns. "I know" she whispered.

"Essie get out and go. Go home I want to follow this one and see where he's going" he said and changed the car from park to drive. Her eyes widened and she took his hand "Daniel what are you crazy? I don't want to go home please. Don't make me" she pleaded. He took a deep breath.

"Just go you'll be fine" he said. For the first time Esselle saw something in Daniel's eyes the way he looked at her. Although the blue was intense his look was soft and filled with...well...she didn't know.

He leaned over slowly in the car and Esselle relaxed and just breathed. He kissed her temple and shut her eyes. The warmth of his mouth of her skin made goose bumps form but in a good way. Her entire body began to tingle and she was shot with adrenaline.

He gently sat back down "Its alright I'm here I'm watching" he said.

Esselle bit her lip and looked back outside the window. He nodded. She hesitantly took her hand and opened the car door keeping her bag in her other hand. She stepped out and shut the door behind her.

"Essie I'm right here. Nothing is going to happen. I'll watch until you go in alright?" he said. Esselle felt her hands grip her bag tighter and the sweat drench her back. She nodded and hopped onto the sidewalk. She looked back a few times and he hadn't moved. Finally she just kept walking down the block. She saw the black Audi park. The person inside was all in black and she couldn't see his face. She looked forward. She heard a car door open. She turned her head and from behind her across the street she could see the car door open and the man in all black step out. Her heart stopped and she turned around fully.

"Daniel" she said. But he wasn't there. Esselle wanted to run for him scream out his name and cry. Why had he left her? How could he leave her? he said he'd stay there with her! Esselle saw the man in black cross the street. She looked around frantically but kept walking. Maybe Daniel made another U-turn. He was nowhere to be seen. She looked up the block and no sign of Daniel. She swallowed hard. She glanced back and the man

Somewhere in Time- trilogy part 2

began walking faster and so did she. Daniel, Daniel, Daniel, Daniel. Was running through her mind. Why when she needed him he was gone? She saw her house growing closer but so did the man. She worked up to a pace. She noticed that the shades to her parents windows were open. They weren't home. How could Esselle have forgotten? They weren't going to be home tonight. Finally she felt she was ready to die and she work up to a jog and so did he behind her. She looked and notice people in black waiting in around the area of her house. She couldn't see their faces in the dark. Esselle could scream but she couldn't find the air. She couldn't climb back into her bedroom window. It would never work there was one already there.

"Daniel" she said. She wish he were here. There was only one person that could make her feel safe. It was him. The one behind her ran and so did she. She screamed a bit and turned the corner.

"Daniel!" she called and looked behind her. He would never hear her. He was probably long gone.

"Daniel!" she tried again. Nothing happened. She looked behind her. They were growing so close now it was three. Still looking back she turned the corner and landed in someone's arms. She looked up and despite trembling with fear she felt relived.

"Ess, thank God" Daniel said. She sighed and let herself go willingly into his arms and practically sob.

"Daniel" she said.

"I notice something wrong with that guy." he said

"Why did you leave me Daniel! You scared me half to death I was calling for you! You weren't there!" Esselle said.

"Ess I'd never leave you. Ever" he said. "There was some cop giving out late night tickets I had to drive around the perimeter I was parked near a fire hydrant. are you alright?" he asked. She nodded. She just felt safer there with him. He wrapped an arm around her and walked away quickly glancing behind them.

"Daniel what if they come for me again?" she asked.

'I'll be damned" he said and looked behind him again.

"Daniel they were at my house-!" she said.

"I know" he said cutting her off. "We have to go somewhere they won't find us. We can't go headquarters we'll lead them right to it" he said and opened the car door for her.

He thought for a moment then smiled like a bad little child. Esselle knew the look already.

"What the hell are you thinking of?" she said.

"Well, I can't take you home or headquarters, you'd definitely object to a hotel" he said.

Esselle nodded hit wide eyes and a raised eyebrow "That's right" he said.

"Don't get weirded out but I'll just take you to the new apartment I just got assigned. They won't look for us there" he said and shut the door. Esselle rolled her eyes.

"I bet the buggy man is your roommate" she said.

He smiled at her "How'd you know?" he asked.

Somewhere in Time- trilogy part 2

"This isn't you apartment" Esselle said. Daniel shut the door and rolled his eyes.

"What part of 'temporary' apartment did you not get the first time I told you" he said. Esselle was not in the same place she had been the day she woke up after Daniel had saved her. It was a warm looking place. It was a mix of earth tones and a modern look. Esselle was really getting sick of 2045's modern. It was annoying ugly. For that she should just go back to 2015 contemporary.

"Its nice. But this God awful modern 2045 look is really getting on my nerves" she said.

Daniel laughed and took her sweater.

"Trust me you'll get used to it" he said.

It didn't shock Esselle much that Daniel had the penthouse. He probably used a lot of his charm to get it. Two walls carved around the perimeter of the apartment and were made of glass in which you could see outside into the city. There was a fire place in the living room along with a chocolate colored coach two side seats, two lamps, a coffee table, and two side stands. There was a huge TV mounted onto the wall. Esselle looked up and the ceiling was concave and the lighting fixtures hung. The kitchen was all stainless steel appliances and a huge long island with a sink making out the shape of the kitchen. there was an arc in the wall on the far left corner that lead to the living room. There was a hallway that lead to guest rooms and a bathroom. There were spiraling steps that lead up stairs to the main bedrooms and bathrooms.

Esselle sighed "What now?" she asked. This had all been driving Esselle up the wall. It made her insane. She felt helpless and defenseless. It might have been obvious in the look on her face because Daniel's face changed too. He actually looked human.
HE walked over and put his hand on her arm.
He took in a deep breath and looked down at her "I don't know Ess" he said.
Esselle looked away and she could hear Daniel inhale. He clasped his hands together and rubbed them.
"Come on" he said. He reached over to the kitchen counter and grabbed the remote. "Let's watch a movie" he said. He hopped right over the couch and landed on his feet. Esselle smiled.
Daniel looked back at her "Well? You coming?" he asked. Esselle looked around but couldn't help it when she smiled and said "Sure"

****

The lights were all off in the apartment and Esselle sat on the couch with her legs crossed. "So what are we watching?" Esselle asked.
"Reruns!" Daniel shouted from the kitchen and she laughed.
"Oh how exciting!" she said.
"Listen kid I'm on a budget so no renting movies plus" he said and he was standing behind her and handed her a bowl "The movies nowadays really such" Daniel walked around the couch and fell into his seat by Esselle's side.
She looked down at her bowl and smiled "You like chocolate ice cream?" she asked. He nodded making a face.
"I hate that God awful vanilla. Its forbidden in this house hold"

he said and grabbed the remote.

"Thank you!" Esselle said. Daniel looked at her with a funny smile. "I think vanilla is gross!" she said.

"Oh no how about strawberry?" he said. They both looked at each other and made a face.

"No" they said in unison and laughed.

"You know before I was frozen my friends and I used to eat ice cream with milk" she said.

Daniel looked at her "Milk?" he said.

It was the Daniel had said it, Esselle decided, that made her burst into laughter. "Yes milk" she said.

"Why in God's name would anyone mix ice cream with milk?" he asked.

"Oh I don't know! It started when we were 12 bored and wanted to give ourselves a stomach ache so we didn't have to go to school the next day and present our project" she said.

Esselle noticed the look on Daniel's face changed again in the TV light. The blue in his eyes just popped. He got up and walked to the kitchen and Esselle followed him with her eyes.

He scoured the cabinets.

"Heads up" he said and tossed her something. Esselle quickly put her bowl down and grabbed it. She smiled.

"Yum chocolate syrup" she said.

"Oh no there's more" he said. He grabbed a cup tossed it behind him which Esselle caught and right after tossed another which Esselle caught. He went into the drawer and grabbed straws and went into the fridge and grabbed a gallon of milk. Esselle laughed when he held it up in front of her.

"I'm going against my better judgment here trying this out" he

Somewhere in Time- trilogy part 2

said.

Esselle nodded "Yes that you are doing" she said and they poured milk and chocolate into glasses.

"You know I could just imagine you a very odd teen back in a day" he said sitting next to her.

Esselle shrugged "I see you being a very hot popular kid" she said. For a moment it didn't click in her mind until she ran the sentence again her mind. She just called him hot. Sure it was true but a girl never says that!

Daniel just laughed "You're face just went pale" eh said.

Her lips scrunched up when she looked at him "Did not!" she snapped.

he made a face and nodded "Ya ok" he said. The screen began to run with colors and images and he sat back.

She gasped "You watch reruns of Tom and Jerry?" she asked.

He nodded "Duh, best cartoon ever" he said.

Esselle sat back and laughed a bit. "You know if only I'd met you sooner" she said and he looked at her. Esselle was running her mouth again saying stupid stuff she shouldn't.

Finally the silence was annoying Esselle and she looked at the TV "Funny how they use pink to color in a strawberry" she said.

Daniel made a face "Ugh, I hate strawberry. Especially strawberry milk its awful" he said.

She giggled and looked down at her fingers.

"Mardrin used to like strawberry milk" she said softly.

He looked at her. She really hadn't meant to say that either. Her big fat mouth was on a roll today.

"Who?" he said and she looked at him.

"Oh um the uh..." she laughed a bit "The one with the office" she said.

He nodded "Ahhh! I see" he said reaching over and putting his cup of milk on the table. Esselle with her spoon moved the lumps of chocolate ice cream around in her bowl.

"You're still in love with him" he said.

"Yes! No! Maybe...Ugh" Esselle said and put her bowl down "I don't know" she said.

"Well let's talk about" he said and she looked at him "Tell me a story of deep delight" he said. Esselle laughed a bit.

"That's one of my favorites by Robert Penn Warren" she said. HE shrugged "figured you might" he said.

Esselle took in and let out a deep breath "I had known him ever since I was little. I had known him all my life. He was the first and only man I had ever found myself to love. He was kind, and generous, and smart, and just..." she sighed "Everything I thought I wanted in life. Now I'm not even sure of what I want. I had always had my life planned out for me always. It was absolute perfection. I was happy we were happy." she laughed a bit "You know when I didn't feel like had to be the person he wanted me to be" she joked.

Daniel shook his head "Why should you change for anyone?" he asked.

Esselle made a face "it wasn't that I had to change. It was like how do I put it? Like one time he got mad when I cut and dyed my hair. Or like one time we got into an argument over what to do for Christmas so I just decided I didn't care and didn't bother saying anything because I didn't want to lose the person that mattered to me because of something I said" she said and looked at him "Just stupid stuff really"

Somewhere in Time- trilogy part 2

Daniel turned in his seat to face Esselle. "To hell with what he wants and thinks you are your own person. If he loved you he wouldn't want you to change! For anything! Be who you are and say what you feel, because those who mind don't matter, and those who matter don't mind." he said and Esselle smiled.
"Oh so now you're trying Bernard M. Baruch on me?" she teased. He just looked at her.
"This guy just sounds stupid to me" he says and Esselle laughed. 'What like you were never in love before?" she asked. His eye lids fell and the blue in his eyes became dull when he spoke. Like it pained him to do so but the pain didn't faze him anymore.
"I was" he said "Once"
Esselle smiled. She turned and leaned in closer and placed her hand in her palm. She grabbed a pillow and scouted closer to him. He laughed a bit.
"Her name was Alice" he said.
"Sounds like a sweet name" Esselle said.
"She was sweet. As sweet as can be. She had light red hair. Not that tacky orange or yellow or ginger!" he said and Esselle laughed "Like a light apple red kind of hair. She had very, very light skin I used to call her a ghost" he said and Esselle giggled. "Her eyes were like a ginger color and she had very light freckles around her nose and cheek bones. When it was cold out her lips turned red and her cheeks grew pink" he said. Esselle had been mesmerized by the way he spoke of her. With so much yet so little emotion.
"I first saw her on a trip out in the city where the big library was at now I don't even remember. She had a camera in her hands and she was sitting on the steps with her hair tied up but it was

Somewhere in Time- trilogy part 2

falling out her messy bun." he said gesturing in the air with his hands what her hair looked like.

"It was love at first sight then" Esselle said and something in her heart felt odd. Like a tingeing feeling.

"No, not at all actually. But I knew it was something special. SO I just looked at her the entire time" he said. Esselle folded her arms on the back of the couch and rested her head there.

"Where is she now? How come you haven't looked for her?" Esselle asked.

Daniel looked at his hands. They were strong and then he looked at her. "Because she died. A long time ago. round four of five years after they shoved me in a freezer" he said.

"Daniel I..." she said and reached for him. He looked away and she brought her hand back in feeling her heart burn. "I don't even know what to say about losing someone you love its awful" she said.

"There is nothing to say. Its done and over with" he said.

Esselle looked away and felt herself slowly choking. She could not believe what she was about to say "I lost my sister" and yet she said it anyway.

He looked at her and his eyebrows pressed together. "What?" he asked. Esselle nodded and held the pillow closer to her. "I thought you were an only child?" he asked and she laughed without humor.

"Most people think that" she said and the TV went silent. "I was five years old and Eliza was three" Esselle said and her palms grew sweaty.

She felt the tears burning and her throat felt as if someone were cutting into her "My mother went inside to get the phone and she

Somewhere in Time- trilogy part 2

told us to stay away from the pool" she said and Daniel grew closer to listen "But I didn't listen to her instead I sat by the 8 foot part and put my feet into the water. Eliza always did what I did and so she sat next to me and did the same. I had on my floaties so I got into the water and I could float. Eliza didn't" Esselle said. Daniel squeezed her arm and she smiled to fight back the tears. 'And so she said she wanted to come in with me and jumped and I..." Esselle looked away. "I couldn't save her and she drowned"

Daniel remained silent for a moment. He opened his mouth to speak but shut his mouth.

"I've never told anyone that before" Esselle said coming to the realization. She looked at him "Mardrin didn't even know I had a sister he was in France for her birth and death and I didn't meet Selena and Stephen until September of that year when I was in kindergarten" she said.

"My parents don't even know what really happened" she said and twisted a loose thread around her long pretty slim fingers. "I had kept the truth to myself for years...until now" she said and looked at him.

"That's not your fault" he said finally and she snorted.

"Of course it is!" she said but her voice wasn't loud nor angry just tired "You sometimes I used to wonder if when I was 17 I could of had a 14 year old sister to taunt and tease and go get my nails painted with or when I was bored go to the movies or when our parents wouldn't home go to Broadway and just see some random show we had seen a million times before" Esselle said and her hair fell in her face. Before she could reach up and push it away Daniel did so and tugged it behind her ear. She felt her

Somewhere in Time- trilogy part 2

heart race for a single second and her skin go tingling.
"In the words of Robert Frost 'In three words I can sum up everything I've learned about life: it goes on.' That's just how you need to think of it" he said.
"How can I even begin..." she said and trailed off "It was my fault" she said.
"No it wasn't" he insisted
"yes it was!" she argued back "If I had been watching her and did what I was supposed to I could have done something anything!" Esselle said and fell back into the couch. she sighed.
"You know what's your fault is when the love of your sister's life is shot and killed because you didn't do anything to warn him" he said and his voice was low and deep.
"What?" Esselle asked. For the first time in Esselle's life she felt safe with someone and despite her having wonderful friends she felt as if she had finally found someone with whom she could confide in freely without judgment. Release all of her deepest secrets. She had never felt that way with anyone else. But now this person who for some crazy unknown reason she found herself trusting had a secret of his own. And now he was about to tell her.
He sighed "Ever wondered why I'm so protective with Jasmine?" he asked. Esselle nodded. Poor Jasmine as feisty as she was she was still held on by leash by her older brother. He didn't allow to go on any type of fun mission, or whatever they called it, that Daniel could go on. Esselle would watch as Jasmine would watch Daniel leave without her. Daniel you could tell clearly hated it when his sister would mingle with the other boys in the facility. Oh yes. He was protective indeed.

Somewhere in Time- trilogy part 2

"Well she was 16. She was in love with this guy Evan. But she was just...in love with him. She loved him with everything she had and I'm pretty sure after what happened to him he loved her. I couldn't stand him though. I always thought she deserved better. He was just your typical hot shot high school kid. I knew those kind I was one of them. I wanted him no where near my sister. Absolutely no where. So it was the summer time and he came to drop her off from going to the movies. I was infuriated it was 2 am and I had been waiting for her for hours. I told him don't get the hell out and not to show his face again. So that night he left. See I had connections with some people. This guy his older brother did drugs but he swore he was clean. I didn't believe him. I knew where they met. His older brother got his drugs from this huge guy in the industry that touched upon just about every type of crime out there. And Evan knew them all and was pretty close. Now these guys were apart of the Irish mob. They aren't like the Italian mod. The Irish are ruthless killers. They'll kill your wife and your kids. So Evan before he left said he was going over there to there hang out. I knew that was a bad idea already. I heard his brother got into some trouble with them because he owed a lot of money. If Evan showed his face they'd take him hold him hostage as leverage then kill him in front of his brother to teach him a lesson. I knew this and didn't say anything. Jasmine went ballistic when she heard where he was going. But I held her down until he left. She was hysterical in tears. I knew right then and there that she hated me. I prayed to God one day she'd understand what I had done for her. She was screaming about why I wouldn't let her go after him so I told her what I knew. She just went cold then lost it. Pushed me out the way and grabbed the car keys. She drove after him. What happened went just as I said only the other way around. On the way driving there Jasmine was blinded by tears and the damn car broke down. She got into a minor accident with someone else. It turned out to be Fenton O'Connell the hot shot planning on killing Evan. He knew she was Evan's girlfriend. He figured why not kill her to send a message. I was driving but I didn't make it on time. He shot her and she was bleeding out in my arms. Fenton was nowhere to be seen. Against my wishes some people in silver uniforms came and took her away and froze her. I hadn't known the were going to freeze her I thought they were apart of the government or something. She was still breathing but barely when they took her away" he said.

Esselle blinked a few times. She had not believed he shared something like that with her. Something so personal. Then again she did the same. And yet it was alright between the both of them. No awkwardness no intensity just the urge to take each other in each others arms and feel the soothing effect it always has.

"It wasn't a life ISN'T a life being frozen then brought back that I wanted for my sister. I still don't want it." he said.

"That wasn't your fault-" Esselle began

"Yes it was" he said cutting her off

"You were just trying to protect her" she said

"And if I hadn't?" he said in a snap growing so close Esselle could feel him breathe "If I hadn't hated him so much. If I hadn't casted him away he might have decided to go home. Jasmine would not have ran after him and got shot. Jasmine was not experimented on fully so had she not died and been frozen the virus would have worn off and lost tis power in her body and she would have lived a normal life. And what is the worst part is she forgave me!" He said. "She gets up every morning and she laughs and she smiles and she loves me the way all sisters loves their brothers. She adores me. Yet I was the one who's fault it was" he said.

Esselle opened her mouth to speak but the words never came. Instead she leaned closer and gently placed her hand on his feeling the electricity. She shook her head.

"She loves you and she forgave you. That's the only thing that should matter" she said

He shook his head "Don't you understand Ess? It doesn't matter to me. The guilt never goes away and its..." he said and trailed off when Esselle took his face in her hand.

"Would you just stop that already? I'd give anything to have my sister. I don't even remember what it was like having a sister. But you have yours. She's right there in front of you. It was a stupid mistake from a long time get over it she has. Now all you know to do now is do better this time around. You have a second chance to do right by your sister. Use it." Esselle said.

"How do you do it?" He asked.

Esselle's eyebrows pressed together "Do what?" she asked.

Esselle still had her hand on his face and he put his hand over those. He frowned "Look and talk just like that. I've seen anyone quite like you before" he said.

"I'm a little scared" she said and he laughed.

"Why?" he asked.

"Because I don't know whether to take that as a complement or an insult" she said. He smiled with shut eyes and gently shook

Somewhere in Time- trilogy part 2

his head.

"We'll see" he said and his eyes opened. The only light in the room was the diming light from the TV as the colors changed the moonlight and the light his eyes gave off when he looked at her. The moon reflected in his blue eyes and they resembled that of a sapphire. Esselle didn't know what she was doing and didn't know what the feeling was making her stomach turn her eyes flutter her skin tingle and heart race a thousand miles. But either way she had never felt something of the sort and despite her feeling light headed it all felt sweet. And she liked it. It seemed friendly enough. Their tones were friendly. To them they were just friends talking to anyone else well...Esselle didn't know what anyone else seeing them would think. Esselle had never felt that way before. Not about anyway. Someone that with just looking at them could for some reason make her mind drift and when they touched her. So much as her hand it made her heart soar. Esselle tried to suppress the feeling and fight it back. Ignoring it Esselle took in deep breath. Then she realized all Daniel was doing was looking at her. Just looking at her and she tilted her head a bit. Esselle began to love the way he looked at her. And a lot. He was rubbing his thumb across her hand when Esselle slowly fell forward. She placed her hand on his shoulder and he came closer to her. Esselle's eye lids slowly began to fall. Daniel took his other hand and touched her shoulder then her neck pushing the hair from her face. Daniel's hand was on the back of Esselle's neck bringing her closer in fact she didn't mind. Whatever was on the television was coming to an end and the screen was slowly fading to black. When finally she shut her eyes and she could just feel the electricity and his warm coming closer. Finally the room fell entirely black. It was only for a split second when the door opened.

"Phew!" someone said and the light from outside was peeking through "Why is it so dark in here?" Jasmine said. Esselle had in a snap became embarrassed and pulled away.

"We were watching a movie" Daniel said looking back at his sister. She stuck her tongue out and flicked on the lights.

"Gee thanks for inviting me!" she said and tossed her bag on to the kitchen counter.

"It was kind of last minute" Daniel said rising from his seat on the coach. He looked at Esselle and she looked back. Finally the burn of his stare was too much and she looked away.

"Well I for one couldn't sleep so I figured I'd come bother you" she said and fell unto the coach next to Esselle. Jasmine smiled "So how's that guy going?" she asked and Esselle felt her cheeks instantly burn red.

Daniel laughed but there was something odd about his laugh that threw Esselle off "What guy?" he asked and he was standing in the kitchen.

Jasmine turned in the couch "You know! That guy she's in love with hello!" she said and Daniel raised an eyebrow. Esselle quickly looked away.

"Jasmine" she said softly

"Gees Daniel keep up! that guy she was gonna marry before she got stuck in the freezer? That he is like still madly in love her! You know! That guy!" she said. Esselle slammed her hand on her forehead.

"Oh that guy" Daniel said turning on the faucet. He had a

Somewhere in Time- trilogy part 2

mischievous little smirk on. Its not like anything happened. Why did he have to look at her like that? She didn't do anything wrong! Or was he just messing and teasing Esselle to get a rise out of her? He does that a lot.

"Jasmine I don't feel that way for him anymore. He's married with a fie and children and-" Esselle said but Daniel cut her off "And you still love him and decide to go see him anyway?" he said and shut the faucet off with just a hint of annoyance.

Jasmine rolled her eyes "Ignore him. He was never good with romance" she said making a face. Daniel laughed a bit.

"Ya cuz you were so goo in that department Jas" he said and she shrugged.

"I'm just saying" she said and her voice turned dreamy when she smiled at Esselle "I think its sweet and romantic that after all this time all he ever thought about was you" Esselle looked at Daniel and he gave her a look of indifference. She sighed and stood up.

"I think its safe for me to go home now" she said.

"I can take you to headquarters" Daniel offered and she quickly blew the idea off.

"No" she said aiming for the door "I'd much rather go home" she said grabbing her bag "And cry to my pillow in piece" she muttered and stepped out the door only after wondering if anyone heard.

Somewhere in Time- trilogy part 2

Esselle wondered is lanyard was out of style nowadays as made a cobra. She had done the boxes, zipper, and Chinese stair case already. Esselle sat under her and Mardrin's tree. She had missed him and when the world had shifted and the mar breeze blew the leaves around and through her hair she missed him more. Esselle didn't have it in her to go to his office again. Forget about being in love she just wanted someone to talk to. She needed someone to talk to. He was the one she wanted to talk to. she hadn't seen Selena for the past couple of days. Her cobra was purple (her favorite color) and blue. The color of his eyes. As much as Esselle tried she couldn't his annoying face out of her mind all weekend. It was annoying the crap out of her. He was just distracting her. Esselle wanted to concentrate on what she was going to do about Mardrin. and him roaming around the back of her mind wasn't helping. All day she found herself thinking of him and all night she found him somewhere in her dreams. That's how Esselle knew there was something wrong. Her dreams were a sacred and sweet place in which she can freely mourn her separation from

Mardrin and dream she were in his arms the way she used to be. Esselle sighed and put her hands on her lap. She had to stop with these insane thoughts. They were flooding her mind with insanity. She heard crunching in the leaves from behind her. she swallowed hard and pretended to ignore it. Even when there was a male shadow present in front of her.
"We're worried you aren't coming back Ess" Daniel said and Esselle ignored. Esselle had done what she did best. Seclude herself in depressing times. She hadn't been to headquarters in days.
"Maybe I'm not coming back" Esselle said continuing to work on her lanyard.
He sighed and bent down next to her "Essie I know its hard but you have to come back. How are you ever going to find out what really happened to you?" he asked. Esselle ignored him but stopped her work. She took in a deep breath and turned to face him.
"Let me guess" she said and her eyes fell on his mouth "You are going to try to convince me to go back" she shifted in her place suddenly uncomfortable and looked away.
"I'm not going back" she said finally.
He rolled his big eyes and plopped down in the spot next to her. He swung his arms around his outstretched knees and looked at her. "You're just as stubborn as I am" he said.
She ignored him and continued with her lanyard. He sighed and grabbed string himself. He vigorously went to work and Esselle couldn't keep her eyes off his hands. How quickly and precisely they worked. he was making something. Something she had never seen before. He grabbed more string and just continued

tying, wrapping, and weaving on string through the other. Esselle pretended to be working on hers so she could watch him. He seemed calm and tranquil while he fiddled with the string. The light hit his hair as the sun in the sky began shifting. The light added dimensions to his face and his skin began to glow. Esselle tilted her head and just looked at him. She watched as his chest slowly rose and fell. She'd love to hear the sound of his heart pound against her ear. He looked more than human. Like something angelic. Odd as it was there was no denying Daniel was more than beautiful. Even Mardrin couldn't stand next to him. Because Daniel was beautiful in ways if not all that was Mardrin was not. Even though Esselle felt as if she were falling it was a wonderful feeling. A feeling she had never experienced before. And she was scared. It made her scared every time he was within touching distance and he made her feel that way. She could feel her heart beat. She was fragile at the moment and broken. But he looked at her and everything in the way he looked at her said otherwise. Esselle wasn't one to stare. But it was easy to stare at Daniel. She could do it all day. So she watched as his hands finally came to a stop and held something up.

He had made a red rose. her favorite and he twisted it in his fingers.

A small smile stretched across Esselle's mouth and he handed it to her. He took in a deep breath and stared out into the park.

"I know its hard. Being awake one day then wake up the other decades later. Its hard it really is I get it. But secluding yourself does not help. Once you find out what happened to you you'll find peace with it trust me. And it'll only get easier after that. Let me help you Ess" he said and looked at her "Just let me help you"

"Where would I even begin?" she asked.

he pressed his lips together and looked away. "I guess we will just have to find that out for ourselves" he said and Esselle looked at him. He stood up and extended his hand. "Together"

Esselle for the first time allowed herself to let go a bit. She reached up and gently placed her hand in his. He held it softly as she got to her feet and the warmth of his hand around his made it burn. But in a good way.

"Come on" he said and she turned to follow him down the hill. Then Esselle heard it and she whipped her head around. She would know that laugh anywhere. She took a few steps forward and Daniel was right there behind her. Down the hill she saw Mardrin laughing.

"Mardrin!" she said. She hadn't seen him in a while and would give anything just to speak to him. She needed a familiar face.

"Ess" Daniel said.

"Mardrin!" she said and began to ran. Daniel took a step forward and grabbed her arm.

"Essie" he said.

"Daniel let me go!" she said with wide shocked eyes.

'I can't" he said.

Esselle's smile was fading away and her mind began to cloud.

"What are talking about Daniel its Mardrin!" she said and yanked her arm but he held on tighter. He pulled her close to him and grabbed her other arm.

'Ess look" he said and Esselle turned around.

Coming out from behind a tree Mardrin was smiling at Martha with his hand in both of hers. She had never seen him look more happy. Finally Esselle stopped fighting back to just stand there in

Somewhere in Time- trilogy part 2

Daniel's arms and watch.

"Essie" Daniel said. Esselle gently shook him off walking a few steps down the hill. She had her hands folded in front of her as her eyes began to burn. She had never seen Mardrin look so in love before. He was smiling so wide at her and everything in his eyes read that the woman he was looking at was the love of his life. Mardrin had never so much as smiled at Esselle the way he did with Martha. They looked like a match made in heaven.

"Dad!" she heard someone shout.

Esselle looked over.

"Hey sweetheart you made it!" she heard Mardrin shout. A woman slim and of average height with Martha's beautiful long golden white hair and Mardrin's eyes. She looked around 16 or 15 and ran into his arms. They were laughing and smiling.

"Where's your brother?" he asked her. The girl looked behind her and a boy around 17 came up behind her. He looked just like Martha but just like Mardrin.

"Hey dad" he said and embraced his parents. They looked like such a beautiful family. It turned out that Mardrin had the two children he had always wanted. One boy and one girl. And for once Esselle didn't feel like it should have been her. She just felt like the way she did at the beach and a huge wave came knocking her out and bringing her out to shore. Like some kind of big realization hit her. They began walking Mardrin's arm around his daughter and his son around his mother while Mardrin and Martha held hands in the middle. They were talking about something Esselle could not hear. Something about how school was. Mardrin looked at his children with such a beautiful love. With such a sparkle and twinkle in his eyes. Mardrin looked at

Martha with a smile that spread all the way to his eyes and he looked so at peace so blissful and the smile took years off of his appearance. Esselle noticed that whenever he was around Martha he had somehow seemed so much lighter happier and just plainly and simply in love. And then he leaned down to kiss her and it had been the most beautiful thing in the world. His children began to laugh and Martha pulled away with a smile and turned to her son and pinched his cheek hard to tease him. Esselle was not at all envious. She just wanted something like that for herself. With someone she loved. But the thing was she wasn't sure of who that was anymore. because one thing was for sure. It definitely was not Mardrin. Esselle came to the thought and realization that maybe he never really was and it hurt because she had probably been blind for so long.

She turned to face Daniel and his eyes said it all. She sighed. "And at last I see" she said and walked past him. Daniel sighed and placed his hand on her arm. She stopped to look at him. He opened his mouth to speak but shut it again. Instead he grabbed her and took her in his arms. Esselle wrapped her arms around his neck and took in the scent of him while burying her face in his shoulder. She hadn't cried just stood there and let him hold her close. She stood there and listened to the sound of his heart beat against his chest and into his ear. She liked the way it sounded.

"Elle" Mardrin said. Esselle smiled and shut his office door shut behind her.

"Hey" she said.

"What are you doing here?" he asks taking off his glasses.

"Oh nothing I just..." she said and sat in the seat across from him. She smiled "Tell me about them" she said.

Mardrin blinked a few times and looked at her "What?" he asked. Esselle sat up in her chair and tilted her head "Tell me about them. Your wife your children. Tell me about your life" she said. He pressed his eyebrows together and looked at her.

"I-" he said and stopped. He looked around then at her. Finally he smiled a bit. He put his glasses back on and went into the bottom drawer of his desk. He pulled out a book and handed it to her. She smiled a bit and took it.

"You keep an album in your office Mr. CEO?" she said and he laughed a bit.

"Just when the days get rough. Their faces always get me through it" he said.

Esselle opened up the book and got to the prom first. She laughed out loud when she saw Stephen and Selena. She flipped some more and saw graduation. Turns out Martha had moved back to the U.S after living in France and transferred to our school. Esselle's favorite picture was the one where with all the chaos and flying hats around Martha and Mardrin are smiling at each other. It was a beautiful picture. For a split second Esselle imagined herself at graduation and then the thought was gone. She turned to pictures of college. The campus. college friends parties laughter and smiles. Martha was in a few and he looked as if when ever he saw her the words I love you were dying to come out. Even when in one they were at a campus party she was sitting on his lap and they were smiling at each other. This did not look like the distraught Mardrin Esselle had painted for her. This looked like a happy and in love Mardrin. She flipped to wedding pictures. Esselle swallowed hard and looked at the look on Mardrin's face when Martha was in his arms dancing. He just looked so at peace and happy. It was as if he only looked like that when he was around her. It despite Esselle trying made her stomach turn a bit. She turned to pictures of a honeymoon. It just looked like Mardrin was laughing and Martha looked annoyed but still smiling. They were in front of the Eiffel Tower. The pictures of a pretty house. Then what looked like a picture on an ultra sound taped inside. Esselle looked at Mardrin and he smiled.

"My son" he said. Esselle nodded and went back to the book. She flipped more pages and saw a baby shower. Martha sitting at a chair with a happy shocked look. Mardrin was kissing her cheek. She had that beautiful new mother look to her and Mardrin just seemed blissful. Then pictures of a beautiful newborn baby and Esselle smiled. Then a first birthday party another ultra sound

Somewhere in Time- trilogy part 2

picture.

"That was for my daughter" Mardrin said and Esselle nodded concentrated on the pictures. A pregnant Martha and Mardrin holding a two year old boy laughing. Simply laughing. They didn't even have to smile for the camera they just looked like all they did was smile. Esselle's favorite part was watching his children grow in pictures. She smiled.

"You're son looks like a mix of the two of you. And your daughter she's beautiful" Esselle said and turned the pages. She loved seeing birthdays and wedding anniversaries and family vacations. Even if they weren't hers she odd enough felt happy for Mardrin that he got everything he wanted in life.

"My son and daughter attend private school but one where they live on campus. Now that their schooling is done for the year they're home for the summer" he said and Esselle smiled.

"That's wonderful" she said.

"I would like if they met you" he said and at that Esselle's heart stopped.

"What?" Esselle asked. Mardrin leaned over and put his elbows on his desk.

"I want you to meet them Elle" he said.

"Have your lost your mind?" Esselle asked.

Mardrin rolled his eyes and got up walked around the desk and stood above her.

"I'm serious" he said and took the book.

"So am I!" she said. Mardrin took in a deep breath and put the book away.

"Elle I want them to meet you and I want you to meet them" he said and took her hand.

Somewhere in Time- trilogy part 2

Esselle made a face. She knew Mardrin all too well "I'm not getting out of this one am I?" she asked and he laughed.
"No you're not" he said.
Esselle bit her lip then took his hand in both of hers "Alright" she said.

Dawn whipped her long knife in the air and sliced the mannequins throat. When she was done she whipped her forehead and smiled.
"So what do you think?" she asked.
Jasmine continued to play with her blade and Esselle smiled.
"Nice" she said. Dawn hopped off the plat form and opened up her arms.
"I just kicked ass and all i get is nice?" she said and both jasmine and Esselle laughed.
"We've been watching you kick as all day" Esselle said. She had her elbows up behind her and was sitting on a bench next to Jasmine. That day it was a hot one and they were all inside the training facility keeping cool. Except for Dawn who felt the need to kick ass on the hottest days of the year. Trevor walked over cleaning his machete and nodded.
"You did well" he said. Dawn made a face.
"Well, isn't good enough either" she said and grabbed her water bottle. Trevor laughed. he had tan skin grey eyes and dark brown hair.
Jasmine was smiling but Esselle could ten she was tensing up

everywhere. Esselle laughed and Dawn looked clueless.

"What?" Dawn asked and Trevor walked over to the weapons wall.

"Esselle stop" Jasmine said and Esselle laughed harder.

Dawn walked over and ran her fingers through her hair.

"What is it?" she asked frustrated.

"Jasmine likes Trevor" Esselle said. Dawn made a smile where her lips went into her mouth and Jasmine shot up with a straight back in her seat.

'Do not!" she said "Say it any louder and he'll hear you!" she said and bit her lip looking over. Dawn fell into the seat on the stool and laughed with Esselle. Esselle began tapping her feet in rhythm and Dawn raised an eyebrow.

"Someone likes to dance" she said. Esselle looked up and smiled.

"I haven't dance in 28 years" she said.

At that moment Daniel and Carmin came in. Carmin was one of the older Hispanic ladies that worked with everyone else. She was in charge of translating for those that didn't speak English. She was short a bit plump by very voluptuous so it looked good. She had very light brown skin long wavy black hair and caramel colored eyes.

"Hey is there a radio here?" Esselle asked.

Dawn nodded "Carmin keeps it on that table" she said and pointed. Carmin took a seat at the table and on top was a modern day radio. "She likes her music when she fills out her paper work."

Esselle stood up and fixed her jeans.

Jasmine laughed "I'm sorry but your butt looks awesome in those" she said. With wide eyes Esselle turned to face her but she and Dawn just laughed. Esselle had on her black high-waisted Colombian jeans. Selena had bought them for her one Christmas. Esselle wanted to laugh while recapping the memory Selena had said "These are made for Spanish girls with bodies like yours. Because lets face it. I have no body. Especially compared to you" she had said to Esselle. Esselle wore a dark blue sheer shirt. The shoulders and chest was bare but it had long pirate sleeves and ruffles at the wrist. Esselle wore her jet black ankle boots with the really high heel. Esselle felt the need to be tall that day.

"Carmin corazon" Esselle said and Daniel approached them. Esselle felt very comfortable talking her native language. She grew up around it all her life.

"What are you doing?" Daniel asked and he looked over. Daniel was dressed all in black as usual.

Carmin looked over "Que paso corazon?" she said.

Daniel raised an eyebrow.

"Me puedes hacer un favor y poner en Vivir mi Vida por Marc Anthony?" she asked and pushed her hair from her face. Carmin smiled.

"Mi madre solía tocar esa canción para mí cuando era más joven" she said and Esselle smiled. Carmin began pressing buttons on the radio. She faced Daniel.

She smiled "Want to dance with me?" she asked and held out her hands.

He put on a funny smile and tossed his weapons belt on the floor.

"Are you sure?" he asked.

"Why? You scared?" she asked. He stepped up to her so close their noses could have been touching. He smirked.

"As if" he said.

Esselle put on the same face when she looked him in the eyes.
"Perfect" she said and she could hear Jasmine laugh.
"My mom used to love listening to this guy" she said and Esselle looked back at Jasmine with her eyebrows furrowed.
"You-" she said but was cut off by Carmin.
"Listo?" she said.
Esselle looked at Daniel trying not laugh.
"Now don't think this is weird" she said taking his hands and placing them on her hips. "But this is how I was taught to dance" she said.
"Oh I no" he said and with a flick of his wrist brought Esselle falling into him and she gasped. He eyes flickered when he smiled "So was I" he said and the music came on.
Jasmine hooted "WOOOO!!!!" she said and Dawn laughed.
Esselle had been a very good dancer when she was younger. She had hoped she kept her skill.
It was true Daniel could dance. Just like her father would with her mother.
Dawn's jaw dropped "Look at those hips go" she said and Esselle laughed. Esselle's feet moved back and forth and she could hear Carmin clapping to the beat. Esselle hips swayed back and forth. She remembered as a child watching her mother doing the same thing. they made sharp curves as she moved then twirled.
"I didn't know you could dance this way" Esselle said and Daniels hand went on her waist again as her hips sharply moved back and forth. He shrugged.
"Watching your parents you kinda pick up on a few things" he said. Esselle pulled out still holding his hand and they danced on their own until he pulled her back again.

"Esselle teach me please how to move my body like that! I have no rhythm!" Dawn said and Esselle laughed again.

"She isn't that good" Daniel said and smiled at Esselle "I've seen better" he teased.

Esselle narrowed her eyes at him and she didn't realize when her legs began moving faster back and forth and in every direction below her. Her heels clicked as it repeatedly touched the floor. She turned on the balls of her feet and moved her arms back and forth. Daniel crossed his eyes and she laughed.

"Daniel you remember when mom used to try and get me to dance like that?" Jasmine said and Daniel smiled a bit "I was way too shy" she said.

"Ya I remember" Daniel said. He flicked his wrist and brought Esselle into him wrapping his arm around her waist again. Esselle smiled.

"Why didn't you tell me you could dance?" she asked and he twirled her.

"You didn't ask" he said and spun her again.

"Wepa!" Carmin said and Esselle broke out into a giggle. Esselle narrowed her eyes at Daniel and he did the same. Was he competing with her?

She placed her arms around his neck and he placed his hands on her hips.

"Look at Esselle go" Trevor said walking back over.

Esselle shifted the weight of her body from foot to foot popping each knee each time. Her hips went sharply back and forth until they worked their way to a swivel. She refused to be out danced by Daniel. If that was even a thing. Her knees began to give out below her and she swirled down to the ground and Daniel did the same.

"I've still seen better" he said.

She grinned "I can completely dance better than you" she said coming back up.

"Alright" he said turned her then yanked her close. "Prove it" he said so Esselle did.

Daniel held the tips of her fingers in the air as she slowly turned. "Move those hips!" Trevor shouted and Daniel shot him a look. Esselle didn't quite catch. Esselle carved the air around her with her hips as she danced. She remembered as a teen watching Selena doing the same thing. Selena had said to Esselle once while she was learning "Its all a matter of your hips going in and out" Esselle when she was younger was shy when it came to dancing. But for some reason it had all melted away. So sure maybe she wasn't dancing very appropriately and if her parents saw her they'd have a heart attack but who cared? Right? She twirled once quickly then she came back into Daniel this time with her back up against him and she laughed. He held her hands as they danced together.

jasmine's eye widened "Our parents did *Not* dance like that in front of us" she said and Esselle could feel Daniel laughing against her.

"That's because this is highly inappropriate" he said.

"Hey any closer with the whole moving thing your clothes might get knotted together. I mean personal space!" Dawn said. At that Daniel and Esselle could not help it. They both turned to face each other and laugh. The song came to an end and the heat of every place on Esselle's skin where Daniel touched her felt cold again when his hands fell. Esselle sucked in her breath and shoved her hands in her back pockets.

"I gotta admit you did well Ess" Daniel said.

Esselle smiled "Thanks, I used to love watching my parents dance together" she said.

"So they taught you?" he asked and Esselle nodded.

"Yup!" she said and Carmin had a little smile on her face when she walked back over to the radio and shut it off. "My mother always said 'To dance is to live so do it like a Puerto Rican'" Esselle said and laughed to herself. "It was kind of like the catch phrase in the house while they were teaching me. I wasn't one for such um...ferocious body movements so it took a lot to break out of that shell" she said and Daniel laughed.

"You sure as hell weren't shy just now" he said.

Esselle dipped her head with a soft smile and blushed "Ya well I uh...guess I'm all grown up now" she said and Daniel stood next to her. He touched her shoulder.

"You did good" he said and walked out. Esselle bit her bottom lip still smiling. She took her right hand out of her pocket and chewed on her nail. When she looked up Dawn had on her superior face with a raised eyebrow and Jasmine was smirking with crossed arms.

"What?" Esselle asked.

"mhm" Dawn said sliding off the stool. Jasmine got up from her seat.

"What?" Esselle insisted.

"Uhu" Jasmine said and followed Dawn.

"hey wait a minute what?" Esselle asked following them

"Nothing" Dawn said

"just nothing" Jasmine said and grabbed a towel

"Oh come on!" Esselle said "Tell me!"
"I'm gonna go kick another mannequin's ass" Dawn said.
"You did that like 30 times today!" Esselle said and Dawn looked back at her with a wry smile
"Well then I'll do it 30 more" she said and she and Jasmine walked out. Esselle frustrated threw up her hands and they fell making a smacking noise on her thighs.
She looked over and saw Carmin smiling.
Esselle widened her eyes "Que?" she asked
Carmin stood up with pressed lips and a smile. She grabbed her folder and walked away
"Nada" she said.

Somewhere in Time- trilogy part 2

"I wanna dance and love and dance again"
Esselle spun and her hair covered her face. The song ended and Esselle hit replay. When Esselle was stressed she would play piano. Unfortunate enough for her they didn't have a piano in headquarters but they did have a dancing room for leisurely time. Esselle had taken dance classes her entire life with Selena. Esselle felt comfortable dancing but only in the usual leotard and stockings. Her leotard was plain black and her stockings were skin toned. The dancing room looked like the one in her old dance school with the ballet bar and mirrors. There was a

television screen up in the far left corner. Esselle grabbed the remote to higher the volume and waited for the video to come on. Esselle, in heels mind you, was trying to master the dance moves in the music video. then again who could master Jennifer Lopez's moves in Dance Again? Esselle was good but decided not good again. Esselle was going over to Mardrin's that night to meet his family. She was conflicted and her mind was just a jumble of thoughts. Really not very appropriate of a very certain person. but she decided to not let her mind drown in thoughts such as those.

"Dance, yes (RedOne)

Love, next

Dance, yes (J.Lo)

Love, next" Esselle heard so she got into her position. She saw her reflection in the mirror. She was sweating but for some reason it made her skin glisten and her hair was still wet as she had just washed it before she got there.

"Shimmy Shimmy yah, Shimmy yam

Shimmy yay

I'm a ol' dirty dog all day

No way Jose

Your girl only go one way, ay mi madre

You should check that out

Maybe you ain't turn her out

Maybe it's none of my business

But for now work it out

Let's get this, dale" Esselle smiled. Every time the shimmy came on she wanted to laugh. She always found it funny.

"Nobody knows what I'm feeling inside

Somewhere in Time- trilogy part 2

I find it so stupid
So why should I hide
That I love to make love to you baby
(yeah make love to me)
So many ways wanna touch you tonight
I'm a big girl got no secrets this time
Yeah I love to make love to you baby
(yeah make love to me)" It was coming up to Esselle's favorite part.
"If this would be a perfect world
We'd be together then
(let's do it do it do it)
Only got just one life this I've learned
Who cares what they're gonna say
(let's do it do it do it)
I wanna dance, and love, and dance again
I wanna dance, and love, and dance again
Dance, yes
Love, next
Dance, yes
Love, next" Esselle began to dance. Left, right, kick, arms, hair she thought to herself.
"Baby your fire is lighting me up
The way that you move boy is reason enough
That I love to make love to you baby
(yeah make love to me)
I can't behave
Oh I want you so much
Your lips taste like heaven

So why should I stop?
Yeah I love to make love to you baby
(yeah make love to me)" Esselle made up her own moves similar to the ones shown just to fill in the empty parts.
"If this would be a perfect world
We'd be together then
(let's do it do it do it)
Only got just one life this I've learned
Who cares what they're gonna say
(let's do it do it do it)
I wanna dance, and love, and dance again
I wanna dance, and love, and dance again" Esselle moved as she saw in the video. She had every move memorized. Then the door came in and Daniel's head peeked in. Esselle ignored him. He looked confused with his eyebrows pressed together. He saw her made a face and shut the door.
"What are you doing?" he asked. Esselle had re-winded the video back a few parts to watch again.
"Stress reliever" she said.
"This part the silent part its a duet" he said.
"ya so" Esselle said tugging at the loose parts of her leotard. It was a bit to big on her. Daniel rolled her eyes and stood behind her. The beat started and Esselle watched the screen.
Daniel grabbed her leg and she threw her head back then turned following every move on the television screen. Left, right, grab she thought and grabbed Daniel and he pulled her into him. Esselle had been so stressed she didn't even noticed being touched the way she was. They just seemed concentrated on looking at each other.

Arm, fists, smack, shoulders Esselle thought and moved to the beat. Sharp move, jump, Daniel hands legs she thought and continued to move.

Daniel grabbed her hands and turned her side ways and then turned to the opposite side.

"Mr Worldwide, and the world's most beautiful woman

Modern day Hugh Hef (uh, yes)

Playboy to the death (uh, yes)

Is he really worldwide? (uh, yes)

Mami let me open your treasure chest

Play dates, we play mates

I'm the king at snatching queens, checkmate

What you think?

It's a rumor

I'm really out of this world

Moon, luna

Make woman comfortable

Call me bloomer

Can't even show love cause they'll sue ya

But I told them, 'hallelujah, have a blessed day'

So ahead of myself

Everyday's yesterday

Want the recipe? it's real simple

Little bit of voli, and she'll open sesame"

Esselle could feel herself gasping for air and the sweat on her back making her clothing stick.

"Now dance yes

Love next

Dance yes

Somewhere in Time- trilogy part 2

Love next
If this would be a perfect world
We'd be together then
(let's do it do it do it)
Only got just one life this I've learned
Who cares what they're gonna say
(let's do it do it do it)
I wanna dance, and love, and dance again
I wanna dance, and love, and dance again"

Daniel grabbed Esselle and pulled her into him right when the song ended. Daniel's heart pounded against his chest and Esselle could feel the rhythm as they breathed in and out deeply gasping for air.

'Now Ess" he said and looked down at her to smile "Tell me what's the matter?" he asked.

"Nothing" she said pulling away. Daniel in a snap took his arms wrapped them around her waist and brought her close again.

"No I'm serious there's something wrong I can sense it" he said.

What's wrong? Esselle felt like saying What's wrong is that she was supposed to go meet her ex boyfriends wife and kids officially she just woke up from being asleep 28 years her parents are never home there is a secret society of people she never knew existed that she was now apart of her best friend is grown up and married everyone around her has gone on with their lives she had been frozen in time and she was despite trying not to and despite his difficult character was falling in love- she stopped herself right there. She wasn't about to get that far. The thought terrified her. She had never felt that way about anyone else but Mardrin. So much as even thinking about it made her stomach turn.

"What's wrong?" Esselle said "What's wrong was in a matter of a month I was brought back from the dead the world has gone on without me as has everyone I once knew. I'm stuck as a 17 year old there's something wrong with me I have a glowing mark there's a world I never knew existed that I am now apart of and all I want to do is wake up to a normal day." she said and Daniel's eyelids fell when he looked at her. he examined every feature of her face and Esselle tried keeping her heart from racing. "I want to be able to wake up every morning and be free. Be free to do whatever I want and everything I used to be able to do. I used to love dancing. It was my favorite hobby when I was younger before all this." she said and looked at him

"Daniel I want to Live, Love, Laugh, and Dance again" she said. He nodded as if he understood and without noticing Esselle's arms were resting around his shoulders.

"Ess, I know all you've been doing is sitting around watching lately but I promise first thing Monday morning. We'll start on finding out what happened to you" he said and his nose touched hers. Esselle's eyelids slowly fell.

"You're not alone" he said. Esselle nodded because she knew that. Being alone was not what scared her it was when she was alone who she wanted to be with her.

Esselle could feel something in her stomach flutter. Like butterflies.

She laughed a bit "That's easy for you to say" she said and he looked at and frowned.

"What do you mean?" he asked.

"You have Jasmine. Your sister. Daniel I walk in here everyday and see strangers. Its like being a complete and totally outcast" she said but he was already shaking his head.

"No" he said and stroked his hair. "You know Carmin, Charlotte, Trevor, Dawn, Jasmine" he said and his eyes met his. They were just as blue as the night Esselle first saw them "Me" he said.

"Well you're not all that" Esselle said. Daniel laughed a bit and tipped her chin.

"Oh come on, I'm just about the most stunning thing you've seen in you're entire life!" he said softly.

Esselle without thinking laughed a bit and said "You are" She instantly felt her stomach turn. What is it with him!? He always made her do that! Say what she was thinking but didn't want to say. Daniel took her chin in his fingers and tilted her head back. "So are you" he said. Esselle's eyes fell slowly shut as she felt the warmth surrounded her, her heart began beating, her skin began to itch with anticipation, her eyes flutter, she felt him growing warmer, and...and the kiss Esselle had been dying for never came. The door opened and he instantly let her go and stood up straight as if nothing was happening. He was awfully good at it. Esselle blinked a few times to snap back into reality. Jasmine was smiling with Dawn at her side when she opened the door.

"Daniel!" she said "I've looking for you come on! Time for training!" she said. Daniel looked at Esselle for a moment then back at her sister.

"Oh I see we were interrupting something?" Dawn asked. Her sharp eyebrow was raised and she had a hand on her popped hip.

"No" Esselle said and at the same time Daniel said "Yes"

They looked at each other

"Yes" Esselle said and at the same time Daniel said "No" They looked at each other again. Daniel looked away to speak to his sister.

"I was just talking to Esselle about being trained" he said.

Dawn made a face

"Oh crap I was hoping we were getting into something good. You boring people." she said and walked out of sight.

Daniel walked over to the door and muttered something to Jasmine at which her expression went unchanging. Daniel looked back.

"I'll see you later Essie" he said. Esselle slowly brought her hand up to wave and the door shut. She could feel her stomach turning.

When Esselle was only everything had dawned on her. She was urging to be kissed. By Daniel.

Mardrin had his hand on the small of Esselle's back and she couldn't breathe. She looked up at the door to his apartment in the city and she clutched her bag. He laughed.

"Why so nervous?" he asked. She looked at him. Oh I don't know she felt like telling him maybe because your wife and children are about to meet the woman you are in love with that isn't Martha.

"Wouldn't you be nervous" she asked and he just laughed. Today his eyes were more yellow than green when he looked at her. He leaned over and kissed her forehead.

'You'll do fine. They'll love you" he said and opened the door.

Somewhere in Time- trilogy part 2

Esselle stepped in and she saw three people running around. "Augustine you Parisian rat you ruined me set up!" Mardrin's daughter said. Esselle had remembered it was Jacqueline. She had a very slight french accent to her. Augustine laughed.
"Jacqueline you set up the table as if it were Christmas" he said and walked passed her. Jacqueline rolled her eyes and went into the kitchen.
"Jacqueline, Augustine so help me if your father sees you two fighting again-" Martha began.
"Too late" he said. Martha looked up at Mardrin as he approached her with a funny smile.
"Sweetheart grab a hold of your children" she said. Martha unlike her children had an obvious but beautiful French accent. Her children had very, very soft French accents but were very strong when they said each other's names. Mardrin had a French accent only when he was angry and said certain words. Other than that it was such a soft accent you could barely tell.
Mardrin placed his hands on her shoulders and smiled that smile again at her before he kissed her.
"Jacqueline, Où avez-vous mis l'-" Augustine said coming out of the kitchen and stopped when he saw Esselle.
"Hello" he said and Esselle smiled.
"Augustine can't you do anything without bothering me! Je fais quelque chose!" Jacqueline says coming up behind him and stops dead in her tracks when she looked up. Esselle forced her smile but she could already begin to feel the awkwardness of it all. Esselle hadn't taken the time to examine Mardrin's home. It was huge no doubt. It was very French looking. Like his country house in France the one he grew up in. Esselle had only seen it in

Somewhere in Time- trilogy part 2

pictures but it was beautiful. It had a bit of an open floor plan with a big chandelier and fire place. The couch was royal looking and a beautiful creme color. There were big pretty stairs in the far right corner that led up stairs and you could see the hallway. There was wainscoting and crown molding on the walls very intricate.

Martha smiled at Esselle. She walked over and took her hands in hers. Esselle felt tense everywhere. Selena was right. She had watched Esselle kiss her husband yet she is a good and gracious woman.

"Welcome" she said and embraced her. And now she was welcoming Esselle into her home. Could this be anymore of a wonderful woman? Perhaps Mardrin did deserve her. Had it been Esselle she would have had grabbed a pan and flung it.

"Thank you" Esselle said as she had truly meant it. Martha took Esselle's hand and lead her over to her children.

"Esselle this is my 15 year old daughter. Jacqueline" she said. Jacqueline had a wide beautiful smile when she extended her hand and Esselle shook it.

"Its nice to meet you" Jacqueline said.

"And this is my son Augustine" she said.

Esselle extended her hand and smiled. Augustine shook it.

"Its nice to meet you" Esselle said

"Likewise" he said and Esselle could hear his accent.

Esselle swallowed hard.

"i'm Esselle" she said and looked at Martha "I'm a friend an old friend of your mother and father's" she said and looked at Martha again. Something about what Esselle had said made Martha's face soften and break out into a glossy eyed smile.

Somewhere in Time- trilogy part 2

Maybe out of respect that Esselle acknowledged her as her friend too? Esselle didn't know. All she knew was that Martha was gaining her composure.

"Please sit!" Martha said and pulled out a chair for Esselle. Esselle decided she liked this woman. Even if she were married to Mardrin.

****

Martha and Esselle were alone in the kitchen drying dishes when it was Martha who spoke first.

"I'm so glad you decided to come over" she said and Esselle looked at her with a smile.

"Thank you for having me" she said. Martha looked away and swallowed hard.

"I'd like to apologize" she said. Esselle practically dropped the plate in her hands.

'What?" she asked completely astonished.

"I know it was a long time and I know it is probably much over due but I'd like to apologize for what I did to you 28 years ago" she said and Martha's eyes met Esselle's. "I was young and I didn't know about you I'm so sorry. I didn't mean-" she said and Esselle cut her off. She shook her head and put the plate down.

"No, don't be sorry it isn't your fault" Esselle said

"Sometimes just sometimes I feel as if" Martha said and looked out of the kitchen and into the living room at her family together happy "If I hadn't done what I did this would be your family" she said and looked at Esselle "Not mine"

"That's not true Mardrin loves you!" Esselle said "Probably more than he ever loved me"

Somewhere in Time- trilogy part 2

Martha laughed a bit and turned to face them again "I highly doubt that. Just look at all the things he's done for you. He would never do the same for me" she said and there was a moment of silence.

"You're right" Esselle said looking at Martha. She turned to face her "He would do so much more" Esselle said shaking her head. "You have no idea Martha that man just lives for. In everything he does. Just in the way he, he smiles at you, kisses you, hugs you, loves you, even in the way he says your name its..." and Esselle trailed off when Martha looked at her. "Its beautiful" Martha looked down at her hands then back out into the living room.

"Despite how much Mardrin and I cared for each other as much as it hurts to say we are polar opposites. We have nothing a like. Something if not everything would have eventually driven us apart" Esselle said and even as she said them the words pained her to do so as the realization of it all was too much to bare. Esselle shut her eyes blocking the pain out the way she always did when things became too much. Martha gently touched her hand.

"I'd still like to apologize" she said and Esselle looked at her. "You don't have to" Esselle began but Martha cut her off.

"But I want to" she said "Woman to woman I truly didn't mean to ruin things between the two of you I didn't. I love my husband and my children and even though I would not give them up for the world not anything or anyone I feel as if I at least awe you an apology for taking away your life basically. When Mr. and Mrs. Elunas told me-" she said but Esselle's eyebrows furrowed.

"Elunas?" she said.

Martha nodded "That day I stopped by the lab and came across Mr. and Mrs. Elunas they were scientists that worked with Mardrin's parents. That was a long time ago anyway. They told me he was home and so I went and I guess..." Martha said and her eyes became cloudy with tears "I just left" she said.

Despite Esselle's mind running she swallowed hard. She smiled and squeezed Martha's hand.

"You're a great woman" she said "And I'm glad that he found you"

Somewhere in Time- trilogy part 2

When Esselle walked into the living room of her house her parents were sitting on the couch. Esselle stood there over them and crossed her arms. Her mother was knitting something and her father was reading a newspaper.
"Well?" Esselle said.
Vivienne looked up from her knitting at her daughter.
Esselle raised an eyebrow.
Vivienne looked at her husband and hit his leg. "Henry!" she said and her voice was soft. With a jump Esselle's father looked up from his newspaper. "What?" Henry said.
Vivienne flicked her head at Esselle. "Our daughter is trying to tell us something" she said.
"Oh!" He said quickly and put his newspaper down. Esselle's mother smiled and her father reached over to take his wife's hand.
"Now sweetheart what did you want to tell us?" he asked.
"What happened 28 years ago at the lab?" she asked. Her mother made a face and blinked a few times.
"What?" she asked.

Esselle rolled her eyes and looked at them "Don't play stupid with me! What happened?" she asked.

"Esselle how an Earth are we supposed to remember something from almost 30 years ago?" her father asked.

"28 years ago" Esselle repeated growing impatient. Esselle could just feel her blood boil and the rage becoming so powerful she could feel it ready to burst from her fingertips. "The day I got into my accident Mardrin's wife Martha went to the lab what did you say to her" Esselle asked through gritted teeth.

"Elle I..." her mother said.

"What did you say to her?" Esselle asked.

"It was a long time it shouldn't matter-" her father began

"What are you hiding from me!" Esselle shouted "Tell me what did you say?"

Her mother sighed "Your father and I were working when she came in looking for him." she said.

"Did you know?" Esselle asked crossing her arms. she could hear the strain in her voice and the burn of tears in the back of her throat.

"Know what?" her father asked. Esselle feeling hopeless and on the verge of tears sighed and took a deep breath.

'Did you know" she said her voice breaking and tears about to pour out "That he was in love with her?" she asked and her parents looked at each other a form of silent communication. Her mother looked away in shame and it was Esselle's father that spoke.

"Yes we did" he said.

Esselle smiled looking to the ceiling. She figured if she smiled it wouldn't hurt as much. The tears were big and fat when they came down Esselle's face and she wiped them away.

"She asked where his parents were she wanted to tell them she was back. We told her way Mardrin was" her mother said not meeting her daughter's eye.

"How could you do that to me? How could you have done that I was there! You knew I was there!" Esselle said.

"Esselle we're sorry-" her father began and reached for her. She smacked him away backing up.

"No you're not. You lied to me. What the hell was running through your mind?" Esselle said.

"Esselle" her mother said.

"Get away from me" Esselle said and her tone was deadly. Esselle turned and slammed the front door shut behind her.

Somewhere in Time- trilogy part 2

Esselle traced the rim of her coffee cup with the tip of her finger. Selena with her newspaper in hand was concentrated on the stock report. Esselle and Selena were having lunch in a cafe in the city. Esselle and Selena were sitting outside and Esselle liked watching the hustle and bustle of New York. Everything just kept going and moving nothing ever stopped. Esselle got a latte and Selena got her coffee black the way she always did.
"How are the twins?" Esselle asked breaking the silence.
Selena looked up and smiled "Good, they asked for you the other day what happened?" she said and went back to the news paper.
"Oh I uh went shopping" Esselle said thinking quickly. Over the edge of the newspaper Selena raised and eyebrow.
she put her paper down "Shopping?" she asked.
"Mhm" Esselle said with a nod. Selena sighed and leaned over the table.
"Elle you're wearing something Victoria Justice would have worn back in her day" she said and sat back in her seat.
Esselle made a face "ya well I just didn't feel like wearing something else today!" she said.
"Selena let me ask you something" Esselle said putting her elbows on the table.
"Tell me babe" she said and took a sip of her coffee.
"Did you know Martha was home?" Esselle asked and at that Selena put her paper down completely.
"Did I what?" she asked.
"28 years ago did you know-" Esselle said but she was cut off. Exasperated Selena slammed her hands on the table and rolled her eyes.

"Of course I knew Elle! Everybody knew she was back! Everyone knew she was going to come and find him hello common freaking sense" she snapped.

"huh" Esselle said falling back in her seat. When ever Esselle was extremely annoyed her tongue would scour her right cheek. Esselle looked off to the side. Selena's eyes grew wide with embarrassment and the wish to take back something she had said. Esselle looked at her "So everyone knew but me basically?" she asked.

"Elle-" Selena began

"Did Stefan know?" Esselle cut in.

Selena nodded slowly "He was the one that told me. Mardrin told him"

Esselle was growing furious and was sure enough to lose her temper if she didn't leave. She grabbed her back and pushed out her iron chair.

"I can't believe you lied to me" Esselle said.

"Elle i didn't lie" she said.

"No you did something worse than that you didn't tell me! You say there and watched basically set me up!" she snapped.

"Elle" Selena said turning in her chair to watch her leave.

"Leave me alone Selena" Esselle said and stormed out.

Esselle grew hot and sweaty in her bed under the silk sheets. The balcony doors were open and the summer breeze came blowing into her room but Esselle didn't notice. Her mind was drifting away deep in her dreams. Esselle was looking in the mirror flattening out her dress. She pushed her hair behind her ears. She was in a room that wasn't hers. It looked like the kind of bedroom in a castle. All the colors were champagne, white, gold, and silver. His arms wrap around Esselle's waist and she smiles when he kisses her cheek. Then the scene changes. Esselle could feel the burn on her skin every time and everywhere she's touched. it drover her insane for more. Esselle could see but at the same time she couldn't. Esselle moved around in her bed and the sheets got knotted in her fists. The scent and smell of him was all the same. The feel of his thick hair running through her

fingertips. There's laughing. Esselle was laughing. It all happened in sharp pretty and intense flashes. There kisses and caressing of skin. Esselle could see as a ribbon was gently being tugged and undone while pretty silky fabric fell to the floor. Esselle could hear laughing again. Sweet innocent harmless laughter. Then Esselle felt heat. Like none other before. Esselle's stomach began to turn and she shifted in her bed. her skin began to tickle then sting. She could feel fingertips graze the skin of her leg like a blade. Esselle's head turned sharply. Esselle could taste the sweetness of his lips pressed against hers and she snapped. Her eyes flew open and she sprang out of bed.
"Shh! Daniel said and pushed her back down.
"Do you want your parents to come in and hear you screaming?" he asked. Her bedroom was completely black except for the moonlight outside. Daniel was on top of her with his hand covering her mouth.
"Gees Ess do you always wake up screaming in your sleep?" he asked removing his hand from her mouth.
"What are you doing here?" Esselle asked sitting up in her bed. She felt Exposed. She was in pajamas. Barely pajamas if shorts that should be underwear and a shirt with spaghetti straps and so tight it could be a second skin.
"Its Monday time to work on your case" he said sitting at the edge of her bed.
Esselle reached over for her new cell phone. She looked at him "Its 12:30 am" she said and he shrugged.
"Still Monday technically" he said walking over to the window. "Are you coming or what?" he asked. Esselle rolled her eyes and got out of bed. She heard him laugh.

Somewhere in Time- trilogy part 2

"What?" she asked walking over to her closet.

"Not that I don't love the whole 'bare skin look' but if I were you I'd try to cover up before any other guy that sees you dies of excitement" he said. Esselle grabbed the nearest pillow and dodged it at him. e avoided it laughing then put his finger over his mouth.

"Shh no need to wake mom and dad" he said.

"Uck!" Esselle said walking over to her closet.

"By the way what were you dreaming of? You seemed pretty deep in" he said and Esselle looked back at him with her hand on the closet door frame.

"Nothing" she said. You, was what she meant. She meant to say I was dreaming of you.

Somewhere in Time- trilogy part 2

"Ok Esselle" said Charlotte and dropped a box of files in front of her.
"We're going to do a little research on you" she said and smiled. Esselle laughed a bit.
"Oh how fun" she said and grabbed a folder.
"I hope what we find isn't too much for you to handle Esselle" Jasmine said and grabbed a folder herself. Esselle sighed.
"Me too" she said.
Dawn fell into a chair and grabbed a folder. Dawns hair was wet Esselle assumed she had just showered. They were sitting in Charlotte's office at a big round white table. Esselle began flipping through her school records when it dawned on her.
"Hey where's your annoying brother?" she asked Jasmine and she laughed.
"He and Trevor had an assignment" she said.
"What do you guys even do on these assignments?" Esselle asked.
"Well they hunt down Elights" Charlotte said. She was flipping through Esselle's legal documents.
"Elights? What are those?" Esselle asked.
"They're vague invisibles. Wild and crazy. When they were experimented on something went wrong mentally with them and

they are unstable killers. They're basically malfunctioned and work in odd ways because of wires in their brain" Charlotte said.
'Wires?" Esselle said and Dawn nodded.
"When the government realized they were messed up in the head they sent them to an asylum where they put wires in their brains to try and keep them stable. Didn't work if you can tell" Dawn said with a snort.
"Sometimes they hunt Zelts" Jasmine chimed in and Charlotte gave her the eye.
"Zelts are highly dangerous" she said and Jasmine began to cower behind her folder "You shouldn't be toying with them you'll get yourself killed Jasmine. Besides only warriors can hunt Zelts" she said.
"Hmph!" Dawn said with a prideful smile.
'Daniel hunts them" Jasmien argued.
"Daniel with that boys skill he might as well already be a warrior. He's excellent and special you know that. He's one of the most powerful of them all. With his background and all" Charlotte said.
"I'm lost what are Zelts?" Esselle asked.
"Zelts are the government's puppets. They hunt and kill us therefore we hunt and kill them. That machine you reported seeing the night you were attacked" Charlotte said "That's what they use to kill us. The most difficult of us of course. Remember how I said we became harder to kill?" she asked and Esselle nodded.
"Well they needed special more powerful weapons to kill us so they used that" Dawn said filling in the thought "Its called a diviser" she said.

"Well would ya looky here" Dawn said leaning over the table to put her folder down.

'What?" Esselle asked.

"Check this out December 1, 2013 Esselle your blood was tested" she said and looked at her "For elestron and metal wire capability"

"What does that mean?" Esselle asked.

"Elestron is a substance in the virus. Its what sends the electrical shocks through the blood and enables it to turn into electricity" Jasmine said.

Esselle swallowed hard. "Where are the rest of my medical records?" she asked. Charlotte pocked into the box and pulled out a whole bunch of folders and Esselle quickly reached for one. She began scanning the pages as quickly as she could.

"Look at this" Jasmine said "In 2009 you went to the hospital for a broken arm right?" Jasmine asked.

Esselle nodded "Ya I fell off my bike"

"Well look at this the pain killers you were given contained laxite" she said and her brown eyes widened.

"What's laxite?" Esselle asked.

"Laxite is what we give patients here when they've injured a bone. Since we become part electronic our bones heel differently they heel like computerized fibers. No pain killers on the face of the planet contain laxite" she said.

"Oh and how about this." Charlotte said and dropped a stack of papers on the table with a smack.

"What's this?" Esselle asked taking it in her hands.

"You're death certificate. Signed by your parents although it says cause of death internal bleeding" and Charlotte had an odd smile on her face. jasmine did soon after.

"We got them" Charlotte said.

"But wait I don't understand what does this mean?" Esselle asked.

"It means this death certificate was faked. You 'died' in a car accident that should have been stated but there was no mention of it here." Charlotte said and took a seat examining the papers further.

"Let me explain you look lost babe" Dawn said shifting in her chair to face Esselle "That car accident someone wanted to hide it because car accidents get investigated. Then there would have to be an autopsy where they look at the body. Whoever froze you didn't want that to happen they needed your body to freeze. So they put internal bleeding" she said.

"But what I don't get is why your parents signed these papers they're bogus" Jasmine said.

"I have a feeling they were in on it" Charlotte mumbled.

"Who, who, whoa ok hold on" Esselle said and everyone looked at her,

"My parents had nothing to do with this" she said.

"Esselle we don't know that" jasmine said softly.

"ya, we still don't know who is apart of the circle of scientist that started this epidemic they could be one of them" Dawn said.

Esselle shook her head "No, not them its impossible" she said.

Charlotte looked at Jasmine and Dawn then took in a deep breath.

"Well alright then. For now we'll just do a little more research. I think that's enough for today" she said rising from her chair.

"But we just started" Esselle said.

"Um Esselle I think she's right" Jasmine said rising from her chair.

"I'll see you girls later for training" Charlotte said and left the room.

"Come on. Maybe we can get our hands on your old car" Dawn said.

"They would still have that?" Esselle asked. Jasmine made a face and nodded.

"It goes into our property. We can get it here by tomorrow around the same time" Jasmine said. Esselle sighed.

"Fine I guess" she said. But it all wasn't fine. Esselle was determined to find out what happened to her. Nothing was going to stop her.

Daniel was walking down the hallway laughing with Trevor. Esselle threw her hands in the air and approached them.
"Where the hell were you! I've looked everywhere for you!" Esselle said approaching them.
Daniel looked at her "Well did you check the Empire State Building?" he asked.
"Well" Esselle said "No"
He raised an eyebrow "Well then you didn't look everywhere" he said.

Trevor gave Daniel a look and faced Esselle "Ignore him. He's just moody today" Trevor said.

"What the hell am I a girl?" Daniel asked. Trevor took in a deep breath still looking at Esselle.

"Anyway" Trevor began "Whatsup?" he said.

"My car they got it in. I know its really late and you guys just came back from and assignment and all but since you guys are good with cars I was wondering if you might want to come and give it a look" Esselle said.

Daniel let out an exaggerated sigh "Not that I want to but..." he said "Fine" and he walked passed Esselle.

Esselle rolled her eyes. "What is his problem today?" she thought aloud.

"You" he said and Esselle looked at him "But not in the bad way you think. Daniel tends to be a pain in the ass when he wants something he knows he can't have"

"Who said he couldn't have me?" Esselle asked and Trevor smirked.

"Who said he could? Then again you're right who said it was you Daniel couldn't have" he replied and walked past her.

****

Daniel whistled. "I can't believe you got hold of this" Daniel said walking around Esselle's cold car.

Esselle shrugged "Jasmine said it was easy that this car instantly becomes theirs" she said.

"Well I can tell you one thing" Daniel said sticking his head through the window. Esselle shoved her hands in her back pockets.

Somewhere in Time- trilogy part 2

"What?" she asked. They were in the garage which really was a garage. It was an all white room with a huge opening in which it lead to outside with a huge landing to drop off cars via helicopter of course. There was another huge white door on the left side where when it opened turned into a spiral exit for people to drive their cars out of the building. Kind of like the way it is in malls.
"This car no way did it blow up and cause a fire" he said.
Esselle frowned "How could you tell?" Esselle asked.
"Well first off the car isn't torched plus look at the paint job its still glossy despite all the dents and scratches. This car took a beating yes but there was no fire" he said and go into the driver's seat. Esselle walked over and leaned against the car.
"What?" Daniel asked.
Esselle shook her head. "Nothing just watching" she said. He made a face and went under the steering wheel. When he came back up he had a bunch of wires in his hands.
"Ok so somebody definitely messed with your car intentionally" he said and hoped out of the car. He opened up the car hood.
"This is a disaster" he said and shut it again.
"What do you think?" Esselle asked.
He sighed "I think I look pretty damn good today considering I haven't slept" he said and yanked his gloves off. Esselle rolled her eyes.
"That's not what I meant" she said following him over to the long narrow corner where he put his gloves down. He looked back at her then to the table.
"i think that outfit looks good on you" he said. Esselle pushed a curl behind her ear and swallowed hard.
"But then again" he said turning to face her "That's just my

opinion" he said.

He had a silver colored tool box in his hand and walked back over to Esselle's car.

"What are you doing?" she asked

"I'm going to try and figure out what this person did to your car" he said. He went back under the steering wheel with a tool in his hand and Esselle could hear all the noise of his tool banging against various areas in her car. When Esselle was younger she had a black Maserati with white interior.

Esselle heard a noise and Daniel grunt.

"Got you" she heard him say and his head popped back up. Esselle had her head peeking inside the car and when he came up their faces were far too close. Esselle's eye widened for a moment before she pushed the air from her face and moved back.

"Um, what's that?" she asked.

Daniel was silent for a moment before he shook his head a bit "Uh," he said and took a deep breath "This is an old fashioned accelerator"

Esselle smiled a bit "You're speaking gibberish to me" she said.

"Oh right" he said raising his eyebrows "Basically you stick this in a car and it goes according to a timer. When the time goes off it brings up the speed of the car."

Esselle bent down next to him and took it in her hands.

"Whoever wanted to get rid of you must have put a lot of detail in doing it" he said

"But I don't understand. The night I got into my accident I stormed out of Mardrin's house. How could they have known exactly what time I was going to leave, when to follow me, and how long it would take for me to get to the highway and fly off" she said.

When she looked up she saw his big eyes and her reflection in them.

He shrugged "I don't know, but I'm definitely going to find out" he said jumping out of the car and walking right past her.

"What do you mean I can't go with you?" Esselle asked following Daniel.

Somewhere in Time- trilogy part 2

"What the hell are you insane?" he said looking back at her.
"He's right Elle" Jasmine said slipping on her weapons belt."Its dangerous"
"Girl you lost it!" Dawn said slipping on her black gloves
"Bringing you with us is like a death wish" she said and raised an eyebrow at her.
"So let me get this straight" Esselle said and everyone looked at her "You're going back to where it all began for me the site of my accident and you're not taking me with you?" she asked.
Daniel gave a single nod "yes" he said.
"I'm not letting you leave without me!" she said.
"Esselle I know it seems unfair now but its for your own good" Trevor said.
Esselle threw her arms up. "You're not leaving without me!" she said.
"Alright that's it!" Daniel said. He walked right over to Esselle and threw her over his shoulders. "Let's go Essie" he said.
"Daniel put me down!" she shrieked.
"Where are you taking here?!" Jasmine said frantically following her brother.
"Control him somebody please!" Esselle said.
"Somewhere I know she won't move" Daniel said turning the corner in the long hallway. These hallways in the main part of the building were different looking. They reminded Esselle of the movie Gone with the Wind and how Scarlet O'Hara's house looked. The beautiful dark cherry wood it looked like a castle.
"Daniel so help me if you don't put me down I'll-!" Esselle hollered and he rolled his eyes "Ya, ya, ya, you'll kill me never forgive me blah blah blah" he said and yanked open the closet

door.

"Now so help me God Ess you better stay put" he said. Esselle got on her feet and he shoved her in.

"Daniel!" she said and he shut the door locking it.

Her eyes widened and she looked at him through the side glass. He pointed a finger at her.

"Don't move' he said and looked back at everyone else behind him. "let's go" he said quickly and they ran.

"Daniel!" Esselle shouted and pounded on the door. "Daniel you narcissistic bastard let me out of here!" she shouted and kicked hard at the door with her heels.

"Urghh!" Esselle grunted as she beat at the door until her hands became bloody. She stomped hard on the ground and looked around the closet. There was no way out. Esselle slid down against the wall hitting the ground with a thump. She ran her fingers through her hair and the got knotted in her curls. She looked up and saw something behind a metal rack. She rose to her feet and stepped on top of a box. Her face lit up. There was a vent behind the metal rack. Esselle with all her strength grabbed hold of the metal bars of the rack and yanked it back. With a shattering noise it fell to the floor. Esselle hooked her fingers within the lines of the vent and yanked it right off tossing it on the floor. With wide eyes she looked down. She didn't know she had that kind of strength. Esselle with her big heel stepped on the nearest box to give her a boost. She wiggled her self through the vent and began to crawl.

"Just wait" she said "When I get my hands on him it'll be around his throat"

Esselle turned a few corners when she realized she had no idea where she was going then she heard a noise. A creaking noise. She felt her body give out below her and she screamed. Esselle fell right through the vent and landed in something soft. She frantically moved around and got to her feet. She landed on a bed in the infirmary. Esselle looked over and saw Margaret the nurse with wide eyes.

Esselle gave a funny smile "Hi" she said "Bye!' And she ran out.

****

Esselle had hailed a cab and she was driving down the highway. It was no surprise to Esselle when she had a weird feeling in her gut. Like her stomach was turning. She felt anxious and nervous. Her palms were sweaty and in the back of the yellow taxi cab she struggled to stay calm.

'Stop" she told the taxi driver. He made a face and looked back at her. He was Arabic Esselle could tell.

She widened her eyes "I'm serious pull over right over there" she said.

"Well alright" he said and he had a strong accent. Esselle slipped him a 50 and jumped right out of the taxi and watch him drive away. Esselle swung her leg over the very short cement wall and then the other. She jumped and landed a few feet in the dirt. It was a breezy summer night and Esselle felt at peace when the wind hit her.

"Would you keep up Jas!" She heard Daniel say.

"You do this in heels!" she snapped.

Esselle felt her stomach turn and she jogged off in that direction.

"I for one would not get in heels" Trevor said "Well at least unless you paid me"

"No one wants to see you in heels Trevor" Daniel said and she could see his flashlight light.

"Oh I don't know I think it might be interesting" Esselle said and all eyes turned to her so quickly she could hear their necks crack.

"Ess" Daniel said. "How in the-"

"I climbed through the vent!" Esselle snapped. Daniel rolled his eyes.

"Remind me next time to *nail* your feet to the ground" he said. "God is there no way keeping you put?" he asked.

Esselle rolled her eyes and grabbed the flashlight Jasmine held out to her.

"What did you guys find out so far?" Esselle asked.

"Well we figured out there really was no fire" Trevor said and Esselle approached the tree he was by.

"How can you tell?" she asked.

"Well first off all of these trees look fine" Dawn said "Second even though it was 28 years ago there would still be signs of burning on all of the other surrounding trees"

Esselle nodded "Nice" she said.

"No not nice" Daniel said and Esselle could hear the crunching noise the leaves made when he walked over. His hair looked darker at night. if it was possible.

"I told you to stay at headquarters and you didn't listen to me" he said.

Esselle's jaw dropped "I didn't listen to you?" she said.
"Oh God that's not good" Jasmine muttered.
Dawn gave her a stupid look "No duh!" she snapped in a high whisper.
"We'll just be..." Trevor said backing up
"Over there" Dawn said and they disappeared in a snap.
"No, you didn't listen to me. Essie when I tell you something its not to leave you out of all of the fun because trust me this isn't fun. Its to keep you safe! You have no experience in the field at all! Your case isn't like any other. Whoever did what they did to you 28 years ago is still after you and can be waiting anywhere at any moment!" he said "You just don't understand"
"I don't understand? Daniel you locked me in closet and i don't understand! This is my case this happened to *me* ! not *you* ! me!" Esselle snapped."You won't even let me help! I just want to find out what happened!"
"You don't think I want the same thing?" he said growing closer. "Ess I'm trying to protect you but your making it harder than it is!"
"Why go through all this trouble to help me! Why protect me? I'm no one special!" she snapped.
"You know Ess its pretty damn obvious!" he shouted back and Esselle sucked in her breath "I don't know maybe we need to get your eyes checked your eyes check or whatever the case maybe because I have just about been bending over backwards for you and you still aren't getting the hint!" he said.
What hint? She felt like screaming back. But then everything around them fell silent. Daniel took in a deep breath and ran his fingers through his hair.

He was saying Esselle wasn't getting the hint but wasn't he getting the hint? All this not getting left behind nonsense Esselle was creating her mind was just an awful excuse to hide the fact that in all reality she just wanted to be near Daniel. But she'd never ever in a million years say that out loud.

"I'm trying" Daniel began and stopped mid sentence. He sighed "I'm trying to well by you Ess. But you're not making it easy at all" he said.

"Well what do you expect me to do? Sit back and watch like a five year old?" she said.

"Oh my god" he said rolling his head back "Nobody said you had to do that Essie! You decided that all on your own! All I'm asking is that you compromise a little!" he said.

"Asking me to compromise is like asking you to stop being so damn arrogant!" Esselle snapped. Daniel rolled his eyes and looked off back to where the highway was. His eyebrows pressed together

"Don't you understand I don't want to sit around while you do everything! You say I have no experience well how I am supposed to learn if you aren't giving me the chance too?" she said.

Daniel wasn't listen. He was concentrating on something he saw in the distance while Esselle continued to rant.

"I for one don't have the slightest clue as to what has happened and I-!" she looked at him. Her blood began to boil as she stomped over to him.

"And you're not even listening to me!" she said. he turned his face to hr but didn't remove his eyes from the highway.

"What are you looking at!" she snapped. Esselle looked up and tilted her head. It looked like silver reflecting in the light.

"What is that?" Esselle asked. Daniel gently shook his head.
"I don't know" he said. He narrowed his eyes "It looks like a-" he said and his eyes widened.
"Ess move!" he shouted and the silver went flying. With all his strength he pushed Esselle to the floor. There was an exploding sound and Esselle screamed covering her ears.
"Shh, I'm right here" Daniel said into her ear "Don't open your eyes keep them shut Ess, please keep them shut" he said and Esselle did so. Daniel was on top of her and with everything Esselle had she tried blocking out the chaos going on around her. Esselle turned over and opened her eyes. She was looking Daniel in the eye and she could see the light of the fire reflect in the blue of his eyes. They were both breathing heavily when the sounds of chaos stopped. Esselle suddenly felt hot as the fire spread.
"Daniel!" she heard Jasmine scream
"Esselle!" Dawn screamed and Esselle could hear their footsteps growing closer.
Esselle was startled and didn't want to move.
"thank you" Esselle chocked out "For saving my life"
Daniel didn't laugh. Still wide eyed he said "Ya well i tend to do that a lot now don't I"
"Oh thank god Daniel!" Jasmine said and Esselle could hear them running over.
"Esselle are you alright?" Dawn shouted.
Esselle swallowed hard and Daniel snapped out of his daze. Daniel rolled over to his side and Esselle got unto her elbows.
"Daniel!" Jasmine said and fell to her knees text to him. "Are you alright?" she asked taking his face in her hands. he gently place his hand on wrist looking off into an oblivion and nodded.

"Ya Jas I'm fine" he said.

"Esselle" Dawn said.

"Here" Trevor said and helped her up.

"Are you alright? We heard the bomb go off and saw the flames so we ran" Dawn said.

"Esselle are you alright?" Jasmine asked.

Esselle swallowed hard and nodded "I'm fine" she said and looked at Daniel.

"Are you alright?" he asked and she nodded.

"Are you?' she asked and something flickered in his eyes.

"Ask me again later" he said. He looked up to the highway.

"Let's go before the cops get here. Don't want to cause a scene" Daniel said starting for the way back.

Esselle hugged herself. Today was a hard day.

"You deliberately disobeyed me!" Charlotte said "I told you specifically I'd send for warriors to explore the grounds! Not you! You are still in training Daniel!"

"Ok in all fairness I kick ass in training" he said with his bloody towel in his hand. Esselle was sitting at the edge of the table in office with an ice pack to her head.

"Don't you even dare try it Daniel! You are not going to charm your way out of this one not this time!" Charlotte said. Despite being angry her accent grew stronger and her voice was still soft but stern.

"not only did you put your life in danger by risking this assignment by going against my orders you brought Jasmine along!" she ranted. Jasmine looked away. "Jasmine is only 16 Daniel! She could have gotten hurt! Do you have no idea the kind of impact the risks your taking can have! And dragging Trevor and Dawn along with you?" she said.

"In all fairness Charlotte we all went willingly. We weren't forced" Dawn said.

Charlotte stood up straight "Well then it was a very foolish move. On all of your behalves. "I'm sorry but that is it with all of your recklessness this past month. I'm passive you know that yer you took advantage not anymore. You are all even you Dawn" she said narrowing her eyes at her "Are on probation"

"But Char-!" Daniel began.

"And!" She said overpowering his voice "You are all officially off of this case"

"Charlotte please!" Jasmine begged.

"You are *not* to leave this building under any circumstances do you understand me?" Charlotte asks.

"Yes" they say in unison. They reminded Esselle of a bunch of bad kids.

"You are to come here to work then back to your assigned apartments or bedrooms and that is it! Understood?" she said.

"Yes" they said again. Charlotte nodded.

'Good" and she examined all their faces. She sighed "Now I'm sorry I had to do this but it is for your own protection" and with that she left.

"What are we going to do now Dan?" Jasmine asked. Daniel tossed his bloody towel on to the table.

"Well for one we're definitely getting back on this case. Second" he said and looked at Trevor

"We have to get back to that site" he said.

"Daniel you heard her we're on probation!" he said.

"Like that ever stopped us before" Dawn said.

"I don't know Charlotte really wasn't kidding this time" Jasmine chimed in "We're screwed"

Daniel marched towards the door. "Right" he teased.

"But Daniel I don't think we should go back there" Esselle said.

He turned around on his heels. His eyebrows were raised and his eyes were wide.

'We?" he said and Esselle nodded.

he opened his mouth but he was at a loss for words. He looked around then finally took Esselle by the elbow and lead her out of the room. They walked down the hallway and turned the corner. The very last door to the last he opened and shut behind him.

'Ok we?" he said. "Did you not just see what happened today?" he asked.

"I'm not blind!" Esselle said. She looked around. They were in a room with super high ceilings and walls covered with shelves of books. They must have been in the library in fact they were. There were a few steps you'd walk up and in the center of that little area was a desk. Esselle walked up the stairs and looked up to marvel at the intricacy of everything in the room. The ceiling was carved covered in murals of angels and heaven. There were arcs in the ceiling painted in gold.

"And what makes you think you're coming with us again?" he asked and Esselle turned her head to look at him.

"Because if you don't I'll just go anyway. Without you when

something worse can happen" she said. he brought his hands up clearly infuriated ready to break something then he just ran his finger tips through his hair and they stood there.

"You are such a pain you know that?" he asked.

Esselle took a step down "Oh I am a pain?" she asked and he nodded.

"Yes you are a major one! There is no way in hell I'm letting you go anywhere with us again! You almost got yourself killed!" he said.

"You can't tell me what to do!" Esselle said.

He snorted "Oh yes I can! I'm in charge of you and your training whether you like it or not Essie" he said and approached the door. Esselle took another step down.

"Hey wait a second I'm talking to you!" she said and he continued to walk across the library to the exit. "Daniel!" she said.

"What!" he snapped.

"Listen to me when I'm talking to you!" she shouted with her hands everywhere. Daniel opened his mouth to speak but just looked away. Instead he looked at her for a moment and just walked towards her. Esselle felt the adrenaline running and her heart the beat she could feel all the way in her stomach. But Daniel starred at her hard as he approached her which made her stomach turn in every which way. When Daniel was in front of her his eyes were so blue she noticed they turned almost violet. They were dark and intense. She swallowed hard awaiting whatever long lecture was coming at her. Instead he took his hands and put them on her waist and squeezed until she was lifted from the ground. She gasped and grabbed his wrist. He

Somewhere in Time- trilogy part 2

walked up the stairs and sat her on the edge of the desk. "Now if I were you I'd just shut up" he said and put his hand on the back of her neck "And just let me kiss you" he said. Esselle grabbed the collar of his shirt and yanked him down pressing her mouth to his so much all it did was hurt for a while and give Esselle a headache with the sound of clattering teeth. He parted her mouth with his and Esselle ran her fingers through his hair. She had always wanted to do that. Esselle had never really kissed anyone but Mardrin. Unless her first kiss in summer camp when she was 13 with some kid she couldn't even remember his name. Daniel ran his hand up her back and eventually his fingers got nodded in her hair. Esselle put her hands on his back bringing him closer. Esselle could feel her heart beat everywhere. It made her sick and happy and dizzy with giddiness. Daniel grabbed Esselle's leg and her heart raced. Esselle wondered if it were wrong. If she was in anyway betraying what she felt for Mardrin. And then it hit her. Esselle quite frankly didn't care. So she wrapped her legs around his waste as he kissed her. Daniel placed his hand on the small of her back bringing her closer. Esselle could feel his heart racing. Daniel reached behind him and with his hand and one swipe threw everything on the desk on the floor clearing it. Esselle slowly moved back. Daniel planted his hand on the desk to keep his balance as he was sure to topple over. Esselle decided kissing Daniel was sweet. She absorbed the scent of him. Like her favorite male cologne. She always loved when a man smelled like that. Especially since every male member of her family always smelled nice. Daniel gently placed Esselle's head on the desk but Esselle got on her elbows. Esselle hard forgotten to breath so she gasped for air. Daniel

kissed her collar bone and her neck then her cheek bone then kissed her lips again. This time Esselle rested her head on the desk and she felt his radiant warmth all over her. Daniel's hands traced every curve of her body then got tangled in her wild hair again. Esselle had a grip tight on his shoulders because she was sure to faint. She had never been kissed that way before. Ever. The intensity of it all made her mind spin. Daniel's hair was thick and black and straight and she loved the silky feel of it through her fingers when her hands got knotted and she tugged. A sound emerged deep in his throat and Esselle's heart jumped. Esselle felt him bight her lip, and hard so hard she could taste blood but for some crazy reason she didn't mind and did the same.
"Daniel?Esselle?" she heard someone call. Esselle gently shrieked gasping for air when she pulled away.
"Who's that" Esselle asked.
Daniel made an annoyed face "My dear little sister" he said and let go of her. Esselle bit the inside of her cheek when Daniel walked over to the door. She reached down to grab her sweater off the floor. She hadn't noticed it got yanked off.
"There you are I've been looking for you" Jasmine said stepping into the doorway. "We got worried you guys were fighting pretty bad"
Daniel stopped next to his sister in the doorway. "Its nothing" he said and walked out.
Jasmine looked at Esselle. She quickly straightened out her hair. Jasmine made a face "Gees you look like a mess" she said and Esselle laughed a bit nervously.
"Ya, bad argument" she said and Jasmine nodded.
"Is your lip bleeding?" Jasmine asked. Esselle's hand instantly

went to her mouth.

"No" Esselle said and ran out.

"You deliberately disobeyed me!" Charlotte said "I told you specifically I'd send for warriors to explore the grounds! Not you! You are still in training Daniel!"

"Ok in all fairness I kick ass in training" he said with his bloody towel in his hand. Esselle was sitting at the edge of the table in office with an ice pack to her head.

"Don't you even dare try it Daniel! You are not going to charm your way out of this one not this time!" Charlotte said. Despite being angry her accent grew stronger and her voice was still soft but stern.

"not only did you put your life in danger by risking this assignment by going against my orders you brought Jasmine along!" she ranted. Jasmine looked away. "Jasmine is only 16 Daniel! She could have gotten hurt! Do you have no idea the kind of impact the risks your taking can have! And dragging Trevor and Dawn along with you?" she said.

"In all fairness Charlotte we all went willingly. We weren't forced" Dawn said.

Charlotte stood up straight "Well then it was a very foolish move. On all of your behalves. "I'm sorry but that is it with all of your recklessness this past month. I'm passive you know that yer you took advantage not anymore. You are all even you Dawn" she said narrowing her eyes at her "Are on probation"

"But Char-!" Daniel began.

"And!" She said overpowering his voice "You are all officially off of this case"

"Charlotte please!" Jasmine begged.

"You are *not* to leave this building under any circumstances do you understand me?" Charlotte asks.

"Yes" they say in unison. They reminded Esselle of a bunch of bad kids.

"You are to come here to work then back to your assigned apartments or bedrooms and that is it! Understood?" she said.

"Yes" they said again. Charlotte nodded.

'Good" and she examined all their faces. She sighed "Now I'm sorry I had to do this but it is for your own protection" and with that she left.

"What are we going to do now Dan?" Jasmine asked. Daniel tossed his bloody towel on to the table.

"Well for one we're definitely getting back on this case. Second" he said and looked at Trevor

"We have to get back to that site" he said.

"Daniel you heard her we're on probation!" he said.

"Like that ever stopped us before" Dawn said.

"I don't know Charlotte really wasn't kidding this time" Jasmine chimed in "We're screwed"

Daniel marched towards the door. "Right" he teased.

"But Daniel I don't think we should go back there" Esselle said. He turned around on his heels. His eyebrows were raised and his eyes were wide.

'We?" he said and Esselle nodded.

he opened his mouth but he was at a loss for words. He looked around then finally took Esselle by the elbow and lead her out of the room. They walked down the hallway and turned the corner. The very last door to the last he opened and shut behind him.

'Ok we?" he said. "Did you not just see what happened today?" he asked.

"I'm not blind!" Esselle said. She looked around. They were in a room with super high ceilings and walls covered with shelves of books. They must have been in the library in fact they were. There were a few steps you'd walk up and in the center of that little area was a desk. Esselle walked up the stairs and looked up to marvel at the intricacy of everything in the room. The ceiling was carved covered in murals of angels and heaven. There were arcs in the ceiling painted in gold.

"And what makes you think you're coming with us again?" he asked and Esselle turned her head to look at him.

"Because if you don't I'll just go anyway. Without you when something worse can happen" she said. he brought his hands up clearly infuriated ready to break something then he just ran his finger tips through his hair and they stood there.

"You are such a pain you know that?" he asked.

Esselle took a step down "Oh I am a pain?" she asked and he nodded.

"Yes you are a major one! There is no way in hell I'm letting you go anywhere with us again! You almost got yourself killed!" he said.

"You can't tell me what to do!" Esselle said.

He snorted "Oh yes I can! I'm in charge of you and your training whether you like it or not Essie" he said and approached the door. Esselle took another step down.

"Hey wait a second I'm talking to you!" she said and he continued to walk across the library to the exit. "Daniel!" she said.

"What!" he snapped.

"Listen to me when I'm talking to you!" she shouted with her hands everywhere. Daniel opened his mouth to speak but just looked away. Instead he looked at her for a moment and just walked towards her. Esselle felt the adrenaline running and her heart the beat she could feel all the way in her stomach. But Daniel starred at her hard as he approached her which made her stomach turn in every which way. When Daniel was in front of her his eyes were so blue she noticed they turned almost violet. They were dark and intense. She swallowed hard awaiting whatever long lecture was coming at her. Instead he took his hands and put them on her waist and squeezed until she was lifted from the ground. She gasped and grabbed his wrist. He walked up the stairs and sat her on the edge of the desk.

"Now if I were you I'd just shut up" he said and put his hand on the back of her neck "And just let me kiss you" he said. Esselle grabbed the collar of his shirt and yanked him down pressing her

Somewhere in Time- trilogy part 2

mouth to his so much all it did was hurt for a while and give Esselle a headache with the sound of clattering teeth. He parted her mouth with his and Esselle ran her fingers through his hair. She had always wanted to do that. Esselle had never really kissed anyone but Mardrin. Unless her first kiss in summer camp when she was 13 with some kid she couldn't even remember his name. Daniel ran his hand up her back and eventually his fingers got nodded in her hair. Esselle put her hands on his back bringing him closer. Esselle could feel her heart beat everywhere. It made her sick and happy and dizzy with giddiness. Daniel grabbed Esselle's leg and her heart raced. Esselle wondered if it were wrong. If she was in anyway betraying what she felt for Mardrin. And then it hit her. Esselle quite frankly didn't care. So she wrapped her legs around his waste as he kissed her. Daniel placed his hand on the small of her back bringing her closer. Esselle could feel his heart racing. Daniel reached behind him and with his hand and one swipe threw everything on the desk on the floor clearing it. Esselle slowly moved back. Daniel planted his hand on the desk to keep his balance as he was sure to topple over. Esselle decided kissing Daniel was sweet. She absorbed the scent of him. Like her favorite male cologne. She always loved when a man smelled like that. Especially since every male member of her family always smelled nice. Daniel gently placed Esselle's head on the desk but Esselle got on her elbows. Esselle hard forgotten to breath so she gasped for air. Daniel kissed her collar bone and her neck then her cheek bone then kissed her lips again. This time Esselle rested her head on the desk and she felt his radiant warmth all over her. Daniel's hands traced every curve of her body then got tangled in her wild hair

Somewhere in Time- trilogy part 2

again. Esselle had a grip tight on his shoulders because she was sure to faint. She had never been kissed that way before. Ever. The intensity of it all made her mind spin. Daniel's hair was thick and black and straight and she loved the silky feel of it through her fingers when her hands got knotted and she tugged. A sound emerged deep in his throat and Esselle's heart jumped. Esselle felt him bight her lip, and hard so hard she could taste blood but for some crazy reason she didn't mind and did the same.
"Daniel?Esselle?" she heard someone call. Esselle gently shrieked gasping for air when she pulled away.
"Who's that" Esselle asked.
Daniel made an annoyed face "My dear little sister" he said and let go of her. Esselle bit the inside of her cheek when Daniel walked over to the door. She reached down to grab her sweater off the floor. She hadn't noticed it got yanked off.
"There you are I've been looking for you" Jasmine said stepping into the doorway. "We got worried you guys were fighting pretty bad"
Daniel stopped next to his sister in the doorway. "Its nothing" he said and walked out.
Jasmine looked at Esselle. She quickly straightened out her hair. Jasmine made a face "Gees you look like a mess" she said and Esselle laughed a bit nervously.
"Ya, bad argument" she said and Jasmine nodded.
"Is your lip bleeding?" Jasmine asked. Esselle's hand instantly went to her mouth.
"No" Esselle said and ran out.

Somewhere in Time- trilogy part 2

"So tell me girl if we touched you get this kind rush baby say yayayaya if you don't wanna take it slow and you just wanna take me home then baby say yayaya and let me kiss you!" Esselle sang into her water bottle. She was giggling standing on top of a mahogany chair in the dance room. She felt as if she were ten again and on the ultimate sugar high. She whipped her hair back and forth and laughed. All day today and yesterday Esselle was giddy as an elf and happy as a kid on Christmas morning. She felt as if she were floating on cloud 9. She was in the dance room with the screen on listening to One Direction. They had been her favorite band when she was a kid. It was nice listening to old music. She felt at home almost. The music was blasting so loud it rang in her ears but she loved it and every part of it. Esselle had black yoga pants on and when of those shirts Dawn always wore with no stomach that basically looked like a bra. She borrowed it for the day.

the same time burning off all the energy she had.

"What re you doing?" Jasmine asked coming in. Essell her hand and pulled her out until the floor.

"So tell me girl if we touched you get this kind rush ba yayayaya if you don't wanna take it slow and you just v me home then baby say yayaya and let me kiss you!" E completely and utterly awful and so out of pitch. Then jumped and twirled gliding around.

Dawn came in laughing"Having a concert without me said. Bobbing her head of wild curls Esselle skipped o humming and took her hands.

"So tell me girl if we touched you get this kind rush ba yayayaya if you don't wanna take it slow and you just v me home then baby say yayaya and let me kiss you!" F hummed and climbed unto her chair again.

She shook her head of locks and laughed.

"And if you you want me too so make a move!" Esselle her water bottle.

"We just need to get you a mic and you can sing for us said.

Making a funny face Esselle swung her hips back and shut her eyes. Her head looked like it was dangling ar her eyes were shut while she just enjoyed the sound o The door opened and Esselle ignored it. The sing ende another one went on.

"Uw!" Esselle said "I like this one! Maybe its the way Straight into my heart and stole it!" She sang with wid

Somewhere in Time- trilogy part 2

a head back facing the ceiling. She heard laughing. She shut her eyes and turned on her chair bobbing her head and dancing. "And we danced all night to the best song ever!" she said and jumped up and down. "Ever heard of the fist pump?" she asked. When Esselle opened her eyes Daniel was leaning against the wall with crossed arms cracking up and Dawn and Jasmine were sitting on the floor with their hands over the stomachs in tears with red faces. They had a case of hysterical giggles.

Esselle's jaw dropped. But she shrugged and continued with her singing.

"I think it went oh oh oh i think it went ya ya ya ya i think it goes ohhh!" she said. Dawn and Jasmine crawled to their feet and it was Dawn who struggled to speak first.

"I need to pee" she said and threw herself out the door. Jasmine went after her. "Wait for me! I can't go too fast! I'll pee my pants!" she said and disappeared.

"You seem awfully happy today" Daniel said. The song ended and another came on.

"Ah!" Esselle shrieked. "Last Friday night ya we danced on table tops and we took too many shots last Friday night!" She sang and twirled. Daniel laughed again.

"Are you high or something?" he asked looking up at her.

"I'm high on life!" she said flinging her arms open. She slipped and laughed when she fell and Daniel grabbed her. She began to giggle hysterically.

"Ok maybe you're drunk" Daniel said but he was still laughing.

"Nope!" Esselle said shaking her head. Daniel keeping one arm around her reached over and shut off the screen with the remote.

"What are you smiling about?" Esselle asked. He just shook his head.

"Come on I'm serious!' she said and punched his shoulder. he just laughed and shook his head.

Esselle was smiling just naturally smiling. Something she had not done in a while.

"Your a real pain in the ass you know that?" she asked. He laughed and pushed the hair away from her face.

"Oh no I know" he said."So I was wondering when you might want to start your training"

"My training?" Esselle asked.

He made a face and nodded "of course your training. Your one of us remember. All of us receive training" he said

"Well then anytime is fine on one condition" she said and wrapped her arms around his neck.

"What's that?" he asked.

"You have to be the one to train me" she said and he laughed.

"Essie" he said and touched her nose with his "I called dibs on you a long time ago" he said.

Esselle smile "So what? I'm just something you can call dibs on? Like the last cupcake?" she asked.

He smiled against her ear when he said "If you were a cupcake I'd choose you first" he said and Esselle laughed.

"Oh how romantic" she teased and he looked at her no longer smiling. Esselle swallowed hard. That probably wasn't the wisest thing to say. Esselle didn't feel so uncomfortable when he took her face in his hand.

"You know you're very slowly working at my will power with those eyes. I'm wearing away" he said.

"Well then don't look at them then" Esselle said and he laughed a bit.

"I just can't help it. I could stare at you all day" he said.

"Oh its cute when a guy does it but when a girl does it, its consider odd" she said rolling her eyes. He laughed and then he kissed her. Esselle felt the jittery feeling coming on again. Ok so sure she wasn't sure what it all meant she didn't know where he and she stood but who cared. Right? SO then Esselle kissed him back and for a moment everything in the world seemed alright and ok. She didn't feel confused or lost or helpless or scared. She felt warm and happy and safe. Safe. Esselle liked the word. She hadn't felt that way in a long time especially with everything going on around her she felt better knowing she had an escape. Then Daniel pulled away and Esselle sighed. It was over.

"Come on" he said lacing his fingers with her he smiled "I want to start on your training"

Esselle laughed a bit "The one time we don't get interrupted you decide to cut it short" she teased.

He laughed and took her chin in his hand "Don't worry" he said and kissed her lightly "We'll have time to practice that too"

Somewhere in Time- trilogy part 2

Somewhere in Time- trilogy part 2

"Disengage" Daniel said and Esselle pulled back.
"Good" he said "Strike" he said and with Esselle's long rod she struck him. He nodded "Good, now try aim and lock" he said. Esselle let out a deep breath. She struck him again twisted her rod and locked it with his yanking him close. He smiled "I'm doing such a great job with you" he said.
"Hey I'm the one doing all of the work!" Esselle said.
He laughed "That's right. You're doing well" he said. Daniel flicked his wrists and Esselle stumbled back losing her balance. His rod swiveled in the air and knocked hers right out of her hands and sent it flying. Daniel caught it and laughed.
"hey give that back!" she said.
He shrugged "Come and get it" he said and turned and ran. Daniel had been training Esselle all weak. Esselle was tired, sweaty, warn out, and yet she never felt more alive holding a weapon in her hand and fighting. Daniel said it was in her blood and now Esselle was starting to believe it.
"Danny!" Esselle said. Daniel flew like nothing across the training room and climbed a latter that lead to long metal rods running across the room with a net below. You were supposed to walk on the metal rods and not loose your balance. He began to glide across the rods. Esselle looked up and stood near the rope.
"Daniel Carter!" she shouted up. He looked down and smiled.
"Essie Elunas!" he shouted back. Esselle stomped hard on the ground.
"Would you stop teasing me and just give me my rod already!" she shouted back.
"Come and catch me first" he said and continued to walk over to

the other side. Esselle sighed and looked around. Something caught her eye as she approached the weapons wall. She jogged over and yanked off the wall what look like a curvy half blade half bat. She walked over and flung it like a boomerang.

It made clank sound when it hit the metal rod. The metal rod began to fumble and eventually fell taking Daniel with it.

"Ha!" Esselle said victoriously.

"Not ha" she heard and looked over. She saw Daniel standing on the other side "Ok first off that was messed up" he said and hopped off the latter. Esselle crossed her arms. "Second ouch that hurt that you tried killing me and third" he said walking over to her. "I already made it to the other side"

"Can I have my rod back?" Esselle asked reaching for it and Daniel put it behind him.

"You're lucky Klaus isn't in charge of training anymore" he said.

"I bet he didn't take people's rods" she said and reached behind him. He brought the rods unto his shoulders.

"No, he actually gave you two" he said.

Esselle stopped "Really?" she asked and he nodded.

"He gave you two but had them tied to your arms and blindfolded you. See at least I'm nice and give you the pleasure of looking at me while you fight" he said.

"Oh how kind of you" she teased

He shrugged "I'm a good guy just don't bother me on days that end in the suffix -day" he said. Esselle thought for a moment.

"All days of the week end in the suffix -day" she said and he smiled.

"Exactly"

"Can I get my rod back?" she asked extending his hand.

Somewhere in Time- trilogy part 2

"No" he said.

Her eyes widened "Come on Danny I want to finish already!" she said.

"Tsk, tsk, tsk" he said shaking his head. "Someone's grouchy today" he said walking past her.

She ran her fingers through her hair. "Ya well training kind of sucks" He looked back at her and started laughing.

"what are you laughing at?' she asked and reached for the rods again.

"You are just so easy to pick on" he said.

She frowned "Am not"

"Don't feel too bad" he said lifting her face by her chin "Sometimes Jasmine cries"

Esselle started to laugh and so did her. "That's mean!" she said and punched his shoulder.

"No whats mean is when she gets her tears all over the floor doesn't even clean them up and when I walk by I slip and bust my ass" he said and Esselle laughed harder.

"If jasmine heard you-" Esselle said.

Daniel made a face "She wouldn't do anything because she knows its true. Actually I'm lying she'd bust out laughing herself." he said.

Still laughing Esselle jumped to try and grab her rod back. "Oh! I almost had it!" she said.

Daniel laughed and grew closer to her face. The door opened and a hysterical Jasmine and Dawn came pouring in. Esselle blew air out of her mouth when she looked over. Daniel made an unpleasant sound and when Esselle looked up she realized he was trying not to laugh. Daniel walked over and put his and

Esselle's rods on a table against the wall.

"What are you laughing at?" Esselle asked.

Jasmine took in a deep breath "Dawn just pranked Trevor" she said.

Dawn smiled "Yup! I put ink inside his water bottle and when he went to drink and got all over his shirt!" she said. The door opened and Trevor covered in black ink and a straight face came waltzing in. Esselle broke out into giggles and smacked her hand over her mouth.

"Daniel" he said and Jasmine and Dawn tried to contain their composure.

Daniel was doing something at the table and he turned the table. "The E.A.I's are here. They want to speak to you" he said. He nodded and went back to what he was doing.

"Alright I'm coming" he sad.

Esselle looked at Trevor "So" Esselle said "You have a little something" she said and gestured to her face.

Trevor nodded "Ya" he said and looked at Dawn "I know" he said and Dawn started to laugh again.

Jasmine sighed "Those guys are back again?" she whispered.

Dawn's face fell serious and Trevor nodded.

Esselle frowned but when she opened her mouth to speak Daniel was already behind her.

"I'll see you guys later" he said nodded at them.

Jasmine licked her lips dry and Dawn swallowed hard. Esselle crossed her arms and looked at Daniel.

"As for you" he said and Esselle looked at him "We'll pick up tomorrow alright?"

Esselle nodded. he placed his hand on her shoulder and kissed

Somewhere in Time- trilogy part 2

her cheek.

Dawn whistled and Esselle's mouth twisted. For a moment his hands locked with hers before he pulled away and left the room. "I'm so glad you've been filling me in!" Dawn said once Daniel had gone.

"What?" Esselle said but she couldn't help but smile.

Dawn made a face and she must have gotten a hair cut because her pixie do looked perfect. Esselle felt something in her fingertips. She looked down and it was a paper. She squeezed her hands shut tight and looked at Jasmine when she spoke.

"Well whatever. I hope you and my brother dearest can go on a double date with Trevor and I" Jasmine said as she slid on to a stool and crossed her legs.

Esselle's eyes widened "Who wait a second I-" she began but Dawn cut her off with a giggle.

"I can totally see them as one of those couples right?' she said. Jasmine began to nod frantically and laugh.

"Yes! That are like always bickering and end up kissing in the end!" Jasmine said.

"Yes!' Dawn said and they gave each other a high five.

"Hold on!" Esselle said and with smiles they looked at her "Who said anything about his together?" Esselle asked.

Dawn made a face "Oh honey he still hasn't asked you yet?" she said and Jasmine flew her hand over her mouth.

"Asked me what?" Esselle said.

"Nothing you know Dawn is mentally unstable" Jasmine said. Esselle rolled her eyes and walked out of the room. When she shut the door she leaned against the wall and looked down either side of the hallway. She took the paper in her hands and unfolded it.

Essie,

Meet me on the rooftop at midnight,

we can see the stars

-Danny

Esselle smiled and covered her mouth with the paper before she went skipping down the hallway.

Esselle pulled the latch to open up the metal door that lead outside. Maybe it wasn't a good idea for Esselle to wear pumps. Then again...it would have completely ruined the essence of her outfit. Dark blue jeans, black pumps, and a sapphire blue shirt. Esselle pushed open the door and climbed out. It was exactly midnight and she hadn't seen Daniel. She walked around and saw Daniel with his elbows on the ledge just looking over the New York City skyline. For once he wasn't wearing all black. His shirt wasn't black this time it was white. Other than that he was pretty much in black again. For the first time Esselle noticed he looked lost in his own little world peaceful and tranquil. Esselle could see fireflies flying around. When Esselle was younger that always in her mind meant Summer was officially here. When Esselle would go to visit her cousin in Ridgewood in Queens they use to catch fireflies and watch them walk on their fingers and then set them free again.

"Hi" Esselle said. Daniel looked back and when he noticed it was her he smiled.

"You're very prompt Essie" he said. Esselle stood with her back to the edge and her hands gripping the bar next to him.

"It runs in the family" she said. "So what do you do here?" she asked.

He took in a deep breath and stood up straight "This is my sanctuary. Kind of like a place to get away and think. An escape from everyone and everything in the world. And Jasmine" he said and Esselle laughed a bit.

Esselle frowned when she saw his right hand.

"What happened to your hand?" she asked.

"Sss" he hissed and shoved his hand in his pocket "Uh, ya that" Daniel said. Esselle reached over taking her hand in his. It was wrapped up in white gauze.

"It was just an accident it was nothing" he said.

"Well what happened tell me" Esselle said.

"Ess" he said and pushed the hair from her face. "I'm fine" Esselle made a face and looked behind her. "Its beautiful up here" she said and swung her legs back in forth when she sat gate.

"Now you know why I come here" he said.

"Why did you ask me to come up here?" she asked.

Daniel looked at her and then just laughed. And then he smiled. Esselle loved it when he smiled. Just naturally and happily.

"Because Essie" he said "I wanted to share this view with you"
"Then that was very sweet of you" she said.
Daniel shrugged "I have my days"
"Daniel when you were younger" Esselle began "What did you want to do with your life? You know before everything" she asked.
Daniel sighed and gripped the bar "Well" he said "I wanted to be an architect"
Esselle smiled. Secretly she had always wanted Mardrin to be an architect. "really?" she asked and he nodded.
"What did you want to be?" he asked.
Esselle straightened out her back with pride "I was going to be a writer"
Daniel laughed "Impressive"
"Yes, well, that dream is long gone" she said.
"Why?" he asked.
Esselle shrugged "Oh well I don't know Daniel maybe because I have a glowing blue tattoo on my arm" she said.
"Correction, its called a mark" he said pointing a finger.
"Point is" Esselle said "That dream got left behind 28 years ago" she said. Esselle shrugged "Its alright though. I have this to concentrate all my time on"
"Doesn't mean you still can't follow your dream Ess" Daniel said and stood next to her looking out into the distance then faced her. "If you love writing as much as you like reading" he teased. Esselle laughed.
"Then there isn't much that should stop you from pursuing your dream" he said.
"Right Daniel because I can just walk up to any publishing

Somewhere in Time- trilogy part 2

company and say I want to be a writer and you're going to publish my stories!" she said. Esselle threw her head back to look at the sky. Every star in the sky seemed to have an extra polished sparkle look. The sky was the darkest shade of blue and the lights from the city lit up the night.

"Look at that star" Esselle said leaning back further. There was a star in the distance that was shining brighter than any other in the sky.

"Where?" Daniel asked.

Esselle tilted her head and leaned further back. She pointed "There" she said. Esselle leaned to far back and slipped letting go of the railing. She shrieked and Daniel instantly grabbed her waist pulling her back in. Esselle began to laugh hysterically when her feet hit the ground.

"Well that was fun" she said. Daniel looked at her with wide eyes as he held her.

"What are you crazy you almost broke your neck!" he said.

Esselle laughed "But I didn't. You caught me"

"Of course I caught you" he said and his fingertips brushed her cheekbone when he pushed her hair from her face. There was that gut wrenching feeling. She could feel her heart literally race and pound in every part of her body. He just had that effect of her. Her veins began to pulse in her fingertips and her toes and everywhere. She felt shivers and the goosebumps surfaced her skin the way waves surface. But he didn't move he just stood there looking at her with those blue eyes of his and it drove Esselle insane.

"Why are you looking at me like that?" she asked. He gently shook his head. Esselle rolled her eyes "If you're going to kiss me get it over with already. The suspense is killing me and quite frankly its irritating" she said and he laughed.

"I'll kiss you" he said "On one condition"

"Oh you have conditions?" Esselle asked and he smiled. "Get out of here!" she said. Daniel took her face in his hands. Esselle wrapped her hand around his neck and kissed him. Esselle didn't odd she just had a lot of questions running around in her mind. Ok first off just a month ago she could not stand this man now its a beautiful summer night on a roof top and she's kissing him. Just two weeks ago this man annoyed the crap out of her. Now odd as it was she felt like she were falling for him and hard. Which made her scared. Terrified. In some odd sick twisted way she felt unfaithful to Mardrin. Esselle felt this kind of loyalty towards him and letting her heart fall into someone's else's hands besides his felt wrong to her. But at the same time Esselle wanted to let go of that part of her life. Despite dreading the thought of letting Mardrin go completely she knew she had to. Did she still love him? Yes but just maybe not in the way Esselle always thought. Esselle wanted to leave her past behind her every part and every aspect. She wanted to find herself here among Daniel's people and find her place in Daniel's world of Invisibles. She belonged there she just hadn't found her place yet. It was warm out and when the breeze hit Esselle shivered. Daniel brought her closer to him and kissed her back. Esselle heard a thump then a vibrating noise. She sighed and buried her face in Daniel's shoulder.

"You know these damn interruptions are really pissing me off" she muttered. She could feel his chest rising and falling. He was laughing. She looked over and it was her phone. It had fallen out of her pocket and her heart stopped when she read the name. It was Mardrin.

"Who's that?" Daniel asked and looked over.

"No one" Esselle said turning his face to look at her.

He raised an eyebrow and looked back down. Esselle felt her stomach turning. She was screwed. Daniel looked at the phone and sighed.

"Ess" he said shaking his head at her. She bit her lip.

He bent down and picked up her phone. "I see he still has you wrapped around his little finger" and he handed her her phone. Esselle held it in her hands.

"Well? Are you going to answer it?" he asked.

"No" Esselle said. She shut her phone off and slipped it in her back pocket.

"Essie" he said.

"Its not what you think I don't even know what he's doing up this late" she said quickly.

"That's not the point. You still don't have him out of your mind" he said walking past her.

"Wait Daniel!" she said grabbing hold of his wrist "Where are you going?"

"To sleep" he said and turned to face her "In case you haven't noticed its late. And your lover is on the phone I figured I'd give you some privacy" he said sarcastically.

"Stop that! Its not like that!" Esselle said but she was screaming. She just sounded desperate. Desperate to convince him otherwise of what he thought.

"Ess" he said and took her face in his hands and he stared down at her hard and the light from the stars made his eyes twinkle.

"I could love you Essie. I could be there for you. I could be your everything. I could be the one you share your hopes and dreams with. I could be the one you cry to and laugh at and love with. I could be your everything Ess. I could love you Esselle in a way that he never could and never will Esselle. Just let him go. Give me the chance to be that for you Esselle that's all I'm asking. I want to be the one to give you the world and wipe away your tears and fight off the bad guys for and punch any smug looking guy that glances at you the wrong way" he said.

Esselle was speechless. She had never thought of it that way. She couldn't manage to get anything out but "That was literally the very first time you ever called me by my awful name" she said.

"That's how you know it just got serious. I actually used your name" he said. Esselle wanted to hear it again. She loved the way he said her name and she could listen to him saying her name forever.

"Don't you have anything to say?" he asked.

"I..." and Esselle trailed off. She hadn't wanted to say anything stupid but the problem was she didn't know what to say. Daniel let go of her and her cheeks began to burn red.

"I see how it is then. All you had to do was say it" he said and turned.

"Daniel" she said.

"I'll see you tomorrow Esselle" he said.

"No! Don't call me that!" Esselle said following him 'Don't call me Esselle" she said and his head turned right around with a snap.

"You're right its highly unprofessional. I'm your trainer obviously nothing more or nothing less to you" he said.

"Daniel" Esselle pleaded.

"Goodnight Ms. Elunas. I'll see you in the training room tomorrow at 8" he said and opened the latch. He jumped through the hole and disappeared. Esselle felt sick. Next time she should just try not being an idiot and actually get the hint. He was trying to say he loved her and Esselle didn't do such a good job saying she loved him back. She had let him leave. Now she was left to wallow in the silence. Alone.

Somewhere in Time- trilogy part 2

Esselle woke up extra early the next morning despite being a sleepless zombie on the way to headquarters. It was very hot out that day. While Esselle approached the Freedom Tower the sun wasn't completely in the sky yet. When Esselle pushed through the training facility doors she heard an awful noise. Like someone was beating the crap out of something. Her eyebrows pressed together and she slid her bag off her shoulder. Esselle pushed back the sliding doors. From the walls hung 100 lb boxing bags lined up across the room. The entire back wall was a glass window and you could see the sun rising. Esselle stepped in and it was hot. Horribly hot as if someone didn't turn the a.c. on. Seriously, its the end of June. Its hot out. Esselle had on her black Capri yoga pants and her black yoga shirt. Then she saw Daniel. Sweating so much his skin was glistening in the sunlight. Esselle begun to feel bad for the punching bag. She has punching at it so hard it was flying all over the place. Esselle bit the inside of her cheek and walked over. He probably didn't hear her come in the noise was loud with him pounding at the thing and everything. He didn't have a shirt on which made Esselle's stomach turn. Ok so Esselle completely pissed him off yesterday she had that much sorted out. But she just had to convince her self it was ok to think he looked pretty damn sexy. Her stomach began to turn again. She was sure to faint where she stood. He didn't have gloves on which made Esselle think his hands must be killing him. His skin looked golden and glistened like glitter in the light. He seemed content on hitting the punching bag so Esselle didn't say anything. Daniel's abdomen was muscular. Like, super gorgeous Tv hottie you would swoon over when you were 13, muscular. Like the angels carved it out themselves. His skin looked soft and tone. Daniel gave one last hard punch. There was a cracking noise. The metal links holding the punching bag cracked broke and the punching bag hit the floor. Daniel was breathing heavily standing at an angle where Esselle could see the sweat drenching his black hair making it glisten in the sunlight. Like something out of an imax movie in the theaters. Where everything just looks polished in gold. What Daniel just did was both sexy and terrifying. A whole new thing for him. He looked over and saw Esselle. For a second his eyes widened then his expression turned cold.

"What are you doing here at 6:30 in the morning" he said and walked over to the next punching bag on his right. Esselle looked beyond him. There were at least ten other punching bags on the floor. Its official. What he did was totally hot.

"I just um..." Esselle said. She grabbed her hair and tied it in a messy bun "I just thought I'd get an early start"

"Ya well I'm off commission right now see?" he said and pointed to his chest "No shirt means no uniform no uniform means I'm not on duty and when I'm not on duty that means you're screwed and came here for nothing" he said and began to beat at the next punching bag. Esselle looked over to the wall. She walked over and grabbed a pair of boxing gloves and slipped them on. She went over to the punching bag next to Daniel's and looked at me.

"You're angry with me?" she asked and he looked at her before throwing another punch.

"No" he said.

"Then you're indifferent with me" Esselle said and threw a punch.

"Not that either" he said

"Well then Daniel what's wrong?" she asked.

With a grunt he stopped and looked at her "This is usually my alone time Ms. Elunas. I like spending it alone" he said.

"Quit calling me that!" she said.

His jaw tensed and he began to beat at the punching bag again.

Somewhere in Time- trilogy part 2

Frustrated Esselle threw a punch into hers. Then another one and another one and another one. She was getting no where and it was just building up the rage inside her.

"Here" Daniel said and walked over. "The tension is here" he said and placed his hand on the bare skin of ehr stomach. "Try actually keeping your balance and place your feet firmly in the ground" he said and placed his other hand on the small of her back.

"Now concentrate on where you are aiming and put your force there. Don't just punch and then all that force and energy goes flying everywhere and lands in some random place" he said and looked at her.

"Now go" he said. Esselle threw a punch.

"Again" he said and Esselle did so "Again" and then Esselle was doing it on her own making the punching bag shake.

When Esselle looked over Daniel was already back to his spot. Esselle continued to punch then kick. Jasmine was teaching her to kick.

"What the hell is that?" Daniel asked.

Esselle put her hands on her hips "I'm kicking" she said.

"My grandmother can do better" he said and walked over. "You don't kick like that you look like a monkey on a sugar high" he said and Esselle's blood ran hot.

"You know maybe if you weren't so content on being an asshat all the time you could teach me to do it the right way!" she snapped.

"You know Ess its not that hard to kick a damn punching bag!" he shouted.

"That's for you to say! You actually know how to kick this" Esselle shouted and looked at it "Thing!" she screamed and pushed it

Somewhere in Time- trilogy part 2

with all her strength.

"Oh god!" Daniel said "You even push like a girl!"

"That's because I am a girl!" Esselle shouted. "What's your excuse?"

"There is none because I can actually throw a punch! If I wanted to i could send that punching bag flying out the damn window!" he screamed.

'i'd like to see you try!" Esselle hollered so loud she could hear the strain.

"Fine!" Daniel ranted

"Fine!" Esselle shouted back.

Daniel raised his hand with one blow the punching back went flying. The metal links broke and the punching back went with so much force it hit the window shattering a part of the glass.

Both hot headed and enraged they looked at each other.

Then Daniel yanked her wrist and they slammed in to each other with a bang and their mouths collided. Esselle was angry and hot and sweating and ready to blow her top. So she kissed him her lips began to feel sore. Esselle could feel Daniel's skin burning against hers. He must have been hot too. Esselle's hand ran up his chest and got knotted in his hair. Daniel's hand went up and down her back sending shivers through her veins.

"God" Esselle said in between kisses "You are such a jerk sometimes"

"And you" he said and kissed her fiercely "Are a major pain in the ass"

Talk about you kiss and makeup Esselle thought. That's literally what this was about to lead to unless she put her foot down. Which she did eventually. After she kissed him one last time.

"You can't keep doing this to me" Esselle said pulling away.
"Do what?" he asked.
"Be completely wonderful and charming one moment and. and kiss me the way you just did then turn around and lay your wrath upon me" she said.
"In all fairness you kissed me first" he said.
Esselle made a face. Esselle was about to say something when Daniel kissed her hard and long.
"Ok" he said pulling away "maybe I shouldn't have said that"
'You think?" Esselle snapped.
"Hey cool it kid you're not the easiest person in the world to be with either" he said.
Esselle shook her head "Either you're mysterious jerk face or sexy boyfriend you can't be both" she said.
Daniel smiled "You think I'm mysterious? Because sexy I've heard all too many times before but mysterious is a new one I like it" he said.
'Ya well" Esselle said and her cheeks began to burn red. She was beyond embarrassment. She wanted to crawl under something and hide. Maybe he'd missed it.
Daniel smiled wider "You're probably praying I missed it but I didn't. I was just trying to get a rise out of you. Which I did" he said and Esselle narrowed her eyes at him.
He smirked "Did you missy just call me your boyfriend?" he asked.
She swallowed hard. He'd caught that and now she was sure to die of embarrassment.
"Well I" Esselle stuttered.
"Because if you did and that's the case I'll definitely have to have

you call me that more often" he said.

Esselle's eyes widened "You..." she stammered "You want me to call you my boyfriend?" she asked.

He shrugged his shoulders "I mean it makes sense if I'll be calling you my girlfriend. Don't you think it would be just weird if you didn't?" he asked.

Esselle let out a laugh that was mostly air. "So you're my boyfriend now?" she asked.

Daniel thought for a moment. "No" he said.

Esselle raised her eyebrows. "No?" she asked. Was she missing something.

He made a face. 'Ya no" he said "I haven't asked you yet"

Daniel cleared his throat. He took Esselle's hands in his and looked at her with thoughtful blue practically violet eyes.

"Essie" he said 'Will you be my girlfriend?" he asked.

Esselle smiled as she couldn't help it. "Well let me think" she said and Daniel laughed.

She smiled at him thoughtfully and said "Yes, of course. It only took you long enough to ask" she said.

Daniel, laughing, took Esselle in his arms lifting her off her feet and kissed her. Esselle loved being lifted off her feet. It reminded her of flying. He thoughtfully wrapped a curl around his finger. Esselle never felt so in love. Esselle had only ever been with one man her entire life. Now this was her second chance. Her chance to let someone else have her heart. Because Esselle wasn't scared anymore. She wasn't afraid of letting go. When Esselle pulled away she kept her eyes shut and took in a deep breath. Daniel pressed his forehead to hers.

"You know everyone is going to be on our case" Esselle said.

Somewhere in Time- trilogy part 2

"I know" Daniel said.

"We're going to have to keep it a secret for a while if we want any shot at a normal relationship" he said.

"I know" she said.

Esselle opened one of her eyes. "You hear that?" she asked.

"I don't hear anything" he said.

'Exactly. Its quiet too quiet" she said.

"We are here alone" he said.

"Sh!" she said and walked over to the door "We can't even hear the a.c. going on next door someone turned it off" Esselle said. She walked over to the door and Daniel was at her side. Esselle put her finger to her lip and she yanked open the door.

Charlotte came tumbling in with a cup in her hand. She quickly cleared her throat and straightened out her vest.

Esselle smiled and put her hands on her hips "Charlotte being sneaky I see?" Esselle said.

Charlotte looked superior "I have no idea what you're talking about" she said. Daniel put his arm up and leaned against the wall.

"Uhu" he said raising and eyebrow.

"I was just doing my early morning run" she said and reached for the control panel. She turned the A.C.'s back on.

"Now if you'll excuse me I have paperwork to do" she said turning on her heels and disappearing. When she did with the tips of Esselle's finger tossed the door and it slammed shut.

Daniel walked over to Esselle and she kissed him. But the laughter was too much they pulled away to laugh. They laughed and laughed and laughed until the sun rose.

Somewhere in Time- trilogy part 2

Somewhere in Time- trilogy part 2

The car door slammed shut and Esselle walked over to the other side. Daniel stuck his elbow out the window and Esselle leaned over to look at him.
She smiled "Thanks" she said.
"So breakfast tomorrow?" he asked.
Esselle nodded "Ya, I don't know where though you chose" she said.
He nodded "I'll pick you up at 8. We have to be back at head quarters at 10 tomorrow" he said.
"Why?" Esselle asked.
"Because tomorrow the council is coming. You're getting fully inducted tomorrow and that's where you really become one of us" he said and pulled down the shoulder of his shirt "Its when you get your first official mark" he said. Esselle's fingertips glided across his skin where the mark was in black. He brought his shirt back up. It was far past midnight and Esselle was at headquarters with Daniel before he took her home.
Esselle sighed "Alright then. I guess we'll be there at ten" she said.
Daniel smiled. He reached out of the car and took Esselle's chin pulling her down to kiss her. "Trust me don't be worried. The council maybe a pain the ass but they're always gracious towards new members" he said and Esselle smiled.
"Let's hope" she said and kissed him again.
"I have to go now. I'm still on probation and if I don't check in

with Charlotte on time for my next mission she'll be on my case" he said.
"Bye" Esselle said.
"Bye Ess" he said and drove away.
Esselle waved as he drove away. She turned on her heels and started to walk towards her house when she stopped. The man in black she saw with the black audi was walking up the stairs to her house. Esselle hid behind a building and watched. The man walked up the steps to her house and rang her bell. Her mother and father came out. She wanted to scream for them to run but they began to talk. Quickly and frantically. The man in black looked around and Esselle hid. She peeked from behind the brick and saw he parents bring the man into the house. Esselle was baffled she had no idea what do. So she stood there and waited. 20 minutes later her parents came out with worried faces and the man said something to them. Then he disappeared into the night and her parents went back inside. Esselle ran. Esselle ran to her front door and yanked out her card to open the door. Esselle first went into the living room and no one was there. Then the dining room and the kitchen empty. She ran upstairs but she heard voices and slowed down. Esselle saw that her parents bedroom door was slightly open.
"Henry if she finds out" she heard her mother say.
"Vivienne stop worrying. We did well by our daughter she'll know" he said.
"But Henry I can't lose her! Not again! We made such an awful mistake Henry we should have never done what we did to her! She'll never forgive us!" she cried.
"Shhh" she heard her father say.

"It'll be alright. As long as they don't find her it'll be alright. And by the way things are looking we have Mardrin and Selena on our side" he said and she heard her mother sniffle.

Mardrin? Selena? What have they done?

"Just go to bed Vivienne. We'll wake her up if she hears us" her father said. Esselle froze. She forgot she snuck out to see Daniel. They thought she was sound asleep.

"Alright" she heard her mother say and the light went out. Now it was official. Esselle was done for.

"Ess hurry up" Daniel said.

Esselle looked at him. "Ih'm Ewing a fas a I cam" she said with a mouthful of her bagel.

Daniel made a face "What?" he asked.

Esselle rolled her eyes "I aid em hewing as fas a I an" she said. Daniel shook his head and yanked the doors of headquarters opened.

"If we're late the council is gonna kick my ass then slice your throat" he said and pulled her along. Esselle swallowed hard and ran towards the elevator with Daniel. With the back of her hand she wiped her face clean. So in all fairness no one told Daniel to decide he wanted bagels for breakfast. Then again no one said for Esselle to decide to chose the busiest bakery in basically the entire to world to get her bagel. So now after waiting an hour on line getting stuck in 45 minutes worth of traffic on the streets of New York the day before the Fourth of July when everyone was going away they were about to be late. Esselle turned around and looked at her reflection in the walls of the elevator. She flattened out her yellow dress and straightened out her necklace. Esselle looked at her hair and yanked the pins out letting her hair fall in curls.She whipped her hair off to the right. It looked awful. she whipped her hair off to the left and she smiled. Much better. Esselle yanked open her bag and slipped on her bangles. Esselle took out her red lipstick and Daniel looked at her quizzically.

"You fit all that in a bag?" he asked.

"Uhuh" she said painting her lips red.

"How do girls even manage to do that?" he asked.

Esselle smiled "Years of going to late night parties on the subway with Selena you learn a trick or two" she said and snapped her bag shut. It was pretty and lacy with a thin metal chain so that it hung on her shoulder.

"So they are going to ask you questions" Daniel said. Esselle nodded. Esselle frowned and reached up to run her fingers through Daniel's hair. He ignored her.

"You have to be very detailed and honest with your answers. are you listening to me?" he asked.

"Hm yup answers detailed" she said and continued to look at his hair. Esselle threw a strand of black hair back.

He looked at her "Keep going!" she said.

"Anyway when they ask you" he said and stopped when Esselle smoothed his black hair down.

"What are you doing!?" he asked.

Esselle tilted her head "I'm fixing your hair now stay still" she said and reached for his hair again. Daniel stepped back making a face.

"Oh God don't tell me we're going to be one of those couples" he said.

Esselle let out a deep breath and her hands fell to her side.

"Would you stay still?" she snapped.

"No!" Daniel said taking a step back. He looked at his reflection. He turned his head either side and made a face "I don't know but the light in this elevator is doing wonders for my skin. What do you think?" he asked.

Esselle looked around just taken back. "Like prince charming" she said putting her hand on her hip.

"Oh no I know that" he said running his fingers through his hair "Today I just look more mysterious bad boy then hunky savior" he said. Esselle opened her mouth to speak when the elevator

Somewhere in Time- trilogy part 2

door opened. Daniel already grabbed her hand and was dashing down the hallways.

"I swear Ess if you made us late" he began

Esselle's jaw dropped "Uh hey no one said to want bagels for breakfast!" she argued

"No one said to chose just about the busiest place in New York to get one! Dunkin Donuts is fine!" he said and pounded the pass code on the control panel. The sliding doors parted and he ran pulling Esselle along with him. Struggling to keep up Esselle tried running too. Until she realized her feet were basically not even touching the ground. She was flying.

"You know what I'm not even going to bother" Esselle said and stopped running. Sure enough she was flying. Literally.

****
****

"This is the heart of headquarters" Daniel said. They were in front of two high, like sky high, beautiful cherry wood doors that reminded Esselle of something in a Gothic cathedral.

"This room is called the "Sancum" like a shortened version of sanctuary. This where all of the important meetings take place. We don't use it other than that. Its really cool inside reminds you of those magical movies with the cool over lord and scary looking council" he said.

Fear began to grow inside of Esselle. She looked at him with big eyes and he looked back at her.

"You're not helping" she said.

Daniel made a face "Sorry. I forgot you're not fearless" he said.

"No one is!" Esselle said frantically.

"I am" he said.

Esselle felt her stomach turning and her heart hit the floor. She felt as if there was no gravity she felt that sick. Like when you go on those upside down roller coasters and you feel like you're flying when you're not. That's hoe Esselle felt and she could barely see straight. Not only was she ready to faint but the cold a.c. air from the floor vents made goosebumps surface her skin. "Alright you better get in there" he said and Esselle looked at him/
"You're not going in with me?" she asked.
Daniel shook his head "Of course not" he said with an obvious tone "I can't go in with you"
Esselle began to cower behind him. She reached out to grab his arm and her heart began skipping beats. "I'm not going in there alone" she said. Daniel sighed and pushed her towards the door. "You'll be fine. We don't even have to train when you get out today. You can just go home or we can watch reruns of Tom and Jerry in the screening room" he said turning the long curvy door handle.
"What if they don't like me?" she asked looking back at him. He sighed and pushed the doors open.
"Ess you'll do fine really. There's nothing to it" he said and kissed her. "Just" he said and looked her up and down.
"Try and be I don't know you!" he said. He grabbed the handles and began to shut the doors "Now go"
"Wait!" she whispered and grabbed the doors. "What if mess up?" she asked.
He kissed her forehead "You won't. I have to go now Ess. I'll be right here waiting for you when you get out" he said pulling them closed.

"But-!" Esselle began.

"Go" he said and shut the doors. Now Esselle was all alone.

****
****

"Please state your full name for the record" The man said. Esselle swallowed hard.

"Esselle Mariasol Elunas" she said. The man was tall with dark hair, brown eyes, a narrow face, and a big nose. He was definitely scary looking. Esselle straightened her back out even more and tugged her dress past her crossed legs. He was standing over her in a white and black uniform with a silver and cold collar.

"Please state your birth date for the record" he said. His voice was so loud it sounded like a microphone and chilled Esselle to the bone.

"April 1, 2000" she said.

He looked down at her "Please state the date of your death for the record" he said. Esselle looked over at Charlotte. Her blonde hair was put up in a pretty messy do. She had her arms crossed and was in her black uniform vest. it was very flattering. She gave a gentle nod of the head and Esselle looked at the man again.

"May 15, 2017" she said. The man tapped it into his tablet. The tablets nowadays were odd looking. They looked like a glowing translucent white hunk of glass.

"Please state the date of your awakening" he said.

Esselle swallowed hard. The date of her awakening was always that of a foggy one.

He raised an eyebrow at her "Please state the day of your awakening for the record" he repeated.

Esselle opened her mouth to speak but nothing came out. She

Somewhere in Time- trilogy part 2

didn't even know what today's date was. Then again that was a lie. Today was July 3 but she never asked her parents the actual date of her awakening.

"I don't know" Esselle said. Whispers began to run through the room like a domino effect. One person turned their head to talk to the other. The room was a semi-circle with people sitting in slots and chairs in the walls feet into the air. There was a narrow table of straight backed people on the floor about 15 feet away from her. They all had black and white uniforms on but some of them had silver and gold collars and others had bronze and amethyst colored collars.

"Your Honor" Charlotte said stepping forward. The man standing over Esselle looked at her. "Her memory is still foggy"

"Its been a month. Her memory should be fine by now" the man said and looked down at Esselle again.

"June 4, 2045 was when we found her" Charlotte said and she looked at Esselle.

"I was awake for 5 days before that" Esselle said softly.

Charlotte gave the man a look "There you have it. The day of her awakening was May 31, 2045" she said and stood back in her spot.

The man cleared his throat. "Esselle Mariasol Elunas. Are you being trained?" he asked.

Esselle nodded "Yes" she said.

"For how long?" he asked. Esselle thought to herself.

"Its been about a week and half" she said.

The man went vigorously typing away on his tablet.

"Are you being trained by a warrior?" he asked.

Esselle began to stutter "I, um, uh" she said and looked over at

Charlotte. She shook her head "No" Esselle said.

The man nodded "And who is overseeing that your training is going according to standards" he asked.

Esselle peeked over at Charlotte. She gently pointed to herself. "Charlotte Miles" she said. The man nodded. He fixed his glasses and looked at Esselle.

"And by whom are you being trained?" he asked.

Now see Esselle knew this one. "Daniel Carter" she said.

The man rolled his eyes "Oh God that one" he muttered.

A woman sitting at the narrow table raised an eyebrow. "Careful counselor" she said.

The man looked at her then back at his tablet. Esselle looked over at the woman. She had jet black hair blue eyes and light skin. She had a square bu very beautiful face. She was smiling and winked at Esselle.

"Have you gone through your tests?" he asked.

Esselle frowned "No" she said.

The man looked over at Charlotte and made a face. "And when do you plan on doing so?" he asked.

Charlotte stood her ground "When and I and the girl are good and ready" she remarked. Esselle fought back a smirk. You go Charlotte she thought.

"Do you have the mark?" he asked rolling his eyes.

"Yes" Esselle said. The man nodded and went typing away again.

"Now, do you wish to be trained?" he asked.

Esselle frowned "Of course" she said.

"Are you entering this lifestyle willingly?" he asked.

"Yes I am" Esselle said feeling offended. She was here wasn't she?

"Are you willing to dedicate yourself to this lifestyle in every way shape and form?" he asked.

"Yes I am" she answered.

"Are you devoted? Dedicated?" he asked.

Esselle nodded growing impatient"Of course" she said. He gave he a look and the fear began to surface. She humbly sat back in her chair.

"Now, at the beginning of this initiation you were read your rights by your overseer Charlotte correct?" he asked.

Esselle nodded.

The man sighed and pulled off his glasses holding them he said "Now child you *are* fully aware of what this lifestyle is like correct? You are willing to receive training" he said and Esselle nodded "Receive a new form of education" he continued and Esselle nodded with his words "And abide by our rules" he said. Esselle nodded one last time and the man sighed.

"Alright then" he said and slipped his glasses back on."Let's continue"

A man and woman came forward with a box in their hands. They had what looked like visors but in mask form covering their face all except their mouths and chins.

"Are you willing to receive your first mark?" the man asked.

Esselle nodded despite feeling the only stomach cramps coming on. She was sick to her stomach.

The man bowed his hands once and the man came forward with the woman. Esselle could tell she was pretty.

"Now" she said and her voice was soft but stern "Where would you like it?" she asked. Esselle thought. Where was she to have her mark? she didn't want to ask for it in any awkward place

because well....it just wouldn't work. She wanted it somewhere she'd know but that no one she didn't want to see it would. So Esselle took her hair in her hands and pushed off to the side.
"I don't want the wrong people to be able to see it" she said and turned in her chair so her back was to them "I want it somewhere they can't see it. I want it on the back of my neck" she said and gently turned her head. The woman seemed to be smiling with approval.
"Alright then" she said.
****
****
Esselle could feel the burn of the mark on the back of her neck when she put her hair back in place. She had her eyes open the entire time but the inside of her cheek was pretty sore from all the biting down she did. The cherry colored wood of the intricate walls began to glow in the mid-day sunlight peeking in through the stain glass windows. Esselle fully turned in her seat to face forward again and looked at the man.
"Congratulations. You have fully been initiated" he said. Esselle smiled and sprung out of her chair. He extended his hand. Esselle's smile was glowing and she took his hand shook it frantically. The man let out a bit of a deep chuckle he seemed caught off guard. Esselle looked over at Charlotte and she gave a soft smile and tilted her head. Esselle had done well. The people in the seats within the walls rose and left. The people sitting at the narrow table approached Charlotte and others approached Esselle just to shake her hand. Esselle was ready to talk to Charlotte when the woman with black hair stepped in front of her.

Somewhere in Time- trilogy part 2

"Oh" Esselle said coming to a stop. She smiled "I'm sorry" she said.

The woman extended her hand and Esselle graciously took it. "You did very well for someone so new to this" she said. Her tone was a tad bit on the deeper side compared to all the high pitched girls Esselle knew. She hand the kind of voice that made anything come out of her mouth sound wise.

"Thank you" Esselle said.

"You know most people go through months or preparation even a year to do what you just pulled off" she said and released Esselle's hand.

Esselle's eyes widened a bit "Really?" she asked and the woman nodded. She had a very kind mature look to her. She had to be around Charlotte's age. "I didn't think it took that much. My trainer he just-" Esselle said and the woman had a look on her face Not a bad one but she was softly smiling and she had a slightly raised eyebrow. Esselle couldn't help but think that she reminded her a bit of Daniel when he was about to give a snarky remark.

"You're trainer yes" she said and her voice was silky smooth "Tell me" she said and shifted where she stood. She looked to the ground for a moment then back at Esselle. She seemed like she had a burning question inside of her but she was doing her best to keep her composure.

"How is?" she asked "You're trainer Daniel Carter"

Esselle was taken aback "Daniel?" she asked.

The woman smirked and raised an eyebrow "That is so odd how you don't refer to him professionally. Everyone does" she said and Esselle's cheeks burned red. She hadn't noticed she said something wrong.

"Right uh," Esselle said "Mr.Carter" she said slowly and the woman still smiling gently rose her head and eyebrows.

"He's doing quite alright" she said.

"Are you sure?" she asked in a bit lower turn. Esselle grew suspicious. She frowned and nodded.

"He hasn't been getting in trouble has he?" she asked as if she already knew. Esselle sighed.

"I'd be lying if I said no" she said and the woman laughed a bit. To Esselle's surprise this woman had actually found it amusing. "Well that definitely sounds alright as long as its not to much trouble" she said. Her eyes met Esselle's. Esselle noticed how a deep a blue they were. "Now tell me child is he in love yet?" she asked.

Esselle's eyes instantly widened as the woman grew closer. She had a secretive smile on her face and Esselle's heart quickly skipped a beat and her cheeks began to burn.

"I uh" Esselle stuttered and she couldn't find the words. The woman laughed.

"Oh I see" she said nodding "That she is you"

Esselle swallowed hard. "Me? Well i wouldn't per say but" Esselle said and she was cut off by the woman's laughter. It was most air a very light and sweet laugh.

"Sweetheart" she said and took Esselle's hands in hers "You're secret is safe with me. Just..." the woman began and then she just trailed off. She grew closer to Esselle and her eyes became so dark and intense they grew violet. She seemed serious.

"Just keep an eye on him for me will you? And keep any eye out for yourself. There are many upcoming dangers I'll do my best to shield you both from. but I am one person and I can't do much" she whispered. Her tone became hard serious and urgent.

"I don't understand" Esselle whispered back.

'Child listen to me" she said growing closer "Watch your back. I don't have time to explain his honor its coming" she said and in a snap moved away from her. "Remember what I told you she said and disappeared into the crowd.

"But-" Esselle began but she was already gone. Esselle whipped her head around and Charlotte with the counselor were behind her. Charlotte smiled.

"You did very well" she said.

Esselle smiled back despite feeling unsettled "Thank you" she said. She looked at counselor. He looked a little nicer. You know when he was't interrogating Esselle.

"You were excellent. I'm surprised you did so well. Your performance deserves praise" he said.

Esselle took a deep breath still smiling. She felt a little more at ease. "Oh thank you" she said.

He bowed his head a bit "Although having that walking disaster as a trainer you're doing pretty well" he said and Esselle flinched. 'Excuse me?' she said.

"Then again we'll just hope that one doesn't rub off on you. That child's head is so big he can barely fit it through the door" he said and chuckled.

"Oh and because I suppose you know him so well?" Esselle said.

He shrugged "What's there to know? He's young and too excellent for his own good. he's an arrogant self righteous little thing that if you let him would rule the world" he said.

"You're right you don't know him at all" Esselle snapped "You don't know who he is the kind of person he is and what's he been through. So if he wants to be a little prideful and arrogant then by hell he has a right too. There's a lot he has to be proud of. He has done countless things for this society countless times more then you allow yourself to admit. You are self righteous and high and mighty. Not him. In fact I think he is modest and humble about all that he's done" Esselle said. The counselor was wide eyed and speechless.

"I am very proud to call him my trainer and very proud of his accomplishments. They are that of abundant and many. Unfortunately something I most likely cannot say for you" Esselle said. Esselle looked superior and everyone around was looking and whispering. Yet she didn't care. She'll be damned anyone said anything like that about Daniel. Not in front of her. "If you'll excuse me I have other business to attend to" she said and walked right past him through the exit. What an idiot that man was.

Somewhere in Time- trilogy part 2

Somewhere in Time- trilogy part 2

When Esselle stepped out and shut the doors behind her she gasped for air keeping the door handles in her grip behind her. She hadn't noticed how fast her breathing was. Esselle had been shaking so much you would have thought there was an earthquake going on. She was so concentrated on trying to bring the speed of her heart rate down she hadn't Daniel wasn't outside waiting waiting for her. She stepped away from the door and pressed her palms to her cheeks cooling them down. She looked down either way in the hallway and he still wasn't there. She took a step forward and heard a crunching sound beneath her feet. She brought her heel up from the ground and saw a letter. She bent over and reached for it. She sighed. Notes are only cute sometimes Daniel she thought. It read:

-Essie
Ok, so I know how I promised I'd be here waiting for you when you came out. In all fairness at first I was. But then Trevor came. So this is all his fault. He said there was a new shipment in the weapons room. In all fairness Trevor forced me. I'll be waiting for you there promise. Don't worry Ess, I knew you did well. I had faith in you. Just thought you should know that since I kind of should have been waiting for you.

Somewhere in Time- trilogy part 2

-Danny

Esselle smiled a bit. Ok so maybe it was a little cute she thought and slipped the note into a hidden pocket in her dress. ow the only problem was Esselle had no idea where in this castle looking building the weapons room was.

****

Esselle had wondered around the building for what felt like hours. In reality it was about only one hour when she checked her watch. Finally the entire decor of this building had Esselle's mind spinning. one moment it looked like a romantic Victorian goth castle. Then she passed through sliding doors and everything was super modern.

Finally after walking around in circles Esselle bumped into Margaret and asked her where the weapons room was. Her details were extremely helpful. Esselle stood in front of a huge door and a plaque next to it read in silver

Weaponry

Esselle pushed the door open and a rush of air hit her. The walls were covered in weaponry and in the far left corner were a bunch of empty boxes pilled high and boxes have full surrounded them. Esselle took a few steps looking around and the echo of her heels filled the room when they clicked against the marble floors. Esselle turned around and in an instant someone pounded into her. Esselle grasped but she was already feet in the air being twirled.

"God you magnificent woman!" Daniel ranted. Esselle felt as if she were ready to fall and she grabbed Daniel's hands around her waist.

"What is it?" she asked. He put her down still holding her and his face was radiant with a smile.

"You are on badass you know that?' he said and kissed her cheek.

"God I could just squeeze you to death right now" he said and kissed her other cheek.

"Wait slow down my head is spinning!" she said and he laughed.

"You think we didn't hear? Dawn practically cried her eyes out and Jasmine was rolling all over the floor" he said.

"I'm still lost" she said and he just laughed and pulled her closer.

"You know you have a lot of nerve telling off the counselor" he said.

Esselle's widened "Oh that!" she said when it had dawned on her "Ya I don't think he likes me or the matter you very much" she said.

Daniel still smiling shook his head "I can't believe you told him off Ess. God, I love it. I knew I'd like you the moment you woke up and the first thing out of your mouth was that I was arrogant" he said and Esselle laughed at the memory.

'Oh right by the way did I ever apologize for that? Because I should have" she said.

He shook his head "Don't. I find it very attractive" he said "Just as attractive as you sticking up for me" and a wry smile crossed his face.

Esselle's cheeks began to burn red. "Did not" she said and he made a face.

"Right' Daniel said.

"He just the counselor guy said you were a walking disaster and I said you weren't" Esselle said.

Somewhere in Time- trilogy part 2

Daniel was nodding sarcastically. He really didn't believe her and Esselle knew.

"Really? So nothing about my accomplishments skill?" he teased. Esselle shook her head. "nope"

"The kind of person I am?" he said and Esselle shook her head again "My modesty?" he asked and Esselle burst into laughter.

"What?" Daniel asked smiling.

"That's how you know its a lie. You are in no way shape or form modest or humble at all" Esselle said and his eyes twinkled.

"While that maybe true I didn't tell you anything about my being humble" he said and smiled wider when Esselle's eyes widened.

'You little buger you tricked me!" she said and punched his shoulder hard. After words she bit her lip because her knuckles began to sting. Hitting him was like hitting a rock.

"I did no such thing" Daniel said and his eyes turned violet.

"You did too!" Esselle and struggled to leave his grip. HE laughed and held her tighter.

"Did" he said and held the back of her neck "Not" and he kissed her. Esselle gave up on fighting back. It was no use. Just him anywhere near her made her knees go weak. She always felt as if she were collapsing to the ground. Esselle began to wonder is every time Daniel kissed her he felt the same thing she did. Esselle felt like the entire world disappeared. That nervous feeling was there. Like a million butterflies in her stomach and a billion things running around her mind not to mention her heart beating so loud it could cause an earthquake. She wondered if every time they touched he got this feeling like he was walking on air. Because she did. She always did. Then Esselle wondered if he felt the same way for her that she felt for him. She wondered if

Esselle had the same effect on him as Daniel had on her. It was hard for her to not to think of these things. They haunted her mind late at night when she tried to sleep. Along with other things she had no desire to admit too. He pulled away and looked at her.

"I still can't believe you said all that" he said with a chuckle. Esselle laughed too "Ya well" she and punched his shoulder slight "I had to defend my boyfriend" she said and he laughed.

Daniel let out a deep chuckle "Oh did you now?" he asked and she nodded.

"Yup i don't know if you know him" she said

"I might" he replied.

"He's very gorgeous" Esselle began in a taunting tone.

'Oh is he now? What else?" he asked.

'Well he kind of has a huge crush on me" Esselle said and fought back the oncoming laughter. Daniel's face changed completely.

"Well tell me his name so I can kick his ass. I don't like the sound of this guy" he said and Esselle realized eh took her seriously. Esselle burst into laughter and ran her fingers through his hair.

"Its you, you jackass I'm talking about you!" she said and his face softened.

"Oh" he said. Esselle laughed and kissed him again.

"Cough I knew it Cough" Esselle heard and she pulled away. Dawn was rocking back and forth on her heels with raised eyebrows looking around. Jasmine stood side by side with Trevor. Trevor looked like he had a kind of "I totally knew it" look on his face and Jasmine looked ready to burst rainbows.

"Oh look who's here ruining the moment" Daniel said and turned to face them. He had let her go completely and Esselle looked down folding her hands in front of her.

"I see you're a bit busy. Sorry to interrupt" Dawn said walking over.

"You weren't interrupting anything because nothing was happening" he said and shoved his hands in his front pockets. Dawn made a face "Right" she said and Daniel lifted a shoulder. Esselle's hair fell covering her face and she bit her lip. had he been ashamed or embarrassed to be seen with her He did say he didn't want anyone to know.

"Uck oh whatever!" Dawn said growing annoyed. She turned on her heels and disappeared into a row blades.

"I don't know I just find it odd" Trevor said as he and Jasmine walked over to the rows with guns.

"Find what odd?" Daniel asked. Esselle felt her stomach turn. She didn't even know what to feel or think.

"Oh I don't know two completely normal people all alone talking" Jasmine teased and walked right passed them.

"I wasn't just talking to any other person" Daniel said. Esselle noticed Trevor and Jasmine walking awfully close to each other. Jasmine and Trevor's eyebrows were pressed together when they looked at him.

"I was talking" Daniel said and to Esselle's surprise he reached over wrapping and arm around Esselle's waist and yanking her over so hard she stumbled "My girlfriend" he said and looked at her. Esselle pressed her lips together but smiled anyway. Dawn was sticking her head out from behind the shelves and Esselle's heart skipped a beat. he had said it in front of them. he called her his girlfriend. Then he pulled her away and down the row of bows and arrows. Odd enough they actually used them.

"You scared me for a minute there" Esselle said. Daniel laughed and kissed her hair.

"I adore this woman" he said with a chuckle. adore Esselle thought. he adored her.

Esselle had had a nightmare. It was that of an awful one but strange enough she had, despite every night dreaming of Daniel, dreamt of Mardrin. She had dreamt she was in the ballroom at The Plaza hotel. When Mardrin and Esselle were together they had always said how they would love to have their wedding reception there. She was dancing with him and in Esselle's dream she felt an overwhelming joy. Then that joy she had felt that happiness melted away. Esselle missed being with Mardrin because she did. If she said otherwise she would be lying. The light was dim and Esselle could hear the click of her heels against the floors. Esselle looked over and saw a radio sitting on top of a pile of stacked chairs.

"No, No, no, I don't want you sending that over" she heard and Esselle looked over. Had she heard the voice she just thought she did. When it was silent Esselle went back to the radio. She flipped the switch and the music went on. She could hear the radio woman speaking.

"All the greatest hits you grew up from 2000-2020 this is the legit channel" the woman said and Esselle laughed. She wondered if kids nowadays said legit.

"Harold absolutely not!" she heard someone rant and her head turned around in a snap. There she saw coming into the room Mardrin. He had a suit on and he looked annoyed. Esselle loved the way he looked when he was annoyed he look adorable. His

Somewhere in Time- trilogy part 2

hair was slicked back and seemed to be longer than the way it did last time she saw him.

"Alright I'll talk to you later then" he said and hung up his phone. "You know you make a very dashing business man" Esselle said and he looked over her in shock as if he thought he were alone "You just might make the woman swoon" she said and he smiled. "Elle" he said and walked over "What are you doing here?" Esselle him half way and embraced him. She hadn't done so in a very long time. He smelled of lemons and fabric softener because of his clothing. His smell was the same 28 years ago and still is today. Embracing him reminded Esselle of all the days after school she'd run down the hill and fall into his arms with a laugh and she'd always ask him how his day was and he'd always say that it was better now that he was with her. That was real. A kind of beautiful love Esselle had and sometimes wished she could go back to. Then she thought about Daniel and then she just became confused. So she tried not thinking of either.

"I was just walking through the city and found myself here" she said when they pulled away. She laughed a bit "It reminded me of you"

Mardrin smiled and ran his fingers through his hair. "Ya well we always did say we wanted to get married here" he said and they looked at each other and laughed. Mardrin looked like it was a nervous laugh but he laughed anyway.

"Aw memories" Esselle teased and walked back over to the radio "SO what are you doing here Mr.CEO!" she said and he smiled.

"I had to meet a client here" he said.

Esselle nodded and brought up the volume of the radio.

"On the Fourth of July Mardrin? You should be home

Somewhere in Time- trilogy part 2

barbecuing" Esselle said and he laughed a bit.

"Ya well you have to do what you have to do" he said. A regrettable choice of words she thought.

Esselle's eyebrows pressed together.

"What's wrong?" he asked.

Esselle made a funny smile.

"Listen" Esselle said and brought up the volume.

"You remember when you were 13 and you danced to this song at a summer dance with your crush? Well here it is Almost Is Never Enough by Ariana Grande and Nathan Sykes from guess what that's right your favorite movie when you were a kid The Mortal Instruments City of Bones! Enjoy" the woman said and Esselle let out a soft laugh. She looked at Mardrin and his yellow-green eyes seemed radiant. She missed looking into them. He flicked his head.

"Come on" he said and Esselle's face fell.

"What?" she said.

"Come on" Mardrin said pulling pulling her unto the dance floor. He took her hand in his and placed the other on the small of her back and smiled. "Let's dance. This is our song after all" he said and Esselle smiled softly.

"This is such a beautiful song" Esselle said with her dress swaying back and forth. She looked up at him "You remember when we first danced to this song?" she asked and he laughed.

"Yes! I do how could I forget!" he said and looked at her. His face was no longer radiant with a smile. His smile grew soft and his eyelids softly fell.

"You had a red rose in your hair" he said and stroked Esselle's locks "We 14 and it was the Valentine's Day dance at our school"

Esselle shut her eyes and smiled "You are very good" she said. "You were wearing the violet dress the one I loved with the lace and angel wing sleeves. You were wearing one or your first pair of heels" he said and Esselle laughed.

"First in many!" she said and he smiled. Esselle thought about the lyrics to the song. How perfectly they described her and Mardrin.

"The second time we danced to this song was when we crashed the 11th grade homecoming when we were in 10th grade" he said and they begun to laugh.

"That's when after officially becoming my boyfriend at 14 you said you loved me" Esselle said and her voice grew soft.

"And meant it" he said and twirled her once then bringing her closer than she was before.

"Then the last time" Esselle said and Mardrin's face grew serious.

"The last time it was your 17 birthday." he said and gently touched her face. Esselle's heart felt and she pressed her face into his hand. She could just feel the tears coming on. She remembered and all too clearly. The memory felt fresh in her mind. Mardrin's hair was shorter much shorter. She had her pretty blue dress on and that was when-

"It was when I decided I wanted to spend the rest of my life with you" he said and Esselle looked at him "We were in love. once before all of this Esselle" he said.

Esselle was smiling but it was painful so she shut her head and nodded.

"Yes, I remember" she said. She laughed a bit and felt the tears coming "I guess this song really does explain us now" she said and he took her face in his hand.

Somewhere in Time- trilogy part 2

"That's not true" he said.

"Yes it is Mardrin look at where were are now" she said.

"Esselle if only I had known. We were so close, so close to everything we wanted and one stupid night ruined it all" he said."I don't maybe just maybe there could still be a chance for us somehow in someway even if it isn't in the way we want" he said. Esselle opened her mouth but all that came out was air. "Mardrin how...I couldn't do that. You couldn't do that to your wife and I couldn't do that to..." she said and trailed off. To Daniel she thought. She couldn't do that to Daniel.

"Esselle you have no idea how hard it is having you back but not having you back" he said and Esselle understood. She understood completely. It was like Esselle was slowly falling to pieces everyday she wasn't with him because before she was frozen she spent almost everyday of her life in love with him.

"Almost will never be enough with you Esselle ever. I could have spent eternity with you" he said.

"And I would have let you" Esselle said and it fell silent for a moment. Mardrin was rubbing his thumb across her cheek bone. Esselle wanted to cry but she did her best not to. He had no idea how much this broke her heart. It broke her heart even more when he took her in his arms and kissed her. It hurt even more when she kissed him back. It hurt because Esselle knew that no matter what it would never be enough. Not ever. There was one point in Esselle's life where all she wanted to be was right where she was and then there was a moment when she thought that was all she was going to do. Now she was just torn. Not just torn, broken, shatter, crushed into a million pieces because she loved him. No matter how much she tried denying it or suppressing the feeling she loved with everything she had she always did. Almost of all fo the most beautiful memories Esselle ever had were attached to him. And now she was surely screwed. But how could she think such thoughts when she ran her fingers through her hair and he traced circles on her back. That was one thing about Mardrin that never changed. The security she felt around him and the tracing of circles. One of the many things she loved about him and would never stop. Kissing him was sweet like honeysuckle. Esselle couldn't help but think that perhaps in a different time and a different future they could have been doing this having been married not torn. Esselle felt her love and life with Mardrin was such a tease. It was true what this song that Esselle loved so much said. Almost is never enough. It truly wasn't and never would be.

Somewhere in Time- trilogy part 2

Daniel was the kind of guy that got what he wanted when he wanted it. It was easy for him. He was gorgeous and witty and overall complete swoon material. Then again he knew that which led to his arrogance. But no one ever really cared. Its was one of the many things that made him so God damn sexy. And he knew that too. He was the kind of guy that saw a girl wanted her had her and when he was done kinda got rid of her. Daniel never payed much attention to the girls he had flings with anyway. He always had Alice in the back of his mind. Sure it had been a long time ago but he couldn't help it. Of the tons of girls Daniel had met in his years of being awaken not one of them had the same affect on him that Alice did. Not one of them had the wholesomeness or sweetness about them that he liked in Alice. The streets of New York City were packed in the afternoon. It was lunch hour and the sun was just scorching Daniel's skin. Daniel loved days like these. He loved the heat. But Alice didn't. She liked when it was cold out. She loved sitting by the fire place in her worn out red robe and fuzzy socks watching the snow fall. No matter how many new robes Daniel bought her she always wore the red one the very first one he got her. He could remember her smile when she looked at him. It still haunted his dreams at night. Just like the look on Jasmine's face when she died the first time. That look haunted his dreams at night. The look of the way his mother's tombstone in the moonlight that haunted his dreams every night. The look on his father's face when the bullet went right through him. He stopped himself right then and there. He wasn't going to revisit the nightmare he had two nights ago no way in hell. Sometimes Daniel would stay up nights on end because he just couldn't sleep. he'd wonder and think about his

Somewhere in Time- trilogy part 2

life and every mistake he ever made. And there were a lot of them. Just about far too many to count. Daniel would walk around the city at night and just look at the lights. He'd hop in a taxi and drive to his old house in Brooklyn. Then he'd lean against the lamppost and just stand there from nightfall to sunrise looking at the building. it was empty now no one lived there. Daniel yanked open the doors to headquarters and ran his fingers through his hair. But all of that awful mopping around like a lifeless zombie ended yesterday when he found her. For the first time since he had awaken he had actually slept an entire night through. And odd enough he saw her in his dreams. She was in the alley where he found her and then his alarm went off and he woke up. Daniel wasn't sure but he liked this girl. She was interesting. New. Like a breath of fresh air. Just thinking about her he wanted to laugh. She had called him arrogant. It was the first thing she had said when she woke up. He couldn't get over it. The amount of nerve she had was incredible. She was just as blunt as he was. He liked that. Now he didn't like like her. Per say. Sure she was beautiful. But not your typical beautiful her beauty was...different. It didn't stem from her pretty face or her body or the way she looked. It kind of stemmed from something else Daniel couldn't quite put his finger on. Either way he liked it. Daniel knew he was going to have fun with this one. Daniel like the king he was in headquarters just walked down the hallways like a boss. And yes odd enough kids nowadays still said it. Sure every girl looked his way when he passed by and smiled and giggled and waved. Why wouldn't they? He was awfully gorgeous.

"Morning Daniel" Kelly said. She was one of the younger nurses around 18 and she had her uniform on. God did Daniel love the nurses uniforms. She was carrying a box of towels and Daniel winked at her.

"Morning Kelly" he said and she smirked looking the other way. It was amazing being him wasn't it?

"Daniel" he heard from behind him. he turned on his heels and started walking backwards.

"In the flesh" he said and gave a crooked smile.

Chelsea made a face and walked towards him. She was one of the trainers Daniel's age. She looked a bit irritated but happy to see him. Wasn't she always?

"I need you to get that paperwork for the Paula case" she said and Daniel smiled.

"Oh Charlotte didn't tell you the little joke I cracked yesterday? POLO" he said and she raised an eyebrow. He laughed a bit and began to walk away.

"Paula only lived once" he said and winked. She had called him a jackass yesterday for saying POLO. Daniel tried hard not to laugh.

Daniel pushed the doors open to the conference room and opened his arms wide.

"Lord Dashing has arrived" he said.

Jasmine rolled her eyes and continued with her yo-yo.

"Oh yay" she said. Jasmine was Daniel's younger sister. Which made her even more annoying. he walked past her and ruffled her hair.

"Quit it jerkface" she snapped and he smiled.

"SO" he said and fell into Charlotte's seat at the head of the table. he kicked his feet up putting them on the edge and put his hands

Somewhere in Time- trilogy part 2

behind his head.

"What do my subjects have for me today?" he asked and Trevor choked on his apple. Daniel laughed but made no noise.

"Badass is here" and the doors slammed open so hard they hit the walls. Dawn came in like nothing and tossed her empty coffee cup in the trash can all the way across the room.

Daniel hooted "Ho, ho, ho, score babe!" he said. Dawn passing by gave him a high fave.

"Damn straight" she said and fell into her chair. She had the boots with the spikes in them on and a black mini skirt with a tube top. She had cut her hair the other day and she looked as Dawn as ever.

"Liking the new hair Dee?' Daniel asked. She looked up and smiled.

"Its so easy the handle in the morning" she said and the room lit up with laughter.

Daniel felt a tight pinch and pull at his ear and he winced.

"I see you've found yourself in my chair again young Daniel" he heard a very pretty welsh accent say.

"Ouch" Daniel said and looked up at Charlotte.

She smiled and raised an eyebrow. Daniel made a face.

"In all fairness the pretty people usually sit at the head of the table" he said and the look on Charlotte's face made him break out into a smile.

'Out" she said and he moved to the seat at Charlotte's side.

"So first order of business" she began.

Daniel pointed a finger interrupting her. "Yes" he said and his sarcasm was too much. It made Jasmine break out into a grin.

"Essie" he said.

Somewhere in Time- trilogy part 2

Trevor made a face "Who?" he asked.
"Essie, you know the girl with the curly brown hair and killer eyes" Daniel said. Trevor made a face. Amazing how Daniel could easily make someone smart look dumb.
Jasmine made a face and smiled "You think she has killer eyes?" she asked and Daniel shrugged.
"Her eyes are gorgeous so?" he said and played with his fingers.
"Essie?" Trevor said again slowly.
Daniel exasperated rolled his eyes and said "Yes! Trevor Essie! You know feisty little thing with the pretty curvy body big lips long hair and a bit of an attitude" he said and Jasmine fell back in her chair laughing.
"This should be good" Dawn said leaning into the table.
"Ok so now that we have established I called dibs on her" Daniel began.
Charlotte rolled her eyes but she was still smiling. All of them were like Charlotte's children. Dawn was the badass, Jasmine was the sweetheart, Trevor was the damn goody goody, and Daniel was the super hot witty one that is always trying to fight off his inner demons and is beautiful but broken and hides whats really going on on the inside by being a totally sexy jackass that all the girls love. Daniel needed more love and attention.
"Yes, you called dibs Daniel" she said.
"Anyway I say I go get her" Daniel said.
Charlotte shook her head "We said we'd give her till tonight" she argued.
Daniel made a face "So what? She'll thrilled to see me and not like she really isn't going to want to come back after last night" Daniel said.

Jasmine nodded "he's right. About the coming back thing not the thrilled to see him thing" she said.

"Actually I think we should get her but send Daniel. We could use his pretty face" Dawn said and turned to Trevor.

"Sorry Trevor" she said and Daniel smiled.

Trevor sighed "Yes we all now I'm not as devastatingly handsome as Daniel is" he said and fell back in his chair.

"Oh come on Trevor! You can be my handsome partner in crime!" Daniel said and Charlotte looked at him. It was one those looks that tell you to be nice.

"I think it would be fine Charlotte" Jasmine said.

"Ok so all in favor" Daniel said.

"I" everyone said in unison except Charlotte. She opened her mouth to speak but Daniel sprang out of his chair.

"Well good enough for me I'll see you" he said and was already out the door.

"Daniel! BE careful!" Charlotte said after him after gently rising from her chair. But Daniel waved a hand behind him and said "Yep!" Charlotte made a face and fell back into her chair. What were they to do with dear old Daniel?

Selena was always a smart woman for her age. She was always one to look on the bright side and try to make sense out things. No matter how much of a wise ass she was. But this was one thing she could never make sense of. one thing she never would. Selena would never understand why Esselle had to die. Why she had to lose her best friend in the entire world. Why because of such a stupid thing. Such a stupid thing of Selena's dishonesty. Selena should have been honest about what was going on. Selena should have told Esselle what Mardrin knew of what was happening to her. If only...if only. If only Esselle hadn't died. Selena couldn't get that conversation on that phone out of her head she had it memorized word for word. And she would for the rest of her life. All Selena did the past four days was cry. Just cry her eyes. Selena felt as if there was this empty whole in her chest. And when Esselle died she took that piece with her. Selena couldn't even put her makeup on the tears kept streaking her face. Eventually she gave up slammed everything threw it across her room shattered her mirror and whimpered. Her mother had come in and knelt down by her side. Selena would give anything for another moment with Esselle. Just to tell her how much she meant to her and how sorry she was. Selena's mother eventually had to put her make up and use waterproof.

Now, she was standing all dressed in black with a veil covering most of her face and sunglasses on. She was squeezing Stephen's hand so hard she could see his jaw tense. If Esselle were here with Selena she would laugh. Esselle knew how much Selena hated black. It was god awful miserable looking. Because it was perfect. Selena was miserable. And she deserved to be. After what she did to Esselle not to Esselle's knowledge she didn't deserve to be happy. Never again. Who cares if she was 17 and had the rest of her life Selena was broken. Forever broken a piece of her heart torn out. Then Selena sighed when they lowered her casket. Burned to death that's what happened to Esselle. To beautiful happy fun loving Esselle. She burned to death. Selena couldn't even look at herself in the mirror every morning let along this. She winced and looked away. Selena glanced at Esselle's parents then quickly looked away. She wouldn't even be able to stand the sight of them. When it was all over and people prepared to go home Selena stopped by Mardrin and placed her hand on his shoulder.

"Mardrin" Selena said but he didn't look at her. Selena was a very strong woman. She did all her mourning in private where she could double over in pain in peace. Her tone was hard and her grip on his shoulder was strong. But she was slowly breaking and slipping away. Even with Stephen by her side holding onto her wasn't enough anymore to keep her strong. Not like this. Mardrin didn't look at her. His short hair Esselle noticed grew out a little bit. Esselle loved his hair short. Never long. His eyes seemed empty and probably the place where his heart should be was empty also. That girl was that mans world. She never knew to the full extent how much he loved her. And now she never will. Because of them.

Mardrin was staring hard at the floor and wouldn't look up.

Selena pressed her lips together "Mardrin" she said again the time her voice softer.

Selena felt the tears beginning to burn. She shook him a bit.

"Mardrin" she croaked and she felt the tears burning. "Mardrin please" she pleaded and grabbed his other shoulder when a tear streaked her face. "Mardrin please look at me" she said and his eyes finally met hers. It was a cloudy foggy muggy nasty day out and the look in his eyes made the day look all the more grey.

"Esselle" was all he said and Selena nodded.

"I know" she said and she could see his eyes beginning to burn red.

"Please don't cry Mardrin please" she begged but the tears were already escaping her eyes. She held him close and he buried his face in her shoulder. Selena sobbed and whimpered and she could feel his tears soaking the fabric of her dress. His chest was rising and falling quickly and Selena winced in pain from all the crying. Selena slammed her hand over her mouth to stop another cry of pain from escaping her mouth and she squeezed her eyes shut tight. Selena felt her knees go out below her and she fell to the ground doubling over and pain. Almost instantly Stephen was by her side

and Mardrin was on her knees with her.
"I'm so sorry this happened" Selena whispered and Stephen swallowed hard. She looked over at him and tears streaked his face and his jaw was clenched. Selena sighed and looked at Mardrin. he was just looking at his hands.
"If I had known..." he began and they heard something.
"Mardrin" someone said and they stood behind him. Her voice was sugary sweet and velvety smooth. She gently kneel down and placed her hand on his shoulder and he instantly took her hand in his. it was Martha. Selena felt the rage boiling up inside as she quickly rose to her feet. Mardrin got to his feet and embraced her. Martha let out a small gasp of surprise but hugged him back. A single tear slid down her perfect face.
"Mardrin i am so sorry" she whispered.
Selena couldn't help it. She wanted to rip her throat out. When they pulled away Selena felt her wrath escape her mouth.
"You have a lot of nerve showing your face here" she said through clenched teeth.
"Selena" Mardrin said in a warning. He was tired so tired Selena could tell.
"No its alright" Martha said and faced Selena "I just came to pay my respects and to give my condolences. I can't help but feel this is all my fault."
"Ya well it is" Selena snapped.
"Selena that's enough" Mardrin said and placed his hand on his shoulder.

"Mardrin stop" Martha said "It was my fault and I'm sorry. I am so sorry. I am so sorry I took away the person you loved I am I didn't know. I know that right now my reason is no excuse for her death because it isn't but just know if I could take it all back I would. I really truly would. But I can't" she said and Selena froze where she stood.

Martha straightened out her back "I've apologized once and I meant it. I don't expect you to forgive me just respect that fact that I did apologize and get on with it" she said and turned on her heels. Mardrin put an arm around her but she shook her head and he nodded.

They walked down the hill in silence.

Soon enough Selena and Stephen did the same and Selena began to cry again.

"I can't believe this" she said and Stephen squeezed her hand.

"Neither can I Sel" he said and she stopped in front of him.

"Stephen I can't i can't so this anymore" she said and he thoughtfully stroked her hair.

"Its our fault its all our fault" she whimpered.

"Stop saying that" he said.

'if only we had warned her! If only we had told her what was really going on everything! What they were doing to her-!" she said and he took her face in his hands.

"Sel, stop. Stop talking like that its over now. We made a mistake that we'll just have to live it. Please Selena you have to stop now" he said.

Selena swallowed hard and shut her eyes. She nodded and he sighed.
"It'll be alright Selena" he said and she nodded. He kissed her and slipped his hand in hers. They went home in silence.

Somewhere in Time- trilogy part 2

"Daniel so help me if I trip and fall" Esselle began. "Calm down you're not!" he said. Esselle sighed and held on tight to his hands over her eyes. As soon as Esselle stepped into the building Daniel swept her up and wouldn't tell her where they were going. She knew it had to be somewhere outside because the wind was hitting her. He was covering her eyes and guiding her. "Ok so" Daniel began and Esselle smiled.
"I'm telling you now if you're playing a prank on me you're not going to live to see tomorrow" she said. Daniel let out a dramatic sigh. "Would you be quite already? You're ruining the moment" he said. Esselle smiled.
"Fine, fine, fine" she said.
"Careful" Daniel said and guided her sideways "You'll trip and fall we're high up"
Esselle stopped dead in her tracks and her heart fell. "We're high up?" she said and Daniel laughed "What the hell Danny are you trying to kill me?"
Daniel began to chuckle "Kill you?" he said.
"Is it because I ate the last purple Popsicle? because if that's the case Dawn didn't tell me it was yours until after the fact" she said.
"No it's not because of the-!" Daniel said and stopped mid-sentence and frowned "You ate my Popsicle?" he

asked and Esselle felt her cheeks go red.
"What no?" she said quickly.
Daniel rolled his eyes "Anyway! Watch your step here" he said and Esselle did her best no to fall. Wherever she was.
Daniel came to a stop and Esselle could tell by the tone of his voice he was smiling. "So now that we're officially boyfriend and girlfriend now" he said and Esselle laughed.
"I thought it be fit to finally take you out on our first date" he said and removed his hands from her eyes "And what better place to do it on then the Freedom Tower on the fourth of July. You like fireworks don't you?"
Esselle gasped and her hands covered her mouth. "Oh Danny" They were on the roof top and its was lit up with sparkling tights.
"Its beautiful" she said. On the highest landing there was a blanket laid out in her favorite color and you could see right over the entire city and more. There were candles and a radio with a pretty basket. She turned to look at him and he was smiling.
"So that's why you totally blew me off for lunch this afternoon" she said and punched his shoulder. He just laughed and held something behind his back.
Esselle raised an eyebrow.
"What's that?" she asked and he shrugged.
"What's what?" he said.
"That behind your back" she said and reached for him

but he turned away.

"I have no idea what you're talking about" he said.

Esselle knew that look on his face. The crooked little grin. as good as it looked on his face it was just screaming trouble.

"Come on Danny let me see" she said and he jumped to the side shaking his head.

"There's nothing behind my back" he said.

Esselle laughed and struggled to reach behind him. He just laughed and easily dodged her every attempt. Esselle wrapped her arms around his neck and kissed him. No one had ever done such a special thing like that for her before. Ever. The nicest thing anyone had ever done for her was by her parents. It was on her 16 birthday and they surprised her by getting her the car she wanted. This beat that by far. Especially since Esselle had grown extremely distant from her parents. Esselle felt something come between them and she let go.

Daniel brushed the rose petals over her nose and handed the bouquet to her.

"Since you insist on knowing what's behind my back" he said and she laughed.

"These are my favorite" she said and Daniel wrapped an arm around her waist.

"Oh I know he said.

"This is the nicest thing anyone's ever done for me" she said and he looked at her for a moment guiding her to where the blanket was laid out.

Somewhere in Time- trilogy part 2

"Ya well don't go telling anyone. I don't people thinking I've gone soft" he said and Esselle laughed. Oh yes, that was her Danny alright.

He climbed up unto the landing and hoped over the railing. Daniel grabbed Esselle by the waist helping her up. When she turned her head she caught sight of the city.

"Wow" she said and walked down the platform "Its beautiful" she said in awe. Since it was the Fourth of July the Freedom Tower was lit up in red white and blue. Esselle could see the beautiful water in the distance. Well...as beautiful as New York City water gets. Esselle saw the World Trade center and below her the lights from cars and lampposts looked like rapid strips of speed and light just zipping by. Esselle looked out over the water and in the distance saw the Brooklyn Bridge. That was her favorite bridge. Her second was the Verrazano.

Esselle put her roses down and walked over placing her hands on the railing. The view took her breath. She wanted to speak but couldn't. She turned around and Daniel had the same little smirk on his face and he had a glass bottle in his hands.

"Ok so technically you're old enough to drink and technically you're not but!" he said and Esselle laughed when the cork made a huge pop and shot out of the bottle. "You seemed like a sparkling cider kind of girl" he said.

"Yes, is it grape?" she asked and he made a face when

he put the bottle down.

"Duh" he said.

Esselle was smiling when she glanced back at the skyline then she looked back at Daniel and walked over.

"I didn't know you had a soft side" Esselle teased and Daniel's face instantly scrunched up.

"Oh no I don't have a soft side nope!" he said.

Esselle laughed and stopped a few steps away from him.

Daniel put his hands on his chest dramatically and said "i am in no way shape or form soft" he said.

Esselle threw her arms around his neck and hugged him with a laugh and she was lifted off her feet. She stood there for a moment before she spoke.

"Thank you" she said and he looked at her. He looked up at the sky and his eyes changed color.

"Look" he said and Esselle turned around. Sounds of explosion filled the world around them and colorful lights filled the night sky. The firework show begun. Esselle looked over and Daniel ad turn the radio on so they could hear what was going on. He handed her a glass and she smiled.

"You know your eyes change color" Esselle said. Daniel made a funny smile before he wrapped an arm around her waist.

"They do?" he asked and she nodded.

"Sometimes they turn violet" she said and he laughed.

"That's because I'm a very *violent* person" he said. Esselle rolled her eyes and continued to look at the sky.

Somewhere in Time- trilogy part 2

****

"That firework looks punch in the face" Daniel said and Esselle made a face.

"It does not it looks like a chrysanthemum!" Esselle argued.

Daniel rolled his eyes "Next one!" he said. After a while Daniel and Esselle laid down on the blankets and were now trying to make figures out of the fireworks in the sky. Esselle let out a deep breath and her hands were folded over her stomach. Esselle tilted her head when a red and orange firework exploded in the sky. Her hands fell to her side. One of her hands hit Daniel. She looked over and pulled it back but he reached over and grabbed her hand and their fingers laced together. She smiled and looked at him but he was looking at the sky and so did she.

"That one looks like a marshmallow!" they both said in unison when their hands flung to the sky to point to a firework. They looked at each other and burst into laughter.

"Ok how about that one" Daniel said looking to the sky. Esselle thought "They're all starting to look the same" she said and they laughed again.

"And here's The National Anthem the last song of the night! Happy 269th Birthday America and to many more!" the man on the radio said and the song began.

"I remember when I was thirteen" Esselle began and Daniel looked at her. "My mother and father they took my to see the fireworks" she continued and laughed a bit "I got to watch Katy Perry perform live and I remember thinking it was just about the coolest thing ever how i got to see all the celebrities up close performing"

Daniel made a face "Who?" he said and Esselle looked at him.

Esselle's eye widened "You don't know who Katy Perry is?" she asked.

Daniel made a face of distaste and shook his head "How am I supposed to know all those 2017 artists" he said.

Esselle grew confused "Daniel Katy Perry was from like summer of 2008 when she hit it big how do you...?" she said and trailed off.

"Oh" she said and Daniel grew silent.

"You were frozen already at that time weren't you" she asked and Daniel didn't say anything just sat up.

"I don't want to talk about it" he said.

"But Daniel that means" she said and tried to search for the words "I thought I was older than you but you're older than me!" she said and he looked at her.

"Duh" he said.

"Daniel how long were you frozen for?' she asked.

"Esselle-" Daniel said letting out a deep breath but she cut him off.

"I'm not letting you blow this off I'm serious" she said grabbing hold of his wrist when he sat up.

"I don't see how it matters I don't want to talk about it" he said and Esselle frowned.

"That's not fair" she said and he looked at her.
'What's not fair?"
Esselle shook her head "You're not telling me. I willingly told you I'd answer any question you'd ask me" she said.
"In all fairness I didn't ask" he said.
"Daniel!" she snapped and he laughed.
Esselle crossed her arms and blew air from her mouth. Daniel sat back on his elbows "You're mad?" he asked.
"Annoyed"
At that Daniel sprang up "Why?"
"Because you're not telling me. Its like you have something to hide" she said.
"Dear God!' he said and ran his fingers through his hair.
"How old are you?" she asked and he looked take back.
"What?"
Esselle rolled her eyes "How old are you its not rocket science! I'm 17" she said and he snorted.
"You're not 17" he said.
"Technically I am" she argued pointing a finger.
"Well, technically but..." he said and trailed off. He looked Esselle in the eyes and rolled his eyes.
"Which age" he said.
"The amount of years you've aged" she said and his head popped up.
"Oh that's easy!" he said waving a hand "21 so technically either way when I step into a bar the ass at the counter can't say jack" he said with a grin.

Esselle despite herself smiled. "You must have been awake a long time then" she said and he looked at her and winced.

"Ya well four years is a long time" he said.

Esselle's eyes widened "You've been awake four years?" she asked and he nodded.

"I was frozen when I was your age Ess" he said.

"Hu" she said and sat back on her elbows "See I did not know that"

"Its really not a big deal" he said and sat back on his elbows with her.

"How long were you frozen then?" Esselle asked and he looked at her "You know since you won't tell me when" Daniel sighed and looked out into the distance again.

The last fireworks lit the night sky until they came to a stop.

Daniel looked at her and his eyes grew violet. Esselle began to love when they did that.

Daniel opened his mouth to speak but there was a huge bang. And it wasn't more fireworks.

Daniel sprang up and Charlotte came pouring in out of breath. Daniel sighed rolling his eyes.

"Charlotte you scared the crap out of me" he said sitting back down.

Charlotte was out of breath when she spoke. The look on her face was enough to make Esselle's stomach turn.

"Its Burn" she said and Daniel's face went white and red at the same time and his eyes instantly went black when his body tensed.

Somewhere in Time- trilogy part 2

Charlotte gasped for air and the only expression of fear and worry clouded her naturally pretty face.
"He's here"

"What the hell do you mean Burn is here?" Daniel asked and Esselle was practically flying down the hallways.
"Daniel slow down" she said.
"The system failed. We don't know how when or by who we just know it went down. He might have been the one to cause it but he's here" Charlotte said and Daniel had steam coming out of his ears. Daniel and Charlotte were rushing down the hallway at lightening speed. Daniel had hold of Esselle's wrist and was basically pulling her along.
"Wait until i get a hold of him" Daniel snarled.
"No, stop. He maybe alone but Daniel he knows you too well. He knows you'll come after him and kill him the first chance you get" she said.
'I don't care" h snapped.
Charlotte sighed and she looked like a worried mother. "Daniel I didn't tell you he was here so you could kill him. I told you he was here so you can drive him out. You're the only one he'll listen to"
"Charlotte I want the son of a bitch out and I want him out now" he said and stopped in front of a door "And if killing him is what it takes then so be it"
He flung the doors open and it was a closet of weapons. He started grabbing things and shoving them in his pocket and

Charlotte looked ready to break a sweat.
"Daniel" she said and stood close next to him while he ignored her."Daniel please I'm begging you don't go through with this" she pleaded. Esselle had never heard Charlotte whisper so low and sound so vulnerable. It almost broke Esselle's heart. The problem here was Daniel was about to do something Charlotte clearly didn't want him to do. He was probably going to get hurt. And Charlotte loved him. He was like her son.
"Charlotte get Jasmine tell her to take Esselle home" Daniel said and at that Esselle's eyes were wide awake and alert along with her ears. "I want her out of here. Tell Kevin at the guard I want this entire building on lock down. No one goes in or a=out. I don't want Jasmine within a 100 mile radius of this building do I make myself clear?" he asked and looked at her.
Esselle had to slow down. Daniel no matter how much of a strong character he was always stood down to Charlotte. She made the calls she made the rules. For god's sake he was still on probation Charlotte had removed everyone else but him. Now Charlotte's face was white she was messing with her fingers and she swallowed hard. Finally she nodded.
"Fine" she said looking away.
"Yes hello hi!" Esselle said "Newbie here remember? Who's Burn?" she asked and all heads turned on her.
"Charlotte!" someone screamed and everyone looked down the hallway.
"He's infiltrating the computers" a red head shouted.
Charlotte practically sprang down the hallway but Daniel grabbed her arm and she looked at him.
"Char" he said "Be careful" She nodded and caught a glimpse of

Esselle.

"Get her out of here" she said and stepped closer to him. She placed her hand on the side of his face and her eyes were burning with power "Do what you have to do and finish him off"

Daniel nodded and she sprang off following the red head.

"Daniel!" Esselle heard. When she turned around she saw Jasmine let out a sigh of relief. She jogged over and fell into his arms.

"Are you alright?" he asked and she nodded.

"Are you?" she asked and looked at him.

"Don't ask" he said and she nodded.

"I want you out of here you understand me?" he said and Jasmine sighed but nodded. "Take Esselle wit you I don't even want you in New York. Get out. Get out and don't come back until I send for you" he said turning on his heels.

"Whoa whoa wait a second you want me to just leave?" Esselle ranted.

Daniel turned around and made a face. He opened his mouth but clammed shut. He took hold of her arm and walked down the next hallway looking either way before he grabbed a door opened it and shoved them both inside.

"Ok" he said and gave the eye. They were in a closet and there was barely any light "You need to please this one time just try not being so god damned stubborn and leave"

"Have you lost your mind?" she sad and he stood straight "You're about to do God knows what with God knows who but I'm pretty sure its going to get your ass killed!" she said and pointed a finger at him "It was bad enough to get Charlotte to abide by your rules and you expect me just walk out like that? You're

crazy! I don't even know what's going on!" she snapped.
Daniel opened his mouth but Esselle cut him off 'Oh right and I forgot not like you'd tell me anyway. Since you know you have this little thing going on when you don't tell me shi-!" but she was cut off. Daniel took Esselle in his arms squeezing her tight and kissed her. Esselle tried wiggling her arms free and she pounded on his chest.
"Leave now" he said pulling away.
"Daniel let me go" she moaned and he squeezed her tighter.
"Not until you promise you'll leave" he said and she looked at him.
"I don't make promises I can't keep" she said. He kissed her again long and hard but Esselle couldn't wiggle out of his grip so eventually Esselle gave up and he looked at her.
"Ess please you don't understand you have to go. if something happened to you..." he said and trailed off.
"Daniel!" Jasmine called from outside.
"Tomorrow I'll meet you" he said and Esselle breathed in "At noon on 34th street alright?" he said.
Esselle knotted her fist in his shirt "You're scaring me" she said and he smiled.
"I should be" he said and opened the door.
He practically dragged her out of the closet with her clinging to him.
Jasmine ran past them then came to a staggering stop.
"There you are!" she said. She had a tank top on and Esselle could see the marks on her upper arm.
"You know what to do" Daniel said pushing Esselle to Jasmine. Jasmine grabbed hold of Esselle's arm. Esselle got the feeling she

was feeling like a child.

"Burn" Jasmine said "He's well you know"

Daniel nodded and disappeared.

Jasmine was strong for 16 and pulled Esselle down the hallway. "I don't suppose you're going to tell me what's happening here?" she asked and Jasmine looked at her when she pounded on the elevator button.

"Its Burn" Jasmine said and he eyebrows narrowed "He was one of the first Invisibles. He's practically impossible to kill. He's all mechanics" she said and the elevator door opened and they were on ground level. Jasmine walked out filling a gun with bullets and Esselle looked at her.

"The only part of him that is still human is his heart. But its covered in steel" she said and yanked the doors to headquarters open.

"But what was it with everything Charlotte said about him and Daniel?" Esselle asked and Jasmine hailed a cab.

She snorted "Burn was his name and burn he shall do the world down that is" and a cab stopped in front of them.

The taxi cabs image flashed in front of Esselle the way the city did. It went from yellow to a glowing blue and black then went back.

Jasmine looked at her "He's one of us. You can tell you saw didn't you?" she asked and opened the car door. Esselle nodded.

'So you guys are everywhere aren't you?" she asked and stepped in.

"We have to" Jasmine said and caught a glimpse of the car driver. He had dark brown skin broad shoulders dark eyes and short hair. "Its Burn" she said and his eyes widened.

"I understand" he said.

"Take her anywhere but here. Bring her to the New Jersey branch. Tell them what happened and that she is allowed to come back in the morning" Jasmine said and Esselle caught her wrist.

"You're not coming?" she asked and Jasmine sighed. Her eyes grew darker.

"No I'm sorry. Just please trust me when I do this" she said.

"But Daniel said to leave" Esselle said.

Jasmine filled another gun with bullets "Daniel feels the need to protect everyone and always take the fall. This time. Burn is going have his work cut out for him with me" she said.

'But why?" Esselle pleaded. Jasmine shook free of Esselle's grip and grabbed the car door.

"Because Esselle" Jasmine began "The bastard killed my father" with that she slammed the car door shut and Esselle drove away.

Esselle hadn't been crying but she wanted to. All she wanted to do was go home. She wanted to go home and she wanted her

Somewhere in Time- trilogy part 2

father to take her in his arms and she wanted her mother to stroke her hair when she was younger. She wanted her big warn out blanket with the fushia flowers Mardrin had bought her when she turned 15 and the slippers Selena bought her when she was 12. She wanted to sit in her living room with a bowl of cereal and watch reruns of her favorite shows because quite frankly the shows nowadays sucked. They were crossing the Verrazano Bridge and the cab driver kept looking at her through the mirror.
"The New Jersey Branch really isn't that bad. Especially the one in Hoboken its really nice." he said and Esselle looked up.
She gave a sad smile "I'm sure it is" she said and went back to leaning against the window.
"Tell me you reside in headquarters right? do you know if Klaus is still there?" he asked.
"Klaus?" Esselle said. She had heard Daniel mention him once during training. "No, at least I don't think so"
He frowned "Oh because you see before I got transferred over to Connecticut I spent the first half of my training in New York 4 years ago. Then left for Connecticut then recently came back to New York" he said.
Something sparked in the bag of Esselle's mind. There was lots of traffic and they came to a stop.
"Did you say 4 years ago?" Esselle asked.
The man nodded "Yup"
"Then you must know my boy- uh trainer" Esselle stumbled.
The man raised an eyebrow "Maybe what's his name?" he asked.
"Daniel, his name is Daniel" Esselle said sitting on the edge of the seat.
"Daniel Carter?" he asked and Esselle nodded.

"Well of course I know him! I was with Klaus when they found him" he said and Esselle broke out into a smile.

"Really?" she asked and the guy nodded.

"Ya! We were friends! Joel Matthews at your service" he says and extends his hand.

Esselle laughs and shook it "Esselle Elunas" she said and he smiled.

"That's a very pretty name" he said.

"Thank you! I wish Daniel thought so" she joked.

Joel made a face "Psh! Girl he hates everyone's name" he said and moved up a little further the traffic was awful.

"Does he have a nickname for you?" he asked with a smile "Pretty sure he does"

Esselle laughed an rolled her eyes "Yes, its Essie not to forget sometimes Ess for sure but mostly Essie"

Joel made a face "Girl, that nickname gon stick wit chu for the rest of your life"he said. He had a bit of an accent to him. A definite New Yorker from Brooklyn accent. Esselle liked it it made her laugh.

"You said he was your trainer right?" Joel asked raising an eyebrow. Esselle nodded and he moved up a few feet.

"Mhm" he said looking at her "Just your trainer?" he asked. Esselle was blushing but laughing. "What's that supposed to mean?" she asked.

"Girl who you think you playing? You are talking to the wrong guy!" he said and moved up a few more feet while Esselle burst into hysteria.

"I have no idea what you're talking about" she joked.

"I'm not stupid ou obvious have it for him" he said and looked her up and down "And bad!"

"I do not!" Esselle argued.

"Oh yes you do. And by the looks of it the fact that he lets you call him by his name while he's training you says he's got it bad for you too" he said and the cars started moving a bit quicker.

Esselle was sitting sideways in the car on the edge just barely sitting early kneeling. She stood up tall with her shy little smile of pride and straightened out her outfit.

"Well I don't know" she said and sat back in her chair.

"Want to know what really gave it away?" he asked looking back as the car began moving in normal speed.

"You almost called him your boyfriend" he said.

Esselle's jaw dropped but she was smiling and he was laughing. Esselle didn't know what to say so she just sat back and crossed her arms. This guy was funny. SO it was official. She liked him.

"Ok changing the topic" Esselle said. She could see him smirking through the window.

"Tell me about you" she said.

"Well I've been awaken about almost 5 yeas now. I was frozen around 22 years ago when I was 20 so now I've aged a total of 25 years. Klaus was the one that found me. He was a good man. He trained Daniel and I. But after I left I lost contact with him" he said.

"Why'd you leave?" she asked.

"Well because I was originally from New York but I found out after my death my family moved to Connecticut so I asked for a transfer so I could be closer. My family and I grew apart so for the past few months I came back home. This city is where I belong" he said and Esselle smiled. She knew how he felt.

Somewhere in Time- trilogy part 2

"Anyway my girl is here. SO it worked out in the end" he said and Esselle smiled.

"Uwww" she said and he laughed a bit shy.

"Well don't uww yet we aren't together" he said.

"Why not?"Esselle asked.

He winced "Its complicated kid. You'll learn when you've been awake a few more years"

Esselle nodded and sighed. "May I ask you something?" she asked after they had been driving a while.

"Sure" he said.

"Daniel when you found him..." and Esselle trailed off "What was he like?"

They came to a read light and Joel looked back raising and eyebrow.

"Is he still an arrogant sarcastic narcissistic bastard?" he asked and Esselle smiled.

She nodded "Yup that's him"

"Well then there's your answer" he said and his eyes locked with the rode. "But aside from all that he seemed a bit broken and warn down" he said and Esselle began to listen.

"I'll never forget the look on his face when he came back after seeing his mother's tombstone-" and Esselle cut him off.

"His mother's dead?" she asked.

Joel nodded and his look seemed morbid "Shot and killed" Esselle shivered.

"Anyway he was just so gray. Then what really was the icing on the cake was when he found Alice" Joel said and made a left.

"Alice?" Esselle repeated.

Joel nodded and they began driving local. Esselle saw a sign that

Somewhere in Time- trilogy part 2

read

Welcome to Hoboken

"His sister had already been awaken we found her a few months after him. His sister warned him not to go but he insisted. It turned out this Alice he was in love with her. After they froze him they killed her looking for him. After that it was history thank God for his sister because after that" he said and shook his head "He had never been the same"

The car came a stop and Esselle looked up. They were in front of City Hall. The town had been a cute one with pretty humble homes and hills.

Joel turned around in the car and handed Esselle a card.

"If you ever need anything you call that number got that?" he said and Esselle nodded "I'm serious"

"But why are we here?" Esselle asked.

"Us Invisible are everywhere. Some of the most important buildings in the country are just a hiding place for us. This is one of them" he said and met Esselle's eye. "Now go"

"But how do I-" she began

"You're one of us. They'll know you have the mark just open the door it'll let you in" he said. Esselle stepped out of the car and felt her heart beat everywhere. She stood next to his window.

"Take care kid" he said "And call me if you need anything. I like you. You're different from the rest of them" he said eyeballing the building. And like that he drove off leaving Esselle alone in the dark at night.

Somewhere in Time- trilogy part 2

Esselle's heart was pounding so hard it made her sick to her stomach. She was hesitant. She didn't know whether or not it would be a good idea to knock on those doors. Esselle secretly wanted to turn around and go home. Then again Esselle wasn't sure if turning back would be the smartest thing to do. So besides herself she gently touched the long curvy door handle and grabbed it. Esselle felt something on her inner arm where her mark was and she looked down. It was her mark. It was glowing vibrant and blue. Esselle heard something from within the building like a grandfather clock ticking and then with out Esselle trying the door opened and she pushed. A gust of wind hit Esselle making her hair fly awry. She gently pushed the door opened and stepped into City Hall glancing back at the big clock in front of the building. Before the door shut behind her and it was dark and she was all alone. The lights turned on just lightly and Esselle was standing in the foyer. The building was beautiful

Somewhere in Time- trilogy part 2

and old with a long descending staircase and the hallway was long and wide. The floor was made of granite and marble with different corresponding patterns. The ceiling was arched and carved with different designs and the walls were a warm tan with wooden door frames and pictures hung on the walls. Joel was right. The Hoboken branch was that of a nice one. There were two candelabras on either side of Esselle just a foot below her height and sconces hanging on the walls. The entire building look lit by candlelight.
"Hello?" Esselle said and her voice begun to echo. "Hello?" she said again and sighed when there was no response.
"Hello" Esselle heard.
She shrieked and turned around. She hadn't expected a response. A woman smiled at her. "Hello"
"Um," Esselle said and straightened out "Hi" she said.
The woman was probably young. She was skin model pretty with blonde hair and dull blue eyes. She was average height and nice and slender. She had on knee high black boots with major heels black leather pants a black vest and black tank top. Her long blonde hair was pulled up into a high ponytail and she had delicate looking hands folded in front of her. She was standing with a popped leg and was smiling at Esselle.
"Um this is the Hoboken branch right?" Esselle looking around. She nodded and walked over to Esselle, her heels making clicking noises that echoed through the building.
"Yes it is, you must be from Headquarters" she said and Esselle looked at her. She had a very pretty southern accent.
"How'd you know?" Esselle asked.
The woman smiled "There was distress call sent out. You must be

Esselle" she said extending her hand. Esselle shook her hand.

"Yes" Esselle said and looked around again. The place was a lot to take in.

"Where's the other one?" she asked raising an eyebrow.

Esselle shook her head "Back in New York where she stood after she shoved me in a taxi"

The woman sighed "That sure sounds like her. You're new. They tend to protect the newer ones quicker than themselves" she said and released Esselle's hand. She flicked her head.

"Come let's talk" she said and lead Esselle down the long wide hallway.

"Us Invisible are a dying bread of human rare and invincible. But there are fewer and fewer of us as our numbers shrink" she said.

"I don't understand" Esselle said.

"That's why they were so quick to protect you. That and by the why Agent Carter spoke of you" she said and stopped "They must love you"

Esselle watched as the woman reached over and opened a door.

"You should get settled in. I know you don't have anything just open the drawers there should be something there. I'll meet you in an hour in my quarters." she said and Esselle stepped into the room.

"But wait" Esselle said looking back "I don't know you're name"

She smiled "SueAnne" she said "SueAnne Donnor"

Somewhere in Time- trilogy part 2

Esselle was all alone in a room that looked like it was ripped out of the Victorian Era and shoved into 2045. The bed was huge. Just about so big it could fit four people. The bed frame was huge and made of dark wood with intricate carvings. The bed sheets were brown and tan and the pillows were satin. There were four tall posts apart of the bed and a small chandelier giving light. There were two night stands with blue and green Tiffany lamps sitting on them. There was one large french window with beautiful red curtains. There was an a huge wardrobe and two doors. One was a closet and the other led to a bathroom. Esselle got cleaned up. She washed the scent of fireworks from her hair and slipped into an outfit she found in the drawers. Odd enough Esselle felt as if all these people wore was black. And it was true. At least her heels were black to match the rest.

****
****

It took Esselle a lot of wandering around to find SueAnne's office. And yet she still couldn't find her way. Luckily it was late and everyone was asleep. She had not wanted to bump into anyone then explain why she was there. After a while Esselle wished she had bumped to someone. Anyone. So they could help her find her way. There were no signs no directions no map on the wall like in malls. Nothing. Sometimes Esselle wondered. How did people think Esselle was to find her way? By magic?

There was a long corridor Esselle found herself in. The light was dim and there were shadows taking shape of the things in her surroundings. The moonlight gave the corridor a blue light kind of feeling and Esselle had an unsettling feeling in her gut. She was lost. Completely and utterly lost and now she was screwed. Now she really wished she had bumped into someone. Esselle banged her head against the wall behind her and looked either way. Had she been going in circles or did everything just look the same?

"Are you lost?" someone asked. Esselle jumped with a gasp and looked to her left.

"Well?" he said "You look very lost to me"

This guy was cute. Not Daniel status cute but cute. He was probably literally just a tiny bit below Daniel. The only thing that didn't put him at Daniel level was that his eyes were brown. Because if they were a light killer color he'd definitely be Daniel level cute. He had dark brown hair and he was tall. Very tall. He was practically towering over Esselle. He stood at the end of the hallway standing sideways with his hands shoved in his front pockets. His hair was very long and combed to the side he was all in black then again everyone that was one of them was. One of her. His eyes were huge and a light brown like Esselle's mother.

"I Um," Esselle stuttered. He examined her with piercing eyes. Esselle stood up straight and looked at him "I was looking for SueAnne's office. You wouldn't happen to know where it is would you?" she asked.

He tilted his head at her. He looked like a total badass. Complete Dawn status badass he had a blade sticking out of either side of his boots and a few knives shoved through his belt.

Somewhere in Time- trilogy part 2

"I don't think I've seen you here before" he said.

"That's because you haven't" Esselle said and he raised his eyebrows with a nod.

"Well then Welcome" he said.

"Ya well don't get used to me. I'm here for a day and I'll be gone tomorrow" she said walking over to him.

"Well in that case Welcome for today" he said and extended his hand "Terrance"

Esselle was hesitant at first when she looked at him. He smirked and Esselle narrowed her eyes at him taking his hand.

"Esselle" she said.

He nodded "That's a very pretty name" he said and Esselle let go of his hand.

"I know" she said and looked behind "So do you know where I could find her office?" she asked.

Terrance nodded "Right this way kiddo" he said turning on his heels and working a strut down the hallway. Dawn did the same thing. Oh yes. Total badass.

"Are you coming?" he called behind him continuing to walk.

Esselle blinked and followed "Ya well I'm not a kid. I'm probably old enough to be your mother" she said. And at that he laughed.

****

****

Terrance stopped in front of a tall dark cherry wood door. The handles were long and curved probably made of brass or bronze and the hallway was lit by only candles. To Esselle it all looked like something pulled out of a story book. Terrance tapped the silver plaque next the door that read:

Chief SueAnne Donnor

"This is where you'll find our southern belle" he said.
"Is that sarcasm?" Esselle asked and he narrowed his eyes at her.
"No" he said and took a moment to deliberate. He made a so-so face and said "Yes"
Such a Dawn thing to say Esselle thought.
Esselle sucked in her breath and reached for the door. He quickly blocked her hand and she looked at him.
"What?" she snapped.
"You don't knock?" he asked. He reached up and grabbed what looked like a metal ring attached to the door and banged it against the wood.
He looked at Esselle and cracked his knuckles. "That's how things are done here new bee" he said.
Esselle made a face "Ya well remember I'm here for a day" she said.
"Come in!" Esselle heard from behind the door.
She looked at Terrance who gave a knock "Now you may open the door" he said and walked passed her.
She turned to look behind her and threw her hands up.
"Thanks!" she said and he waved a hand behind him.
"Your Welcome!" he called back and disappeared into the darkness.
Esselle opened the door and stepped into the room. It was a big square room. One wall was a big arched window. Half made of clear class so you could see outside to a rooftop garden and the other half made of stained glass. On either side the windows were two walls covered in shelves filled with leather bound books. And then there was a desk big with a small lamp sitting on top of it. SueAnne was sitting behind it working vigorously on

Somewhere in Time- trilogy part 2

paper work. Esselle looked to her left and saw an arc in the wall that lead to what looked like a sitting are. There was big middle rug an the fireplace was on. Odd with it being summer. There was another window arched as well but it was entirely stained glass.
"You said you wanted to see me" Esselle said.
SueAnne looked up from her work and smiled.
"Yes I did" she said. She had a gold colored metal pen in her hand and she stuck it back in its place. Her chair was made of dark leather and was glossy in the lamp and candle light.
She pointed to the chair in front of her.
"Sit" she said and Esselle did so.
SueAnne looked tired. Her hair was a mess falling apart in bits and pieces and she had a pencil sticking out from her awfully done bun.
"So" she said and pulled off her reading glasses. "I was recently on the phone with headquarters"
Esselle was sitting on the edge of her seat. "What did they say?" she asked.
SueAnne took in a deep breath and looked away. "Well for starters the situation has been put under control" she said "For now" she quickly added. She yanked open the bottom drawer of her desk. She took out to glasses. They were thick and patterned so that when you look through them the image was disoriented.
"What else happened? Is everyone alright?" Esselle asked.
SueAnne dropped a big bottle of Carmel colored Hennessey on her desk and looked at Esselle with indifferent eyes.
"That depends. What's your definition of alright?" she asked and popped the bottle open running her fingers through her thin

hair.

"Um, alive?" Esselle said hesitantly.

SueAnne nodded distantly and went to pouring "When then yes everyone's per say alright. But Burn took a few confidential files with him hen he attacked" she said and handed her a glass.

"Oh no I can't drink" Esselle said gently putting it back on her desk. SueAnne gave her a look. Esselle stood tall in her chair and folded her hands in her lap.

"I'm not legal yet" she said.

SueAnne opened her mouth to speak but shut it quickly. She shut her eyes and shook her head.

"Child just take it trust me you'll need it after this conversation" she said shutting the bottom drawer of her desk.

Esselle liked SueAnne's southern accent it sounded sweet as honey. Maybe Terrance was right. She did look and talk like a southern belle.

Esselle examined the glass in her hands. It had diamond shaped bumps on it that felt like dull pikes to her skin when she held it. SueAnne caught Esselle looking at it and smiled.

"I see you're examining my daddy's cup" she said and Esselle looked up.

SueAnne pushed her chair in closer to her desk and held her glass in her hands.

"My daddy was your typical Georgia man with land but he always kept his glasses intact. He used to say a good classy southern man always had beautiful glasses in his study" she smiled softly at the glass turning her hand "I inherited these when he died. Along with the ranch and the estate and all the family heirlooms. I was always Daddy's favorite of us seven kids." she said and put

Somewhere in Time- trilogy part 2

her glass down.

"I'm so sorry" Esselle said. Esselle had just met SueAnne yet she felt like she knew her even without knowing her story. Just the look in her eyes made her heart break.

"Its not your fault baby doll. He died of a broken heart." she said and looked at her. SueAnne shrugged. "My Daddy was already an older man when he and Mama had me. So when I was brought back and he saw me his poor little heart couldn't take it. He died smiling holding my hand in his death bead" SueAnne yanked the hair tie from her hair and her locks came cascading past her shoulders. Esselle hadn't notice but she had beautiful hair. Like a doll.

"Now enough about me" she said with a soft smile "Back to headquarters"

Esselle nodded and took a sip from her glass. It burned her throat and her mouth making her eyes water but she didn't care. SueAnne was right. After this conversation Esselle did need a glass. She took the rest down in one gulp and realized she needed another one. SueAnne did the same and filled their glasses again before sitting back in her chair.

"So I was informed you're allowed to leave in the morning" she said and Esselle nodded.

"Preferably so that I can be back before noon" she said and drank from her glass.

SueAnne nodded "Yes I was told that too. Also you are to come back here"

At that Esselle's eyes widened. But SueAnne just finished her glass then swung it back and forth between her fingertips.

"What do you mean come back here?" Esselle asked.

Somewhere in Time- trilogy part 2

"Child" SueAnne said and planted her elbows on her desk. "I was going through your reports your a special one. The rest of your documents are getting shipped out here first thing tomorrow morning"

Esselle began to tremble in horror.

"You are being relocated over here for the time being. Finish up some more of your training before you can be properly transferred to the Los Angeles branch in California." she said.

"California!" Esselle blurted out. "Why are they shipping me anywhere in the first place?"

"We have reason to believe that your are the one that set the chain reaction almost thirty years ago. You haven't even received your tests besides. California is excellent for specialty cases like yours. There is more space for training and its safer especially in remote areas. Headquarters isn't safe for you anymore. Someone's bound to find out who you and where you've been and when that happens we want to make sure you're as far away as possible." SueAnne said and her eyes grew a duller blue.

SueAnne was very logical when she spoke and was careful to properly state her facts.

"But I don't understand. I feel like my mind is spinning! No one ever tells me anything and when they do its some half ass story and then I get hit over the head with stuff like this and I'm completely unprepared!" Esselle ranted. Or maybe it was the Hennessey talking. Either way Esselle was furious.

"I understand this is hard-" SueAnne began calmly but Esselle cut her off.

"Hard? Hard? What the hell I'm supposed to do? Disappear into thin air? My family is here my friends that know I'm alive what

are they going to think when I disappear again? Its hard enough as it is with my parents already on my case about never being home how am I supposed to explain my absence?" she asked.
"That's the thing Ms. Elunas" SueAnne said "Us Invisible this is a tough lifestyle. One I wish people didn't have to live but its the truth. That's the whole point. You're supposed to disappear. You will in the eyes of society literally become invisible" she said.
Esselle couldn't believe it. She needed more information more time. She needed to straighten things out and she sure as hell had to do everything she could to keep herself from going anywhere especially Los Angeles. She needed to talk to Daniel. As soon as possible. But she would have to wait till tomorrow. Until then Esselle had to squeeze out as much as she could from SueAnne first.
"Ok let's start from the beginning. Who is Burn?" Esselle asked.
"Ah" SueAnne said and pushed in her chair again. "Burn is one of the elite"
"Who are the elite?" Esselle asked.
"The Elite are the first ten people frozen. Ever. All the way back in 1995. He was the fifth one frozen and fifth to be awaken." SueAnne said.
"Ok why did he attack headquarters?" Esselle asked leaning in to hear.
"He attacked headquarters because around let me see 25 years ago he was out casted. This happened because Burn wanted to take down the government and reveal the identity of the Invisible. He wanted to expose us and the government for what they did." SueAnne explained.
"Why didn't he?" Esselle asked growing more curious as the story

Somewhere in Time- trilogy part 2

went along.

"The Elite and the council they absolutely forbade it. That lead to the explosion at Highest Point at the universal meeting." SueAnne continued and filled both their glasses again. Esselle took hers gratefully and nodded.

"What's that?" Esselle asked and took a sip.

"High Point is in Miami, Florida. That's where the Universal meeting takes place every single year. That's when all the high leaders of the Invisibles meet to discuss whatever needs to be discussed. Burn planned to sabotage that meeting. He set up a bomb but it malfunctioned and he almost died. That's why he's part metal he was so badly damaged in the bombing" SueAnne said and when she went to drink from her cup she made a face and realized it as empty. Esselle would have smiled but she was too buys processing what she had just heard. See if everyone was as thorough and informative as SueAnne maybe she wouldn't be in the dark.

"See I understand more. Now why was he in headquarters" Esselle asked.

"He was in headquarters trying to access the data base of new Invisible. he's trying to build an army and stole some files. Luckily yours wasn't one of them. He'd have a field day with you" she said and ran her fingers through he hair.

"Does he kill people?" Esselle asked remembering what Jasmine had said about her father.

SueAnne nodded. "He was an assassin for a while"

Esselle nodded as things began to make more sense. "Who did he usually kill?" Esselle asked and SueAnne made a face.

"That is none of our business. He did what he had to do and that was it. No one really looks into that" She said. Esselle sighed and sat back. She looked at her reflection in her drink before finishing it.

"But it won't happen again. It turns out the reason why Burn was able to enter headquarters is because he overridded the system but it won't happen again" she said and looked at the Hennessey bottle which was now empty. She sighed and put everything away.

"Now you have a long day tomorrow better go onto bed" she said. Esselle nodded and left.

****
****

WHile Esselle lie in her bed in the dark she began to wonder and think and try her best to put all the pieces of the puzzle together in her mind. But it didn't work. There was too much missing. But either way everything was unraveling before her eyes.

Somewhere in Time- trilogy part 2

Somewhere in Time- trilogy part 2

Esselle all that night was just thinking of get nightmare. It was with her parelotnts and she tried her best not to think about it. Esselle couldn't get out of get mind wEsselle hat Daniel said to her that time. He had suspected Esselle's parents. He had said to her face he believed get parents were involved he said to look at the facts. Esselle didn't want to believe it. Was she in denial? Maybe. Did she love get parents? Of course. Was it complicated? Absolutely. Was she torn? No doubt. Then she began to think of three conversation she over heard. When her parents thought she was asleep. Selena and Mardrin were in their side. But she had no idea what this meant. Were her parents involved? And if so how? How could they have done this to her? How could they have done this. Their daughter. Their only daughter. It made Esselle sick to her stomach. All those tests they gag done on her. Esselle realized they must have known all along what they were doing to her. They knew they always knew. They were preparing her body for it. What confused Esselle more was the chain reaction. She had no idea what that meant. What she did know was the virus mutated through the years as the government conducted different things in various Invisible but the basics stood the same. Except for her. Except for Esselle. Esselle was different special somehow in someway. She was determined to find out. Which meant one thing. It was time to go home. It was time to confront her parents.

****
****

It was windy in New York. The clouds were dense and greedy and people seemed a lot calmer than usual. Then again it was Friday and they were probably all just relaxed. Esselle when she had gotten dressed this missing was disappointed. All they had was black. Literally. Now Esselle blended in with everyone else's modern day attire. Esselle had to face out sooner or later. She began feeling odd. A very awful unsettling feeling. Almost as if something was off. It was one minute till noon and she turned the corner. She had so many questions that need answers her mind was ready to burst. Then she saw him. It wasn't fair. It was so unfair. It would never be fair. She hated him with every fiber in her being. The way he made her feel every time she saw him. It was sickening and she hated it. She hated it when her heart would skip a beat and her knees would go week. She hated it when her mind would race a mile a minute and all she could think of all she could imagine was him putting his arms around her. She hated the feeling of her stomach turning and the giddy urge to jump for joy every time his eyes met hers. It was an awful feeling Esselle felt that of a feeling and experience she had never had before. Not with anyone. Not anyone but him. So when he stood there nonchalantly with his hands shoved into his front pockets, like he didn't have a care in the world, Esselle wanted to hate him. She wanted to hate him for making her feel the way she did. Then the light would hit him just right and Esselle could feel all of that just melting away. Because all she want to do was smile at him. And all she wanted him to do was smile with her.Back at her. That's all she wanted. That was all she ever wanted. But Esselle just kept walking. She tried to concentrate on breathing. She wanted to run. She wanted to hug him and kiss him and ask him if he was alright. At the same time she wanted to grab him. And punch him and kick him and yell at him and tell him he scared her to death. She wanted to ask him why they were

Somewhere in Time- trilogy part 2

shipping her some place else. She wanted to ask questions and demand answers. Then she wanted to holler at him and scream and yell and complain and nag and ask him why he kept so many things for her. Why he didn't tell her anything. But then that all melted away. She was feet away from her when he looked her way. He let out a deep sigh of relief and turned to face her.
"Ess" Daniel said and Esselle felt the sudden urge to cry. And the sudden urge to punch him in the face. Either way Esselle had been a mess of emotions at the moment. So she just let out the same sigh of relief he did and threw her arms around him.
"Danny" she said because she couldn't say anything else. But he just hugged her back and didn't say a word. Esselle didn't want to yell anymore. She was just tired. Sick and tired. She had an awful migraine just pounding against the inside of her head and she felt dizzy. Daniel wasted no time. He took Esselle's face in his hands and kissed her. Now Esselle was angry. Now Esselle wanted to smack and yell at him and shout to him and ask him why? But right after she'd kissed him back. For a moment Esselle let the world dissolve and she just froze in the moment and time where everyone for just a second was alright and safe. Then she pulled away and kept her eyes shut for a moment before looking at him.
"California Daniel? Really?" she asked. "Because you couldn't send me any farther away?"
Daniel quickly looked around as if he could feel the burn of people's eyes resting upon him. He grabbed Esselle's arm and rushed into an alley way. Esselle leaned against a brick wall before he frantically looked both ways then at her and grabbed her shoulders.

"Who told you?" he asked.
"Chief Donnor" Esselle said and he sighed.
"Oh right" he said and his hands fell to his side "I forgot"
"Daniel have you lost it? Shipping me off to California when I barely know what's going on? Its like your sending me into the lion's den completely blind" Esselle said softly but urgently. She had no time to waste and had to talk quickly.
"The less you know the better" he said and his eyes were as blue as ever. But no not violet. Not yet. The sun was hitting him. Enough to make his hair glisten like a pool of black diamonds.
"No Daniel the less I know the worse. You have kept me in the dark for too long you can't keep doing that. Keeping me in the dark is the worst thing to do don't you know that?" Esselle said and her voice had a pleading tone to it "I'm oblivious to everything going on around me. What is it are you hiding something from me?" she asked.
At that he blinked a few times at her and his entire demeanor changed. He looked almost disgusted by what he had said to her. He looked as if Esselle had spit in his face or stabbed in the back.
"Hitting something from you?" he said and his tone was deadly.
"I have just about been busting my ass to keep you safe and you think I'm hiding something from you?" he quickly shook his head.
"No now you've lost it"
"I've lost it?" Esselle was baffled "The hell if I know if you're lying! I'm barely with you enough to know the difference anyway!" she snapped.
"That's not fair" he said pointing a finger at her "You have no idea what goes on"

"In case you haven't noticed that's the problem here!" Esselle realized she had begun to shout "I'm over here playing the pretty little damsel in distress meanwhile everyone else is doing what they have to protect me, to help me, to find out what happened to me, yet me!" Esselle said with her hands frantically pointing to herself "Doesn't have a God damned clue as to what's going on!" and she flung her arms in the air. Esselle was angry. She was furious and she could feel the tears beginning to burn the back of her eyes but she ferociously fought them back. She was not about to cry. At all.

"Your ass is getting shipped off to California first thing next week that's it period amen!" he shouted at her. It sent a shiver through Esselle's body making her feel numb and cold. His voice was so deep when he yelled at her it reminded her of the voice of the monsters in kid movies.

Now Esselle was crying. But they were burning red hot angry tears streaking her face like claw marks.

"It's not fair" she said through gritted teeth trying not to sob through the pain. "You just want me to drop everything and go off to California without another word. What about my car? What about my case? What about my training?" Esselle asked "What about us?"

Daniel took a deep breath and just looked at her.

"Over my dead body are you just shipping me off to the other side of the country without another word! I won't do it! I won't let you make me do it Daniel! I tolerate a lot of your nonsense but this..." she said and sighed "This I won't do. I won't leave you here. I won't leave Jasmine or Dawn or Charlotte or Trevor. I won't leave the ones I love. My mom my dad Selena-" Mardrin.

She was going to say. But she stopped herself and sighed.
"I made promises to these people I intend to keep. I made promises to myself. I missed 28 years of my life. I'm finally catching up with my best friend who thought I was dead for years on end!" Esselle said and wiped a tear from her face. "Daniel Selena has been deprived of me for 28 years. I mean I..." she trailed off and a tear hit the ground. He reached for her and she shoved his hand away.
"I'm finally able to talk to her look at her hold her. I get to watch her children grow even if I am a little late. Her granddaughter Daniel her granddaughter she's beautiful and just a few months I could watch over her. And my parents. They finally have their daughter back" she said and met his eye.
"I can't do that to them. I won't" she said.
"Texas" Daniel said and she shook her head.
"New York" she said.
"Florida"
"New York"
Daniel rolled his eyes and exasperated and his jaw tensed. "D.C" he said.
"New York" Esselle said softly pronouncing each word clearly.
He sighed and twisted one of her curls through his fingers.
"New Jersey" he said and Esselle fell against the brick wall behind her.
"What?" she asked.
"There's no way in hell I'm letting you stay in New York. At least you can stay Hoboken" he said.
Esselle sighed. This was as close as she was going to get. "Fine" she said and took his hand in hers. Esselle grew tired of yelling

and screaming she had an awful headache.

"When's the next time i see you?" she asks and he looks at her "You know since I'm on exile and all" and her tone was far too bitter than anticipated.

Daniel sighed "Once a year" he said and Esselle's eyes widened.

"Are you kidding me?" she asked and he shook his head.

"Essie this can go on forever" he said.

She shook her head "5 times a day" she said and he laughed looking out into the street.

"2 a year" he said.

"4 times a day" she protested.

"Once a month he suggested.

"Three times a day. We can have meals together" she said and despite her being rather seriously he laughed but without humor.

"Once every two weeks" he said.

Esselle shook her head "twice a day"

"Once a week" he said narrowing his eyes at her.

"Every other day" Esselle said and this time she wouldn't budge.

Daniel just shook his head "Absolutely not" he said.

"Either you find me or I find you" Esselle said and tilted her head "Your choice"

Daniel shut his eyes for a moment and looked away. Was this killing him inside? Esselle didn't know. But she had wanted to know. Then he broke out to a smile and rubbed his jaw and chin when he looked at her and chuckled soundlessly. Esselle would give anything to know what he was thinking at that moment. Daniel grew closer to her and pressed his forehead to hers shutting his eyes. He let out a deep breath and Esselle could tell he was about to do something he hadn't want to.

"Fine" he muttered. Esselle bit back a smile.
"See not that hard now was it?" she asked and he pulled away from her.
"Esselle sometimes I just wish..." he said and trailed off.
Esselle made a comical face and smiled "Whoa. It just got serious. There goes my awful name"
He didn't laugh "I wish it weren't so hard to please you"
"To please me?" Esselle said and stepped away "You wanted to fly me off across the country without a single world"
Daniel looked around as if he couldn't believe it and his shoulders began to scrunch up.
"What do you want me to do? I'm trying to keep you safe!" he said.
"Oh!" Esselle said rolling her eyes and making a face "Bull shit!" she snapped and he looked at her. "You just don't want to let me into your 'Agent's only' little club or tree house or whatever it is you call it! You just want to be the one to have all the knowledge that's it!" Esselle said.
"What the hell are you talking about!"
"You know what I'm talking about!" she shouted back "Rant all you want about how much you're trying to keep me safe but you fail to tell me exactly how you're doing that!"
Daniel just looked at her bewildered.
"So go ahead!" she said flinging an arm "Keep on hiding things from me Daniel see how that all works out!"
"Hiding things like what!" he screamed at her "Like the fact that your parents are the ones that killed you in the first place then shoved you in a freezer afterwards! You were probably their little experiment! They probably poked around in your head long

enough to finish what they wanted to do with you and then tossed you to the side when they were done and had what they needed!"

Esselle stepped back. She was chocking. Very slowly and painfully dying. Against Esselle's will the tears burned the back of her throat and her eyes as they came pouring down. They were hot and her face was soaked. No use for it now she didn't bother wiping them away. They already ruined her makeup. Her heart was racing so fast she could hear the thump in her ears. How could anyone say anything like that to her? Ever.

Daniel looked at her red hot with anger at first but that quickly melted away as he continued to breathe his face slowly softened until he looked just slightly annoyed. Then his eyes grew wide with realization as if something had just hit him dead in the face. Esselle still shocked and taken aback looked away finding herself struggling with even the thought of looking at him making her stomach turn.

"How could you..." and Esselle trailed off "Say that to me?"

"Esselle" he said and reached for her but she smacked his hand away as if his touch burned. She turned around and ran. She ran out and bumped into people on the way into the streets. Esselle bumped into a man and his wife and when she ran past them they shouted curses behind her. Esselle ran. The city's streets were so dense during lunch hour Esselle could barely see straight.

Esselle pounded into what felt like a cement wall and she looked up.

"Elle" Mardrin said and Esselle swore to herself. Because Manhattan wasn't big enough he just had to find his way and

bump into her.'Esselle quickly looked away and tried to find another way to run but he caught hold of her shoulder's. "Elle?" he said and she looked at him defiantly.
But it didn't woke she broke out into tears again.
"Elle what's wrong?" he asked.
"Nothing!" she said with an obvious tone. She twisted her arm and pushed him away "Let me go!" she said and he grabbed her wrists.
"Not until you tell me why you're running around the streets of Manhattan like a lunatic crying your eyes out!" he said and looked at her hard. His yellow-greens eyes turned color in the sunlight. It reminded Esselle of their first day of high school. He had looked at her when she told him her stomach was turning. But he just smiled at her and squeezed her hand. Then the sunlight drenched him in gold and changed the tone of his eyes. That was exactly the way he looked now.
"Mardrin just leave me alone I don't want to talk about it right now" she said and wiggled free sprinting down 2 avenue.

Somewhere in Time- trilogy part 2

Somewhere in Time- trilogy part 2

Esselle pushed herself through the front doors of her townhouse. To hell with this. To hell with that. To hell with going to New Jersey and to hell with everyone else she wasn't going anywhere. She wanted to be home and stay home. Esselle looked around frantically and noticed the house turning grey as the sun outside in the sky was moving and the clouds began piling in. It was supposed to rain soon.
"Mom!" Esselle shouted and darted to the foot of the stairs
"Dad!" she hollered and ran up the stairs.
Their bedroom. Empty. Esselle flew downstairs. The living room. Empty. Dining room. Empty. Kitchen, balcony, rooftop, basement, attic, everywhere. Empty. Esselle leaned against the hallway wall and pressed her palm to her forehead. She slid against the wall hitting the ground with a thump. She buried her

face in her hands and begun to cry. Esselle had not cried not in a while. She really hadn't taken the time to let her emotions run wild. So she cried. She cried for being frozen. Which was something she had never even given a second thought. Esselle was frozen trapped in a dome for 28 years frozen. She had missed out on her life. Esselle had never noticed before but she was forced to grow up so quickly. Esselle didn't want to be some kind of government toy or some kind of warrior with a glowing tattoo. No. Esselle wanted to be a hormonal, moody, whiny, bratty, immature, selfish, childish, kid. The teenager that she was. Esselle may have been on this Earth 45 years but she had only aged and lived for 17 of them. Meaning she had the mentality of a high school kid. Basically. Esselle breathed in and out deeply and whimpered. She could barely breathe. Esselle heard her front door open and her head darted up.

She heard voices and she stretched her legs out in front of her and turned her body.

"I don't even think that's logical" she heard a woman say.

"I think it is" this time it was a male's voice.

"Dad!" Esselle shouted. The clicking of shoes against the polished floors of downstairs stopped along with the voices. "Mom!" Esselle said again and got on her hands.

"Sweetie?" and this time it was Vivienne calling for her daughter. Esselle hurried to her feet but slipped several times and darted down the hallway. Esselle flung herself at the banister almost falling over. There at the bottom of the stairs her mother stood elegantly gently touching the railing in her lab coat and her father dropping his keys on the table near the door.

"Elle we haven't seen you for days where have you been?" her father said. But Esselle wasn't listening. She flew down the stairs and tripped on the last step.

"Elle" her mother said again. Esselle flung herself into her father's arms and begun to cry again.

Her parents gave each other quizzical looks but she just clung to her father the way magnets cling to each other and she shoved her face into his lab coat and it smelled of downy and tide.

"Daddy" she whimpered and she found herself choking on the tears.

"What's wrong with you?" her mother said and her father frowned and shook his head.

"Mommy" Esselle stuttered gasping for air. She grabbed her mother's arm and tugged her closer. Her mother tried digging her face from her husbands lab coat but she couldn't. And Henry just stroked his daughter's hair with the most lost look on his face. But all the while Esselle wondered how parents like hers could ever do what they did to her. And she wondered what they were thinking the whole time. So then it came to the point where Esselle thought about if her parents really loved her or her only purpose was to serve as their lab rat. So lastly she wondered is her whole life was just a lie.

****
****

Esselle had sat on the couch in her father's arms while her mother braided her hair for hours on end letting the tv run. Then night had fallen and her parents went to bed. Esselle had not spoken a word and her parents had not asked her a question. The moon was full and the night sky odd enough was filled with clouds and an abundance of beautiful shinning stars. Esselle was asleep under her covers when her mind drifted off to a black dark place. A place where Daniel's voice continued to echo in her ears. No matter what she'd there was his voice lingering in her mind. *your parents are the ones that killed you in the first place then shoved you in a freezer afterwards* Was what he had said to her. *You were probably their little experiment* he said. He'd said they poked around in her mind. Thinking about it had made her cry in her sleep. Yet again. It was like he wanted to hurt her. It was like he wanted to take her heart rip it out of her chest and squeeze it until it turned to dust between his fingertips. And he did. That he did. Then Esselle heard a thump. Almost like a tap. Esselle opened her eyes and her eyebrows furrowed. It couldn't have been what she thought it was. Then another one. Esselle this time opened her eyes. Was she going crazy? No. She went back to bed. As if right on cue ten seconds later the third jump. This time Esselle looked up around her bed.

Esselle thought. It wasn't whom she though it was. She wouldn't believe it. It couldn't be? Something like this could not be happening. Not since high school. Esselle waited for the rest of the pattern. It was three thuds ten seconds apart. Then four thuds five seconds apart and lastly five thuds back to back. Esselle waited and counted. 1...2...3...4. 4 thuds five seconds a part. She yanked the blanket off and hesitated to get out of her bed. So she waited. tap, tap, tap, tap, tap. Five thuds back to back. This had been enough for Esselle. She darted out of bed yanking her silk robe along with her and threw open the doors of her balcony and practically flung herself over the railing to look at who was there. And it had been exactly whom she thought. "Mardrin!" she said in a loud frantic whisper.

He smiled "Hey Elle" he looked mischievous.

"What the hell are you doing outside my window in the middle of the night! What are we 17!" she loudly whispered urgently. He laughed.

'Well technically you are" he said and Esselle made a face.

"What are you doing here?" she asked and he walked over to the wall "If my parents caught you they'd kill you"

He grabbed on to a vine growing on the walls and made a face "What are they going to do?" he asked "Make me break up with you?"

At that Esselle laughed. Esselle couldn't help but feel the strangest thing. Almost as if this had all happened before. Before Esselle knew it she had a wry smirk across her face and and Mardrin was smiling sitting on the ledge of her balcony. He extended his arms and smile.

"Feels like deja vu doesn't it?" he asked.

Esselle nodded softly at the memory "Yes" she said "It is"

Mardrin gave a funny smile. "Do you remember when we were 16" he said and Esselle begun to laugh.

"Yes, you don't even have to remind me!" she said and walked over to the other side for the ledge of the balcony and placed her hands on it. The air was sweet when it hit her and she shut her eyes to smile.

"I was 16 years old" she begun "And I had lost the broach my grandmother gave me" Esselle swallowed back any tears that might threaten to come. But he just tilted his head and looked at her thoughtfully.

She took in and let out a deep breath "I was devastated that whole day after words so you came to my window" and Esselle giggled. She flipped her hair from her face and looked at him "And held up a basket" she said demonstrating with her hands "And I'll never forget what you said" she said and shifted on her feet.

"You said to me 'I may not be your grandmother or your broach'" she said and the last part he joined in

"'But at least I can try and make you feel better'" he nodded.

"Exactly" Esselle said "You remember?" she asked and he nodded again.

"How could I forget. You were heartbroken" he said and leaned in a bit "Kind of like now" he said a bit sarcastically and Esselle smiled.

"What are you doing here?" she asked.

He held up a basket and put it on the ledge. He gave it a funny look and sighed then he looked up at her with green eyes that somehow in the moonlight lost most of its yellow.

"You seemed pretty upset" he said.

"Ah!" Esselle said and she tried not to laugh. He was thoughtful. He was always thoughtful she reminded herself. "So since you wouldn't talk to me I figured I'd throw rocks at your window in the middle of the night and figure out what's up" he said and she laughed. She slid unto the ledge of the balcony on the opposite of the basket.

"We used to do lost of stuff like this together" she said tracing the shape of the basket and looked at him "Before"

Mardrin took a deep breath and shifted where he sat "Elle listen we may not be together together anymore but that still doesn't mean I don't care about you. That it doesn't bother me when your hurt or angry" he said and he sounded so logical. Another

thing the man she loved always was. Logical. He tilted his hand back and forth and gently moved his hand when he spoke "We can still be friends" he said and Esselle let out a cold laugh.
"Mardrin" she teased "Are you breaking up with me?" she asked and he laughed uncomfortably.
He placed his hand on the back of his neck and Esselle laughed. She missed watching his emotions change. It was one of her favorite things about him.
"Because when a couple breaks up" she continued "And they say they can still befriends" she scrunched up her face and shook her head "It never really works"
This time he just laughed naturally. She loved the way he laughed. And she loved being the reason why. It made her heart flutter.
It fell silent for a moment and then he had a very soft smile just looking at her.
"What?" she asked.
He just gently raised his shoulders and shook his head "Its just nice to look at you again" he said.
Esselle blushed but she straightened out her back "I do have that kind of effect on people I should have warned you" she said and he laughed. She smiled too but her cheeks still felt warm.
He flicked his head "Come on" he said and Esselle widened her eyes at him.
"What?"
"Come on I said. I'm taking you out. It annoys me when you're depressed" he said and jumped off the ledge to a flat landing.
Esselle turned "Where are we going?" she asked.
He made a face and grabbed the basket. "You have five minutes"

he said holding up his fingers. He jumped and then was out of sight. Esselle looked around for a moment. Was she dreaming. "5 minutes Elle!" Mardrin called up. She looked over the ledge and found herself with a smile. Mardrin had always did things like these with her. You know almost 30 years ago.
****
****

"What are you doing slow down!" Esselle said with a case of hysteria. Mardrin looked back at her and smiled.
"I'm running. Isn't it obvious?" he asked and pulled her by the hand along. They were laughing. Just laughing reminiscing on the past as they walked through central park. The park was warm but also nice and cool at night and the clouds cleared up a bit more and the stars shone brighter than diamonds in the distance. They slowed down while they reached the top of the hill where their tree stood and Esselle squeezed her stomach as she laughed. Mardrin sighed with a smile and looked up at the tree. Esselle was holding the basket and she gently placed it on the ground. She stood next to him and imitated his pose. She stood sideways on one leg and planted both her hands firmly on her hips.
"Do you remember when we named this our tree?" he asked raising an eyebrow. He looked at her but she didn't look at him.
"Yup we were 11" she said and he laughed.
"Our parents were God knows where and we had wondered off" Mardrin said and his eyes scanned the trunk of the tree.
"Then we ended up here" Esselle said and grew closer to the tree
"And I remember you had your jacks with you and we sat her under the branches and played"

"After we always found ourselves at this tree" he said and ran his fingers along the bark. He made a questioning face and looked at her "Do you remember when we carved our names here?" he asked and Esselle laughed.

"Yes that I do remember" she said and stood next to him running her fingers along the bark. "We were 15 and the sky became cloudy and it started pouring rain"

Esselle picked at the bark and continued to scratch at it finding the carving.

"We ended up getting stuck under this tree for a while. I remember you laughed because you said what were the odds of us ending up under our tree" he said and his eyebrows were drawn toward the middle and he looked to the back side of the tree.

"Then to pass the time you carved our names in the bark" Esselle said with a slight chuckle and she continued to scour the tree.

"Where is it?" she said frustrated. He stepped out from behind the tree and looked at her.

"I always knew where it was I knew this tree like the back of my hand" she said frustrated.

"Almost 30 years later Elle the tree's bound to grow" he said and Esselle made a face. Esselle heard him laugh a bit.

"Like our love" she heard him mutter.

It had a tinge of sarcasm but it still made Esselle smile a bit out of sight. She knew it were a joke but at the same time it stung a little. It was too early to make jokes about their failed relationship. Because Esselle hadn't fully healed yet. Not like she ever would but still. Mardrin used to say that to her. That over the years the tree's branches would spread, the leaves would multiply, and the trunk would grow. And so would their love. It was a sweet thought it really was but the pain of the memory made tears burn and sting at Esselle's eyes. So she took that memory kept close and near and dear to her heart and locked it away for another day to think about.

Esselle looked at the tree again and grew aggravated. "This is so freaking annoying" she muttered.

She heard a slight chuckle from the other side. "You're just impatient" Mardrin said.

In a snap Esselle's head was peeking out to the other side and she saw his fingers tracing the carve of the tree.

"I am not impatient" she remarked.

She saw him smile a bit and shake his head. "Yes you are" he said.

Esselle narrowed her eyes at him then went back to looking at the tree. It was true what he said. About Esselle being impatient. She just didn't want to admit he was right. That was why they were always so good together. Mardrin balanced her out. He was very calm and mellow and patient. She on the other hand had very little tolerance and patient. Now without him Esselle didn't have her other half anymore. To keep her calm cool and collective. there was no one in the world that could keep Esselle in check the way Mardrin could. And no one ever could. Esselle used to call it his super power. But he'd just smile and kiss her cheek disregarding it. Mardrin was kind of Esselle's rock in way she couldn't be without him. Not even now 28 years later. Esselle just supposed she needed him and by the way he had been acting he must have really needed her too.

The idea made Esselle blush and bright pink. She wasn't

supposed to think of him that way anymore. He wasn't the same person she loved all that time ago. He didn't even look the same. But for some reason Esselle could still feel her heart skip a beat when she was around him. The corners of Esselle's mouth slowly rose. She still got the tingly feeling in her gut when he was around her. Like when she was younger and she liked him and he didn't know. She could still feel her heart racing from the first time he had kissed her or said I love you to her.

The thought of it though also made her stomach turn. He had said I love you all day everyday to someone else for decades now. Some one else beside her. If you had came to Esselle almost 30 years ago and asked her what would happen if they didn't end up together she would have laughed in their face and not even given it a second thought. She was just that sure. They were always that sure. And then she stormed out of his house. And the last thing she had said was that she hated him. Esselle flinched at the thought. She felt as if she were going to be sick.

"Found it!" she heard Mardrin shout victoriously.

Esselle gasped and realized she hadn't been breathing. She snapped out of her trans and stepped away from the tree. Selena's voice began to ring in her mind. He had come here to this tree every year for 28 years on the anniversary of her death. Esselle shut her eyes when she felt her heart break. Then she wondered how could she have ever done something like that to the one she loved?

"Let me see it" Esselle said still drawn from the world. So she concentrated on sounds to bring her back and relax her heartbeat. The leaves made a crunching noise beneath Esselle's feet when she walked over to Mardrin's side of the tree.

He was standing a few feet away from the tree. He was looking up smiling with pride and he had his hands on his hips. He glanced at Esselle once then back at the tree with a sense of victory.

Esselle smiled a bit. He may have been a grown man but he still looked like that happy pappy jock kid she knew so long ago. The way he looked now reminded her of when she was coming out of school and he was waiting at the corner for her. He looked the exact same way. Esselle had laughed and when she was close enough asked him why he was so happy. And then he had said it was because he had totally creamed his rival team in the game from the night before. The though made Esselle smile a bit. He always took pride in such a little things. She loved that about him. And so what if it were wrong if she still did. It made him look like just about the most adorable thing on the face of the Earth when he glanced at her. She fought back the laughter threatening to erupt.

She stood next to him and took the same stance as he did. He pointed and looked at her.

'Right there" he said with a face and Esselle laughed,

Esselle walked over to the tree with Mardrin close behind and found the carving herself.

"It looks just as I remember it but in a different place" she said and looked at him. He shrugged.

"Trees grow Elle" he said. She heard him walk away but she just stood there as if she weren't able to move. She stuck her fingers in between the dents and holes the carving left; it was beautiful. And yet till today it still stood there unchanging all except its location on the tree. Sooner or later the tree would grow more

and the location would change. The tree would grow until eventually the carving would be so far up and Esselle couldn't see it anymore. And then her heart would surely break. Then again...
Esselle heard a noise. Like the flapping of wings. She walked out from behind the tree and saw Mardrin. he was looking down quizzically and a blanket on the floor with his eyebrows pressed together. He looked up at her.
"Ok, I'm not good with blankets" he said.
Esselle burst into laughter and he smiled.
"No you're not" Esselle said shaking her head. "You never were" Esselle walked over. She flattened out the edges and spread the blanket out nicely. She stood up and smiled.
"There" she said "All better"
"Ok just for the record" Mardrin said slowly taking a seat on the blanket against the tree. He looked up at Esselle "I totally set that blanket up for you"
Esselle laughed and took the seat next to him. "Ya sure!" she said.
He opened up the basket and made a face at Esselle. Her eyebrows pressed together and he pulled out an apple. She laughed and took it from him.
"I figured they were still one of your favorites" he said and she nodded.
"Yes they are" she said. She scouted closer to him and brought her knees closer to her and bit her apple.
She turned the apple in her hands and examined it.
"You know next time I'm picking the apples"
Mardrin seemed to have the basket next to him and Esselle couldn't quite see what he was doing."My dear your apple

picking is quite awful" she said sarcastically.

"Fine then, you're awfully picky" He said.

Esselle had a funny smile and her eyebrows pressed together when she looked at him.

"Mardrin?' she said and he looked at her covering her view of the basket.

"What are you doing?" she asked.

He shook his head "Nothing" he said and shifted.

Esselle extended her head and he smirked moving to block her view.

Her eyes widened "Mardrin!" she said and jumped over him. he started laughing.

"You little snype you brought grapes and didn't tell me!" she said. But he just laughed and moved the basket away from her as she struggled wiggling her way near the basket.

"You're such an idiot" she said giggling and tried grabbing the basket from behind him.

"You don't even like grapes!" he protested.

Esselle laughed "I love grapes! Its the only fruit you're good at picking!" she said and he laughed. Esselle lost her balance and shrieked. She fell over in a fit of laughter on his lap and he laughed too.

"This is because you won't share your grapes!" she said and flung her apple.

"Why can't you ever eat the strawberries?" he said still laughing.

"Because I hate strawberries!" she ranted and sat up.

Esselle realized she was looking Mardrin right and the eye and he was too close for comfort. Esselle used to sit like this all the time. On the terrace at his house, on the couch in Selena's house, in

Stephan's backyard. Now it just sent out an awkward vibe and the laughter died down. And quickly. Mardrin, as if nothing, just took her hair and tugged it behind her ear. Esselle reminded herself over and over again he was married. It was a heartrending feeling thinking about it. Esselle missed Mardrin's hair shorter. It annoyed her seeing it so long. It wasn't him. She flattened out his hair.

"Why did you grow it out so long?" she asked and he smiled a bit. "Because Elle you were the only one that liked it short" he said and the smile slipped from his face and shrugged. "I kept my hair short for a while but then I just gave up on it and let it grow out" he said. Esselle tilted her head and just ran her fingers through his hair absentmindedly.

"I miss it short" she said and took his head in her hands and smiled "Your hair is long it turns into locks at the bottom" she teased and ruffled his hair. He laughed.

For anyone else walking by it might have been odd. Seeing two people so late at night in Central Park. Such a young youthful pretty looking girl sitting on the lap of someone who could might as well be her father. But it wasn't odd to her not at ll. To her it just looked like how it always been. Mardrin and Esselle. Esselle and Mardrin. All day everyday. Forever and Always. Perfection.

"You know I never got around to asking you" Esselle began "Why do you look so young" she said and they both chuckled.

"Well you know that's what our parents specialized in. Staying youthful. There's this shot you get in your cheekbones that keeps you from aging for twenty years. I did it and so did pretty much everyone else. I wanted to chose an age where I looked young but not too young that I couldn't get a drink if I wanted" he said and

Somewhere in Time- trilogy part 2

Esselle laughed.

"So I chose 29" he said and Esselle nodded. It made sense.

"That's why you looked so much the same!" Esselle said.

He nodded "You looked the same. Not like a kid but the same" she said.

"Like a grown up version of yourself" they both said and he smiled.

"Exactly" and Mardrin smiled "Take it like a matured 17 year old look"

Esselle smiled "You don't look 17 to me" she said and pushed his hair from his ace "But you still kid of do its odd its like..." and she trailed off as they looked at each other.

She sighed "Its almost as if you were frozen in time with me" she said and his eye lids fell.

'Ya." he said "Kind of"

He was a wife Esselle reminded herself. He took her face in his hand. He has a wife Esselle she reminded herself again. She swallowed hard. And you have a boyfriend she finally said. Esselle had a boyfriend. She was sure to go to hell for this. Then again...Esselle begun to not care anymore. Look at where caring got her. Esselle could feel her stomach but then a radiant warmth came over her and she felt at peace again. It had been a very long time that she ever felt that way. A long time. Esselle gently leaned in and Mardrin's mouth brushed her like a tease. And then he kissed her. Esselle should have felt the only guilt, the only desire to push away, and the only craving to scream. But she didn't. Maybe it as wrong if Esselle kissed him back but she just didn't care anymore. She was sick and tired of being cautious and considerate and think about the consequences of her actions it annoyed her. So for once even if it were only one time she let herself melt away as he enveloped her in his arms. Esselle wrapped her arms around him and her mind was spinning. All she could think of were laughs and smiles and happy times. The times where every night she'd dream of him and everyday she'd be with him and they were just always happy. Esselle some how felt calmer around him like he toned her down. He always managed to make her worries slip way. He traced circles on her back and she wrapped his long locks around her fingers. Esselle could give anything, anything in the world just for the chance to be able to say 'I love you' to him again without the threat of death. She'd truly give anything. She wondered if he would too. Things were becoming too much for her she realized probably too much for her to bare. He pulled her closer deepening their kiss and her heart began pounding fiercely against her chest. She supposed after all this time his will power was slowly slipping away. She wasn't going to lie so was hers and she squeezed him tight. She felt his hands go up her back below her sweater and she shivered despite the warmth outside.

Then at hat moment Esselle was ready to die. Before anything got too serious she felt her phone vibrate and they very slowly pulled away. She pressed her forehead to his and sighed. She reached for her phone in her back pocket and Mardrin kept his eyes shut.

"What happened?" he asked.

Esselle wanted to know the same thing. Who ever was calling her she was sure to kick their ass tomorrow. Her heart dropped. It was Daniel. She quickly put her phone away and swallowed hard. "It was nothing" she said.

"Who's calling you this late?" he asked.

Esselle had to think quick. "Nothing just one of those notifications to update your phone.

He chuckled a bit "I hate those" Esselle was annoyed when she slid off his lap.

"Me too" she muttered trying to hide her annoyance.

"By the way" she said and he looked at her. She felt herself smile. "I totally took your grapes" she said and held up the bag.

"You did not!' he said but Esselle was already running down the hill.

Mardrin laughed and ran after her.

He lifted her off her feet and she shrieked. They both fell to the ground in a fit of laughter and soon enough they were looking at the stars with their hands locked together.

"You know" Esselle began shoving a grape in her mouth "I would love to touch a star" she said and he laughed.

"Me too Elle" he said and squeezed her hand "Me too"

"I think about you all the time I see you in my dreams" Esselle hummed and giggled. She stood on her tip toes and turned looking at her reflection in her mirror.
"Baby Boy you stay on my mind full fill my fantasies" she hummed and grabbed bobbie pins.
"Baby Boy not a day goes" she sang and giggled. She grabbed her hair and pinned it up in a messy bun. She softly smiled to herself and the morning light went pouring into her bedroom. It was morning and Esselle had been giddy. Ok so maybe what she had

done the night before was totally wrong. She knew it and she acknowledged it but she loved the feeling of being happy and walking on air. That's how she felt in the morning when she woke up. She was walking on air. Esselle had some of her old music on and she took a step forward and danced in place and took another step and moved her hips.

"Oh na na na" she sung and she smiled to herself as she continued to dance.

"I think about you all the time" she sang and floated over to her closet.

"Baby Boy you stay on my mind" she sang and her eyes scanned her closet.

She frowned "Baby Boy won't you be mine" she hummed and pulled out a bright white and yellow dress. Her nose wrinkled at the sight of it and she exchanged it for a beautiful white blouse and pretty frilly yellow skirt. She slipped on her wedges and flew down the stairs.

She sighed and opened her arms with a wide smile when she stepped into the kitchen.

"Good morning!" she said softly and sweetly.

Her mother looked up at her with a funny smile.

"Aren't you happy" she said.

"Isn't it just another beautiful day of life?" she asked. Her father was sitting on a stool reading his newspaper and Esselle smiled. She gently placed her hands on his shoulders and kissed his head.

"Morning dad" she said and glided towards the fridge.

He looked up "Good morning Elle" he said with the same smile as his wife's.

Somewhere in Time- trilogy part 2

Esselle hummed and swayed her hips back and forth as she looked at the contents of the fridge. Nothing stood out except for the vanilla yogurt. She wasn't a fan of vanilla but it looked good so she grabbed it and with her hips swung the fridge door shut. She yanked open the drawer grabbed a spoon and with a swing of her hips it slammed shut and she worked a strut across the kitchen. Esselle was humming and dancing as she walked around.

"You're love's got me looking so crazy right now" she hummed and her parents looked at her.

"oh oh oh oh oh oh oh oh" hummed and kicked her feet forward and back.

"You are way to hyper this morning" her mother said with a chuckle as she scoured the cabinets.

Esselle with a funny smile shrugged her shoulders. She sighed "Its such a lovely sunny day" she said and her father laughed.

"If I didn't know any better I would say she were drunk" he said and went back to his newspaper. For a moment he had a slight smile reading the stock report then his face fell and it dawned on him. He looked at his daughter.

"You're not drunk are you?' he asked and Esselle laughed.

"No better!" she said and danced again.

"Ok, ok now come take your vitamins" her mother said with a chuckle. Esselle stopped here she stood and saw her mother put the bottle on the counter. Esselle slowly walked over. She ran all the possibilities in her mind. These vitamins. It made her head spin. If she didn't take them they'd grow suspicious. She swallowed hard and opened the bottle. She shook them out and her mother looked at her.

Somewhere in Time- trilogy part 2

'What? No dancing?' her mother teased. Esselle looked down at the vitamins and shoved them in her mouth. She had to act normal now she thought. She broke out into a sing and dance and her parents laughed amused. Esselle would give anything for the chance to spit these out.

"So what do you plan on doing today?" her mother asked. Esselle slid into the stool next to her father.

Esselle hadn't known what to do. Then it hit her,

"I'm going to see Selena today" she said "Visit the kids"

Her father smiled "Sounds like a great idea"

Esselle swallowed hard for a moment when she stood in front of the door to Selena's house. Esselle's energy had been drained out her completely and totally. She was wrong. She was so so so so so wrong. She shouldn't have kissed Mardrin yesterday. Esselle acting just so stupid lately. She had been acting like a spoiled little whiny brat. It was almost like the world was teasing her from behind shut doors. Boo hoo hoo poor Esselle has an

awesome boyfriend but still goes after a man that is married with two beautiful children and a beautiful family because she wanted too. Instead of acting like an idiot Esselle should have been in New Jersey. She should have been in Hoboken everything she could have possibly done to finish up her training and find out what happened to her to put all her lingering questions to rest. But no. Esselle felt like such a fool. Like a moron an idiot. Like the kind of stupid girl she'd be yelling at in a movie she were watching or a book she were reading. Esselle needed to get a hold of herself. She felt disgusted with herself. The least she could this morning make herself useful to the world and go see Selena who hadn't seen her in days and probably thinks she's dead again. Esselle rang the bell. She wanted to talk to Selena because she had been on her mind for a while. Esselle wanted to know what her parents meant that night when they said they had Selena on her side.
The door opened and Selena looked at Esselle wide eyed.
"Elle" she said and Esselle smiled.
"Hey Sel" she said.
Selena sighed and pulled Esselle into her arms.
"So help me God" Selena said and Esselle laughed a bit "If you ever got that long without calling me or talking to me or seeing me again like that ever again I will hunt you down like a dog and just might kill you myself" she said.
Esselle shut her eyes and hugged her friend back.
"I know, I'm sorry" she said and Esselle was. She was truly sorry. Selena pulled away and looked at her with a straight face.
Selena laughed a bit and took a chunk of Esselle's hair in her hands. "Copying my style now are you?' she asked and Esselle

laughed.

Selena was known for her luscious long thick dark gorgeous hair. When Esselle straightened her hair like she had done that morning they looked more like sisters than friends.

"I'm rocking the Selena look" she said and the friends laughed.

Selena flicked her head and stood out of the doorway.

"Come on the kids have been asking for you" she said. Esselle walked in and a rush of cool a.c. air hit her and Selena with the tips of her fingers gently slammed the door shut.

Esselle heard the pitter patter of feet zooming down the stairs. Selena crossed her arms and walked out into the living room.

"Guys no running I-' Selena called up the stair case but it was too late. Esselle was already smiling and got to her knees and Diana and John came rushing into the living room with the widest smiles.

"Titi Elle!" they ranted and fell into Esselle's arms.

"No running" Selena said with a sigh finishing her sentence. She made a face "Well so much for disciplining my children" she said and Esselle laughed.

"Where have you been?" Dianna asked and Esselle smiled at her niece smoothing out her hair.

"Titi has been a bit busy lately sweety" she said.

"We got our report cards you missed it!" John said "We both got into honors for fifth grade!" he said and Esselle gasped.

"You did!" she said and he nodded frantically.

Selena was quietly observing from a distance with one her signature smiles.

"We go to summer camp now!" Dianna ranted.

Esselle was just wide eyed with a smile "You do?' she asked and

Somewhere in Time- trilogy part 2

john chimed in.

"We do! We made you something!" he said.

"No!" Esselle said and put her hands on her hips "You didn't!' she teased.

"Yesssss!!!!!" john said bobbing his head up and down. She chuckled.

"Come on" Diana said taking her hand and pulling her along.

"We'll show you" she said and John grabbed Esselle's other hand. She was shocked with how strong they were and how easy it was for them to pull her up on her feet and away. Selena watched and laughed.

****

Esselle was softly smiling and moving the bracelets around on her wrist. Diana and John each made her one and Esselle put them on her wrist. Now Selena was drinking her coffee on the balcony with Esselle and finally Selena broke the silence with a chuckle.

"You really love it don't you?" she asked.

Esselle looked up and smiled "I do"

"You were always so good with children" Selena replied.

Esselle was softly smiling and shrugged "I always loved children" Selena took on a soft smile and put her cup down "You were always good mother material. You were always great with kids you just oozed love and affection" she said.

Esselle crossed her legs and looked out at the skyline. The subtle breeze hit her and the wind made her shiver "I always wanted to be a mother you" she said and Selena tilted her head and listened attentively. "I had always wanted to feel the joy of holding a baby

Somewhere in Time- trilogy part 2

in your arms and cradle them there" she said and formed the shape with her arms.

"I always wanted to look down on a little face and know that I was the one that brought that miracle into the world. I wanted to push my child in a stroller in the park and fix their outfit on the first day of kindergarten" she said and her arms fell. She looked off again.

"Now I feel like those dreams are so far" she said.

"That's not true" Selena said quickly leaning over in her chair.

'Yes it is" Esselle said. She looked down and sighed "Selena I don't ever think I'll ever have kids not even if I wanted to" Esselle ran her fingers through her thick straight long hair.

Selena sat back and sighed "Elle just take it a day at a time" she said.

Esselle licked her lips dry and looked at Selena. "Sel I have to ask you something" she said.

Selena shrugged. "Sure' Selena was dresses casually today Esselle noticed. She had on dark blue high rise jeans with a pretty green shirt black ballet flats and her hair was in a high pony tail. Selena looked young like Selena. The one she knew before.

"Did you ever notice anything odd about my parents?" she asked and Selena raised an eyebrow.

"Odd?" she said and laughed "Odd like how they still treat you like you're five odd or odd like movie bad guy odd"

"no I mean-" Esselle stopped "I'm not five!" she said and Selena laughed.

"Oh come on Elle admit they do" she said.

"So what. My mom still makes me breakfast" she said and Selena giggled "My dad pays for everything because I'm the little princess" she said and broke out into a smile "All the cleaning gets done for me I take my vitamins like a good girl-" and Esselle was cut off.

"Vitamins?" Selena asked. Her tone and demeanor were alarming and changed so instantly. It made Esselle a bit tense.

"Yes" Esselle said and her body froze "Why?" she asked.

Selena looked both ways and leaned over the table.

"Before Stephan gets home" she said and Esselle leaned into listen "Esselle I am so sorry i can't I have to be honest with you" she said and shut her eyes shut as if in pain.

"It was a long time ago. I made a mistake I shouldn't have done what i had done kept what I did from you the way I did I thought I was protecting you. I lied that's the thing" she said and Esselle's eyebrows furrowed.

"I've been trying to redeem myself with you but its so hard" Selena shifted in her chair and moved closer "Stop taking those damn vitamins and now like asap." she said and her voice was hard and cold.

"But why?" she asked.

"Your parents thought they love you aren't who you think they are. Stop taking them throw them out spit them up do whatever just don't let them give them to you" she said and before Esselle could question what Esselle said Stephan came in and smiled. Selena stood from her chair and plastered on a smile.

"Hey girls" Stephan said.

"Hey babe you're home early" Selena said and kissed her husband.

"Eh it was slow today" he said and Esselle smiled to greet him.

"So girls what are you guys doing?" he asked.

Somewhere in Time- trilogy part 2

"Oh nothing" Esselle said.

"Elle was just leaving she came to visit" Selena said and shoot her a look.

"So soon?" He asked.

Esselle didn't know what to do. Selena raised an eyebrow so she decided to just play along.

"Ya sorry I just came for a little bit" she said.

Stephan smiled "Alright then but come over again tomorrow you can stay for dinner" he said.

Esselle already had her bag in hand and was standing near the doors.

She smiled and nodded "Sure" she said and gave Selena a second glance before walking out. What did Selena mean? Esselle knew one thing. She had to see Daniel tomorrow. And it wasn't going to be a good thing either.

Esselle's heart had been racing as she walked further and further away from Selena's house. She needed to get to headquarters. She needed to find someone do something anything useful. The vitamins. So that's how they did it. Maybe Esselle didn't know. Her parents the thought still made her sick to her stomach. Esselle needed to act on what she knew. But at the same exact time she couldn't because then what happened if Esselle found something her heart just could not handle? What if she just broke? She needed to distract herself it was all in all far too much for one person to absorb in just one visit to Selena's house. She wanted to jump in a car and drive just drive fast. Better yet she needed someone to talk to. To keep her mind off of her own problems. Esselle when she was in high school was the go to gal for problem fixing. She needed to fix someone else's problems to help her calm down. Like asap.

"Hey!" Esselle heard. She looked around. Was she hallucinating? "Hey Esselle!" she heard again this time it came from the street. Esselle saw a yellow taxi cab strolling up next to her and she smiled when the window went all the way down.

"Hey Joel!" she said and he laughed.

"Hey I knew that was you! Almost didn't recognize you with the new hair!" he said and she gently stroked her hair. He smiled and nodded "It looks good" he said.

She smiled and leaned against the car.

"Hey what are you doing here?" she asked.

He smiled "What do you think i'm doing here kid? It's New York City I'm driving around!" he said and she smiled.

"Yes well I'm just walking around" she said and crossed her arms.

"Kid where you heading? You need a ride?" he asked.

"Oh no Joel I'm just going where the wind takes me" she said with a smile. She liked Joel. He was like a breath of fresh air. Like that one good fun friend you needed in your life to just pull you away from the chaos and make you laugh.

"So where you headin'?" Esselle asked.

He smiled a bit bashfully "I was just heading down to Union Square" he said.

She smirked "What's down in Union Square?" she asked.

Somewhere in Time- trilogy part 2

He shied away a bit still smiling "Just a Barnes and Nobel" he said.
She nodded "Oh" she said "Mind if I tag along?" he shook his head.
"Come right along!" he said. Esselle smiled and opened the car door.

****

Joel pulled over and rubbed his hands together. They were parked out side of Barnes and Nobel and the blue in his cotton t-shirt shone brighter when the sunlight hit him. The sun was low and golden orange in the sky and cast shadows along the buildings making some seem longer and others shorter.
"So this is it" he said.
Esselle nodded and unbuckled her seat belt.
"Cool so what book are you getting?' she asked but he just stared out his window.
His eyes seemed to sparkle a bit and he seemed worlds away. Esselle's eyes pressed together and she looked out his window. Then it hit Esselle. it was a girl. He was looking a t a girl. She was a beautiful one. She had coffee colored long dark hair and glowing bronze skin. She had light eyes like a cat and the prettiest face.
"Oh I see" Esselle said and he sighed.
"Yup that's her" he said.
Esselle smiled a bit 'What's her name?" she asked
He looked at her "Kara" he said and looked over again "Her name is Kara"
Esselle knew that look on his face. The droopy eyes filled with

longing and emotion. The way his shoulders dropped and his distant look.

"You're in love with this girl Kara" she said "You love her"

He chuckled and nodded "Is it that obvious?" he asked.

"What happened?" she asked. He let out a deep breath that sounded like a hiss.

"We were close" he said and pulled out his wallet. "Then I transferred over to Connecticut" he handed her a picture. It was of her and Esselle smiled. It was sweet he had kept a picture of her.

"Anyways she is not one of us. I didn't want to endanger her with this kind of would and life style. She is just too beautiful a person" he said and Esselle handed him back the picture. he moved it in his hands and stared at it "I couldn't do that to her" and he slipped his wallet back into his pocket.

"SO you just watch her?" She asked.

'Its the closet thing to being with her. I do this everyday at the same time just for a few minutes though" he said.

"I think its romantic" Esselle said.

He laughed and put the car into drive. "Ya well" he said and they began to drive away.

Esselle turned in her chair to face him "You know what I think I'm going to help you win her heart" she said and he laughed.

"Good luck kid' he said.

Esselle's face lit up. "So is that a yes?" she asked. He had a smirk on his face when he glanced at her then shook his head and turned to the rode.

"Oh god" he said.

Esselle shrieked "That wasn't a no!" she said and he laughed.

Somewhere in Time- trilogy part 2

Somewhere in Time- trilogy part 2

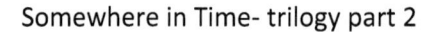

Joel and Esselle were laughing and pretty hard too. Esselle enjoyed listening to Joel's stories. They were soothing. After leaving Kara they drove around a little longer until they realized something. They were starving. So they stopped at the nearest place. The ended up on a rooftop lace just a block away from the

Somewhere in Time- trilogy part 2

Empire State building. It had the most beautiful view of the skyline. Esselle still giggling looked over the ledge and saw the setting sun cut the sky in half and cast golden shadows over New York.
"So tell me" Esselle said and Joel's laughter calmed down "What was it like when you first woke up, life in general I mean"
Joel's eyebrows pressed together and he nodded "Good question" he said and shifted in his chair.
He put his elbow on the arm of the chair and looked out into the sunset. He let out a deep breath and looked at Esselle.
"It was like walking on air" he said and Esselle smiled. "Imagine one second you're in your house then someone breaks in you get shot and you think you're dead only to awaken and realize you have been given this second chance at life"
Esselle ran her fingers through her hair and sighed "I wish it were that way for me" she said.
"It could be" he said and put his elbows on the table.
"No it can't I'm a major screw up. I'm such an idiot moping around feeling pity on myself" she said and he laughed.
"Of course you're going to feel that way" he said and she looked at him. 'Listen Esselle its only normal at some point in all our lives Invisible or not we are bound to feel that way. Now?" and he sat back in his chair like he were at the beach. Esselle smiled a bit.
"Now you just know that you need to change that. Turn your life around Esselle you've been given a second chance. Get your training and education done. Close your case found out what happened to you and move on with your life. I'm not going to lie its hard because it is. it was for me. But you get this only feeling

Somewhere in Time- trilogy part 2

of the weight of the world being lifted off your shoulders when you do so" he said and Esselle smiled at the skyline.

"You know if only more people in my life thought the way you did" she said and he laughed.

"Hey well you've got Daniel" he said and Esselle let out something that was a cross between a laugh and a snort.

"Oh ya Captain optimistic over here" she said and he made a face.

"Ok so maybe he's a bit of a jackass-" he said and Esselle raised her eyebrows.

"A bit?" she said baffled and he burst into laughter. She blew air out of her mouth "I don't think we know the same Daniel" she said and looked at the white table cloth.

"Ok so ya maybe he's a total jackass but!" he said and she looked at him.

"That guy's been through hell and back you know. And he's still able to get up in the morning it boggles my mind" he said and Esselle kept her eyes locked on the table. She was fiddling with her napkin because she couldn't stand to look him in the face. She heard him sigh and he leaned over the table and her eyes slowly rose to look at him.

"He's a great guy he really is kid just give him a chance to prove it to you" he said softly "It may not be all its cracked up to be now but just give it a little time. He'll change trust me"

"I don't know" Esselle said and twisted the ring on her finger.

"What do you mean you don't know?" he asked and Esselle placed her hand on her forehead.

"I don't know" she said again "its just so hard being with him makes it so damn difficult" she said. Joel stood quiet and just nodded.

"I know I'm new I get that. I know I'm not fully trained or educated and I'm probably in the most danger than any other person in the country I know that. But he just never gives me the chance. He won't give me the chance to learn or prove it to myself. How am i supposed to learn if I never try and screw up or make mistakes how? It won't work. He hides things from me all the time and expects things to be ok when they're not" and Esselle's face was buried in her hands.

She heard Joel sigh. he hissed through his teeth. "Ya" he said and sat back in his chair. "I see"

"And now I'm avoiding him because he doesn't want me in headquarters for 'safety reasons' he almost shipped me off to California but I fought it and now he wants me to stay in Hoboken as compromise I feel like we're miles apart" Esselle said and took her glass in her hands.

"He's doing it because he loves you" he said plain and simple. Esselle's dropped her glass and looked at Joel.

"What?" she asked and Joel shrugged his blue cotton shirt scrunching up at the shoulders.

"He's in love with you so he'll do anything to protect you and that's how he's best. You may see it as him hiding things from you which he is don't get me wrong but there are also a lot of things in the this lifestyle that he doesn't want you to see. He wants to preserve your innocence so he'll do as he sees is necessary whether you agree or not. You'll understand one day the extent people will go to for love" he said and looked off into the distance. Joel stood silent for a moment before looking at her again.

"You're hurt I get it any normal person would be. Just try seeing it the way he does. He doesn't want to hurt you by telling you everything so he does what he can. But by the way you speak of him I can tell you're wearing thin on him" he chuckled "I have to say I never thought in a million years there would be a girl that could wrap Daniel around their little finger the way you do" he said and Esselle smiled a bit.

"Well I don't know" she said and looked at him "He pretty much has me wrapped around his" she said and he laughed. Just laughed.

Somewhere in Time- trilogy part 2

Somewhere in Time- trilogy part 2

Esselle lie awake in her bed in the middle of the night. She stared at the ceiling. She sighed and turned to her side. She could see the night sky and the full moon. The sky was abundant with beautiful stars twinkling bringing the night light. Esselle hadn't been able to sleep. She kept running her and Joel's conversation over and over again in her mind. She moaned and hid under the blanket. Esselle hadn't slept for days now not being able to. Sleep had just refused to come to her. And sooner or later the sun will show and Esselle would have to get up and walk around like a sleepless zombie. It also been 2 days since her big falling out with Daniel and she'd have to see him again at noon. That was another thing. Noon. She wasn't sure if she could face him no after what she did the other night it made her sick and nauseous. She regretted it big time. Even after what Joel told her it just made her feel worse about seeing him. Now Esselle had gotten herself into a deeper whole then she already was in. Just because she was stupid. A stupid idiot. No wonder Daniel didn't tell her anything he probably knew better. He probably knew she was going to screw it up anyway. Esselle grabbed her pillow and crushed her face in between the mattress and pillow. She could wait. She could definitely wait until noon. The sun will show soon Esselle knew and she'd be screwed. She squinted and took a peek out her window. A speck of sunlight was in the distance. She groaned and slammed her face into her pillow. It would be a very

Somewhere in Time- trilogy part 2

long day.

****

Ultimately Esselle hadn't slept a wink. Then again who could? so by the time the sun had shown Esselle was already up and out of bed. Pacing back and forth in her bedroom chewing down on her once flawless beautiful nails. Her french manicure was now chipped and her nails were bit down. The sky outside was orange when Esselle glanced out her window. Then she went back to acing. She was up to her pointer finger on her right hand and she was currently chewing down. She was in her lose booty shorts. The ones that were sky blue with white puffy clouds and she had her beige cami on with it. Her left hand was placed firmly on her her hip and her feet were brushing across her white plush area rug. She hadn't none what to do. She had till noon when she was to see Daniel again. Ok, so maybe she kind of wanted to see him again. Ok, so maybe she wanted to after their last argument resolve things. Esselle didn't do well with conflict. It didn't match her character. Esselle was all hugs kisses happiness smiles and love. She had always been that way. Daniel had to have been the very first person to ever made Esselle angry. That intrigued her yet worried her. Either way his character was a bit uh...what was the word? Outside of the box for her. Yes, that's the perfect way to explain him. The A.C. had been on full blast all night and her bedroom was like a meat locker. Esselle hadn't noticed though. It happens when she's tense. Esselle looked over. Behind the silky sheer curtains partially covering her bedroom she could see the sky's orange was become more muted as it grew green yellow and barely blue. There had been a cat purring scratching at her

window. She sighed and walked over to the door unhinging the lock. The cat worked a strut into her bedroom and walked circles around her feet. She bent down and gently patted it's head.
"What are you doing here?" she said and the cat purred against her leg again.
"Are you lost little thing?" she asked. It was a beautiful blackish-grey cat with big eyes and soft fur. Esselle could see the way the cat looked at her and she frowned.
"It's ok little thing" she said "So am I" and at that the cat worked a strut back out unto the balcony and disappeared off the ledge. Oh how Esselle wished she could disappear too. Disappear into thin air.
****
****

It turned out that high-waisted pants in 2045 were the new low riders. Completely in style. Or at least that was what the most recent fashion magazine that came in the mail said. SO she wore the white high-waisted shorts she had. She wore her flowery wedges and the pretty sheer baggy shirt with ruffles. When Esselle came into the kitchen her mother laughed.
"It's about time you finally adapted to today's style" Vivienne said. Esselle made a face and tossed her bag onto the table.
Her father Henry looked up and smiled.
"You look like a kid again" he said. Esselle smiled a bit and kissed his forehead.
She walked over to the refrigerator and yanked the door open.
"So" Esselle said and grabbed the grape juice.
"What are you guys doing today?" she asked and then grabbed yogurt. Sure it wasn't the best mix but when Esselle was up to

Somewhere in Time- trilogy part 2

something and tense she had strange food cravings. She shut the fridge door and her mother was smiling in her bleach white lad coat with her coffee mug in hand (the one Esselle got her for mother's day when she turned 10) and she was leaning against the sink.

The day was a sunny one but the sun was huge and low in the sky turning the world a sunset orange. Even the light inside of the house changed the appearance of her parents skin making them glow and glisten bronze.

Vivienne shrugged "I don't know sweetheart" she said.

Esselle raised and eyebrow and her father laughed. "You're in your lab coat" she said and looked at her father. "Like always!" she said and they both laughed.

"No it's true" Henry said and shifted in his stool "We're going to the lab for a little while then coming home. We can have lunch together meet us back home at 2? Wherever you're going" he said and winked at his daughter.

"I'm just going to try to little by little *not* get lost using the MTA system" she said and her parents laughed "Plus I need to seriously update on my wardrobe"

Esselle thought for a moment "I might even get a haircut"

"Well whatever you do just be home by 2 alright?" her father said

Esselle grabbed her bag off the counter "Alright see ya" she said and her mother put her coffee down.

"Wait! You forgot to take your vitamins" she said and went into the cabinets.

Esselle stopped and looked over. She swallowed hard. Everything was going according to plan. Now here was the tricky part. She laughed off her emotions.

Somewhere in Time- trilogy part 2

"How old am I mom? 5 that you have to make sure I take my vitamins?" Esselle asked and leaned over the counter. Henry was eyeballing his wife over the rim of his coffee mug.

Vivienne gently shook three vitamins out of the bottle and handed them to Esselle.

Esselle smiled and she felt the thump of her heart pounding ferociously against her chest. So much it made her grow hot in her jean jacket. But she had to wear her jean jacket. Or else it would never work. She had been thinking through her plan all morning. She glanced at the clock. She hadn't much time left until noon.

Her mother looked at her and Esselle rolled her eyes. Her father Henry had an unsettling look and Vivienne forced a soft smile on her face. almost as if slowly Esselle tilted her head back placing her hand over mouth. Her hand came back empty and her parents seemed to have let out a sigh of relief. She swallowed and made a funny face with an open mouth.

"See! she said and they laughed a bit nervously and relieved "Done!" and Esselle sprinted out the door. Of course she remained conscious to not let her dirty little secret escape her sleeve.

****
****

Esselle found it odd. So odd. It was ten past 12 and there was no sign of the boy with black hair anywhere. She had no idea where he could be. He was usually never late for anything. Had he forgotten about Esselle already? Was he angry? Did he not want to see her? Did something happen? Was he just running late? She was oblivious. The summer sun was scorching her skin and she was eager to yank off her jean jacket but she couldn't. She knew she couldn't. She risked loosing it. There was a mesh of people they were all just colors and their bags and arms were brushing against Esselle as the streets were so dense. Esselle tried moving and shifting somewhere else where there wasn't as much traffic. As she arched her head over the crowd she saw a city bus change before her eyes. Again. it happened all the time Esselle semi grew used to it.

While Esselle arched her back to get a better look at people crossing the street she lost her balance. She was yanked and pulled and before she could scream someone was covering her mouth. Then her back hit a few bricks and the hand fell from her face. She let out a sigh.

"Daniel" she said.

"Where in God's name have you been?" he asked.

She rolled her eyes but then remembered. She was tired of fighting.

"It's nice to see you too" she said and he tensed.

"Are you alright?' he asked more calmly.

Esselle's eye brows furrowed. 'What?" she asked.

"No broken bones bumps bruises scratches severe cuts" he said turning her face in his hands.

"I'm fine!" she said.

"You don't look fine" he said.

Esselle looked away and he let go of her face. She began pulling at her jacket sleeve.

"I'm sorry for running off like that" she said and he shook his head.

"No" he began.

"I was angry and I didn't mean to worry you" Esselle tugged one last time at her jacket sleeve and felt all three gently fall into her palm. Her vitamins.

She took her hand in his and gently placed them in her palm. He frowned.

"What are these?" he asked and examined them. That had been her plan all along. To slip them down her sleeve instead of swallowing them. Esselle realized now what the right thing to do was. So now she was just doing it.

"This is me trusting you" she said and he looked at her. "Being away from you even though it wasn't that long of a period of time it felt like forever for me. I realized something. That I just have to trust you. Even when I'm scared to and even when it feels like its impossible to do so because you worry me. I have to trust you if I don't then this all means nothing. And us being together is pointless."

She rubbed her elbow and couldn't meet his eyes. But she felt the burn of his eyes on her.

"I realized that I was just in denial the whole time and didn't want to believe it. That's why I couldn't find myself believing or trusting you. I didn't want to I was scared. Of getting hurt. Its happened all too many times before. I thought of my parents. I would just keep on running through my mind what you had said about them and wonder-" Esselle said but he cut her off.

"I was wrong" he said and she looked at him.

She laughed without humor "You weren't wrong you were right" she said.

"No I was wrong" he said and placed her vitamins back in her hand.

"I stood up hours on end just thinking about what I said to you. I ran it through my mind the different ways it could have happened and the different ways I wished it had happened. And the whole time I just kept thinking about the way you looked at me and how much I regretted it' and Daniel for once Esselle saw her shinning armor slowly melting away. And once it was gone under it all he actually looked like something far more beautiful than he already was. Human.

"How many times I wish I could just go and find you but didn't. How much I wished I hadn't let you go so easily and how much I wished I had ran after you and stopped you and held you in my arms and said I WAS SORRY and that I didn't mean it. That I didn't mean to hurt you" and he took her hand.

"I know you didn't" she said stressing each word carefully.

"That's the point. I still did. And I didn't want to. I was just angry and I wanted to hurt you the way you hurt me and that was badly." and he looked at her "By the way that stays between you and I"

Esselle laughed and he smiled a bit.

After a moment of silence passed Esselle spoke "I want you take these and test them" she said shifting the vitamins back into his hand.

"I know now that you're right. For now it's going to hurt a lot. And badly. Right now I still don't believe it I'm trying not to but I'm just asking you to do this for me. TO finally put it to rest and figure out what happens next and i'll handle it. Whatever comes my way I'll figure out a way to deal with it" she said.

"You say it like you'll be going through this all on your own" he said "Have you forgotten that I'm right here?"

"You?" she said.

He shifted where he stood and winced. He looked beautiful in the light. She felt the need to point that out.

"Ess, you're not alone. I'm here. You'll never be alone again" he said and pushed the hair form her face.

"I'm sorry" she joked out "I'm sorry I accused you of lying to me and hiding something from me when you were just trying to protect me" That was another thing that thanks to Joel she realized. It was Daniel's form of protection.

"Well you were half wrong and half right. i wasn't lying. But I was hiding stuff from you" he took a moment to think "And a lot" Esselle besides herself laughed even though she pushed him hard. It was difficult to not laugh the way he said certain things. It was just his view of the world that made her laugh.

"Like what things?" she asked.

The deep breath he took through his mouth hissed through his teeth. "The things I wanted to do to you when i first saw you but would never say because you'd skin me" he said "Stuff like that"

It was the look on her face that made Daniel laugh.

"we're having a serious conversation" Esselle began just taken back and Daniel cut her off.

"It was your fault for asking in all fairness" he said.

Esselle sighed "What do we do now?" she asked.

Daniel had a twisted look on his face. Like he was thinking something he really shouldn't be thinking but because he was Daniel he didn't care and thought it anyway with no shame. He pushed her against the brick wall and took her face in his hand. 'This is the part where we kiss and make up" he said and leaned down to kiss her. She smiled and turned her face where he kissed her cheek.

"I'm not kissing you" she said detaching herself from the wall. "I'm still mad with you" she said.

His jaw dropped and he threw his arms up. "What do you want me to grovel on me knees?" he asked.

Esselle took a moment to think. Then after a moment of silent with a simple nod of her head she spoke and said "Yes"

Daniel gave her face and she smiled. He looked down at the vitamins in his hand and looked at her the serious side of him kicking in.

"Are you sure you want me to do this?" he asked.

Esselle swallowed hard and yanked her jacket off. She nodded. "As much as I'd *love* to expose the bastards for what they did this all depends on you. As long as these don't get tested your parents are a hundred percent innocent" he said and she looked at him "I know how much their innocence means to you"

"I know" Esselle stepped up to him. She held out his hands in front of him and closed them tight around the capsules in his hands. "its hard for me but i'll manage. The faster we get this over with the better right?" she asked and he didn't say anything. He tilted his head and just looked at her. "I admire your courage you know that?" he said and she smiled.

"Doesn't everyone?" she said.

Somewhere in Time- trilogy part 2

Somewhere in Time- trilogy part 2

Esselle swallowed hard and sat in the cold metal chair in the testing room. She gripped the arms of the chair as Charlotte laced the weird contraption on her head. It was silver in color the shape of a helmet with different wires and sleek colors forming signs. Daniel was kneeling down in front of her and she reached out to grab his hand.
"Char" he said and she looked at him "Do you mind?" he asked. Charlotte nodded and left the room.
Daniel watched Charlotte shut the door and his eyes rested on the steel door before his head gently turned to face Esselle.
"Are you sure you want to do this?" he asked. Esselle was

squeezing his hand when he looked at them. He placed his other hand on top of hers and she shut her eyes.

"of course i do" she said.

It took her a moment to realize but he was stroking the back of her hand with his thumb.

"Because I can talk to the council. Get them to look you over. I've done it before all I have to do is tell them I'll behave for an entire day and they're on their knees"

"Daniel" Esselle said quickly.

"Essie, trust me when I tell you this is a God awful experience. I've administered this test more than enough times to know' he said.

"So what's the point of this test anyway?" she asked.

"It tells us what you're made of. How your mind and body functioned. It tells us exactly how your body transformed and the transitions its gone through. It tell us what makes you an Invisible. it even tests your blood" he says and taps the wire in Esselle's arm.

"How was yours?" she asked.

He stood silent for a moment and looked at her "I'm different Ess. So my testing was a lot different then those on average" he said.

Esselle frowned "Different?" she asked "Is that another thing you kept from me?"

He smiled a bit "I'll tell you as soon as you're out" he said and kissed her cheek. "Until them I'll be overseeing the testing process being run on those vitamins you brought in. That's if"

Esselle looked up at him "yes Daniel I want to get this over with already" she said. She smirked "But I have to admit the whole

Somewhere in Time- trilogy part 2

worried boyfriend side of you is adorable" she teased.

He gave her a twisted grin that most likely read 'Not cool watch my ego'

Esselle laughed and eventually he broke out into a wider smile. He got back down on his knees in front of her and raised an eyebrow.

"Now listen here kid" he said and she laughed "I won't have you going around making me look soft. Go it?" Esselle leaned over and looked at him.

"Of course not" she said and tapped his nose "You're tough as nails!" she said in her best manly voice.

Daniel laughed he semi rose to his feet and kissed her. Without noticing Esselle kissed him back. When she pulled away she looked at him.

"Hey! I said I wasn't going to kiss you!" she said and punched his shoulder.

He shrugged "Opps?" he tried.

Esselle made a face but she saw him smile anyway. A smile that spread all the way to his eyes. They were as blue as ever. So blue with a trick of the light they could have been mistaken for a lovely shade of violet.

There was a banging on the glass and Esselle looked behind Daniel. It was Jasmine. The room they were in was white with a table of odd looking things the chair Esselle was in a computer screen and another stool for someone else. In front of her was a long rectangular cut out in the wall with an odd kind of glass window were everything was tinted brown.

Daniel frowned and Jasmine ran over to the door and yanked it open.

Somewhere in Time- trilogy part 2

"Daniel" she said and she seemed out of breath. Her long thick straight almost wavy ink black hair was in a high ponytail. Her skin seemed light then usual and her beauty seemed subdued for some odd reason. As if her face was so clouded with emotion it drained out her beauty.

"What?" he asked and Esselle grabbed hold of his wrist out of instinct.

"The testing they're doing" she said and gasped for air. She froze for a moment slowly taking in air and examined their faces. Last she looked at her brother and said.

"Those capsules you brought in" she said "I think you should see this"

****

Esselle was looking over Daniel's shoulder as Doctor Matlock in his uniform and silver hair turned the computer screen on his desk to face Daniel and dropped folders on his desk. The room was light in black light and had several aluminum racks filling up the space. There were wires and screens everywhere. There were bottles of colorful water and Esselle felt her eyes burn from the fumes.

Daniel's eyebrows were pressed together as he scanned the screen. jasmine was standing with an almost sour look on her face and crossed arms. It wasn't until then did Esselle realize how long her hair was. It looked like a cascading waterfall of black over her shoulder and past her waist. Beautiful. Her hair was so beautiful. Daniel and his sister were both stunning. Esselle guessed it was just genetics even though it wasn't fair. No human beings should be that beautiful. Ever.

"I told you" Jasmine said and Esselle snapped out of her daze. Daniel sat back in his chair with a ghostly daze and his hand over his mouth. Esselle knew that position. he was thinking. But of what? Esselle looked at the computer screen and took a folder in her hands. It looked like a mumble jumble of words on paper and different formulas and signs on a computer screen. Esselle was smart. Just not Einstein smart.

"I guess we've literally found your match" Doctor Matlock said and Daniel's eyes shifted to look at him.

"Are you sure?" he asked.

Doctor Matlock nodded. "Oh I'm sure. Ran this through the system at least ten times I didn't believe it myself" he said and Charlotte walked in.

"What is this I hear about-?!" she began and her eyes fell on Esselle. She quickly stiffened and flattened out her vest.

She realized something. Charlotte's accent grew very strong when she was angry about something. Her accent wasn't light and sweet like honey suckle.

"Char" Daniel said and he was distant. "She needs to get tested. And now"

"Well wait" Esselle said softly "What's going on I'm lost"

Everyone just looked at her. Daniel seemed distant not disgusted really just like he couldn't stand to be there like it made him sick to his stomach. like he was ready to die where he was. Or maybe like he just found something he wished he hadn't. Something he wished he didn't and could have gone his whole life not knowing. He let out a deep breath and shut his eyes. After a little he ran his fingers through his hair and looked at Esselle.

"Well?" she said again 'Tell me what happened what was in those things?" she asked.

"Just tell her" Jasmine said and Charlotte shot her a venomous look that read 'shut your mouth'

"Ess you remember that time Char and Jas explained to you the forms in which we change? The forms in which we obtain the virus? by shot or by consumption?" he asked.

Esselle frowned and nodded. It's not true. It isn't true. It at least hasn't been true until now. Esselle was scared. She felt nauseous and sick to her stomach.

"There's um...a lot of explaining I have to do with these results but first and foremost you should know that..." he sighed and shut his eyes again.

'Essie I'm sorry' he whispered. It hit Esselle. He wouldn't say it. he couldn't. It must not be true. As long as he didn't say it it wouldn't be true. It would be all she could hold on to.

She softly shook her head mortified.

"No" she said sliding away.

"Essie-" he said and she shook her head more.

"No" she said "No! Don't say it!" she repeated.

"Ess" he said and reached for her. She quickly covered her eyes.

"No don't say it" she said through gritted teeth fighting back the tears. 'Its not true. They love me. They wouldn't do that to me. As long as you don't say it it won't be true" she said and put her feet on her chair.

"Ess I'm sorry I tried warning you. The tests came back" he said and she looked at him. "Positive"

Esselle broke and the tears came down. She clammed her mouth shut and breathed in and out deeply running her hands through her hair. Her tears gathered at her nose and fell off.

"No" she said and sucked in air. He stood over her and she squeezed her jaw shut "No" she whimpered and broke out into sobs.

"So you're telling me" and this time Charlotte spoke. Her voice was back to normal. "That for x amount of time her parents gave her these and that's how she transformed?"

Doctor Matlock nodded. But Esselle wasn't paying attention. Daniel knelled down in front of her and tugged at her wrists pulling them away from her face.

"Hey" he said.

"Of course this is a very unfamiliar form of virus I have seen. I have only ever seen it once" and he looked at Daniel. Except Daniel didn't look back. He was concentrated on Esselle.

"But after her blood work goes through and her test can I later determine what she is. I have never seen her form of Invisible before. Ever" Doctor Matlock said.

Daniel was content with pulling at Esselle's wrist.

"Hey look at me" he said and Esselle continued to cry. Oh great. Not only did Esselle have really screwed up parents but they turned her into some form of Invisible unknown to the greatest doctor in headquarters. Just. Great.

Finally Esselle looked at Daniel and the corner of his mouth rose. "That's better" he said. In a moment Esselle looked at him then flung herself in his arms. He held her tightly and she cried into his shoulder and he stroked her hair.

"I'm sorry" he said in her hair "I really am"

"I can't...believe...they'd do this to me" she stuttered.

"Shh" he said and Esselle whimpered a bit more. "You're fine" Esselle shook her head. "No I'm not" she said and sniffled "I'm broken"

****

Wherever Esselle was it was dark. She felt little electrical shots pulsing through her body. Then images flashes pictures signs symbols just flashing before her eyes. Then they felt like pinches burns. Florescent blue lighting forming before her eyes then disappearing as fast as they had come. Then her eyes flung open. Esselle looked over in her chair and saw Charlotte absolutely shocked sitting in her stool in front of the computer screen. She very slowly removed her helmet and was looking at Esselle so strangely. Esselle slowly sat up as much as she could on the inclined chair. She was practically lying down. She took the helmet thing off her head and put it down.

"Charlotte" she said slowly "What's wrong?" She heard noise. She looked over to the glass and saw Jasmine shuffling for the door. Daniel was just standing there with crossed arms and a puzzled look until he slowly followed his sister.

Jasmine came pouring into the room and quickly stood next to Charlotte reading the screen.

Charlotte looked at her silently until Jasmine's eyes widened and they looked at each other.

"What?" Esselle asked and Daniel stood behind Charlotte.

"It's her. I didn't think we were right at first but I...I didn't think..." and Jasmine looked at Daniel "She'd be so much like you"

"Daniel I don't think we should wait to inform the council" Charlotte said.

Daniel was reading the screen until his eyes grew wide and black.

Somewhere in Time- trilogy part 2

"What!' Esselle repeated.

"Its like you designed for each other" Jasmine said in a loud whisper.

He looked at his sister with wide eyes "Like hell we were what is this?" he asked.

"Daniel I'm telling you the system does not fail look at exactly what its telling us!" Charlotte said.

'I don't give a damn what the system is telling us we are not exactly alike!" he snapped.

Esselle groaned and stood from her chair muttering unlady like things and pushed past them to the screen.

"Ughh!" Esselle snapped. She strained to read what the screen meant but she had no idea what the words and symbols meant along with the numbers.

She looked at Daniel and pointed at the screen "Would you like to tell me what this means?"

Daniel still had his arms crossed and he snorted. "It means you're my twin" he said.

****

"What the hell do you mean twin? I'm pretty sure I was born by myself!" Esselle said half running half walking down the hallways to keep up with Daniel.

"Ya well" he said and Esselle grew sick to her stomach and she slowed down.

'Dear God my parents are your" and she stopped herself. He turned around with a quick sharp move and looked disgusted.

"Dear God no not like that what the he;; are you thinking!" he said stopping dead in his tracks.

Somewhere in Time- trilogy part 2

"Well twins are-' she said.

He shook his head "Twins are different in our terms" he said and continued to zoom down the hallways. Charlotte was in front of him and Jasmine was behind Esselle.

"Then what do twins mean in your terms?" she asked.

She heard him sigh "Twins here means that two people were made the exact same way and most likely by the same exact people" he said glancing back at her.

"Here's the art where you get to know more about me Ess" he said "I'm the only Invisible of my kind. My blood my body the way I work and function my abilities are far different than any other invisibles. We thought I was the only one like this. You see over time Ess we have evolved there are different forms of us. Some rarer then other because of time period. But never one single person all on their own. I knew something was wrong right away when you weren't screaming in excruciating pain during your test. It's extremely painful. I didn't feel pain either during mine" he said.

"So you mean we were made the same way?" she asked. They were in the training room. Esselle could see Charlotte up front look totally badass. She had never seen that side of the motherly figure before. She yanked open a door to a room. The same room Esselle had gone into to see Dawn's marks.

"In" Charlotte said and they stopped to look at her "Now, and don't make me repeat myself" they all obeyed and marked in. Charlotte slammed the door shut behind them and the light was. Jasmine was near the control panel. She was rapidly pressing buttons and Charlotte had her arms crossed. Until the lighting changed. Esselle felt her mark glow on her inner arm. it had been

Somewhere in Time- trilogy part 2

the first time she'd seen it since she found out she had one. it was still beautiful. Esselle saw Jasmine's mark. Beautiful. Until she saw Charlotte. Charlotte had marks all over her body. She looked like a warrior. The look on her face when she saw Esselle examining her changed. Charlotte looked not beautiful but not ugly with her marks. Esselle slowly approached her and Charlotte gave her a small smile.

"Years of being a fighter like me Esselle gets your marks like these" she said.

'But how-?" she began and Charlotte spoke.

"I was one of the first Invisible remember" she moved her arms. "I have the history of our people written across my body. My arms legs stomach back. Everywhere"

"It's so different from mine from ours' Esselle said and Charlotte smiled.

"Of course it is dear. We were the first" she said.

"What are we here for again?" Jasmine asked.

Charlotte cleared her throat and brought Daniel and Esselle to the center of the room. Esselle could very slightly see the outline of a circle.

Esselle could see Daniel's mark sticking out from the collar of his shirt. He had quite a few. jasmine only had around four or five.

"Why do you have so many marks?" Esselle asked.

"The more we accomplish the more marks we get" Daniel said.

"Take each other's hands" Charlotte said and Daniel made a face.

"What is this? A fantasy movie?" he asked and Charlotte's patience Esselle could tell was wearing thin.

"DO it or I'll cut your ear off" she said in a deadly calm. If only for a second Esselle saw it. Daniel's eyes widened and he shivered a bit. Esselle looked at him and extended her hands. He rolled his eyes and took Esselle's hands. There was a spark. Like electricity and they quickly staggered back.

Daniel had a wild look on his face and his black hair slightly covered his flawless face as he looked at his hands.

"What the hell was that?" he said. Jasmine and Charlotte were side by side and slowly backing away from them. Charlotte had a knowing look on her hand.

"Do it" she said slowly "Again" almost as if she were hesitant. Daniel and Esselle looked at each other. Esselle looked at her hands again. What had just happened? it felt like a spark going off. A thousand volts of electricity made her head ring and explode like fireworks.

They slowly reached out for each other and took each others hands. That's when Esselle saw it. The marks. They were running across Daniel's skin then circling and enter winning continuing on Esselle's skin. It was beautiful. In a rainbow of beautiful colors. The colors blue, red, yellow, orange, green, and purple all in harmony in beautiful designs covering their skin. Burning the form they were in on their skin. Then there was something glowing beneath them. The light dim then grew brighter then slightly dimmer and even brighter until Esselle saw it. A mark. A mark that looked like something she had never seen before. With sharp defining edges and beautiful curves lit up in between the circle they were both standing in. Then the room began spinning. Literally. The blue and green and yellow red purple orange began traveling along the floor and up the walls like electricity or fire spreading. Eventually the walls and floor were lit up in colors and light. The looked like images. Signs symbols.

Somewhere in Time- trilogy part 2

Charlotte looked around in awe and Jasmine just seemed mesmerized.

"Wow" Jasmine gasped.

'I have never seen a pair quite like you too before" Charlotte said and looked at them her soft beauty look fierce in the light "never a pair quite so powerful before"

Then as if on Que the colors were being stripped from the walls and floors until it ended up back in the circle it started. But Daniel and Esselle were just looking at each other. Then the marks on their bodies slowly began to fade away. Until it was completely black and dim in the room. Esselle could feel the warmth grow.

The lighting in the room changed and Esselle could slightly see the outline of everyone the way she had before the light and mark phenomenon.

Esselle felt a burning at her side and she winced. So did Daniel. Esselle pulled up her shirt on her side was a mark glowing. It looked like something you'd see carved into the walls of some ancient secret building. a language unknown to her.

She looked over and Daniel was doing the same thing. He had the same exact mark as her. She gently ran her finger tips over his skin absent minded and her mind clouded with confusion.

'What the hell did your parents do to you" she heard Jasmine mutter.

At that moment the lights went on completely and she could see everyone. Charlotte stood the superior figure she was with her hands folded in front of her.

"Daniel" she said and they both distant.

"Yes" he said.

'You said that whoever turned us did it the same exact way right?" she asked.

"Yeah" he replied

"It also means it was done by the same exact people" Charlotte said and they looked at her. She shook her head "Impossible two different people did what they did to you impossible. You're both to uniquely different from the rest of us so intricate. Your basics aren't even the same as ours. The foundation on which you were both altered is complicated from ours" she said.

"But" Esselle said and looked at Daniel "My parents' and she chocked on the word.

'Did what they did to me that means..." she trailed off. Daniel and everyone in the room gave her a worried look. Esselle could feel the rage and anger burn up inside of her. She marched off towards the door.

"Ess" she heard Daniel call after her. He she could tell was trying to compose himself. Bad enough they did what they did to their daughter but to a complete innocent person. Esselle was now beyond repair. She was ready to burn their home to ashes.

"Ess!" she heard Daniel yell. But it was too late. She was already running.

****
****

Esselle snorted. "Like hell I will" she said. She turned the corner on her block and glanced out the window.

She had her cell phone pressed against her ear and Daniel was arguing with her on the other line. She had grabbed his car keys and ran out of headquarters. They lost her a couple dozen blocks behind. Night had fallen when Esselle left headquarters. Well at least almost. It was sunset and the sky was half and half. It had not hit Esselle that she was late for lunch by hours until she left headquarters. She pulled up in front of her house and yanked the key out of the ignition.

"Ess whatever you think about doing-" she heard Daniel say and she snorted.

"Oh please" she said. She hung up her phone and tossed it into her bag. She stepped out and slammed the car door close behind her. Esselle was fuming. Esselle didn't know how they did it or why but they did. That's why she saw that man in black go to her house that time. He knew her parents. Because they hired him to kill their daughter 28 years ago. They killed her to complete their little experiment. She was never their daughter they never loved her. She was their toy and when they were done with her they tossed her to the side. She had once said to Daniel that she wasn't titanium. Maybe she was and she just didn't know it. Esselle was still in one piece despite being and angry emotional wreck but she was still somehow functioning. She somehow managed to do so. She slammed the door open to her house and slammed it shut. She heard a scream. Her mother. Esselle threw her bag and marched right into the kitchen. She heard rushed footsteps.

Soon enough her mother was standing under the arc in the kitchen.

She sighed 'Esselle we've been worried sick. Where have you been?" she asked. Esselle wasn't listening. She was drowning out the sound of her mother's voice with the sounds of her screams the day of her death.

She yanked open the cabinets searching frantically for the bottle that ruined her life. She started throwing things and she heard her mother shriek as Esselle threw the glass jar of sugar behind her and it shattered. how could they. They took everything away from her. First off they took away her life! 28 years of living she lost her teen years she never fully got to be a crazy wild kid! She never finished school everyone who once knew her thought she was dead!That's why no matter what they always gave Esselle vitamins. Her whole life shoving them down by the bottle down her throat. They took away her happiness. They took away her best friend and they took her away from her best friend. She lost Mardrin because of them. One of the only men she had ever loved. If you asked Esselle just a few weeks ago the person she would die for she would have answered Mardrin. Just don't ask her again now who the love of her life is. The world is messed up as it is.

Soon enough her father came in. All the way in the back of the cabinet was a little door. She opened it and bottles and bottles of vitamins were there. She was burning a bloody red. She pulled a bottle out and turned around.

"What the hell are you doing!" her mother said clearly furious.

"What is this?" Esselle asked and her father's face froze.

Her mother still enraged froze and her eyes widened with something Esselle didn't even recognize in her own mother. Esselle screamed in anguish and grabbed more bottles.

"What is this!" she demanded.

"Its not what you think" her mother said.

Esselle gave an evil smile "Oh its not what I think?" she snapped she opened up the bottles and poured the capsules everywhere and threw the empty bottles hard against the counter. Her mother jumped.

"For my entire life you shoved these things down my throat! What the hell did you think I wasn't going to find out what was going!" she screamed. She emptied out the cabinet making a disastrous mess and all the anger she felt bottling up was exploding out of her. And she couldn't stop it from coming. Not at all.

"Esselle stop!' her mother said walking around the counter.

"Don't tell me stop to hell with you! You screwed around in your kids head for her entire life and you want me to calm down? You turned me into one of your freak experiments!" she shouted.

"Esselle we love you you know that-" her father said.

"Bull shit!" she snapped and her parents eyes widened. She had never really cursed in front of them before.

Her mother reached for her and she staggered back. "I swear to god if you get anywhere closer to me you'll force me to tell you to fuck off!" Esselle said and her mother's cheeks were bright red.

'I don't appreciate how your talking to your mother!" she said.

"You are not my mother" she spat "And you are not my father" Esselle felt sick to her stomach "I don't understand! I'm your only daughter! How did you even...i can't..." Esselle ran her fingers through her hair and walked off. Then it hit her. Something she had failed to think about before. Mardrin.

"Mardrin" she said and her father looked at her.

"What about him?" he asked.

Esselle was so enraged her chest bubbled with laughter and it came out. She placed her hand on her hip and looked at her.

"So that's how you did it?' she asked.

'Did what!" her mother asked.

'Killed me! That's how you killed your daughter!" Esselle shouted.

"You knew Martha. You knew she was coming back. Everyone knew Mardrin told everyone. But me!" and Esselle had a bitter taste in her mouth. Her words were poisonous. "You knew the first place she would go was to the office. I mean its obvious Mardrin is there all the time. His parents weren't working that day I remember they went out to dinner that's why we were at his house. When Martha came you'd send her there. Because you knew" Esselle looked to the ceiling. "You knew how could you have know. Your own daughter! You set up your own daughter! Dear God!" she said.

"Elle-" her father began and she shot him a look that read shut up.

"Then you knew I'd run out right on cue. That's why you had that man there in the black car. Waiting just waiting. He must have just installed that bomb thing whatever it was in my car when I ran out. He followed me. Ran me off the road and I died just enough for you stick me in a freaking freezer!" she yelled enraged.

Her parents faces were blank and defeated. Like the color had been drained out of them.

"How did you know what we were doing in the first place?" her mother asked choking on each word.

"Does it matter point is you did it! In cold blood too I have half mind by everything I have to ki-!" she said and Esselle was cut off.

"Stop!" she heard and she turned around. She saw Mardrin standing in the doorway.

Somewhere in Time- trilogy part 2

Esselle's mind was now spinning. Now what the hell was he doing here! Did he hear everything?

"Mardrin what are you-?" but he finished the question off fore her.

"Doing here? I was talking to your parents before you stormed in. i figured I'd stay quiet until you left but this is too much for me to hear" he said.

"What are you doing here in the first place?" she asked.

"Talking about your health" he said.

Esselle staggered back "My health?" she asked and he went white.

"I meant-" he said and reached for her. She smacked him dead across the face making such a loud noise she heard her mother let out a little shriek. It was so hard Esselle felt her hand throbbing but she didn't care she was so beyond words she didn't care. There was a huge swelling red mark across his face and he looked at her shocked. Esselle let out a sound of disgust.

"You knew?" she asked.

He swallowed hard "Elle please find it in you to forgive me I-" he said and Esselle smacked him again.

"ugh!" she said as she was unable to say anything else she stomped frantically. "Ugh!" she screamed.

"You knew! It doesn't matter you knew and you didn't tell me Mardrin! You didn't tell me!' she screamed so loud and hard it sounded like she were screaming bloody Mary.

"Elle if I could have done something anything to stop what was happening I would have! I didn't know to the extent-" he said but she cut him off again.

"But you knew!' and her screams sounded like pleas "Mardrin

you knew and you didn't tell me! You tricked me you lied! I trusted you I loved you more than anything in the world don't you get that? I would have died for you Mardrin! Had it been me I would have said something! I would have tried to help you to save you to do anything!" she screamed.

"The damage was already done Esselle what the hell was I supposed to do! God knows it killed me I loved you Esselle you thought it was easy for me watching you suffer?" he shouted back.

"It was your own fault!" she growled and ranted growing exasperated. "Had you opened your freaking mouth and said something maybe I wouldn't be where I am now! you coward you moron you idiot! You call that love? You call that protecting the one you love? You I just I can't!" she said and stepped a few steps back.

'Was it all real anyway or were you just part of their little plan to shove me in a freezer?" she asked.

"Of course it was!" he snapped "How could you even ask such a question I did everything I could to convince your parents to stop! What do you think i sat on my ass all those years?"

Esselle's eyes widened "Years?" she asked "So you knew from the beginning?" she asked.

He sighed and ran his fingers through his hair "Elle we knew. We all knew from the beginning."

"I will never forgive you" Esselle said shaking her head.

'Elle" Mardrin said.

"Don't!" she shouted forcefully "Mardrin don't!"

"That's not how it is!" he argued.

Esselle gasped "Oh Mardrin that's ok because i'll tell you how it

Somewhere in Time- trilogy part 2

is!" she snapped "You!" she said and pointed a finger at him. "Don't tell the love of your life that her parents are poking around in her mind! 28 years later she's back and you fail to tell her again you let her down!" she said and poked his chest. "You tell her you love her you kiss her you talk to her you do all of this for and at the end of the day you go home to your wife!" she said and punched his chest hard "And kids!" she screamed and punched him hard again.

"That's the way it is!" she screamed.

Esselle heard the front door open and Daniel came in like.

"Like hell when I find that girl-" and he stopped dead in his tracks. "Crap" she heard him mutter.

'Daniel" Esselle gasped "What are you doing here?' she asked.

"Looking for y-!" she heard and Jasmine stopped dead in her tracks behind him.

"Uh awkward" she said and Daniel eyeballed her. "I'll be outside" she said and ran before Daniel could grab hold of her shirt. He winced when the fabric slipped between his fingertips.

"You" she heard Mardrin mutter so softly it took her a second to decipher his word.

"Oh look what a nice little reunion" he said and nonchalantly shoved his hands in his front pockets.

"What in the hell are you doing here?" Mardrin said.

Daniel gave a smile. Esselle knew that smile. She was ready to die in her place.

"Well look at you all grown up. Honestly I never thought I'd see you again. Then again" he looked at Esselle "Its a small world"

"You know each other?" she asked and stood next to Daniel.

"Vaguely" he said and Esselle's parents were approaching.

"Its you? Of all people our daughter found her way to you?" her mother asked.

Esselle looked at Daniel. "Daniel?" she said.

"Well in all fairness the last time I saw them I was seventeen" he said.

"17?" Esselle repeated. She turned on her heels and ran her fingers through her hair. "I can't believe this" she said to herself.

"What i'd like to know is what he's doing here" she ehard Mardrin mutter.

Esselle stopped dead in her tracks to look at them. "What I'd like to know is who the hell invited you into *my* house anyway!" she snapped.

She heard Daniel laughed and ehr mother looked mortified.

"I don't remember him recieving an invitation" Mardrin remarked.

Daniel let out a snort and Esselle realized he was trying not to laugh. She turned on her heels and shot him a look.

"What do you find so amusing about this!" she said clearly curious.

He shurgged "I find it funny how your parents seem silent in all this" he pointed a finger at them "Parent of the year award winners 17 years running. Then again until your daughter died. But you see enevr in a million years did I think y paths would cross with you again" he said and looked at Esselle.

"Until I met you" and he pointed at Esselle. "So now" he said and shoved his hands back in his pockets. "I guess we're all screwed."

"We did well with you didn't we?" Vivenne asked.

Daniel made a so-so face and waved a hand in the air. "Well considering I was alreadyperfect before you did ok. The strength was just a bonus"

"I can't believe this" Esselle budded in after ignoring her boyfriend's sarcasm "Not only did you screw around in my head you screwed around his. This is ridiculous" she said and looked at Mardrin 'And you knew you knew the whole time" and the betrayl began seeping into her voice.

"Ell I-!" Mardrin began clearing growing annoyed.

Esselle shook her head and stepped back. "no, what you did to me was just a betrayl beyond words. I could never forgive you for that" she said.

"Elle" he said and took her shoulder. She quickly shook him off.

"I've had enough don't touch me" she said and ran off past Daniel.

"Elle!" Mardrin called after her.

Daniel quickly made a side step and stopped dead in front of Mardrin blocking his way. They were both intimidating looking and around the same hieght.

Daniel had such a calm yet serious look on his face.

"She said not to touch her" he said and it was eep scratchy and soft. The two men now rivals looked at each other for a moment before Daniel turned around and ran off.

"Ess!" he shouted. He ran outside and Esselle was struggling with getting the car door open across the street.

"Essie" he said and jogged towards her.

"This damn car!" she said and kicked the door.

"That's because you're turning the key the wrong way" he said and did it for her.

She stomed inside and she shoved the key in the ignition.

"I don't believe this" she muttered when he got in. "They didn't even apologive they just..."

Daniel grabbed her hand and yanked the keys out.

She turned to look at him. "What are you doing?" she snapped.

"You're seriously driving in this condition?" he asked.

She yanked the keys back and went 100 miles an hour down the street. "I don't care" she said through gritted teeth.

"Well I do! Listen I'm not ready to have you be an idiot speeding down the road besides!" he grabbed the steeringwheel and they stopped in some alley between buildings where trucks drop off cargo "It'd be a shame to see a pretty face like this leave the world twice too soon"

Esselle swallowed hard and yanked the car keys from the ignition. HE was right. Her head was a clouded mess she couldn't even think straight. All the questions she had before disappeared because she was just to busy hurting. Her mind heart soul body everything. She had an awful headache coming on and she banged on the steering wheel hard. Twice three times four times five. And she didn't stop. Finally without crying to her surprise she just burried her face in her hands and breathed.

"Are you done yet?' Daniel asked and Esselle realized he was still there. He hadn't left. Even though it probably would have been easier to leave he didn't. He was still by her side. She couldn't say that about not one other person she thought was important in her life. It said a lot. And definitely showed her more.

"Why did you let me bang on that thing" she said and looked down at her hands "it really hurt.

She saw Daniel smile. He took her hands in his and rubbed them together. "Because I figured you were angry and hurt and i shouldn't bother stopping you from chanelling you angry

Somewhere in Time- trilogy part 2

anyway"" he said and she nodded "Plus I didn't want you chanelling your anger on my face. I kind of need it"

Esselle laughed a bit. Then her laughter slowly died down until they were in the silenc of the car. Esselle could feel the tears coming on but she fought them back. She had already cied too much she felt weak and athetic. Especially if she shed one more tear. As if reading her mind Daniel said

"If you want to cry just do it. Emotions are relentless bastards. they demand to be present felt and shown in every way shape and form possible. I don't blame you"

Esselle took one deep breath nodded and shut her eyes while the tears began to streak her face. And before she knew it Daniel had in her in his arms and she was ready to die from the pain. Until it dawned on her.

"Daniel?" she sobbed nto his cotton shirt.

"Yes" he replied

"Can I be honest with you about something?" she asked.

She felt him smile "Of course anything"

"Ok well then good. Because we kind of forgot Jasmine" she said and he laughed.

Somewhere in Time- trilogy part 2

"Esselle I'm sorry" Jasmine said and gently placed Esselle's hands in hers.

Esselle smiled "I left you there rememebr?" she said.

Jasmien laughed and embraced Esselle "I forgive you. Besides you were angry" and she pulled away "When I first found out who did what they did to me it came a a huge shock. But I could never imagne it being my own parents though"

"How did it happen to you?" Esselle asked.

Jasmine shifted in her seat. They were sitting in a room with a big circle table. Esselle was sitting at the head of the table and Jasmine was sitting at the seat on her left. The table was a dark cherry wood and the walls were covered in warm light brown paint and beautiful shelves of leather bound books.

"Me?" she said and examined the room. "I was young. They didn't get to do a lot to me. It was my doctor. I had the right blood type for the experiment and he noticed. He was part of the outer circle though of scientists. Not the elite group. Anyways he didn't get to do much with me because I noticed something wrong and switched doctors"

Esselle nodded as she listened attentively.

"But then I died" and Esselle already knew that part of the story but she waited for Jasmine to say so but she didn't. And Esselle kept her mouth shut. "See had I not died the virus would have worn off. I could have been normal. But since I died they had no choice but to freeze me and they did. Later when I woke up I was extremely weak and frail. They had to finish me off. Instilled the rest of the virus in me. I had awaken too early i was premature. After a few months they froze me again. I just recently wok up the second time around"

"You were frozen twice?" Esselle asked and she nodded. It did make sense she guessed. Jasmine was only 16 yet Joel had said she woken up a few months after Daniel. Daniel woke up years ago now. SO Jasmine as frozen again. Esselle had a better understanding of why Daniel was so hard on himself when it came to his sister. Now she knew. But Jasmine seemed like a ray of sunshine always. She didn't seem to hold it against him.

"But that was ancient history" she said pushing stray black hairs behind her ear. "Now we have to figure out what to do with you"

"If I knew I wouldn't be here" Esselle said looking around. At that moment the door opened. Charlotte came in and smiled softly.

"Hello Esselle" she said. She had her knew high black boots on and same black leather vest on as usual. "Things haven't been very normal lately have they?" she asked and walked over making the silent room echo with the click of her heels.

"Yes it has" Esselle said.

Charlotte had her signature warm smile stood over Esselle and ran her hand down her hair. "Tell me child what are you thinking?" she asked.

Esselle sighed. She was thinking it would be a really nice time to jump off the Empire State Building. Then again. "I don't know what to do next" Esselle finally managed to say.

"Well we contacted the council. They should be here tomorrow. You've already been fully inducted. Next we'll just try getting you on a normal schedule its the best we can do for now. Your parents you have been informed disappeared"

Esselle nodded. They had told her that hours ago. Daniel had told her and then he kissed her said he'd be back and left. That was 4 hours ago and he wasn't back.

"We'll finish up your training give you a normal and formal education and try our best to treat you like the rest of us" Charlotte said.

"But I'm not like the rest of you" Esselle said. Charlotte bent down next to Esselle and listened to her. "You remember what happened with my tests. What my parents did-" Esselle said but Charlotte cut her off.

"You and Daniel are *both* different. You'll have to get through it together. Imagine Esselle he had to go through this by himself the past four years. Now he has you" she said.

Esselle thought for her moment. Esselle could barely get through this and she had a support system. Daniel however...was on his own. Maybe he were stronger than she thought. And not just physically.

at that moment before Esselle could reply the doors busted open and Dawn came in.

She looked at Esselle and gave her a half smile. "Hey kid" she said and walked over. From head to toe she was in all black. A black tank top with a plunging neckline black leather pants with a hanging metal chain her black gloves and the platform boots. The ones with the studs.

Esselle smiled a bit back at her when she grabbed a chair and pushed it close to hers. Dawn kicked up her feet dropping them on another chair and held onto Esselle's arm snuggling her head on her. "How ya doin'?" she asked.

Esselle smiled a bit and stroked Dawn's hair. "I've been better"
"On a scale from one to ten?" she asked and Charlotte smiled. Esselle thought "1-10?' she asked "Well right now I'm just about at you living the rest of your life with wearing spikes being against the law"
She heard Dawn gasp a bit and give her a heartbreaking look with sad eyes. As if it were a very serious painful thing. Esselle laughed very amused as did Jasmine. Dawn went back to snuggling against Esselle's arm and Charlotte began to speak.
"So I'm assuming you don't want to go home" she said.
Esselle snorted "The street sounds better"
"Well Esselle I don't know what we can do. You might have to live there" Charlotte said.
'What do you mean?" Esselle asked and Dawn looked up at her.
"Oh ya" she said and their eyes met for a second before Charlotte spoke again.
"Well although the council knows already in can take you weeks maybe even a few months to run you through the system and give you a permanent assigned place to live. It was Daniel and he only just finally got a permanent apartment. Its a process" Charlotte said and as she spoke Esselle's headache grew.
"Are you kidding me" she said and looked at Jasmine who was nodding with raised eyebrows.
"As you know there is a living quarters here but that will take weeks for you to get assigned to live in one of the rooms" she said.
"Is the living quarters the castle looking part of this place? Because to be honest that always confused me" Esselle said. Charlotte laughed. "Well that's the way I wanted it. I have very

exquisite taste"

Esselle frowned "You wanted it?" she asked.

Charlotte smiled with shut eyes and sat at the edge of the table. "When they were almost done building the Freedom Tower Esselle I had awaken. The Invisibles were just beginning. They right away assigned me to the overseer in headquarters. They wanted this hideous decor I absolutely forbade it. I allowed the training quarters to be extremely modern as it had to be. But in the living quarters I wanted it almost palace like. It's the same everywhere else' she straightened her back out with pride "I turned it into a trend"

The girls smiled and the door opened.

Trevor came in and he had an irritated look on his face. He was covered in mud. He walked over to the table and slammed what looked like piece of a rusted bike on the table.

He pointed at Jasmine "Do you mind telling

your *brother* something" he said.

Jasmine laughed "he's your best friend. Why is he always my brother when he did something wrong" she said.

"Because he's your brother!" he said. Esselle had begun to braid Dawn's very short hair. Esselle noticed his voice was getting squeaky high. Like when Daniel gets annoyed. But Daniel couldn't get that high in his life. His tone was too deep.

Jasmine swung an arm around to point at the tranquil Esselle braiding Dawn's hair.

"He's her boyfriend!" she said and her voice was squeaky high too.

Esselle looked up defensive as Charlotte and Dawn chuckled. "I didn't even do anything wrong!" and this time her voice was

Somewhere in Time- trilogy part 2

squeaky high.
"BUt Daniel did" Jasmine and Trevor said in unison.
"How's that my fault? I'm just sitting here all calm and quite-!" Esselle began to rant when the doors opened.
Daniel came in. He glanced over once and his eyes fell on Trevor. Trevor had a face and Daniel broke out into a smile and a fit of silent hysteria.
We walked over to Trevor and shook his shoulder.
He sighed and stopped laughing. His smile was wide big and bright and his eyes were twinkling. He pointed a finger at Trevor. "You look good kid" he said.
Charlotte raised an eyebrow but she was smiling. "Daniel what did you do this time?" she asked.
Daniel's jaw dropped and he gently place a hand on his chest "Why I didn't do anything!" he said.
In that moment every head in the room turned with a crack to look at him. he examined each face with the same look. He finally gave up and gave a crooked grin.
"Kicked a couple of zelt ass is all" he said.
What did I tell you about that?" Charlotte asked.
"Char but listen. It was *sick* I'm telling you I looked so good doing it I wish I were someone else to watch" he said. Esselle wanted to laugh.
"I used this rubber band I found on the floor and a few pebbles. I have killer aim! I just need someone to grab the rocks for me. grabbed the nearest fool" he said.
Trevor's eyes widened "That was me!" he ranted.
Daniel smiled "Why were you standing next to me?" he asked.
Trevor with wide eyes and a wide mouth looked around with

rising shoulders and a red face beneath the mud. "I was walking WITH you!" he said. Trevor face everyone else The bastard had me climb a whole bunch of huge rocks in central park slipped and fell and landed in the mud near the water!" he said and Daniel chuckled.

"You looked very attractive while doing it though" he said.

"Aw" jasmine said "I'm sure you did" and the room lit up with smiles and subtle laughter.

"Anyways you told Ess about her house yet?" Trevor asked and fell into a chair.

"What about my house?" she asked.

"Nothing" Daniel said quickly.

"Oh you didn't know?" Trevor said innocently.

"Shit" she heard Dawn mutter when she slammed her hand on her forehead.

Charlotte cleared her throat. "Uh Trevor sweetheart" she said. Trevor grabbed an apple from the bowl in the middle of the table and took a bite.

"Trev" Daniel muttered and smacked the back of his chair.

"What?" he said in a nagging tone. "They're tearing your house apart from the inside" he said and took a bite.

"What?" Esselle said growing mortified.

"Yup" Trevor said with a mouthful.

Jasmine was waving her hands in silent motion but he didn't see.

"They have to for evidence and stuff like that. Taking everything and the house will be put under quarantine" he said and bit the apple again.

"Trevor!" Daniel said in a deep whisper.

"Probably getting ready right now" Trevor said.

Somewhere in Time- trilogy part 2

At that moment Daniel smacked his hand on his forehead and turned around and as did everyone muttering things like "Hell" and "Dear God"

"They can't do that!" Esselle said springing out of her chair.

"Oh!" Dawn shrieked and she fell back into Esselle's now empty seat.

"Watch it here precious cargo!" she snapped rubbing her head.

"But all of my things are there!" Esselle said.

"You can buy new clothes" Daniel said.

She shook her head "No, no, no its not that. other stuff. Sentimental things I can't lose!' she said walking around the table.

'I have to go back!"

"Esselle that's not a good idea" Charlotte said standing from her seat.

"I want be long I promise!" she quickly turned "Daniel please!" she begged.

He made a face "I really don't think its a good idea." he said.

She folded her hands in front of her face "Please! I'll be quick I promise!" she said.

He rolled his eyes and looked at Charlotte.

"Look I know its a lot to ask but I'm starting over here. A fresh slate. It's going to be hard and having something from before to hold onto will help me get through it all!" she tried "Right?"

Daniel looked at Charlotte again whom shrugged. "You have an hour" she said.

Somewhere in Time- trilogy part 2

Esselle's bedroom door slowly opened and she stepped inside. The light from outside made her room look blue and she sighed. This was the place she had been raised grown up her whole life. The next time she would see it her room would be empty.
"You know I'm going to miss this place" she said and approached her vanity.
Daniel leaned against the far left wall and crossed his arms.
"Of course you are. Its the logical thing of course" he said.
Esselle quickly found a very small box. The size of around your average school desk.
She turned around and face Daniel. She bit her lip "I need your help" she said.

Somewhere in Time- trilogy part 2

He raised an eyebrow. He looked mysterious in this lightening. "Why?" he asked.

"Because what I need is kind of under my mattress" she said.

He let out a deep breath and smiled. "Of course what you need is under your mattress" he said walking over.

He picked up the corner lifting it with ease. Esselle got down to her knees and stuck her hand between the mattress. She pulled her hand out. In it was a huge thick scrapbook.

She smiled at it and held the book close to her life. "In this book is every great moment in my life. Its also the last piece of my sisters existence" she said and looked at the pretty flowery glittery cover.

Daniel nodded and dropped the mattress. "It's a big book" he said with the same charisma he's always had.

Esselle laughed a bit "Yes. I was a very happy girl once' she said stroking the lace on the cover. She tossed the book into her box and went on her way. She mostly took family heirlooms she didn't want other people getting their sticky fingers on. She was going through her jewelry box when through the mirror of the vanity she saw Daniel glancing at the pictures on her nightstand. She smiled just waiting for him to pick one up. He picked up one of her favorites. Of her and Mardrin smiling at each other the one she always kept there.S he pretended to not know and went on her business when he glanced at her cautiously and looked at the other photos. She had hoped he would look at them. Esselle was going through a small little bock when she found a locket. One that Mardrin had gave her. She felt her heart fall. As angry as she was she could not bear to see that locket go. It was the first gift he ever got her. They were thirteen. And now Esselle felt like a

fool being so sentimental. But ti didn't stop her from dropping it into the box. No one needed to know. It could just be between herself and no one else. She cleared her throat grabbing her box and turning around. She smiled. He was still examining the photos. With no shame he looked at her and said.
"I'm surprised you kept these" and his voice oozed honesty. She was just smiling. "You have no idea how many times I wanted to fling those out a window" she said and dropped the now full box on her bed. She stood next to him and grabbed another picture frame. "I would have taken them down but I was scared my parents might find it odd."
She put the photo on the floor and stomped on it hard shattering the glass. She smiled.
"now that that's over with" she said and plucked the frame from Daniel's hands. She tossed it on the floor did the same cleaned her hands off.
"Don't be jealous though" she said.
'Why would I be jealous?" he said with a face.
"Don't worry. I made sure my *boyfriend* was still being represented" she said. She reached over her bed slipping her hand under her pillow. When she pulled her hand back there was a pretty frame in her hands. She was still smiling when she handed it over to him.
"Used to look at it every night. Never left that spot" she said grabbing her box and heading for the door.
"Come on Daniel!" she called behind her. When she was gone Daniel smiled at the empty hallway in her wake. What a woman she was.

Somewhere in Time- trilogy part 2

"Coming" he called back making sure to take the picture frame ,with a photograph of the two of them laughing, with him.

Esselle plopped herself on the couch in Daniel's apartment and her box was on the kitchen counter. Jasmine had left not too long ago. All they did was sit in silence talking here and there about what to do next. Esselle ran her hands through her hair and Daniel sat in the seat next to her.
"What are you thinking about?" he asked. It was too late. The tears were just falling out of Esselle's eyes. She wasn't sobbing they were just pouring out and her entire body ached from the pain.
"Ess?" he said and she sniffled "But Ess why are you crying?" he asked and wrapped an arm around her.
"Because" she said. Now she was beginning to sob. "I don't know what to do now"
Daniel pulled her over and she rested her head on his shoulder.
"What am i supposed to do now? Where do I go? My house is off

limits. My founds well, I have none. The world thinks I died remember. I have no other family but my parents and they've fled." she said and wiped her tears away.

"I mean you heard what Charlotte said. It can take weeks for them to assign me somewhere" she said and he looked at her "Its like I can't get a break. Ever! No matter what i do something always comes over and bangs me over the head!"

"Essie you'll be fine" he said.

"No I won't" she said covering her face "I'm gonna get stuck living on the L train" she spoke her voice muffled through her hands.

He laughed "Of course not that's ridiculous. You'll be living right here" he said.

Esselle looked at him. He was smiling. Not mischievously but sweetly. She liked it. "But I don't..." she said and trailed off.

"Live? With you?" she said and he laughed.

"Ya. The couch actually isn't that bad you know. I guess its safe to say you've taken over my bedroom. I like the couch anyway. You know I found this thing in Philly?" he said.

Esselle's eyebrows furrowed. "Philly?" she said and he nodded.

"Yup. I could take you there one day-well-if I weren't banned from the lovely state of Pennsylvania" he said. Before Esselle could reply he said "But that's a whole other story. I'll you though. One day" he said.

Esselle took a moment of silence before she began to laugh. And eventually he did too.

"You don't have to do that for me" she said fiddling with the collar of his shirt.

"I don't mind. jasmine offered but I figured I'd save you the

Somewhere in Time- trilogy part 2

suicide attempts" he said and Esselle widened her eyes.
He nodded "She has that effect on people trust me" he said.
Esselle laughed again. And then she just laughed and laughed and laughed until she couldn't anymore.
Finally the sun had risen again and Esselle and Daniel were still on the couch watching reruns of Tom and Jerry.
"You know" Daniel said breaking the silence. Esselle was lying on his chest with her feet stretched out over the couch when she looked up at him. He had an arm around her and he made a face "I have something to tell you"
She shrugged "Hit me kid" she said. He smiled a bit.
"You see I don't know how to put this exactly t there is someone I have been meaning to tell something to" he said.
Esselle smiled 'Oh really?" she teased.
he nodded and looked down at her "You see I've been meaning to tell her I love her. I just haven't figured out how to do so yet"
Esselle's smile fell and she felt her heart race. She swallowed hard and pushed the hair from his face. "Why don't you just do it then?" she asked.
He shrugged "Guess I'm wondering if she'll say it back" he said.
Esselle bit back a soft smile. "Well then" she said and laid back down. "You're worried for nothing"
"Am I?" he asked.
She nodded without looking at him but smiled anyway "Because if you weren't so afraid to tell her" she said "She would have said she loved you too"
Daniel laughed.
"Then again that's what you get for being a chicken" she teased and this time he laughed louder.

"Oh no I'm no chicken" he said and she smiled at him. He smiled back "You know I love you right?" he said.
Esselle smiled wide and just laid her head back down. "Oh I know" she said "I love you too"
Then he just laughed.

4 weeks later.........

So Esselle had kind of taken over Daniel's apartment. But he really didn't mind. He said he had liked what she did with the place anyway. Jasmine came in at all the wrong times as usual. She did live right below them. Them. It was strange thinking of it. Esselle had never even thought in a millions years she'd like Daniel. Let along love him. It was a whole new feeling for her. Kind of like getting to live all over again. Which was exactly what she was doing. Living again. Things hadn't exactly been normal per-say. But they were still great. Esselle rushed down the street running right past a yellow taxi. The sun was shinning bright and beautiful. The summer air was warm and sweet. Esselle felt as if she could finally breathe again. It was a beautiful feeling.
Esselle stopped at a flower shop and picked up a dozen lilies. They were Charlotte's favorite. They were celebrating her birthday today. Everyone was in charge of something. Jasmine and Dawn decorating. Esselle flowers. Trevor cake. Joel gift. It turned out Joel decided to hang around headquarters more often. Esselle liked it. Daniel was just in charge of showing up and showing his pretty face because God knows if anyone gave

Somewhere in Time- trilogy part 2

anything he'd forget. Then they'd have to kick his ass. Then he'd give a confusing speech and make people love him and forget they were mad in the first place they figured they'd avoid that.
"Hey!" Esselle heard someone shout. She looked over and saw a taxi flash colors before her eyes. She smiled.
"hey Joel!" she said.
"Hey you coming for the party right?" he asked.
"Yes! Don't forget the gift please!" she said and he laughed.
"I'm going to pick it up right now!" he shouted back.
Esselle waved "See ya there!" she called out as he drove away.
Esselle was walking on air everyday she woke up. All the days had been bright and sunny and breezy. Esselle had not been so happy before. At least not in a while.
She crossed the street when the light turned and grabbed the flowers tighter. They were slipping through her sweaty fingertips. She glanced across the street saw a blonde headed halo and looked back. She stopped dead in her tracks. Did she see who she thought she saw? Because Manhattan wasn't big enough.
She very gently turned her head trying not to make it obvious. She hadn't realized she found her self walking right past the block his office was at. Finally she decided to turn half her body around and look back. There he was. Leaning against the building with his phone in hand. He had a white loose button down and beige pants. He looked stunning. Esselle had always loved the way the sunlight made him shine like gold. The yellow-green in his eyes were bright even from a distance. His hair shone like white gold. Esselle slowly fully turned around slightly tilting her hair and just looked at Mardrin. it had been weeks. But as long as he didn't see her looking it was alright. Right?

Somewhere in Time- trilogy part 2

Esselle was rethinking looking at him. She was thinking of turning around and walking away. Then he turned his face and his eyes fell on hers. His mouth stopped moving and he straightened out. Esselle had realized something. She had done this to Mardrin very often in the past. That day in her house when they argued she failed to let him explain himself. She was too hurt too think straight. She had done the same thing 28 years ago and she lost him. Maybe through this all Esselle had learned her lesson. Just maybe. She when she softly smile and gently waved it was an offer of friendship. He softly smiled and waved back giving her the same look. Esselle loved this man. Once. Now she loved someone else. Even though she may not have been completely over him she was content where she was. Happy. That was more than enough for Esselle. More than she could ask for. The wind blew and her hair blew along with the wind. Maybe a friendship a real one after this moment could blossom. But not now. Just not now. She had something to do. So she very gracefully turned and walked away making sure she glanced back one or twice. She had hoped that maybe just maybe he caught the flash of the locket around her throat. As she never took it off.
****

"Happy Birthday to you! WOOOO!!!" Everyone cheered. Charlotte was smiling glowing in fact. She blew out her candles and the lights went back on.

"No wonder you children have been missing lately" she said and all of headquarters vibrated with laughter. Daniel pulled Esselle closer to him and she continued to clap and laugh.

"New Jersey people coming through!" Esselle heard a lovely

Somewhere in Time- trilogy part 2

southern accent shout. Shoving through the crowd a big wide beautiful smile came with a box in her hands appeared.
"SueAnne!" Esselle said.
"As lovely as always I'm here peaches" she gushed and Charlotte and SueAnne engaged in small talk. Behind her master badass came.
Esselle smiled "Hey Terrance nice to see badass is here!" she called out over the crowd. Terrance looked over confused. When he saw Esselle he smiled and tipped his hat.
"I'm the only badass here" Dawn said coming up behind him. Terrance and Dawn stopped for a moment and looked at each other both up and down. Daniel and Esselle laughed. They were both all black spikes and attitude. I guess they finally found their match.
Daniel took Esselle's hand and they walked outside onto the balcony.
"I'm very proud of you" Esselle said and he looked at her.
"Why?" he asked.
She bumped him with her hip and smiled "Because" she said "You managed to get them here"
He smiled in the moonlight. "Yes well" he said and looked at her "I figured I could do something"
Esselle despite wearing heels had rise a bit on her toes to reach him. She kissed his cheek and smiled.
"You did good Danny" she said.
He smiled "Thanks Ess" he bent down and kissed her. For a moment if just a moment the chaos inside melted away. And all there was was a beautiful summer night.
"Hey sexy!" someone shouted. They pulled away and looked over.

Somewhere in Time- trilogy part 2

Jasmine was smirking looking at them. "You want cake or what?" she asked.

Trevor showed up behind her and she smiled when he took her by the waste.

Daniel nodded as if in approval. "What?" Esselle asked.

"Nice to know he grew some balls" he said and Esselle burst into laughter.

"But he hurts her i'll hurt him" he said.

Esselle rolled her eyes and pulled Daniel along.

"I think she is more than capable than doing that herself" Esselle said and they stepped back inside.

When Esselle got inside she saw Terrance and Dawn next to each other leaning against a table.

"So" she heard Dawn say. Terrance with big eyes looked at her. She flicked her head towards his belt "You like knives?" she asked.

He nodded "You like spikes?" he asked pointing to her high heels. She smiled 'Yup" they both looked separate ways for a moment smiling a bit.

"I think I'm going to like you" they said in unison.

Esselle laughed but she didn't have much time because Daniel pulled he onto the dance floor. He took her in his arms and the music blasted in her ears making the room vibrate. He kissed her and she laughed.

"Let's show them how its done" he said. Esselle nodded.

"Let's go babe' she said. He smiled. They danced the night away to the sound of loud music laughter and love. Something Esselle loved. Just the way she loved to be alive. This time around was going to be different. She was going to live life right. She had everything she needed and more. But especially more than anything else she had the most important thing. Something that was real. Love.

Somewhere in Time- trilogy part 2

Printed in Great Britain
by Amazon